LAST HILL OF ARIRANG

For Judi
with best wishes,
Beverly Paik

In memory of
Arthur Boniface

LAST HILL OF ARIRANG

A Story of Korea

By Beverly Paik

Writer's Showcase
San Jose New York Lincoln Shanghai

Last Hill of Arirang
A Story of Korea

Writer's Showcase
an imprint of iUniverse, Inc.

For information address:
iUniverse, Inc.
5220 S. 16th St., Suite 200
Lincoln, NE 68512
www.iuniverse.com

Any resemblance to actual people and events is purely coincidental.
This is a work of fiction.

ISBN: 0-595-24098-4

Printed in the United States of America

Cover design by
Harkjoon Paik

For the memory of Ohmanee,
whose life encompassed these years and events

Contents

Acknowledgements

For their helpful criticism, encouragement, humor and patience throughout all our years together I thank my writing friends, Joan and Tom Condon, William Drake, Jim Greenan, Joyce and George Hahn, Mary Krainik, and Evelyn Smart, and also honor the memory of Dr. Tom Ainsworth and Helen Parker.

Song of Arirang

Arirang, Arirang, Arario!
As you proceed along Arirang Pass
You, my loved one, who me have forsaken
Pained be your feet at the end of a mile.

Arirang, Arirang, Arario!
As you proceed along Arirang Pass
The moon comes up and the stars come out
Who is that laughing behind the clouds?

Arirang, Arirang, Arario!
Crossing the hills of Arirang
Many stars deep in the sky,
Many crimes in the life of man.

Arirang, Arirang, Arario!
Crossing the hills of Arirang,
Arirang hills are the mountains of sorrow.
There are twelve hills of Arirang.

Preface

Most Korean folk songs have evolved from feelings of melancholia, nostalgia, anguish or frustrated love, but without a doubt the greatest expression of these sentiments is found in their most well known, the "Song of Arirang."

Arirang—a symbol of mankind's journey through time. Even if one is in Korea for a short visit only, nearly every foreigner, soldier, diplomat, businessman or tourist sooner or later becomes familiar with its hypnotic beat. Its roots are obscure and the source has varied explanations, but it is agreed that this song first gained wide popularity near the close of the nineteenth century when Korea was first opened to western influences. It was a time of social and political change when national identity became a passionate concern for many and this simple folksong epitomized that emerging spirit. It seemed to touch a deeply respondent chord in the Korean psyche, the long tradition of inevitable sad parting.

When the singing of the Korean national anthem was banned by the Japanese in the early years of their occupation of Korea "Arirang" replaced it in a surreptitious way, especially among the members of the underground movement.

"Arirang" is often sung with plaintive drama by professional musicians and in treble tones by children, but it can be no more infectious in its vivacious rhythm that when it is borne by the voice of good friends toward the end of an evening when they feel replete with food and drink. In such a setting the listener, though he may be a stranger, will find himself impulsively clapping his hands, even impelled to join in the chorus, though he may not speak the language or be able to carry a tune.

The most common legend of its origin is that in the early Yi dynasty there was a hill near Seoul on which a solitary giant pine tree stood. It became the official site of execution for all enemies of the regime—bandits, common criminals, political dissidents and youthful rebels. One such young victim first sang this song as he trudged up that hill. Condemned men afterwards sang this song in farewell to earthly joys and sorrows. So it has come to symbolize the tragedy of Korea, of the constant climb over obstacles, only to find death at the end. But death is not defeat, for out of many deaths victory may be born.

So to sing the "Song of Arirang" is to sing of Korea.

Part One
1910 to 1921

Sun Yi stood in the narrow side street of Taegu, waiting for the signal that would begin the rebellion. She bore no weapon but the flagpole, and it was heavy. Perhaps it was a mistake that she had offered to carry it. But its burden could be no greater than the past nine years of oppression by Japan that her country, Korea, had endured.

Today, March 1, 1919, she would show them this flag, forbidden symbol of Korea's lost independence. She would wave it in their faces if the police dared to interfere with this peaceful march. What could they do to her? She shouldn't be afraid. Yet she was.

She listened to the restless, shuffling feet around her. There were hundreds of other students, some even younger than her seventeen years, and many of them standing with her only because of her own enthusiastic persuasion. If only she could depend on them to stay together!

The entire plan courted danger. How would their rulers react when Koreans in every city and village, at the stroke of twelve, began to shout in the streets for freedom? The chance they took would be daring, for no one knew.

If Grandfather could see her now! He believed, to the end of his life, that a proper young woman of her class should be confined within the walls of her family home. This I do for you, Grandfather, she thought. Revenge for every insult you suffered. Will you forgive me now? Do you see that my defiance of your authority has helped to produce this grand result? She hoisted the flag higher, for the noon hour was near.

The younger girls moved closer to Sun Yi, as if by standing in her shadow they might absorb her confidence. She must not show her fear. They were trying to be silent as she had warned. Surprise was vital. Someone muffled a cough. Everyone waited.

Sun Yi tossed her long black braid over her shoulder and gripped the staff of her flag more securely. Sudden chill winds whipped the full white chima against her legs. She shivered. Why was she shaking?

Her danger was nothing compared to that faced by the thirty-three men who dared to sign the Declaration of Independence that would be read in Seoul's Pagoda Park today. They were certain to be arrested. The shield of a thousand anonymous faces protected her.

Turning to watch the twisting line of white-clad figures behind her, she caught the eyes of her friend, Lee Yong Soon. She smiled and received that mischievous grin that recalled their hours of conspiracy. The infectious spirit in Yong Soon's sparkling eyes kindled a response in Sun Yi, as it had from the day of their first meeting at the Christian mission school. She raised the flag higher. They could not fail.

The flag was beautiful, this forbidden banner of her country. Since that day in 1910 when Japan annexed Korea, taking her homeland in bondage, no one had seen it until today. The circle of blue and red, the yin and yang, on a background of white with narrow bars of black in each corner, unfurled in the wind that blew just as the first bells sounded.

"Now!" Sun Yi shouted. Ringing, tolling, chiming, every bell in Taegu combined with a raucous intensity that sent her blood racing. Yong Soon shoved her forward.

"The time has come!" she cried.

Behind Sun Yi the crowd surged, propelling her into the main street. First she stumbled, then caught her balance and was carried along in the stream, buoyed by the voices shouting "Mansei!" "Long life to our country" "Tahahn dockeip mansei!" "May Korea live ten thousand years!"

People dressed in traditional white flowed into the market center from every side, faces glowing with happiness. Old men and young, farmers and yangban, who were marching together for the first time.

Sun Yi called to Yong Soon, still beside her, "See all the women!"

Such a triumph! Elation overwhelmed her. When, in all of Korea's long history, had women dared to participate as they were doing now? Never! And she had helped to make it happen!

Sun Yi moved forward, all sense of fear banished. Her voice rose with the others. Imagine a woman shouting in the public streets! Surely no one had ever dared before. Even Yong Soon's voice, she who always spoke in soft, controlled tones, could be heard among all the others. "Mansei!"

Louder and louder. The crowd seemed intoxicated with this new freedom.

"Isn't it wonderful?"

Sun Yi nodded, calling over the tumult, "Just as we hoped!" She waved the banner faster, stretching to push it higher. The protest had turned into a great festival. Crowds still flowed into the broad avenue. A tide of white in motion, dust rising from their feet, voices crying out, arms waving handmade Korean flags.

All we have are our flags and our voices, yet see what we have accomplished, in peace. Sun Yi exulted, recalling her daring in helping to inform these people so they'd be here today. The directions to the people had been clear and all were following the edict: "You must be peaceful. Do not insult the Japanese. Do not hit with your fists. Do not throw stones. These are the acts of barbarians."

She waved the flag again, delighting in the sight of it as it flashed over her head, just as she saw the first of the police taking their places along the sides of the avenue. They stood motionless, staring at the crowd. She turned to say to Yong Soon, "We surprised them! We did! They can do nothing that will stop us now."

At that same moment an explosion of gunfire shattered the air and stunned the jubilant voices of the great milling throng. A volley of shots followed. The procession broke ranks. The black uniforms of the police mingled with the white hanbok of the protestors, as if a giant chess table had been spilled.

First the police struck down the young men on the front ranks, those who carried the largest flags. Dozens of emblems dropped into the dust and were trampled, along with the crumpled bodies of those who had borne them. Sabers flashed amidst the screaming voices, striking again and again. There was a dull thud as each wooden club pummeled unprotected flesh, blending with shrieks and cries of the injured.

Sun Yi was trapped. She could not move. Those behind her thrust the girl forward, while those in front fell back against her. She could suffocate! Was there no way out? She sensed rather than heard her own cry of panic. There was no one to help her. In the great melee she fell to her knees, so she did not see the wooden club poised above her head. It struck her skull, blow after blow, until she slid into unconsciousness.

The pain peeled away, layer after layer, then returned in endless throbbing vibrations that pressed down on her temples, draining the strength from her. She opened her eyes. She saw only a stone wall, marking the boundary of someone's home. Sounds, muffled, no longer filled with joy, terrible moans of fear and agony, came to her from the street. Then she felt a touch on her shoulder and being raised to a sitting position. Through her glazed sight she finally recognized Yong Soon, kneeling beside her.

"No! I can't move," Sun Yi protested, sliding down again.

"You must!"

"Who brought me here?"

"I did. Get up! We have to get out of this place. It's not safe. We must get back to the school."

Yong Soon pulled Sun Yi to her feet. Blood from the gash on her own head blended with tears, streaming down her cheeks in muddy streaks.

Sporadic gunfire still echoed through the street. People ran about aimlessly. The two young women, arms about each other's shoulders, struggled, pushing through the crowd.

"The police are everywhere," Yong Soon warned in a hoarse whisper. She pulled Sun Yi into a narrow passageway. "Perhaps we won't be seen if we go this way."

Sun Yi stopped to peer out.

"Don't look! Do you want to be beaten again?"

When Sun Yi looked at her reproachfully Yong Soon relented. "All right. Can you walk? No? Well, hang onto me." She half-carried, half-dragged Sun YI, stopping every few steps, then moving forward.

In the morning Sun Yi could not move. All the bruises made her slightest motion painful. She remained in her bed in the dormitory, where she had been deposited when she and Yong Soon finally reached the school. She knew that only Yong Soon's persistence made that possible. Without her, Sun Yi admitted, I'd still be lying in the street. Or somewhere else. And I thought I was the strong one.

Martha Adams, the headmistress, looked in. Sun Yi beckoned to her.

"Yong Soon? Where is she?"

"Her mother took her home." She shook her head. The hair, blonde when she had arrived in Korea, was streaked with gray, pulled back into a severe knot. "Why you girls thought you could help by taking to the streets is beyond my understanding."

Sun Yi once thought Miss Adams a difficult, demanding woman. The blue eyes still made her feel uncomfortable. She could see in them only a bottomless depth. But the two developed a truce. After four years a strange kind of friendship grew, that of two strong personalities who recognize each other's determination and respect the boundaries over which neither will step.

"Tell me," Sun Yi begged, "what is happening? The march was intended to be peaceful. Did we fail?"

"If you are asking, 'was the message heard?' the answer is no. You certainly did not fail. Only the police are using violence. But what you have begun." She shook her head again. "Do you know that one young woman, a student from Ewha College, was shot? You might have been, also." She leaned closer, speaking softly. "Thousands and thousands of your countrymen are still protesting. Everywhere. All of the workers and farmers have joined with your people. They will not be stopped, not even with bullets." She paused, then repeated, "Only the police have used force."

"Then it is happening just as Yong Soon's father told us it would."

In her excitement Sun Yi forgot her pain and sat up. "Rev. Lee said if we cried with one voice our call for freedom would be heard on the other side of the ocean. President Wilson will help us." She winced and lay back, exhausted but satisfied.

Yong Soon returned after a few days. The long scar on the side of her face was beginning to heal but still looked raw and ugly. There was a greater change, though, which Sun Yi noticed at once. Her friend's eyes no longer sparkled. She never smiled.

"My father disappeared on the first day," she told Sun Yi. "We can't learn anything about him. There are so many others still missing. No one has time to try to trace him." She added with a bit of her former spirit, "I know he would tell me it doesn't matter. It's part of the price of our success."

"Success?"

"Yes. Look around at what is happening. The protests continue. Shops are closed. There is no business being done, anywhere. Now everyone dares to defy the Japanese. Can they put an entire nation into prison?"

They have, Sun Yi answered silently. They already have. She heard that thousands of people died since March 1. The police were arresting more each day. Prisons were overflowing. Would she and her friend be next?

But when a few more days passed she began to feel more secure. After all, no one but Yong Soon and her father knew of the actual involvement she had with the independence movement. And who would be bothered with a mere schoolgirl?

Just one week passed before she received the summons. Two Japanese policemen were waiting in the school office. Martha Adams, who had sent her the message, stood nearby. Her arms hung at her sides, her hands clenched in anger, but Sun Yi knew that she was helpless.

"I'm so sorry, Sun Yi," she whispered. "They threatened to close the school if I did not cooperate."

"Yu Sun Yi?" One of the men, short and stocky, shook his finger in her face. She took a step back, looking down at the officer. She nodded, the tightening of her throat choking her voice so that she could not make a sound.

"You are under arrest. You will follow me." He reached out to loop a rope around her waist.

Suddenly the words exploded. "Why? What am I charged with? You can't arrest me without a reason."

At the same time the headmistress cried out, "Oh, no! You must not do that to my girl. She will obey you. I promise. But no rope!"

Angered by their defiance, he jerked the cord tighter, ignoring their pleas and shoving Sun Yi toward the door.

Outside, she stumbled after the men, forced to keep up with their brisk marching strides. Tears stung her eyes. Everyone in the street was looking at her. Such shame! Then she turned aside, realizing that her teacher had caught up to her. Martha Adams walked with Sun Yi, together every step of the way through the streets of Taegu, only stopping when they reached the entrance to the prison. There her way was barred. She clasped Sun Yi by the shoulders, whispering, "I'll reach your family, tell them what has happened to you. Don't despair. You'll not be forgotten."

Her teacher's kind face, wrenched by sorrow, was the girl's last sight before the heavy gates swung shut, imprisoning her. A guard led her to a room so large it seemed like a vast cave. There was a barrier formed by some black metal bars at one end. He shoved her through a gate, pushing her so hard that she fell against the women huddled behind it. No one responded to her mumbled excuses. The faces wore a closed look, sullen, as if each of them were locked into her own cell of fear.

Sun Yi sat on the earthen floor among them and though she was pressed against the bodies of these strangers she'd never felt more alone. Surely I'll be set free soon, she consoled herself. Someone from the school will come to help me. As soon as I tell the authorities who I am there will be apologies and I'll be sent back.

But the hours passed, so many that she lost all notion of time. One by one the others were taken away. Each returned, covered with blood, sobbing, screaming with pain. At last, when it seemed that night must be over, she heard her own name called. She felt stiff. Any movement required great effort, but she pushed herself to her feet, relieved that now she could protest her unjust arrest.

The room to which she was led was in shadow, with only one dim light high overhead, but she could still see the thick ropes, bamboo sticks, rubber hoses, and jars of water. What would they do to her in this place? A man, short, heavy-set, with thick black brows that nearly hid his eyes watched her from behind a table of rough wood at the far end. He flung out an arm silently, indicating the spot on the ground where she was to stand, facing him.

Taking a deep breath of the foul air, she began, "I am Yu Sun Yi of Kyongsang province," in her best school girl Japanese, "and my grandfather was."

"Be silent. Answer only the questions," he interrupted. "You are charged with leading all of the students from your school in that unfortunate incident of March 1. Do not attempt to deny it. There is complete evidence implicating you."

Informers, thought Sun Yi. I always knew there were some like that around. If that is all that is known about me I will be fortunate. But I will tell them nothing.

He demanded to know the names of the others in her group, the names of her contacts. Sun Yi raised her brown eyes to his face boldly, the gold lights within them flashing her defiance, but she remained silent. Only the hands clasped with whitened knuckles might betray her emotion, but they were hidden in the folds of her chima and he could not see them.

At last, slamming his fist on the table, her interrogator bellowed some words. Immediately two slender women dressed in chimas of drab gray scurried to his side.

"Take her away," he ordered. "Give her the usual treatment. She'll soon speak."

The women led her to another room, smaller, darker. She felt her quivering knees begin to give way. Could she remain strong? Sun Yi had never known women such as these. Low born, surely or they would never perform such degrading tasks. Yet they were unlike the servants in her home. She detected a peculiar kind of arrogance in their manner, almost as if they found her contemptible. Well, she would show them the fine cloth of which she was made.

"What are you looking for?" she demanded. One of these women was tugging at her clothing, unfastening the knot of Sun Yi's chogori. Next she pulled the girl's arms from the sleeves and picked up a small but sharp looking knife. The captive girl winced before she realized that it was being used only to slice apart the ties that held her chima over her bare shoulders. The long skirt fell to the floor in a heap around her feet. Sun Yi's face burned as four hands touched every part of her, the fingers crawling like spider legs, up and down. The humiliation was too much. She wanted to scream when the probing and pressing moved forward and back over all of her private parts.

Instead, she spat in the face nearest her. The female guard straightened up, wiping the saliva from her cheek, then swung the flat of her hand across Sun Yi's face. She shoved the girl into a dusty corner and tossed her clothing after her.

Sun Yi crouched, stunned by the blow, waiting, expecting another to follow it.

"Put them on," the guard hissed, in Korean, addressing Sun Yi in the lowest of low forms, that one would not use even toward a servant.

Sun Yi struggled to cover herself. When she had done her best with the torn clothing the woman pinned a large paper bearing a number to the front of her dress. She jabbed the pin through to her skin, piercing the tender skin of her breast beneath, and the guard's eyes met her for a fraction of a second. Again Sun Yi felt the sting of contempt and hatred burning within them, toward her. Why?

The cell was, perhaps, six feet square. When she lay full length on the filthy quilt there was still a narrow space between her feet and moist rock of the wall. Sun Yi looked up at the ceiling where a yellow light bulb in one corner remained on all of the time. She'd turn it out if she could, but it was too high for her to reach.

Every muscle in her body felt stiff, tense. She stretched out her arms in an attempt to release the strain and touched a mass of soft, tangled cobwebs. More hung over her head. They were draped from wall to wall, and some brushed her face.

The year was 1910. The apple blossoms, pink and white, floated down with the gentle wind on the hillside. Some brushed her face while others rested on her shiny, tightly plaited braids. Sun Yi sat alone beneath the branches of the ancient tree, holding out her small hands to catch some of the petals. This place was her favorite. No one noticed her leaving the courtyard to come here. Now she sat in this forbidden place, her nostrils quivering with delight as she inhaled the sweet air and gazed around. She could see the Naktong River winding through the valley below, and the ridge of hills that rose beyond it, blue in the haze of late afternoon, with dark spots in the fields where the oxen were still working. She loved the special quiet here, with no voices to interrupt her daydreams.

She knelt on the grass; taking care not to crush the stiff silk of the dress she wore for this special day, and stared at the purple shrouded hills. In her daydream she was rising, lifted high by the wind, carried over those far hills, swooping, gliding, just as the birds flew, following those great, free creatures that could fade from sight into the distant land. But the hills came no closer and she frowned. Seven years old, Sun Yi had always lived in this place, Kyongsangdo, lush green province of southern Korea. Would she never leave it, see the mysteries that surely lay beyond?

"Sun Yi!" The calling voice bounced and echoed. "Little mistress!"

Forgetting the dress, Sun Yi flattened herself, pressing into the grass. The voice called again, closer this time. Poor Auntie. She chuckled, picturing the stout old woman climbing this steep hillside. Still she lay in silence, basking in the warmth of the sun on her tanned cheeks. Her eyes, brown gilded with flecks of gold, sparkled with her mischievous thoughts. She was mean, forcing her kind nursemaid to stumble on, searching for her. Should she jump up, cry out, "Here I am!" No!

"I don't care," she whispered, testing the strength of her defiance. She wanted to be here, alone on this beautiful, peaceful South Mountain one more time. If that meant punishment later the price was fair.

But no one would be cross on this day, the celebration of Grandfather's hwegap. Sixty years old. It was a time for singing, feasting, to honor him on attainment of such an important milestone. Today Sun Yi knew she could be as naughty as she pleased and no one would notice or care.

Mother would not know. How could she? Yesterday, when Sun YI peeked into the room where she lay, before the maid found her and carried her away, she saw her mother's eyes closed, her face pale. Covered by the ibul, she looked as tiny as her daughter did.

Sun Yi sat up; chin resting on her knees. If Ohmanee had called to her the maid would not have been allowed to take her child away. Mother would have beckoned to her, held her, singing, crooning the lullaby while she stroked the hair from her forehead, and told her not to be sad, even though she was a girl. "Ohmanee always loves you." That's what she would have said.

"Bad child! Why do you cause me so much trouble?" Strong hands pulled Sun Yi to her feet, brushing bits of dried grass from her dress. The bright stripes of yellow, red and green were all crumpled, creased. "Everyone is looking for you," the old woman scolded.

Sun Yi looked down, pretending to feel shame. That's not true, she thought. You are the only one looking for me. She glanced from the corners of her eyes at her nursemaid. The woman was fanning herself. Her breath, heavy with the scent of garlic, came in great deep gulps. Her white cotton hanbok was snagged with burrs from the weeds of the hillside.

"Naughty child! Why must you be the only one who leaves the courtyard?"

"I wanted to see the mountains again.' But she wasn't listening. Sun Yi followed her, stumbling as they hurried down, her small hand engulfed by the grip of the larger one. "From our house I can see only the branches of trees. I want to see the whole world!"

"Born in the year of the tiger. Hopeless. Impossible to tame. What will become of you?"

The child's feet dragged, trampling the wild sweet grasses.

"All of your cousins bowed to your grandfather. You were the only one missing. They blamed me. From today you must stay inside the gate with the other women, always. You are now too old to roam by yourself any longer."

But no one looked her way when they passed through the wide wooden gate. She heard the voices of the men, loud booming sounds, coming from the direction of the ondol room. The male relatives and neighboring yangban sat in there with Grandfather.

The colors stopped her. All that glorious fruit displayed in heaps on a long low table in the center of the courtyard. Glossy red apples, gigantic yellow pears round as moons and rare tangerines and oranges carried, she'd heard, all of the way from Chejudo, the island far to the south where winds blew warm over rocky shores.

Clouds of smoke drifted from the kitchen. Just at that moment a maid emerged, bringing a platter of steaming bul kogi and Sun Yi paused to inhale the delicious aroma of charcoal broiled meat. Perhaps it was, after all, a good time to return. She was, suddenly, ravenous with hunger.

Curiosity was greater, however, and she crept close to the great hall of the sarang, the men's quarters where Grandfather entertained his guests. Careful to keep out of their sight, she peeked through a narrow crack between the sliding doors. He was seated on a silk cushion and wearing a fine white silk jacket and pantaloons that were bound at his ankles, full at the sides. His tall black hat, woven of the finest horsehair, was tied under his chin. It glistened atop his long coil of hair, still black.

Sun Yi caught her breath. He was magnificent. No wonder all of the other yangban honored him the most.

Words drifted out with the smoke of their pipes and the sound gripped Sun Yi with a sudden fear, tight and heavy, though she knew nothing of their meaning. Annexation. Occupation by the Japanese. A king with no power. End of the Yi dynasty. It was the tone, the sadness that chilled her, this fearless child. She shivered and ran, seeking the consoling warmth of sunlight.

Sunlight. Would she ever see it again? Nine years had passed since that happy day of celebration. Sun Yi stretched out her legs, rubbing her calves. They were numb. The cold from the stones beneath penetrated throughout her entire body. Was it possible that she would freeze to death before anyone came to help her? The day of Grandfather's hwegap was the last happy time she could remember. From that day nothing had been the same.

Her village, close to the town of Andong in the southern province of Kyongsang, had survived for hundreds of years in isolation. Life was a peaceful routine, following the traditions of their ancestors, with no concern for the intrigues, conspiracies and power struggles of the royal court in the capitol city far to the north.

For as long as anyone could remember all of the land in Korea belonged to the Emperor. Most people never saw him. They all knew that he lived in Kyongbok Palace in the capitol city but that was beyond any dream of travel. More important to those who worked the land was the landholder, the steward who collected part of their harvest in taxes each season. A large share of the grain produced by each tenant farmer went to him. If the chungin worked for the yangban. he also received from him such help and protection as he might need. The system worked well. Life was hard for most, but seldom did anyone suffer from hunger.

Even among the other yangban of Kyongsangdo, Sun Yi's Grandfather commanded greater respect because he was a learned man, a scholar, as well as the steward of vast lands. He was wise and he was fair. For three hundred years his ancestors oversaw this portion of Korea, since the time when that first one was forced to leave the Royal Court after losing a power struggle.

The full impact of Japan's control was felt soon after the hwegap where Sun Yi listened to the anguish of her elders. Four thousand, two hundred and forty-three years after its legendary founding annexation came and those men were powerless. They could not save their country from domination by the ones they called weanom. The island savages.

First the Japanese made a survey of their land. Individual ownership replaced the king's rule but few Korean farmers understood the concept. When they failed to comply with new registration laws great parcels of their land were divided and purchased, or simply taken, by recent immigrants from Japan.

With the sound of heavy booted feet marching by, right outside her cell, Sun Yi's mind returned to the present. She leaped up, grate-

ful even that the long period of silence was finally broken. The rattle
of keys was closer. Perhaps someone was there, coming to free her!

Although the rhythmic tramping stopped, her door did not open.
Instead a voice called to her through the small opening near the top
of it.

"You must kneel. Face the door. Don't move." The voice was
harsh. "Or you will be beaten."

Sun Yi slumped forward. The threat struck her like a physical
blow. Then she rose to her knees, complying with the order, growing
more uncomfortable with each moment, shivering. Was someone
watching her? Would the door open without warning if she moved?
Soon her feet tingled. Prickling needles raced up and down her legs
and her flesh began to swell until the skin stretched taut as a drum
cover. Waves of drowsiness swept over her and she slept, upright,
struggling from time to time to rouse herself. This was no time for
sleep, but instead a time to try to recall when she'd laid her head in a
far different place.

She was only thirteen then and still with her family. Sun Yi wished
she could remain in her bed. The layer of soft ibuls was comfortable,
warm, and the rosy light of morning just beginning to lighten the
rice paper window. But she did not dare. The aunts would be cross.
She jumped up, rolled her sleeping quilts into a bundle, and tossed
them into a closet behind a sliding door.

She cast aside her nightdress, slipped into a chima and chogori,
tugging at the ribbons that fastened the long and full skirt over her
shoulders, and shoved her feet into the straw slippers waiting on the
maru outside. Then she moved swiftly along that narrow wooden
porch along the inner wall of the house. Ladies did not run. Not even
those who were only thirteen, but she must hurry. There was much
to be done and with no mother or grandmother to share the work
Sun Yi performed more of it than most girls of her age did. There
were the wives of the uncles and the maids, of course. And her

father's new wife, but she was occupied with the baby at this time of day. Sun Yi had no time to think or to linger, even at this early hour.

Later, when she had helped to serve the morning meal to the men, bringing trays with rice, soup and kimchee, she did stand in the courtyard for a time, raising her face to the sun, basking in the brisk but warming air of the October day.

Sun Yi was taller than most girls of her age were and slender as the poplar. Her black hair, glossy from brushing, hung in a single braid that touched her waist. The rosy glow of her cheeks was enhanced by the contrast with the white cotton of her long, full skirt and short jacket.

She inhaled, taking a deep breath of the fresh air, stretching her arms to the blue sky. Then, as she turned back to the kitchen, she noticed some scrolls of paper lying on the ground in the shadow of the maru. Had the wind blown them, or were these left behind by one of the careless boy cousins on his way to school?

She picked one up and unrolled it. Beautiful! Bold strokes in heavy black ink covered the paper from top to bottom. Sun Yi traced the marks with one slender finger. But what did it mean?

"Ouch!" She dropped the scroll and clutched at the corner post of the maru to keep her balance. The sach'on, her eldest boy cousin, held her long braid in his grip.

"What are you doing?"

She grimaced with pain as he continued to pull.

"You can't read!" He snatched the scroll from the ground where it had fallen. "But I can! And, what's more, I wrote this."

Sun Yi glared at him. Her golden brown eyes flashed with anger. He was no taller than she and only one year older. "Take it then, if it is yours. Don't leave it for the wind to play with."

She watched him run from the courtyard. "You think you are wonderful. Just because you are a boy and can attend school. It's only a village school," she called after him. But he had already disappeared and silence swallowed her words. The girl turned toward the kitchen, the sadness in her heart stealing the light from her eyes.

Her father's new wife was there, alone, chopping vegetables. She smiled when she saw Sun Yi and beckoned.

"Won't you help me?"

The request was gentle, unlike the commands of her aunts.

"I must finish this," she motioned to the heaps of garlic, onion, carrots, daikon, that she was mixing with red chili peppers, "so it will be ready when the cabbages arrive in the morning."

Sun Yi knelt beside her, taking up a knife, while she listened to the chatter of her stepmother. She was comfortable with her when they were alone. Almost like being with a sister.

"When I was younger I always thought kimchee making was the best time of the year," Sun Yi confided. "When those carts come rolling into the yard, wheels creaking, packed to the top with cabbages. We children loved to watch the drivers tossing them down. Hundreds and hundreds of cabbages! How many do you think there are?"

"Oh, there must be at least fifty for each person in our household. How could we survive without plenty of kimchee?"

Sun Yi scraped another daikon and added it to the stack. "Now when I hear the sound of the il yukkas early in the morning I know it means only lots of hard work for me. The boys know nothing of this. They're all in school." She leaned closer and whispered, "Did you ever guess, when you came to live with us two years ago, that you would have to work all day long like this?"

Kum Seung was wrapped in a large apron, her long braid wound into a tight coil at the back of her head to indicate her married status, but her smooth face looked almost as young as Sun Yi's. She paused to push in more securely the white jade pinja that held the coil in place, then resumed chopping up and down in a clean rhythm before replying. Neat thin slivers of vegetables joined the others in an ever-higher mound.

"Oh, yes. I watched my own mother. She never stopped, from morning to night, even though she had many to help. How can you think of any other life for women?"

"Well, I do. Sometimes. I even pretend that I can read and study, just as the boys do." Sun Yi related the incident of that morning in the courtyard. "Kum Seung, I think I have an impossible dream, but I can't stop my wishing for it."

The older girl's name was a secret between the two. No one else used it, for Kum Seung had given up her little name with her childhood on the day she married. Now she was known simply as Ohmanee, mother of Han Ju. But the sound of it brought a smile to her face and she nodded in understanding, although she had never been to school, either.

"Some girls are being educated, I've heard. In Taegu. There's a school where girls live and study together. Missionaries from America are their teachers." She stopped the knife in mid-air. "I heard talk of it in my own village before I left. One family had dared to send their daughter. Everyone else said it was outrageous. They would be sorry. It was even said that the girl would never find a husband. No one wants an educated wife to stir up trouble, you know."

The knife chopped down with swift, vicious strokes and her eyes turned solemn, as though a veil had dropped to hide their sparkle.

"How well you manage this work," Sun Yi said, prompting her to speak again. "I am so clumsy. I'll probably never be of any use in the kitchen. And with the baby to care for. You have so much to do."

The knife paused again. "You'll learn soon enough when you marry."

Sun Yi laughed. "That's a long time away."

"Your marriage may be sooner than you realize."

The laughter ceased. Kim Seung looked serious and her words sounded like a warning.

"There is a rumor," she continued, "and I've heard it myself. It is said the Japanese may force our young girls to marry their sons.

Many betrothals are being arranged at an early age, to prevent such a tragedy. Your own turn may not be far off."

"Oh, no! It couldn't happen to me. Grandfather would never allow such a thing. I'm too young." After a moment she added, "Why, if that should happen I would never have a chance of going to school."

The baby woke with a howl. He had been asleep in the corner. When she lifted him to her shoulder his bright eyes fastened on Sun Yi. He is sweet, she thought, when he clung to her. She nuzzled her face in his soft, dark hair, inhaling the sweet baby fragrance. Han Ju had been born in the springtime. What would it be like to have the care of a child, even one so delightful as he? She knew the answer. She did not hesitate to let him go when Kum Seung reached out for the squirming form.

"How far do you think it is from here?"

Startled, Kum Seung looked up, distracting the baby from his feeding. He howled with impatience.

"Taegu. How far from here?"

"Oh, it's far to the south." Kum Seung guided the demanding mouth to her breast once more. "But there is a train. It passes through Andong."

"Can the journey be made in one day?"

"Yes. I think so. If one started early. Why do you want to know? Do you plan on such a journey?"

Kum Seung began to laugh but she stopped as soon as she realized from Sun Yi's solemn expression that her question was serious.

"I'm going to speak to Haraboji," the younger girl told her, and she ran from the kitchen.

Her grandfather should be in his room at this time of day. Sun Yi was certain, for he talked with her father each morning, even though Abuji handled all of the daily business matters since the hwegap.

Waiting outside the door, she trembled, unable to control her apprehension. The grandfather often sounded angry when she listened to him speaking with the other men of the family. It would be easier to make her request when he was alone, perhaps. She thought he was growing older and sadder each day. She dreaded to interrupt him, even though she was his only granddaughter and he'd always treated her kindly. If only he could be as happy as he once was. Now he seemed to find contentment only when he shared a pipe with old friends and engaged in endless games of chess with them.

Sun Yi had no choice, for he must be the one to decide. He was still the head of their family. He must listen to her today. In the past when she'd spoken of her desire to become a student he'd always said, "You are still a child." Today would be different. It had to be. She'd have no other chance.

Please may he be alone.

He was not. A man stepped from the ondol room with him. A foreigner, wearing a uniform of a dark color. Sun Yi retreated a few steps. No Japanese had ever been allowed inside their gate before.

Grandfather stood on the top stair. He was shaking with rage and his face, flushed with anger, frightened her so that she felt, in a rush, that he had turned into a stranger, also. Even worse, he was shouting.

"Get out! Get out!"

"I leave now, but I'll soon return." The man's calm reply made his words even more ominous. "And when I do, you will be pleased to accept any price that I offer. And it will be less." He marched out the gate without a backward look.

Grandfather raised his fist, though the man was out of sight, then dropped it when he saw Sun Yi watching him.

"What are you doing here?"

Perhaps speaking now was a mistake. But if she did not, when would she? Soon the time would be past. Forever.

The child bowed low before the old man, taking time to rise.

"Well?"

Sun Yi gave him the morning greeting, then asked quickly, "Why does that man intrude into our home?" She looked up, just far enough to see the chokki, watching its amber buttons dangling from his vest. She dared not to see his face, yet. His turamagi, the long traditional coat of a country gentleman, reminded the girl of his authority over her. Slowly she raised her head, seeing first his white beard, and then the tired eyes and finally the black horsehair hat with the high peak that made him appear like a giant above her. His voice was calmer but she shivered at its sound.

"He came to buy our land."

"You would not sell it!"

"No, not today."

"Will our land be sold. Ever?" She asked the question with her boldness increasing. "Where would all the farmers go, Haraboji?"

"To the north, to Manchuria, where the others have gone already," he answered, turning away.

Sun Yi took a deep breath.

"Grandfather! Grandfather, I came to ask that you consider sending me to school."

One foot was rising to the doorstep. It came down. He turned, his eyes focusing on the top of her head. But he was listening.

"All of the grandchildren,the boys, anyway, are learning to read. I wish to learn, also."

"You?" The tall black hat swung from side to side. "No, such learning is not for women. You have no time to read."

Inhaling another great gulp of air, Sun Yi spoke, still wondering at her daring. "Some girls are going to school."

"A mistake." He frowned. "Their families will have cause for regret." He turned to go inside.

"Please, Grandfather. Send me to school!" The words, uncontrollable now, leapt out.

"You are a daughter of this house and it is your duty to maintain its traditions." His voice rising shrilly struck her ears like the raucous shrieks of crows. "I know that change is all around us. There is little we can do to resist." He was silent for a long time, looking beyond her, and Sun Yi began to hope, but then he thundered, "However, there are some parts of our lives that we may still control. No, you will not leave this house until you are a married woman."

"A married woman!" Then Kum Seung was right. The words pierced like needles and she cried out in pain.

"Grandfather, I want to go to school. I don't want to be married. Don't lock me inside these walls forever!"

She clapped her hand to her mouth, but it was too late. He seized her by the ear, pulling her into the ondol room; his face turned monstrous with rage. She froze, fascinated, watching his hand reach for the leather strap, sensing the blur of motion when it swung toward her.

Only then did Sun Yi feel the blows. On her shoulders, her arms, her back. Again. Over and over again. A swish, a crack, then a cringe she could not prevent. The dull heat spread all over her body. The thin cotton of her chogori shredded and she fell to her knees. Shock silenced her voice. The strap continued to strike. She struggled to stand, dodging its swinging arc.

Finally she ran. Out of the room. Across the courtyard. Tears blinding, instinct propelled her to the kitchen garden. There she threw herself into Kum Seung's arms, clutching fiercely at the older girl. Then, only then, with her shoulders heaving, did the sobs break through.

Kum Seung rocked her, soothing, crooning words of comfort, stroking her head with a touch that reminded Sun Yi of her mother's hands, long ago.

She calmed at last, but the welts on her back, swelling where the torn cloth bared the skin, burned with a searing, constant heat. "It is hopeless for me. Truly hopeless," she whispered. "I know now that Grandfather will never let me go. What shall I do?"

Sun Yi looked up at Kum Seung's face and saw an extraordinary expression. Defiance.

"You must leave! Before it is too late. I've heard of betrothals arranged for girls of your same age."

"What shall I do?" Anguish choked her words. Her chest tightened as if she were wrapped in a rope.

"I will help you." Kum Seung spoke the words more to herself than to the girl in her arms. "You will go to that school in Taegu. It is your only chance."

"It's a big city."

"That doesn't matter. Someone will show you the way. Only you must leave soon."

"But how?" A thousand silent years passed while she waited for the answer.

"Of course! The ox carts."

An oxcart? Was she joking, after all this? The ox carts brought cabbages and radishes for making kimchee. How could they help a young girl?

"It will be perfect," Kum Seung insisted. "No one will guess. It will be early. Tomorrow. You must be ready," she warned. "The carts arrive even before the daylight."

"Oh, I will," Sun Yi managed to answer with assurance, but she wondered how this could happen. Only Kum Seung's enthusiasm made the idea seem possible. She listened to the plans, nearly forgetting her pain.

"The other women will be rushing around, one taking the dried red chili peppers down from the rafters in the storeroom, another filling the toks with cabbage, pouring in salt brine." She continued the litany, ending with "Nobody will even notice that you are gone."

Perhaps she was right. Perhaps it was the perfect time. Even if it wasn't, Sun Yi had no other choice.

Later she laid out her few necessities, all she could carry, and wrapped everything in a square of strong silk, crossing and tying the four corners to make a handle. Then she placed the gold rings that had once been her mother's in a pocket and pinned it closed.

When she'd finished she looked around. This house is beautiful, she thought. I love the roof of gray tiles and the upturned eaves with the bright designs painted on the wood. I'll miss it. Can I really leave my home?

The door slid open softly and Kum Seung came in. She pressed a small purse into Sun Yi's hands. It was heavy.

"This is mine," she whispered. "It is all I have but I don't need it here, and you will. Remember, the cart will take you to Andong. There you must get on the train. When it stops at Yongchon you must get off and wait for the train that goes to Taegu. I heard my brothers speaking of this." She nodded her head and her eyes were shining.

Why, she looks almost as if she were planning this journey for herself, Sun Yi realized. I must go! All doubts and hesitation melted, leaving confidence in their place.

Yet she could not sleep. She was committing an act of the greatest disobedience. Could she risk it? Suppose someone stopped her? It was her only chance. Nothing in her life would improve. If she did not leave now she would soon be shut within the walls of a strange house, married to a man she would not even meet until the day of her wedding. The prospect terrified her. But, if she were to become a student in this school that Kum Seung spoke of, who could tell what her future might be?

In her mind Sun Yi saw the tree on the top of South Mountain. It was her secret refuge since she was a tiny child, the only place where she could be alone with her thoughts amidst the beauty of the trees in blossom among the wildflowers, with the beckoning mountains in the distance, forever shrouded in mist. What if she never went up there again? Well, she wasn't allowed there any longer now that she was older. It didn't matter, really.

The sound of the creaking wheels woke her. She heard the lowing of the oxen. The carts must be at the kitchen gate already! She jumped up. There was no more time to think.

When she draped the sigachima around her shoulders the long hooded cape covered her completely. She looked like any proper woman who must appear in public. Only her darting eyes and tiny hands and feet were visible.

She tiptoed to the gate, though she saw no one about. Then she slipped through, careful not to let it creak.

Kum Seung was outside already, speaking to the driver, putting something into his hand. She helped Sun Yi to climb up, then handed her bundle to her. The tall sides of the cart would shield Sun Yi from discovery. Then she spoke one last fierce word of farewell.

"Someday, come back and teach me!"

The sky of early dawn was already clear and blue. Hanuri nopda. The time of high skies. Sun Yi's spirits soared with the morning sun. Peering through the narrow openings between the wooden slats of the cart she looked at the passing countryside. Every sight was new, fascinating. Tall, straight rows of golden poplars lined the rutted path, with water flowing in the open irrigation canals to the low lying rice fields on either side. Dry fields of the higher hills, interspersed with groves of bamboo, surrounded the villages of thatched huts. All of this Sun Yi looked upon for the first time.

This is the beginning of the rest of the world; she exulted, feeling a great impatience to see more.

When, at last, the cart rumbled into Andong Sun Yi did not look back. With some of Kum Seung's precious coins she purchased her ticket. Then she waited, her eyes intent on the track, and the first sight of the train, repeating to herself the words of the old saying. It was the teaching of her nursemaid.

"Blame yourself, not the stream, if you fall into the water."

Andong lay in a narrow valley some sixty miles north of Taegu. The Naktong River cut through the mountain ridges nearby to turn westward from the Taebaek Range for the run of three hundred miles or more to the East Sea near Pusan. This place had long been the local center of the opposition yangban aristocracy who had, after 1600, been barred from holding office or living in Seoul. It was for that reason Sun Yi's ancestors settled in the region.

"Not to worry," the station master reassured her. "There's only one train a day and you'll hear it before you see it."

Still, it was difficult to be patient when she thought someone might come looking for her at any moment. What would she do then?

Her relief when the train arrived was so great that she failed to be frightened by the shudders and steaming belches it gave out. The step leading into the wooden coach looked high as a mountain peak to her, though, and she landed with a bump on the bench that ran the length of the compartment. Nothing could prepare her for the sensation of its motion. The car trembled. Sun Yi trembled.

The only other passengers were three elderly gentlemen. They stared at her so she pulled her head back into the hood of the dark green sigachima, wishing she might disappear like a turtle into its shell. Turning away from them, she watched the villages from the open window. Andong had been a real town, with a street of small shuttered shops. Now she saw only small settlements passing by so swiftly that they seemed close together, though there were great open spaces between each. The huts were made of wood and mud, their roofs of thatched grass. Most had two or three rooms in a round or egg shaped design. Occasionally she saw a farmer following his oxen as they pulled an iron plow across the rich brown soil. Only once did Sun Yi see a house like her own with a roof of tile and high walls of wood and mud surrounding it. This made her think of home and she wondered if anyone there missed her yet.

She didn't even dare to think again of the possible consequences of her disobedience. That time had passed. Now she thought only of the future, of the school that awaited her in Taegu.

It was an enormous city. She had to push through the crowds of people in the street. She'd never seen so many persons in one place before. Even worse was her feeling that each of them knew their destination. She alone moved without direction.

The day was nearly over and she had to find the school before darkness fell. Men of all ages passed her, their backs bent with loaded chige, the frame that seemed to hold more than the weight of the bearer. Women in long skirts walked erectly with a basket of vegetables, a large jar, or sometimes a single enormous cabbage balanced carelessly on top of their heads. Small children tied in slings on their mothers' backs stared at her with bright dark eyes.

Who could she ask? Who would tell her the way? It was a long time before Sun Yi gathered courage to stop someone and ask directions to the mission school.

But she knew when she saw it that she had reached the right place, for the school perched on a summit of a small hill in the northern section of Taegu. It was the only two-story building in sight, built of solid granite and unlike any other structure in this city of winding streets, narrow alleys and single level tile roofed houses. Did all the buildings in America look like this? She passed by the two large paulonia trees whose broad leaves guarded the entrance, and approached the door.

"This is most unusual." The American woman with the pale face looked kind but worried. Her soft voice spoke firmly and Sun Yi waited, not even daring to consider that she'd be sent away, now that she'd finally reached her goal.

"If you can't pay for your schooling, my dear, you will have to help with the work in the kitchen to earn your way."

"I'll be willing to do that, teacher," Sun Yi replied. She would not reveal or relinquish that small hoard of coins Kum Seung gave her. It was her only link to independence. But she wondered did she travel all this distance simply to work in another kitchen? Aloud she added, "If you will give me the chance I promise to do my best. Please. I do want to stay here." Where else could she go? She looked again into this woman's eyes. Such a strange color, deep blue, just like the high skies.

"Then you shall," Martha Adams promised. "I'll call Yong Soon. She's just the one to help you feel at home here. She'll show you the room where the girls sleep. You can leave that next to your bed." She indicated the silk wrapped bundle that Sun Yi still held close. "Then come back downstairs. You're just in time for the evening meal."

In the days that followed Sun Yi sometimes sat by the window in the second floor dormitory. From there she could see Palgong-san. It looked as lonely as she felt. Perhaps not the tallest mountain but certainly the most interesting on the horizon, it was actually eight separate peaks rising from a single base on the northern edge of Taegu. It was named for a Buddhist monk of the Koryo dynasty, she learned. At its foot flowed the Kimho River, a wide and shallow stream.

She told herself that she should be happy. She was a student now. Her strongest wish had come true. But even the excitement of learning could not erase her guilt. She worried constantly about the disrespect to her family and sometimes her spirit was engulfed in shame that she'd left home when Grandfather expressly forbade her doing so.

Then the most surprising, least expected, thing happened. On a chill winter day when Sun Yi had been in school several months Miss Adams summoned her to the office. The woman's blue eyes were shining.

"A message has arrived from your grandfather," she said. He writes that he gives approval for your quest for education. Furthermore, he sends your tuition for the entire year. You need not work any longer, Sun Yi."

The tall blonde woman placed her hands on the girl's shoulders as she said this. The blue eyes beamed down on her.

"It is truly amazing to witness this progress. In just this short time we've convinced even an elderly yangban gentleman that women are entitled to share in the opportunities given to men in your country."

Her Korean was not flawless but Sun Yi understood the meaning of her words. She kept her own thoughts to herself. Kum Seung must have presented her case well. She'd assured Sun Yi that she'd persuade Grandfather that the girl's ambitions would bring honor to the family. Or had she? More likely the old gentleman used the ruse of acquiescence, the bestowing of his blessing, however late, to avoid the scandal that would come from common knowledge of her disobedience. Grandfather gave in to her wishes and managed to salvage the outward appearances. Disgraceful for a girl to be educated, yes, but infinitely worse to let the world know of her gross disrespect to an elder.

The heavy sense of oppression took wings, replaced by a great surge of satisfaction, filling Sun Yi with a new sense of her own power, a giddy, uplifting sensation. She smiled. She learned a lesson today. From this time on she'd use her own strong will to win whatever she wanted. Never would she doubt the source of power within herself. She made a silent promise.

I'll use this force only to achieve that which I must have.

With more time for her studies Sun Yi excelled, moving rapidly to more advanced subjects. First she had to learn Japanese, for all of the instruction was presented in that language. The missionary teachers followed strict rules enforced by the authorities and even though the school had been established and was still run by the Christians, many of the teachers came from Japan. Consequently, all of her studies focused on the culture of that foreign invader, with no mention of events important in the history of Korea.

Sitting alone in the dormitory during the hour before dinner, Sun Yi snapped her books shut with disgust. She was not learning even one example of the classic literature and poetry of her country. Outside the Siberian winds blew over the snow draped hills. The dreary gray of the sky only reinforced her mood. She was lonely. She had felt better when she had helped with the work.

She wandered into the kitchen where others were helping with the meal preparation. Most of these girls came from homes far simpler than her own. Aware of the difference, they'd shared an initial reluctance to accept her, anticipating her aloof attitude. True, Sun Yi'd detested the kitchen chores when she'd been required to work. Now she used the homely tasks as her key to a warm circle of friendship.

Lee Yong Soon, the daughter of a Presbyterian minister in Taegu, became her closest friend. Sun Yi sensed an energy, like an electoral current, in the presence of this young woman. She was slight in stature, quiet in her motions, yet she inspired confidence in Sun Yi, in much the same way that Kum Seung had done.

"Come home with me tomorrow," Yong Soon suggested toward the end of the week in early spring.

"Will I be allowed?" Sun Yi hesitated. The students were governed by strict rules that did not allow leaving school.

"Don't worry. I know how to arrange everything," Yong Soon promised. "You must meet my family. I know you will like them."

She was right. The atmosphere within her home was unlike any Sun Yi had known. Her father, a second son, had his own small home, with only Yong Soon's mother, her sister and a brother. Yong Soon sat at the same table with her father while he questioned her about her studies. He even drew Sun Yi into the conversation. For the first time she spoke to a man outside of her own family without keeping her eyes lowered.

As she listened to the conversation she realized that both father and daughter knew far more of Korean history than she'd imagined. She began to ask questions, so many that finally Rev. Lee took a book from one of the wooden chests lining the ondol room. The volume was heavy looking and worn with age.

"This book hold many of the answers you seek," he told her, "and much more. I think you must read it for yourself, so you may borrow it. I warn, though, that you must promise to keep it well hidden from others. As you know, books of this kind are forbidden by our present rulers."

He trusts me, Sun Yi thought, and felt suddenly much older. Fascinated, she read of past events and achievements and her pride in her ancestors grew. She learned how hangul, the phonetic alphabet, was first developed five hundred years earlier, giving Koreans a written language system for the first time. Before its invention only the scholars who studied classical Chinese were literate. Since the Chinese language was completely different from Korean, its symbols could not represent the sound and structure of the words spoken in daily life. This hangul was so simple that King Sejong, its creator, was said to describe it as something a talented person could learn to read in a morning and even a fool in ten days.

She discovered, also, that during the reign of this king, Sejong, the first movable type came into use, fifty years before the work of Gutenberg that the westerners praised.

Even the recent occupation of Korea was not the first. One hundred and fifty thousand Japanese under the command of the general Hideyoshi wasted her land for six years in a war that began in 1592. It engendered the animosity between the two peoples that continued to the present time. Only with the ingenuity of Admiral Lee Sun Sin, and his invention of a "turtle ship", an iron clad vessel, were the Japanese finally defeated.

When Sun Yi began to share these stories, after a time, with the few classmates she trusted they decided to make a copy of the book for themselves. Such an act was forbidden but this made no difference. The knowledge should be preserved. The girls worked at the slow and tedious task during the night when everyone believed them to be sleeping. Just before its completion the headmistress again summoned Sun Yi and this time she looked somber.

"Sun Yi," she began, "we've been proud of your progress. You're one of our best students. We hold great hope for your future." She hesitated, then continued in a lower voice. "It is unwise for you to involve yourself in actions that will jeopardize your reputation. No matter how foolish some restrictions may seem, we all must consider the long-term perspective." She paused. "You do understand, don't you?" Without waiting for Sun Yi's reply, she added, "You must remember that it is a privilege for us to conduct this school. Each of you who benefits has a responsibility to help us continue. You must do nothing, nothing, to embarrass us before the authorities, if you wish to remain as a student."

The implication, the threat, in her tone was clear.

"Who could have told?" Sun Yi demanded, describing the confrontation to her friends. "Someone is spying on us!"

"Calm down," interrupted Yong Soon. "No matter who is guilty, our problem now is the book. What shall we do with it?"

"Burn it!

"After all of that work?" Sun Yi objected. "There has to be some way to preserve it."

"We can bury it."

"Yes, why not?" she agreed. "Someday we'll dig it up, when we're free." The idea was not so preposterous. Of course she'd return Rev. Lee's copy to him right away, but the other could be buried. They'd have to be careful. No one must see them.

Late that night the four girls met in the field behind the school. The sky was dark. Only a thin sliver of moon lighted their steps. The air was still but an occasional breeze rustled the leaves of trees as they circled the building.

"No one upstairs can see us on this side," Sun Yi assured them as they climbed the hillside. When the full branches of a willow tree enveloped the girls she regained some of her confidence. The necessity for this escapade was her fault. If they were discovered it would also be her responsibility. She shushed their voices.

The soil was soft from the recent spring rain. The digging, with a shovel taken from the caretaker's shed, was easier than she'd expected. While one girl kept watch the others took turns until they'd made a trench deep enough to hide the book. It was wrapped in silk, with many layers of rough hemp cloth on the outside.

Sun Yi placed it in the hole. Yong Soon and the others helped to cover it with the loose soil, then pushed leaves and grass over it until they thought the natural appearance of the site was restored.

One by one, moving like apparitions, they crept back to their beds.

But who could sleep? Sun Yi lay between her quilts, waiting for their warmth to release the tension in her body. When would that account of Korean history be recovered? Was it's burial a symbol of the fate of her country?

As long as Korea remained under foreign domination the possession of books like that would be incriminating evidence of subversive ideas. But no matter. Those events of a proud past were engraved in her mind. They could not be buried so long as she had life.

New Year's Day, 1919. On this holiday, the most important of all, Sun Yi anticipated having only the American teachers as her companions. It was more than three years since that early morning when she left her family's country home in the clumsy il yukka, and she'd not gone back, even once. When her classmates returned to their homes for the summer recess in August and for the month long interval in midwinter she remained in the suddenly silent dormitory. If she were to return to her home she feared she'd never leave it again.

She stood at the top of her class in the mission school and was recognized by many in her class as a true leader. Soon her studies would be completed and she did not know what she should do next. Teach, perhaps? The girls she'd worked with on copying the contraband account of Korean history never revealed their involvement to anyone else and never learned the identity of their informer.

Today pictures of past New Years flooded her memory. She, with the other cousins, coming to the ondol room early in the morning, each dressed in the brightly colored new clothes and each in turn kneeling before their grandfather. She'd always bowed until her forehead knocked against the polished floor. He gave shiny coins and wishes for their good fortune in return for their obeisance.

On this New Year, far from the scene of those memories, she had a new family. Yong Soon insisted she must join them and stay for several days. The home of her father, Lee Jong Soo, was open, not to only his relatives but to all who knew him. This gentle man, one of the first Koreans to become a Christian minister, welcomed Sun Yi as he did every person who came to his gate with the traditional greeting.

Later in the day there was a feast for all of the men. Seated on the silk cushions, they gathered around a large table in the ondol room while Sun Yi and Yong Soon helped to serve enormous platters of food to them. Yong Soon's parents must have scrimped for many days to save the money for this delicious meal.

She placed a large brass bowl of mandoo, the dumplings filled with meat and still steaming, in the center of the wooden table. Yong Soon followed with a platter; larger still, on which slices of pressed fish cake were arranged in alternating rows with forest mushrooms, floating in a dark broth. Next to it she presented a plate heaped with squares of fresh white fish that had been dipped in an egg batter and fried to a golden color. A great bowl of hot rice contributed its own savory aroma, flanked by three different kinds of kimchee, each swimming in a fiery red liquid.

Yong Soon returned with another platter heaped with thin strips of beef marinated in soy, green onions, and ginger. This was still smoking, having come straight from the grill in the kitchen.

Then her mother brought, in an enormous bowl, the most important dish of a New Year meal, the duk kuk. She served each man the beef broth with thin slices of the soft and glutinous rice cake. Duk kuk must be served in every Korean home on New Year's Day. Who dared begin another year without the traditional omen of good fortune?

Reverend Lee is a generous man, Sun Yi thought as she watched his guests arriving. The table was quite crowded but no one seemed to mind. She listened to their laughter and joking and lively conversation until the meal was served. Then they began the earnest work of consuming the delicacies.

After serving the plates of food Sun Yi retired with the other women of the home to another room where they prepared to enjoy their own portions. She sat in a corner with her feet tucked under her chima. The floor felt deliciously warm on this winter day and she reveled in its comfort. The heat from the fire in the kitchen flowed through tunnels under the floor and spread its warmth in a continuous stream so that even when the wind howled and sent gusts of bitter cold the inside remained a haven of comfort.

Still more of Yong Soon's father's guests arrived. He made room for each at his bountiful table and summoned his wife to bring fresh servings to replace the empty dishes. Her face serene, she darted about, directing the girls who helped her. They glided in and out soundlessly in their soft slippers.

Just as Yong Soon suggested they help her mother to clear away the empty dishes a loud insistent pounding erupted at the outer door. Before Reverend Lee could respond the door sprang open, wind blasting in behind it. Two uniformed policemen entered with the chill draft.

"We are looking for Kim Yong Shik," the taller man proclaimed. "If you just point him out to us, the rest of you can go on with your party."

Everyone looked at him but no one spoke or moved, except for Yong Soon's father. He'd jumped up at the first sign of the intrusion and stood there now, paralyzed by this menacing voice.

"There's good reason for us to believe this man is here," his companion interjected quietly. He spoke in Korean, using the familiar form.

Sun Yi froze. The others stared also, bewildered by the crude disruption. At one moment they'd been enjoying warm companionship. In the next instant the relaxed and friendly atmosphere changed to fear and hostility.

Reverend Lee tried to dispel the mood. "Here you will find no one but my countrymen sharing a New Year meal with me," he responded, moving in front as if he thought his body could shield them.

Sun Yi's eyes swept around the room and widened with surprise. There was one vacant place at the table! A plate containing the vestiges of an unfinished meal lay there.

She glided over to it; her head lowered like a serving girl's, and under the pretense of removing some of the other dishes, pushed that one telltale plate under the table. It was hidden, under the feet of the men who were still seated. Then, just as Yong Soon's father ushered in the officers, she retreated, her head still lowered, with the other platters in her hands.

"As you can see, gentlemen, we are all here together. No one else. What did you say the man's name was? You are welcome to join us in our simple meal."

Heavy steps of mud encrusted boots resounded on the polished floors that shoes had never touched. With rude gestures the intruders demanded identification papers and examined each one by one while silence echoed from every corner.

Sun Yi watched from the doorway and apprehension sliced through her though she had no guilt. So this is the way it happens. Never had she been exposed to these brutal indignities. How did her countrymen endure day after day?

Next the two men pulled open the doors of the wooden chests that lined the room. Did they really expect to find someone curled up and hiding in such small spaces? She wished she dared to challenge them out loud.

Instead, all of the women kept their heads bowed, hiding their faces from the strangers as they brushed past to enter the kitchen. Kettles and pans clattered as they continued to search. They moved next to the men's sleeping quarters with Rev. Lee following and soon emerged. Only the women's rooms remained unexplored. Surely they knew no man dared to enter. Or did they? Perhaps the custom of their country was less civilized.

Dr. Lee broke the silence. "Surely you realize by now that the man you seek is not here," the minister told the intruders. His tone was filled with patience and dignity. How could he remain so calm?

Their response was to push him aside. Then his voice rose in a tightly controlled anger. Its note of warning could not be ignored.

"It is our custom, as you know, to keep our women's rooms sacred from any intrusion by men. Thus, it would be impossible for anyone to enter without my knowledge."

Still the men attempted to push him out of their way.

"You have my word, honorable gentlemen. You need not search these rooms."

Somehow his gentle voice rang with authority. The police hesitated. They heard the sound of the men behind them rising to their feet. The one who was the shorter of the two muttered to his companion in Japanese and the other responded.

Sun Yi could not catch their words but when she saw his shrug and turn back to the main room she felt the thrill of victory. The sheer numbers of their potential opposition intimidated them.

Obviously they would not dare to challenge this basic rule of the Korean household. She heard the taller man speak, this time in Korean. His loud warning rang throughout the house.

"You may be sure, Rev. Lee, that you and everyone else who enters or leaves this place will be observed. And reported. You should be cautious. Follow our rules strictly or you may not avoid trouble in the future." Turning to the men who still sat in silence he barked, "Each of you stands warned as well. So long as you continue to visit this house you will be watched."

Again their boots grated on the floor. The officers stopped at the door and glared at their unwilling host before they left.

No one moved for several minutes after the gate slammed shut. Then one man crashed his fist on the table. The plates and bowls rang with the impact. Immediately he apologized to Yong Soon's father.

"My gesture is useless as well as rude," he told him.

Everyone nodded. They understood, for they, also, felt despondent. The authority was brutal but they were paralyzed by fear of the consequences if it were challenged.

Then someone reached under the table and brought out the plate that Sun Yi had hidden there and she felt all the eyes staring at her. She lowered her own but listened to their approval.

"We're all proud of you." Yong Soon's father said, "Your quick action saved a man from certain suffering and imprisonment. Though you are young you are as brave as any of us."

Praise surprised her. Actually praise was something she'd never heard before. Sun Yi bowed deeply but could say nothing.

The police had disrupted the mood of the celebration and no one remained long. When the last of them departed the girls sat with Yong Soon's father and listened as he told them of his work with the movement for independence. With his words those unexplained servants and delivery persons, all the suspicions Sun Yi gathered from her previous visits to his home, were confirmed now. He explained the operation of the Korean underground. The peddlers and beggars whom she'd seen stopping here were not what they appeared.

"Then those poorly dressed men I observed entering your home were actually carrying messages among the leaders of the movement to free our country!" she exclaimed.

Rev. Lee nodded his head. "And that is how we shall have to disguise our hidden young man, also, before he leaves here tonight." He added in sad resignation, "I'd hoped not to involve you young women in the work of men. Now I realize that your help will be necessary, even vital, to us in the weeks to come. After this incident I will be observed even more carefully. There will be limits to what I can do myself. You two, however, still have an excellent chance of escaping detection. Both of you will have an important role to play, if our plan is to succeed."

He warned Sun Yi and his daughter that they must make this choice for themselves, with a clear understanding of the danger they would face. There would be time to think about the decision.

Sun Yi recalled a conversation she'd had with a classmate not long before. The other girl chided her for her adamant stand against the occupation by the Japanese.

"Don't you see that Japan is becoming more powerful each day?" she'd demanded. "We cannot oppose them. That is useless. We must cooperate so we can share the benefits. It is our destiny."

Sun Yi had bit her lip, trying not to respond to this bait. No, she thought that day and again today. It will never be my destiny.

And with the simple act of hiding a dinner plate to protect an unseen patriot she found she'd made her decision already. From now on she would do everything within her power to help free her country. She committed herself to secure Korea's independence.

Nothing would deter her from that goal.

A few days after the New Year celebration, when snowflakes swirled about and icicles hung from the eaves of every roof, Sun Yi received a letter from home, from Kum Seung. It was not in her own hand, for of course she could not write, but her words had been carefully copied down by one of the boy cousins.

"The grandfather is seriously ill," Sun Yi read. "We understand why you have stayed away for so long, but this may be a time when you wish to be with your family. You may be sure of your welcome if you decide to return."

Sun Yi did believe Kum Seung would welcome her, but what of the others? Did her father or the other elders know of her summons? As she boarded the train for the journey north that would retrace the steps of her escape she was filled with apprehension.

There was one matter on which she was confident. This time she didn't fumble with the coins when she bought her ticket, and the blustery locomotive did not intimidate her as it had before. The winds blew bitter cold and she was grateful to wrap herself in the sigachima that she must still wear in public. It enveloped her student uniform. The white chogori with its full sleeves and the high waisted navy blue chima that billowed over her upturned slippers were discreetly covered by the outer garment failed to disguise her slender profile and unusual height. She was several inches taller than most girls of her age and that quality provided an aura of distinction to her carriage.

The train whisking Sun Yi past the villages and fields, now white, stark and bare, seemed also to carry her back to the time when she was a child. Strange. She'd thought the journey much longer then. The seed of determination to continue her chosen course still remained at the very center of her being but the sharp teeth of doubt nibbled at the edges of her resolve. Would the influence of her home and family now weaken the sense of purpose that she'd nurtured throughout the recent months and years while she became more capable of independent thought and action?

Grandfather was dying. She was glad she'd come home after all, for she had just one moment in which to bow and ask his forgiveness for her disobedience. He may not have recognized his granddaughter but she felt better for it anyway. She was shocked when she realized that she was just one of many family members gathered to honor their patriarch. No one but Kum Seung gave her much attention. It was a stunning reminder of the way in which life could continue in its routine patterns without the presence of one individual.

When the funeral procession formed on the third day following her grandfather's death Sun Yi watched with surprise as many of the tenant farmers who'd worked his lands all during his lifetime came to honor him. The Japanese military government attempted to eliminate the distinctions between upper and lower classes in Korea, not realizing that yangban were revered more because of their classical education than for their propertied status. Such respect could not be destroyed by a simple edict.

The coffin, painted in several colors and decorated with red and blue cloths, was placed on a wooden platform with two parallel carrying poles. Then twelve men carried it from the matang while one other rode on the front of the carrier ringing a handbell with slow strokes that gave a solemn beat.

The man leading the way bore a flag on which Sun Yi's father had painted Grandfather's name. The bell ringer sang each verse of the funeral song, which was then repeated by the twelve bearers.

Sun Yi walked with the other women behind the men of her family. They followed the hearse. A long line of lesser relatives and friends completed the group. They all climbed to the top of a high hill.

This place, selected by her grandfather long ago, offered a panoramic view. It was a place of exceptional beauty. In summer the slopes would be covered by wind swept grasses and patches of wildflowers. Fields, fertile and green, lay in geometric precision, on every side with the line of hills beyond them fading into the distant purple mountains. The winding curve of the Naktong flowed through the valley.

But on this winter day the flatlands and hills lay under a mantle of white. Time stood still and summer was far away.

A deep hole had been chopped in the frozen earth and after the coffin was placed in it, footend sloping downward, Sun Yi watched the younger boys take turns filling in the grave site until it was smooth and level. Food offerings were laid at one end and each of the relatives in turn bowed before it. Then the remainder of the fresh earth was piled over it until the mound reached high above her head. Grandfather was a highly esteemed person in life. The size of his grave would always remain to indicate his importance. Under the layers of snow nearby were similar mounds, gravesites of his father and grandfather that gave proof of her family's long continuity in its native village.

While Sun Yi stood among her relatives all dressed in white on this spot where the memory of her ancestors was honored, observing the traditional practices that had been repeated so many times in the past, her thoughts were already turning to the other life that she lived far from the home of the Yu clan. Would she ever return to this place? She felt all the forces of her new life combining to sweep her away, toward a destiny far different from any that the women of her family had ever known.

Already she had substantial knowledge of the organization that was making secret plans for a day of national protest and mass resistance to the rule of Korea by Japan. Sun Yi was determined to play a role, no matter how insignificant, in that plea for independence.

On the following morning she returned to Taegu.

A few weeks later Sun Yi was roused early one morning from her bed in the school dormitory.

"Wake up!" whispered Yong Soon, shaking Sun Yi by the shoulder.

The dim light of early morning accosted her sleep filled eyes but she woke sufficiently to recognize the urgency in her friend's voice.

Yong Soon repeated the command, adding, "We must go to my father's house. Now!"

Sun Yi struggled into her heavily padded winter clothing and followed as quietly as she could. She must not disturb the sleeping girls around her. Questions would wait until she and Yong Soon were alone.

The city of Taegu, though it lay in the southern portion of Korea, was still in the grip of icy winter and Sun Yi shivered when they left the building, not only from the chill but also from sudden apprehension. It flowed through her veins like a draught of spring water. The anticipated day was at hand. Was she prepared? Could she, at this crucial moment, summon the courage she would need?

"I told the head mistress that we were needed at my home today. Nothing more," Yong Soon explained, shutting the door soundlessly behind them. "It's better for no one at the mission school to know the truth. Total ignorance will be their best and also honest protection."

This pre-dawn summons was no real surprise. Ever since her visit of the previous week to the home of Rev. Lee Sun Yi had rehearsed over and over the reasons to justify her own involvement in this dangerous activity, until she convinced herself without even a glimmer of doubt that she could not relinquish such an opportunity to help the cause of her country's independence. As she walked over the snow encrusted path with Yong Soon the tall and slender young woman looked over her shoulder at the school building only once as it receded into the distance.

As she left its cloisters she cast off, also, the remnants of her childhood. School days were ended. She pulled the sigachima close about her, until only her sparkling and determined eyes could be seen within the folds of its hood.

Yong Soon's father's face had shone with the light of his unrestrained enthusiasm when he last spoke with the girls.

Self-determination for small nations.

These are the words, he said, that the American president, Woodrow Wilson, spoke when he met the leaders in Europe to settle the end of the Great War. In his efforts to promote a just peace, to end the carnage and suffering, he had not forgotten places like Korea.

The words of Wilson stirred hope and lifted from despair every Korean patriot who listened to its promise and saw in it a vision of a future time when Korea would become free once more.

The leaders of the great powers are meeting in Paris now, Rev. Lee told the girls. The Korean government-in-exile, in Shanghai, is sending delegates to the peace conference with a petition, an appeal to recognize the right of Korea to be independent. That's why we must act now. Surely the weight of world opinion will force Japan's leaders to withdraw, if only the truth be known about their cruel domination of us.

He'd listened to the words of Wilson's plea that the power of the world leaders be used "to provide for the freedom of small nations and to prevent the domination of small nation by big ones." It kindled the flames of hope in Rev. Lee and every other Korean patriot, both within the borders of their country and in the foreign cities where exiled men lived by their dreams.

But the petition to Versailles will not be enough, Rev. Lee warned Sun Yi and Yong Soon.

"We must cry out, with one strong voice that will be heard around the world," he exhorted, while they listened, both of their faces glowing with expectation.

A plan had been conceived, first by Korean students in Japan but gathering in momentum after reaching the homeland. It would be a movement on a national scale. The leaders of the Ch'ondogyo religious group approved of participation and enlisted the support of Christians among the Koreans.

"Together we will have a strength that cannot be defeated," Rev. Lee promised. "If each of us carries out our part."

Sun Yi knew she could.

This was the plan: The old former emperor of Korea, Kojong, who had been forced by the Japanese, in 1907, to abdicate his throne, died on January 22 in 1919. Public feelings against the Japanese in Korea were inflamed by the rumors that he had been poisoned because he supported independence efforts, or that he had committed suicide because he was in despair over the enforced marriage of his son to a Japanese princess. Even in the provinces far from the capitol people put on the traditional white hats of mourning. Quickly, these hats became more a symbol of anti-Japanese spirit than a true show of feeling for the last of the Yi dynasty emperors.

Such was the mood on this cold morning near the end of February when Sun Yi arrived at the home of Rev. Lee. The girls heard information of even more startling nature from him.

"The mass resistance plan is ready," he said. "The official funeral for Emperor Kojong is planned for March 3 in Seoul. Thousands of mourners will be traveling into the city for the ceremonies. It will be an ideal situation. The officials will not notice unusual crowds. Still, surprise is most important," the minister emphasized. "That is why this national protest will begin on March 1, two days before the funeral."

While Sun Yi's eyes grew wide, he went on; "Information about this must be carried throughout Korea in advance. You will be among those brave young persons of the Ch'ondogyo and Christian churches who will bring this declaration of independence to every town and village in Korea." His voice ended with a rising note of pride.

Then Sun Yi's eyes met those of Yong Soon. Hers were steady and Sun Yi's own sagging courage was strengthened by the determined will of her friend.

"We must notify everyone of the reading of the Declaration at 2 p.m. on that day in Seoul, in Pagoda Park, so their own participation, wherever they live, may begin at that precise moment,"Rev. Lee continued, "but some towns have been quite effectively sealed off. No one has been able to bring this information to our leaders in those places. Someone is needed to deliver these documents. It must be a person who will arouse the least suspicion of the authorities."

He looked at his daughter and Sun Yi. A half-smile flickered over his face and then the most serious of expressions replaced it.

"There is no one we trust more for this mission than you."

Yong Soon's father opened the doors of a beautiful cabinet, which stood in one corner. It was made of shiny lacquered wood with an intricate inlaid design of iridescent mother-of-pearl on the front panels. Inside lay stacks of newssheets, still smelling of fresh ink. Handing one to each, he asked once more, "Do you truly wish to be part of this?"

Sun Yi held the precious paper in her hand for the first time, reading:

"We herewith proclaim the independence of Korea and the liberty of the Korean people. We tell it to the world in witness of equality of all nations and we pass it on to the posterity as their inherent right."

At the bottom of the page were the instructions:

"At noontime on March l, 1919, the bells of Pagoda Park in Seoul will begin to ring. At that moment everywhere in Korea people should meet in public streets to hear the reading of this declaration and show the strength of their unity behind it. The demonstration must be peaceful. Whatever you do, do not insult the Japanese. Do not hit with your fists. Do not throw stones. These are the acts of barbarians."

Sun Yi's brown eyes burned with excitement as she read these words. It was a noble undertaking. At last something of great importance was about to happen and she would be part of it, helping it to succeed. A peaceful demonstration. No violence. Millions of people. All at the same time. Brilliant! It was the most impressive idea she'd ever heard.

"If you are caught with these papers you will jeopardize the secrecy of the entire plan," Rev. Lee warned. "In addition, you may be jailed, possibly tortured, for your involvement. Do you still want to be a part of this? The choice must be your own."

Could there be any doubt?

She heard his voice tremble and watched, transfixed by the sight of his eyes shining with intensity as he said, "By this notice every Korean will be informed in time to join in the protest. We will speak as one voice. A voice that will be heard by the powerful men of the western world. The only ones that can help us."

He laid the stack of papers on the floor in front of the girls.

Half an hour later Sun Yi laughed at her reflection in the bedroom mirror. Yong Soon, near by, joined in, but their laughter covered nervous trembling. Her mother had helped them to dress, providing the clothing. Sun Yi truly could not recognize her slender self in the image of the rotund and matronly figure who stared back at her. The long black braid was wound in a coronet around her head, the headress of a married woman. White mourning clothing, the short jacket with the bow ties on the right side near her shoulder and a long, full skirt falling over the baggy pantaloons that were bound near her ankles gave Sun Yi a rounded figure.

No wonder, for the many sheets of paper folded and bound close to her skin formed a bulky underlayer. When she wrapped the sigachima around herself she felt well camauflaged. Yet she still worried about how she would slip past the guards when she boarded the train. That each passenger was closely scrutinized, she was well aware.

"What do you think? Will I look like a widow?"

Sun Yi turned around, trying to view herself from all angles.

Yong Soon, though she was shorter, looked much like her, with her bulging figure wrapped in the voluminous white cotton outfit. She whispered back with just a slight tremor.

"You must believe you do. Let's be quick. There isn't much time."

A fellow conspirator took them to the railroad station in his wagon, leaving them around a corner so they could approach it on foot and each alone, as they had planned. Yong Soon would leave on a different train, traveling in the opposite direction. Neither of them knew when, or if, she would see the other again.

From this moment Sun Yi would have no one to rely upon but herself.

After purchasing her ticket she found a wooden bench in the shadow of the station wall where she could sit while waiting for the departure time. Sun Yi hoped desperately that she really looked like the country matron she was attempting to portray. Her heart's pounding drummed so loudly in her own ears that she felt certain her panic would be noticed. She concentrated on sitting quietly, her eyes downcast, and at last she began to relax.

When she joined the long line of passengers waiting to board she averted her face in what she hoped was a becoming modesty with her eyes focused on the ground in front of her. She clutched the peasants' small basket of food for the journey.

The uniformed guard stood next to the gate, staring at each person passing, sometimes asking a question. When her turn came what she had feared most happened. He stepped directly in front so that she could not pass.

"Where are you going?"

"My mother lies dying in the village of Kumho and I must hurry to be with her in her last moments." Sun Yi tried to keep her voice low and deferential. Despite the chill air, beads of perspiration were forming on her forehead and beginning to run down her cheeks.

Surely this man would force her to reveal her true mission at any moment.

But the guard hesitated. "You don't have the look of a married woman," he said, leaning down to stare into her face. Then he signaled to another policeman, this one dressed in ordinary clothing. "Go with this woman. See that she is really going to Kumho, to visit her mother. If she doesn't." he paused, "bring her back."

Once seated on a rough bench inside the train Sun YI turned her face away from her guard, watching as the twisting streets of the city sped past her window. He sat on the opposite side of the aisle. Soon they passed the snow-covered fields of the open countryside. Groves of fruit trees lifted bare branches to gray skies. The distant hills peeked through drifting shrouds of mist.

My beautiful country is hibernating, she thought. Spring will revive the land, but will this sad place ever recover from the oppression its people suffer? The lump of fear within her weighed her to the seat. How would she escape from the sight of this man? She knew she must.

Time passed. Still Sun Yi could not think of any solution to her dilemma. Kumho was near. She grew desperate.

Suddenly the guard stood up. "I'm going to the dining car," he told her, glaring. "Just stay put, my little widow. Don't try jumping off," he added with a twisted smile.

Sun Yi stared at her good fortune with disbelief. But where could she hide? He was right. There was no place on this train where he would not find her. She wished she dared leap from the moving train, as he'd suggested. But she must try something!

She rose, swaying, and walked to the opposite end from which he'd disappeared, then stepped to the next car. There were five more cars behind it and then only the caboose. She would try each one. She would not give up. Her hands sweated, her heart pounded. She looked around her. At least everyone in this car appeared to be Korean. Good! There, at the far end, was a woman holding an infant, a tiny baby. Sun Yi moved toward her, swaying with the motion of the car. Stopping next to her, she whispered, "Please help me. I am being followed and I must hide. Will you let me hold your child?"

The woman started but her surprise was quickly replaced by puzzlement, then understanding. She stood up, motioning for Sun Yi to take her place. Then she laid the small, still bundle in her arms and draped the shawl she had been wearing over Sun Yi's head and around her shoulders. She sat on an empty seat nearby.

Shrouded in the covering, Sun Yi pretended to be nursing the child. Fortunately the baby slept on, satisfied by the warmth of her body. She bent her face over the little one.

Moments later the guard burst in. His face was flushed. He pushed the other passengers aside, moving down the aisle, stopping to look into each face. Closer he came. He was almost next to her.

The train hit a rough spot and shook violently. Cursing, he reached out to keep from falling.

He stopped beside her. She closed her eyes.

Then the car lurched once more. He glanced at the mother and child, reaching out to catch his balance, and passed on to the next compartment.

Sun Yi sat motionless, barely breathing, until the train stopped.

Kumho. It was a small place. She stood up. Only a few passengers were leaving. Would she have to take the child with her? Just as she thought this, its mother whispered that this was her destination also. Sun Yi climbed down, clumsily hanging onto the baby while trying to manage her bulky skirts. The mother followed.

The guard was already outside. He stopped each person passing through the gate. Keeping her head bent over the child in her arms, she brushed past him. Again he gave her only a cursory glance. She walked away rapidly, wanting to run anywhere to distance herself from him.

Turning a corner, she handed the child back to its mother with a deep sigh of relief, then gripped the woman's hand for a moment.

How would the guard explain this to his superior?

But she had no time to think about his fate. The early darkness of a winter day was closing in and she must find the meeting place, a small church near the edge of town.

The strangers with whom she shared her mission welcomed her after she reached Kumho safely with the documents. The reception gave her a great surge of satisfaction. Discovery of the papers hidden within her clothing would have jeopardized the entire independence movement. She had not allowed that to happen. And on the day of protest Kumho would be a part of the nation-wide demonstration because of her efforts.

She hadn't realized that in Taegu, on her return, an even more dangerous assignment awaited her.

So she had come to be in this prison. It is in the morning that you know you are really in such a place. It is not simply part of a bad dream. This was Sun Yi's first thought when she opened her eyes on the day following her arrest.

How could she have slept at all? Around her the chill and damp air, heavy with the must of years past, permeated the gray stone walls and ceiling of the cell. How many others, prisoners kept unjustly as her, had this small space confined?

Sun Yi hurt so much that she knew this was no dream. Aches and stiffness from her bruises, yes, but even more from tossing through the long night, trying to sleep on the hard earthen floor with only a thin quilt beneath her. It was all quite real. But how could it have happened to her?

She was alone, locked into this tiny cell. She heard voices yelling, "Get up! Get up!" and raised her head, still heavy with sleep. Why? It was barely dawn. The light filtering through the small opening near the ceiling was only a dim grayness. The ever-present light bulb emitted a weak yellow glow.

Footsteps approached, sounding louder with each step, until they stopped outside the heavy wooden door that barred her way. Through the small opening in the middle of the door a voice called, reminding her to kneel, facing toward it.

"Don't move. "The voice was harsh and threatening. "Or you will be beaten."

Sun Yi waited. She remained in the uncomfortable position. Was someone watching her? Would the door open suddenly? She dared not to move, even when her feet tingled as though a thousand needles impaled them. Her legs swelled, turning dark from the lack of circulation. Still she waited. She had eaten nothing since this horror began. Despite her pangs of hunger she dreaded another bowl of food if it looked like what had been thrust through the opening in the door on the previous evening. A pasty mixture of boiled soybeans and millet mixed with a bit of salt, it was cold and gritty with sand and it smelled rotten. She could not swallow such a mess! The cup of broth served with it was greasy and salty. Now she was so thirsty that her tongue felt thickened. The wooden bucket was empty but she dared not call for water. The other bucket, pushed as far away from her as possible, she wished was empty. Would no one ever come for it?

Never in her seventeen years had she been assaulted by odors so nauseous as those surrounding her now. Even walking on a country road where the farmers used nightsoil for fertilizer she had never smelled anything like the stench that permeated this prison. It was a large and rambling structure of rough stone, two stories in height, and the entire building reeked of odors more foul than Sun Yi could have imagined. At first she felt she must die if she breathed the vile, gaseous air.

She had not died. After spending an entire night in this stagnant atmosphere she was still alive and somehow managed to sleep from time to time. The strength of her will to survive surprised her. Did any of the others who helped to carry out the protest confront the possibility of imprisonment first? She knew she had not, not really, no matter what Rev. Lee told her. She had not even dreamed that she would end by sitting in this dreary place, believing that sheer numbers alone protected her anonymity. There were countless thousands in the streets.

Those men who signed the declaration, the thirty-three leaders of Ch'ondogyo and Christian churches, they must have known. They waited for their arrest in a public restaurant after sending a copy that contained all of their signatures to the governor-general himself. She had made no such plan but here she was, with no hope but to wait for help and no idea of how long she would remain in this wretched place, but only a determination to survive.

How long ago it seemed since the day she stepped from the train with the borrowed baby in her arms. After she gave the child to its mother she was guided by friends in the underground who were watching for her. They had been cautious in approaching, waiting until she walked some distance from the station. Then she was taken to the home of a Mr. Song, who was the district leader of the Ch'ondogyo. They met in his wife's room within the inner courtyard to prevent eavesdropping. He had been acquainted with her grandfather, she learned, and his daughter was now a student in Sun Yi's school. She told him of the plans for March 1st and gave him the copies of the declaration and other secret documents that she carried hidden under her heavy clothing. She told him that the young patriot, Rhee Syngman, was in America now trying to present Korea's plea to President Wilson, whom he'd known when he was a student at Princeton University.

Mr. Song relayed her information to the educated young men of his town who were also members of the Ch'ondogyo. With so little time the message was relayed mouth to mouth, but with the tight structure of their group such communication was not difficult.

Throughout the following day Sun Yi had moved about the streets helping to transmit her message. To avoid attracting attention she again wore the covering of the sigachima, thinking how ironic it was that she used an old fashioned garment to foster an action and spirit which was quite its opposite. No traditional woman would dare to behave as she did.

When the information was dispersed Sun Yi returned to Taegu again by train and this time caused little notice from the authorities. All the trains were jammed with riders headed for Seoul to participate in the public funeral. She didn't mind standing for it gave her a better opportunity to become lost in the crowd.

Yong Soon returned safely, also, and both felt reasonably certain that their roles in the underground were still undetected. Sun Yi welcomed her additional responsibilities as a student teacher, in preparation for the full-time work she anticipated soon, teaching mathematics to the younger girls. Miss Adams, the headmistress who had once seemed stern and foreign, was now her friend.

Education was not an expansion of her mind. It was an explosion. When she left her village home she'd had a vague yearning to know more of the world beyond the walls of her courtyard. What she'd received was an experience unlike that of any Korean woman in the past. Not only did she study English, Japanese and the Chinese classics, but mathematics, science and geography. Debating skills were introduced to encourage the young women to think for themselves and to express their ideas with force. This was happening for the first time in the history of their ancient country. Sun Yi became aware of events happening in other parts of the world and she developed a strong feeling that both she and her land were a part of all the changes happening in the aftermath of the Great War.

Someone thrust a bowl through the small passage in the cell door. The food on it was just as poor as the last meal served. Only her determination to survive enabled Sun Yi to swallow its contents.

What could she do to fill the hours? If only she had a book to read, or even a paper and pencil! All personal possessions were denied her.

Thoughts and memories remained. The enemy could never take those away.

After three days a guard came in the morning with a clean quilt and some clothing. He told her that a girl had brought it from her school. She would be allowed this privilege on one day each week. It was a bright moment, bringing hope that she was not forgotten, that someone cared about her. The food improved. The rice, mixed though it was with barley, was clean and properly cooked. Her appetite increased and each day she began to feel stronger.

Later Sun Yi learned that it was Miss Adams who was responsible for the change in conditions. She'd begged to be allowed to provide Sun Yi's meals and the authorities relented out of fear and respect for her influence. From time to time Sun Yi was taken from her cell, displayed as an example of the good treatment received by prisoners when missionaries made periodic visits to inspect conditions. She was even taken to the courtyard for a few minutes of fresh air and exercise each day so she would continue to look well.

She was not allowed to speak with anyone.

After some weeks she and the young woman in the adjoining cell discovered they could understand each other by a system of taps on the wall. The guards discovered them when they became brave enough to whisper. The punishment was a day without food and water, and Sun Yi was transferred to the next cell, leaving an empty room between them.

Worse even, a new prisoner was installed in her old cell, one that wailed and screamed and babbled without cessation. Her nightmarish behavior continued for two weeks and during all of this time Sun Yi prayed that her own mind remain sane. For diversion she concentrated hours at a time, transporting herself in spirit to that hillside near her childhood home where she'd run away to sit under the trees in springtime, to watch the blossoms floating in the breeze. At times she actually believed herself to be on that grassy slope, young once more and weaving rings of sweet smelling wildflowers.

Four months later she was taken in an ox cart one day, with several other girls, to a court. Once more she bore the indignity of being led on a rope. Locked inside a cramped prison box of a room, she awaited her turn at a hearing. Many others came before her. When at last she stood before the judge he only delivered a tedious speech on the responsibility of women to be obedient.

"You should be a good wife and mother," he admonished, speaking in rapid Japanese. "You'll get nothing but trouble for yourself if you continue to teach young girls these wild ideas about independence."

Sun Yi dared to hope that this might be the end of her imprisonment but when his harangue ended she was led to an old Ford truck for the return to the jail, along with several others. Among the captives was an old woman. She'd been sentenced to death for her part in the demonstration but she did not understand Japanese. She had no idea of what was said in the courtroom and what was about to happen to her. No one wanted to translate for her.

Sun Yi returned to her cell and resumed the routine of prison life.

Not until some weeks later did Sun Yi again have reason for hope. Early one morning the door opened without warning. Sun Yi had just awakened. She stumbled sleepily behind the guard through the stonewalled corridor, past all those other tightly closed doors on either side of it. When she neared the end of the long walkway the blazing sunlight of the September day struck her eyes. She blinked and slipped on the uneven paving.

Sun Yi had been confined to the dim light of the cell most of the time for the past six months. It took time for her eyes to adjust to the bright world outside. She'd begun to forget it existed. Probably she'd be taken once more to the courtroom where she'd faced that judge earlier in the summer, hoping to gain freedom. But this time the guard only led her across the courtyard to a low building that stood separate from the prison.

She followed slowly, seeking energy to move. Once inside, she saw a man seated behind a desk so large it almost hid him. He had broad shoulders and wore a black uniform, too warm for this late summer day. The visor of the cap he wore low on his forehead mostly covered his glare, when he saw her.

"Aigo!" The expression of her surprise slipped involuntarily from her lips. That American man standing near the desk! She recognized him! He was the minister she'd often seen in the pulpit during services at school. Why was he here? His was the first kindly face she'd looked on since her confinement began. But the officer drew her attention by calling her name abruptly.

"Yu Sun Yi!"

"Yes, sir." She waited for him to continue, the silence that followed droning in her ear like a mosquito.

"Have you repented for your rebellion against Japanese law?"

"I do not recognize Japanese law." The smooth flow of her words, as if she'd rehearsed them, amazed her. She steadied herself for the next question, lifting her head and gazing directly at him. She felt that she had prepared for just this moment. "I am a Korean and I can only be ruled by the laws of Korea. I was not arrested by Korean police."

"Answer the question." As his voice grew louder his round face reddened.

"This is my answer. You Japanese have stolen this country. If Koreans invaded Japan, would you have done differently."

The muscle at his temple twitched. The pencil he held between his stubby fingers snapped in two. "You are here to answer my questions."

The interrogation continued, the same questions or variations of them over and over. Sun Yi answered, her responses similar to her first. She dared not look over at the minister. I can go back to my cell, she told herself. I did not tolerate all of those months to weaken now.

Finally he seemed to realize that she would never capitulate. With a weary voice he told Sun Yi that if she were a man she would receive harsh treatment for those answers but he decided to show mercy since she was only a young girl.

"You should be with your family. Don't you care about them?"

"Of course I do. It is for my family that I have acted, desiring to do whatever is within my power to help my country."

"If I free you, will you swear never again to join in subversive activity against your rulers?"

"If you mean will I never resist Japanese rule, I cannot swear to such a thing, for to me such action is not subversive."

He was a stout man and rivulets of perspiration rolled over his paunchy cheeks as he heaved a great sigh. His shoulders rose and fell with his deep breath. "You deserve a severe sentence for your disobedience. However you are still a mere child, a misguided girl. In time you will mature and realize the wisdom of the Japanese rule in Korea. You will come to see that we Asians were meant to unite and that Japan is a natural leader by destiny. So instead I sentence you to house arrest. You must return to your family home and remain there for one year."

Sun Yi stole a look at the minister. He hadn't said a word in her presence yet she knew it must be he who made this possible. She repeated the words of her sentence silently and felt herself growing faint. With great effort she focused her eyes on the officer, showing no expression. He would not see the effect of his words on her. But shock waves rolled through her brain as he went on.

"Every day you must report to the local police of your village. If you have shown the proper behavior at the end of one year the removal of your sentence will be considered. Remember that you will be closely watched at all times."

He turned away, motioning for the clerk to prepare the papers she must carry with her.

Being at home is certainly better than being in prison, Sun Yi admitted. But how could she continue to work with the underground if she was under constant observation. Was this how the entire movement was weakened? Any attempt on her part to contact her friends would surely cause their identification and entrapment. She would have to be cautious.

She nodded in understanding to the clerk but did not speak or look at the packet of papers that he placed in her hands. Naturally this officer was reluctant to give any prisoner his freedom. What need would there be for him if his jail were empty? He'd lose his reason for being here, be forced to find a new place for himself. There were many such men in this country today filling all the places in offices, pushing stacks of papers, giving orders in harsh Japanese, while the lowly labor was being performed by the Koreans so dominated and intimidated that they would never dare to dissent as individuals.

Slowly the last words spoken became clear. She was free! She could turn around. No bowing, and walk out of this room right now. She would enter once more the world of sunshine and moonlight, hear the noises of the city streets, see the green trees swaying in the wind, watch the hills recede to a distant purple, smell the rain when the clouds swelled. To savor all the sights and smells and sounds that a person free to roam at his own pleasure would calmly accept. That is the meaning of freedom.

Except that she must not leave her own home.

"My words are so poor. They can't express my feelings," Sun Yi told the Rev. Cartwright as they walked out through the iron gate together. The clang as it shut behind her signaled that her ordeal was truly ended. She took a deep breath and then exhaled as if to rid her of all the stale smells she had endured for six months.

"I've tried many times before to persuade them to release you," he explained, "without success or even any encouragement. Today there was a change of luck." He smiled down at her and slowed his stride when he saw that she was nearly running to keep beside him. "We could take a ricksha."

"Oh, no. It's wonderful to just walk and walk. You can't imagine how I've dreamed of doing this." When she'd caught up to him she asked, "What will happen to me now?"

"We promised to return you to your family home. You'll wait there for the year of your sentence and then, if you wish, you may return to the school here. We need young women like you, intelligent and capable. We hope to expand the school. There'll be teaching for you to do."

Sun Yi nodded, listening to the street sounds from the throngs of people on their early morning errands. She'd often imagined such noises in her dreams. Now they were real. That persistent clanking, a tinny vibration, could be none other than the vendor who sold yut, striding along with his long scissors at his side. He was followed by a legion of children clamoring for the chance to trade for his candy. She watched the old man in the white robe stop at each few steps and ceremoniously snip a bit of the pale brown hard candy and exchange it for a bit of plunder, a bit of rubber or some old shoes or some other oddment that he tossed into the sack hanging from his shoulder. Then he continued on, the children of the street trailing at his heels.

Sun Yi stopped to watch, realizing that she was fascinated by a sight that would, a few months earlier, have seemed unworthy of her notice.

Then the two of them, a Korean girl with her long black braid swinging behind her and a tall and thin black coated American man, his head shiny and nearly bald, threaded their way around the carts laden with fruit and vegetables, small Jonathon apples, long white radishes, pale green heads of cabbage, glossy red peppers, heaps of round onions, and more.

Around them she noticed everyone else heading in the direction of this marketplace. I suppose we look strange, she thought, realizing that many were staring at this couple.

"I think I'm hungry," Sun Yi announced as she surveyed the display of tempting food.

"We'll soon be at your school," he reminded her, but he stopped anyway and selected a huge yellow pear from the nearest vendor. "Take this with you. Call it your golden omen of good fortune for the future," he suggested, with a smile.

Sun Yi smiled back. She really felt like smiling, for the first time that she could remember. She tried it again and found that the simple exercise of stretching her lips into an upward curve lifted her feelings, tightly compressed for so long. She cradled the pear in her cupped hands, anticipating the moment when she might take the first bite of its crisp white flesh. Who would think a simple piece of fruit so precious?

"Thank you," she said. "First you give me my freedom and then you provide me a feast." The sudden thought clouded her face. "But the price. Was it great?"

"The pear?" Rev. Cartwright appeared puzzled by her question.

"No. Not that. My freedom."

He nodded. The minister was silent as they continued to walk. Finally he replied. "We all must find it necessary, at times, to conform to the way of our hosts, if we are to remain as welcome guests."

His meaning was clear. Would her family be responsible for the debt she'd incurred?

"I'm so eager to see Miss Adams," she remarked, sensing that this was the time to speak of some other subject. She thought of the last sight of her dear friend, on the day she was imprisoned.

"I'm sorry, Sun Yi. She would have been the happiest of all of us today. She always kept faith that you would survive. You know how difficult conditions are for us here. She was ill and returned to America a month ago. We are all in hope of her recovery."

The sadness in his eyes told Sun Yi another story. I'll never talk with her again, she thought.

The classmates were overwhelmed by her unexpected appearance. They knew she'd suffered for the deeds of each of them. Only Yong Soon was missing. Confined to her home, also, one of them told her, after her own recent release from the prison.

Dinner was a feast of celebration for her, surrounded by friends and served foods that now seemed delicate and delicious. But the ultimate luxury was to sink into the clean, soft ibuls spread on the warm floor. In all the days of her imprisonment she'd not dared to dream of such bliss.

In the morning Rev. Cartwright escorted her to the railroad station. She passed again through the streets of Taegu but this time in a ricksha, bouncing and dodging around the old men bent under the weight of their chige, the A shaped frame laden with sticks of wood or pots and other goods for sale looking far too heavy for their fragile backs.

"Don't forget," he said. "You must return to us when your year is over."

"I will," she said. But she wondered if she would find the courage to leave her home a second time.

The gray tile of the roof was the first reminder of that place. She saw it from the wagon as the oxen pulled them slowly over the last hill and then started down the narrow lane that led to their gate. It looked exactly as she remembered it and suddenly she felt very happy to be there.

She was weary. She needed this place of rest.

Father met her at the railroad station in Andong, for Rev. Cartwright had sent him a telegram. Although her father was now the head of the household he greeted her with a formality that she would not expect an elder to use toward his child, even if she grew to be an old woman. How he has changed, she thought, looking at his lined face. The hair she recalled as black and glossy now flashed with silver.

He wore white cotton pantaloons, bound at the ankles, and the vest and flowing white coat, however, and with the peaked hat of black horsehair to provide an illusion of great height she still looked up to him as she had when she was younger.

First he took her to the police station in Andong. The registration was required by the conditions of her release, he said. Then they turned toward home and it was on the way that he surprised her.

"You are changed."

He did not elaborate but she smiled at his words, pleased that he noticed, and she wondered if now she might have a certain freedom to express herself in his presence.

The wagon jolted on the packed earth, worn deep with ruts where the summer's heavy rains had turned it to mud. Today the hot sun of midday beat down but the air was fresh and clean, the blue sky of autumn cloudless.

"How peaceful," she said to herself, looking from side to side from her perch.

The branches of fruit trees on the floor of the valley hung heavy with red apples, but the persimmons, still hard and green, awaited the first frost to turn their color to orange. Flashes of color dotted the ravines and hillsides where poplar trees changed to gold and flame.

"Are you well?" There was an anxious tone in her father's question.

"Only tired, Abuji," she reassured him. "It's hard for me to think of being idle and useless." After a long silence she added, "I'd like to become useful again."

"You'll find this life quiet, not like the times you've known since you left. We do have a peaceful life, but it's often uneventful as well."

His tone of resignation saddened her, quite suddenly. Have I changed so greatly that my father can speak of such matters to me?

During the months of work with the underground Sun Yi became accustomed to working side by side others of a different social class, even with men. Their common goals forged a sense of equality that was reflected in their manner of speaking. Now her education, she realized, gave even her father a certain kind of respect for her. And it gave her an idea to consider.

If I shall be able to talk with him about the really significant matters, perhaps this year will not be so impossible to endure. I'd like to know if he thinks our efforts made a difference. Has Korea changed at all because of what we did on March 1?

Kum Seung was waiting by the gate. The eyes of her stepmother glistened with tears as she pressed Sun Yi's hand fiercely between her own. "I feared I'd never see you again," she whispered.

Later that day the two women sat in the shade of a small pomegranate bush within the walls of the kitchen garden. In this secluded place for women and children only they watched the three young ones at play on the matang, the large flat area of smooth clay next to the house. It was a pleasant spot on this warm day.

The youngster who had been a new born infant when Sun Yi first left for school was now an impishly lively boy of six, forever running, jumping, bouncing up in unexpected places. He looked at her with his face rosy cheeked, eyes sparkling, pleased to be the center of attention from the new lady he'd been instructed to call elder sister.

His three year old brother sat more quietly on the pavement, engrossed in watching the motion of a trail of ants. He looked up, though, from time to time from his safe distance, and his sharp eyes stared at her, unblinking.

Sun Yi snuggled the youngest baby, a girl, in her arms.

"Next month we'll have the celebration for her first birthday," Kum Seung promised. "You missed the others'. Our house has good fortune. Three healthy babies, and now you are with us again."

She appears well satisfied with her life now, Sun Yi thought, nuzzling her face in the soft hair of the child's small head.

But when the children had been praised and admired, Kum Seung turned to Sun Yi with her face serious and asked, "What will you do now? The matchmakers are sure to be here soon."

Han Ju ran across the courtyard, leaping like a young deer, and flung himself into his sister's lap. Sun Yi raised him by his shoulders and gazed into his sparkling eyes. His sheer joy brought a smile to her face.

Never had she seen a child so free with his emotions as this young half-brother. Since her return he'd stayed close to her side, sharing his small treasures and adventures only with her. The opportunity to become acquainted with the special nature of this boy was the one distinctly good part of her enforced sojourn. Perhaps his devotion evolved from the conditions of the busy household where no one else could spare time to listen to his wild stories with a moment of singular attention. Whatever it was, he had obviously chosen her as his companion and when he talked all of his emotions lay close to the surface, ready to bubble upward, so unlike the restrained expressions of the others. If he stumbled he would cry. If he found amusement he chuckled in his infectious style.

The air was warm on this day in mid-October and aromatic with the perfume of chopped cabbage, garlic and spices, for the time for kimchee making was here. All of the women worked since the early arrival of wagons pulled by bellowing oxen and laden with mounds of turnips, onions, radishes and cabbage freshly harvested.

Kum Seung directed their work, a coarse gray apron thrown over her long dress. Sun Yi offered to help but after watching her clumsy efforts Kum Seung pushed her away. "You are helpless in the kitchen," she laughed. "I'll be finished sooner without your help. Go sit in the shade and watch the babies."

Now Han Ju joined her as she sat under the persimmon tree.

"What have you been up to today?" She gave him a teasing look from the corners of her eyes.

He was sweaty and dusty and his breath came in deep gulps. He'd entered through the outer gate and he stood tall before his sister with his hands clasped behind his back as he told her, "Oh, elder sister, I've been chasing the grasshoppers in the rice fields with my cousins."

"And did you catch any?"

"Well, no,but almost. When we catch them we're going to roast them over the charcoal until their shells pop off. Then we'll eat them!" He waited for the grimacing look of horror to appear on her face.

Han Ju was in that delightful midland where he could still roam freely between the women's courtyard where the babies stayed and the freedom of the open fields beyond the walls, with only sporadic observation of his activities, the prerogative of the male child. His school lessons had not yet begun in earnest.

"Tell me a story. Like the last one, but with tigers in it this time," he begged, settling down beside her. He frowned his disappointment when a young maid approached just as Sun Yi began to speak.

"Your father wishes to see you in the great hall," the girl whispered.

Promising Han Ju that the story would come later, Sun Yi rose and followed her. For two weeks she'd been home and each day passed in a routine of household activities broken only by the arrival of the local police officer to verify her presence. There'd been no further opportunity to speak with her father alone.

So today she hesitated on the steps leading to the ondol room. The glistening light yellow jongpan paper, pressed from mulberry wood, felt warm beneath her slippered feet. The underground flues leading from the kitchen fires brought a comfort that was welcome on this brisk morning.

This room appeared just as it had on that terrible day when she begged her grandfather to send her to school. The quiet dignity was enhanced by a long scroll hanging on the far wall, on which was painted in black and white with etchings of pink the silhouette of a slender stemmed crane dipping its beak into a lily pond. The crane was the symbol of fidelity, honesty, a good conscience. Surely appropriate for the haven of her father.

He was seated in the space between two book chests, behind a long and narrow scholar's desk. How well she remembered the Buddhist designs carved into its side panels! Sun Yi sunk to her knees in a deep bow before him so that all she could see was the carved foot supports that raised the book chests above the heated floor. These chaek jang were, she knew, the finest antique furniture owned by her family. Each tall section, of polished gingko wood, had a flat top that curved upward at both ends, or the yellow brass of the braces and hinges captured and reflected the room's dim light.

"I'm pleased to see you looking so well, my daughter."

She raised her head and he motioned for her to sit on the red and blue brocaded cushions in front of his desk.

"Only two weeks in the country and your good health has returned."

"Yes, Abuji."

She waited patiently for him to continue but he was silent. She could not know that with her smooth, high brow and arched cheek bones, their points of natural high color in contrast to her cream colored complexion, Sun Yi brought sharp memories to him of another face from the time long past. Her mother lived in this house only a brief time and left this daughter, like herself a wilful spirit shrouded by a gentle beauty, as her only legacy.

At last the dignified gentleman broke from his reverie.

"We must consider your future, my child. You are already past the age when your life should become settled into a steady direction. I called you today to discuss your chance for a satisfactory marriage."

Sun Yi nodded, understanding that he must follow his duty in such a matter. She'd anticipated this conversation.

"With respect, Abuji, I should like to say that my life's path has been cast. My education and my work with the independence movement have determined my future. I'm prepared to live in a way that will seem quite unlike most women of my age. I've changed and cannot step back."

It was a long speech. When she finished she caught her breath, fearing the reaction it might provoke, expecting a burst of anger for her daring.

Instead, her father sat in thoughtful silence before he replied.

"The words you speak are true," he admitted, "and that is the reason my task is particularly difficult. However, it still remains my responsibility to secure your future. The life of your daughter and the course of a stream depend on what you do to guide them."

"Life seems like a river to me, Abuji," Sun Yi responded. "Unless it reaches a precipice and tumbles over, it can never make a waterfall, and the higher the cliff the more magnificent will be the display."

She raised her eyes a trifle to gauge his reaction.

"I have an education and I must use it to teach others. Do you know how badly I am needed? The old ways are finished. Soon nearly every young girl will have the chance to learn. Teachers must be ready for them. I must be among the leaders."

He shook his head.

"You cannot depart so easily from long tradition. Even with your education you must still rely upon your family to choose a suitable husband. You know you must trust me. You know that I will never force unhappiness upon you, but understand that I am able to foresee important matters that may not be obvious to you. There are many aspects to be considered in choosing your mate. You must think of the family, of its strength, of the honorable line that you represent, of your descendents. More than your own happiness is at stake."

He spoke slowly and Sun Yi sat with her eyes properly downcast, but she was thinking of that other time when she'd gathered courage to defy familial rule, to pursue her own determined goals. Could she, must she, force herself to such a crucial action again?

Father voice softened.

"Perhaps you can still be a teacher. Still, you must trust my judgment, for I have the wisdom of years, and I represent the traditions of our family." The tone of his voice changed, and he said, "The rule of the alien Japanese is tightening everywhere. Many people who were involved in the recent political activities have fled from our country, if it was possible. You, especially, must be careful. No," he raised his hand to emphasize the seriousness of his next words, "the efforts of so many brave patriots"

Did she detect pride in his voice? Did he include herself among the courageous?

"has not brought about the freedom of our country. Yet. The change of governor-general, the appointment of Admiral Saito, may be an omen of change in the future. It is unlikely you'd be out of prison without his moderating influence. But you can be certain that the Japanese are only more determined to tighten control over every part of our lives. The only difference now is that their way will be subtler. They will not allow us to embarrass them again. If you are to survive in such an atmosphere you must be both wise and cautious in all your actions. That includes your marriage."

Here I go from one prison to another, she thought, admitting that he was right. Sun Yi understood the suspicion of the authorities toward teachers in the Christian mission schools. Their students were among the most fervent nationalists. She felt her spirit plunge to its lowest depth as she sighed with resignation.

Raising her sleek dark head enough to see the toes of his slippers, she pleaded, "If you must choose a husband for me, Abuji, please consider the effect my education will have. I can not bear to live under the rule of a man who will not accept it. Let him be a man who will value me as I am."

Ignoring her last words, he rose, indicating that the conversation was ended. He seemed satisfied that she accepted his role.

Sun Yi rose, also, bowed once more, and left the room quickly.

The sunlight stung her eyes but Sun Yi was aware only of the gloom descending over her earlier cheerfulness. She stood by the door for a moment and then, with a suddenness that shocked even herself, she sped toward the outer gate, pausing only to exchange her slippers for the sturdy shoes worn out of doors before she passed beyond it.

Instinct guided her along the path that led to the hilltop. Eyes blinded by tears, she was not visibly conscious of her destination. Leaving the gray tiled roof far below, she walked with a sure step through the dry grass on the slope. The sun was still high. Early enough. She'd not be missed by anyone.

Since the time when she was a young child South Mountain held a particular fascination. She found a secret world on its summit. It beckoned to her, offering solitude with only the beauty of its natural setting as her companion. She turned to it now while she struggled with the turbulence of her thoughts.

Her father was determined, kind and gentle though he was. She did not doubt that he would resolve the question of her future for her. She was already old, soon too old, at the age of nineteen, for betrothal. And there was the question of her education and her political activities, her time away from the protection of her family, where every properly bred young woman was expected to remain until her marriage. She knew he thought her willful and difficult. She would never fit the role of a Korean wife, dutiful and obedient, first to her father, later to her husband and, eventually, to her son. The defiant desire for knowledge led her to experience a broader life and now she knew the potential for living, as she'd never imagined if she'd not left her home.

Sun Yi, breathing hard from the rapid climb and her agitation, stopped until she felt more calm, then continued upward at a slower pace.

The atmosphere of her school encouraged original thinking, independence, action, strengthened her patriotic fervor. For the first time she played a vital role in events beyond her own life. She became intoxicated with the power that came from acting with a strong purpose. Was all of this to end with nothing?

The wind blew harder at the summit. She brushed stray hairs from her face and shaded her eyes to look down at the valley. How often in prison she'd imagined this scene!

Confined to that cell, she'd hung in a suspended time warp, a void, not knowing what happened outside, deprived of human contact that could nurture her renegade spirit.

Then she was cast back into the mold of her childhood, in a home where nothing changed while she was evolving. She felt as a silkworm must, released from its cocoon and learning to fly when suddenly recaptured and forced to reenter a cast off and outgrown chrysalis. An impossibility.

How could she marry a stranger? There was no doubt that her father would think he was acting in her best interest. He wanted a life for her in which she would be cared for, secure, for how could a woman live without a husband in this country? His way could never be her way. Change was all around them and his generation with its patterns of tradition would soon be no more than a memory. He did not see it. What could she do?

Hold fast long enough for the year to pass! Then she might be safe.

> "Were you to ask me what I'd wish to be
> In the world beyond this world,
> I would answer, a pine tree, tall and hardy
> On the highest peak of Mt. Pongnae

And to be green, alone, green
When snow fills heaven and earth."

Lost in the words of the poem by Song Sam Mun, Sun Yi climbed on until, breathing in gulps of air, she stopped and looked around again. The wind whipped her chima and stung her cheeks into a rosy glow. Far below, the curve of the broad Naktong flowed through the narrow plain, with green squares of terraced fields rising in succession up the gently curving slopes. In higher places the poplar and gingko painted spots of gold. Over all the sky cast its brilliant blueness while the whistling sound of wind punctuated the air.

But another sound pierced the solitude, a song by turns sweet and merry, then sad, and always foreign but lilting, entrancing and luring her on to discover its source.

Sun Yi stopped on the brow of the hill, listening. She was perplexed. She could hear the music still, but from where? Its beauty brought tears and her vision dimmed. The sound floated all around her but she could not see the source of this strange haunting melody.

The sound grew louder as she climbed even higher. Some willows clustered near the crest, their branches spreading outward and touching, drooping close to the grass, forming a cap like an umbrella to provide a refuge of shade.

She walked steadily toward it and then paused, breathless, for she had stopped only briefly on the way up. The vibrant tones continued. Surely she'd discover the source in that grove of trees.

As she approached Sun Yi saw, all at once, the creator of this intensely pure music. He was seated beneath one of the trees, his back toward her, but she could tell by his dark hair that he must be a young man. He wore no hat but his clothing was in the western style, his jacket and trousers etching a sharp profile against the golden grasses that swayed around his seated form.

Sun Yi hesitated. She did not expect to meet another person up here. Everyone she knew was working at this time of day, either in the fields or in the small village shops, or in the courtyards and houses. No one would take a holiday at this time of year but herself. Yet here he was. He must be a stranger. It would be most improper to speak to him, alone as she was in this secluded spot. He had not yet seen her. She could turn and leave.

Despite these thoughts, Sun Yi did not move. Some force she did not question, perhaps only her own strong sense of curiosity, or possibly that same thread of innate rebellion that led her to follow her own will, now compelled her to remain here.

Thus, when he did turn and saw her for the first time her form was outlined against the horizon above the grassy slope, with the gold of the sunlight delineating the curve of her head, and the billowing mass of her chima caught and whipped sidelong by the breezes, as though she might have stepped forward out of the sky itself, bathed in this luminous glow that was a scene of pure fantasy, or some creation of his imagination.

At any rate, the silver flute dropped from his lips, halting the pure sounds in mid-song.

Since they had seen each other she knew she must speak.

"Ah nyun ha sim ni ka."

She did not look directly at him but he responded with the same greeting, rising to his feet at the same moment. She noticed that his height exceeded hers by several inches. He looked down at her when she said, "Forgive my intrusion."

Her voice was soft and he stepped forward to catch the sounds.

"I didn't expect to find Someone else here and then I heard the music. I had to discover how it could be, up here in this solitude."

He held out the instrument. "It's only my flute."

"But what is.flute?" The foreign word was as strange to her as the appearance. Its slender and shiny surface was as different as the sounds it produced. Curiosity drew her closer. She forgot to consider the propriety of her behavior as she studied the source of the melody that drew her to this mountaintop.

He held it out to show her. Her fingers grasped it.

"It's slippery!"

It felt warm from the sunlight that flickered through the net of leaves above them.

"Can you show me how you play this? Its voice is so clear. It does resemble the ok dae guem," she added.

He brought one tip of the silver flute to his lips and an upward scale trilled, his fingers flying agilely, their tips pressing the small openings that cascaded up to the mouthpiece.

Sun Yi shook her head and smiled. "Well, I have seen some musical instruments that are played in this way," she told him, "but none of them ever sounded like that."

"That is because no one else has ever sounded like Mozart," he explained.

"Mozart?"

"The man who composed the music you have heard me playing. He lived in Europe more than one hundred years ago."

"But how do you know about Mozart?" She waved her hand to indicate his appearance. "You don't look like someone from Europe." Now that she was closer she knew that this man was not one of the Japanese, but a Korean like herself.

He responded by taking his western style jacket off and spreading it upon the ground.

"Sit here and I'll explain."

Sun Yi dropped to her knees, uncertainly, and the stranger sat also, facing her with his legs crossed, the shiny flute lying carelessly across his lap. With the collar of his shirt loosened he appeared to her hardly more than a boy and the reserve she'd felt on first approaching him was swept away with the rush of curiosity about the strange words he spoke.

"I learned to play this flute while I was a student in Germany," he began.

"Germany!"

Sun Yi had never met a Korean who'd traveled outside her country.

"It's a good companion to have in a place where you feel alone. I've just returned. I'm here to visit some members of my father's family. They live near Yongju."

Yongju was not far from her family home. So he was not really a stranger.

"So I came out here today, just to enjoy walking and to admire this magnificent view." He spread his arms wide to include the vista she'd always loved. "Why are you here?"

The abrupt, direct question startled her so that she responded in a similar manner rather than taking time to consider her words and phrase them in ambiguous and formal style used between persons not well acquainted.

"I always come to South Mountain when I have a need to be alone, to think about matters important to me."

"Does South Mountain belong to you then?"

"When I was a child I thought it did, but of course now I know better," she smiled, smoothing her chima about her. "But my home is near the foot of this mountain so it's always been close. Even while I was far away this South Mountain stayed close in my thoughts."

He leaned forward with an eager look, asking, "Are you the one? Could you be the one who was imprisoned after the Mansei day?

"How do you know about that?"

He drew back as if stung by her rebuke.

Sun Yi resented the intrusion of her private life. None of her actions for the independence movement were carried out to draw attention to herself.

"Everyone in the home of my relatives knows about you. Most of them have great pride. It is a distinguished honor to produce a patriot from your own province. They say you were quite brave."

Sun Yi frowned. "And the others? What do they say? That I stepped out of my proper place?"

"There are some who say that. Not me."

"Well, what about yourself? Wouldn't you have done the same? Where were you on Mansei day?"

"If I'd been here. But I was on a ship in the middle of the Indian Ocean on March 1."

How could this be? That she, Yu Sun Yi, should be sitting on a hillside, engaged in an intellectual fencing match with a man she'd just met! She didn't even know his name, or that of his family! Had her independent nature carried her this far from the traditional upbringing of her childhood? She was speaking to this man as if he were one of her classmates preparing for an academic debate. Her sense of proper behavior should propel her onto her feet and send her straight down to the walls of her courtyard right now, without one backward glance.

Instead, she remained as she was. Never had she held such a conversation and she was far too intrigued to break it off at this point.

"I was once a mission school student myself," he continued, "in Seoul. My teachers encouraged me to study western medicine and some of them helped me to find a place at the university in Munich. That's in Bavaria, a part of Germany."

"I know that," she retorted. When he raised his eyebrows she said, "Girls study far more than the skills of the home in my school." This young man provoked antagonizing responses. She couldn't help herself.

He only shrugged and continued, "The Great War began soon after I arrived in Munich. Since travel was impossible, I remained there and completed my studies. And I learned to play this." He picked up the flute and laid it upon his lips again, playing a cheerful little song. "From The Magic Flute," he told her when he'd finished. "That is an opera, also written by Mozart. After the war ended I was able to return to my home here."

"Oh, what was it like? Would you tell me about Munich, and Bavaria, and Germany? All of it! Is it very different from our country?"

The golden lights in Sun Yi's eyes flashed with intensity. Some time later, after she listened to his descriptions and stories and they'd laughed together over some of his misadventures in a strange culture, she asked, "What will you do now?" Sun Yi's interest in this stranger replaced her earlier antagonism when she thought he'd attempted to demonstrate his superior knowledge.

His face turned serious. "I am returning to Seoul next week. I hope to open a medical clinic there where I can use the skills I have learned."

"Do you expect to be successful with your western medicine? I believe most Korean people still prefer the ancient methods of hanyak."

She knew the younger men were reluctant to challenge the beliefs of their elders. In fact the practices introduced by the American missionary doctors were slow in gaining acceptance.

He laid down his flute. Placing his fingertips together, he spread out his hands before her. Slender and long, blunt tipped, with a delicate look that belied their strength.

"With these Korean hands I hope to persuade my countrymen, sooner or later, that we can make good use of foreign ideas while still retaining the essence of our customs and traditions. It's not necessary to lose the best of the ancient ways while cultivating the most useful of the new, even though they come to us from the West."

The hands of a skilled surgeon, Sun Yi thought, but also the hands of a musician. A sudden thought caused her to lean toward him and ask, "Will the Japanese allow you such freedom?"

"That's one of the more promising reasons for becoming a physician in Korea today," he told her. "Skilled medical care is one kind of training that the Japanese need as much as anyone. Since I can be of use to them they'll give me a measure of respect and freedom. It helps that I wasn't part of the Mansei demonstration. I'll be trusted. So I can be effective, and help to preserve our country at the same time."

The sun's rays, low on the horizon, pierced the branches of the willow tree and Sun Yi jumped up.

"It's late! How long have I been here?" She would have to hurry or she would surely be missed. "I must go. Your interesting new ideas have distracted me and I stayed to listen when I had no intention of committing such indiscreet behavior. I hope you will forgive me this one time of immodesty."

Her words brought a quick smile to his face and his direct look caused her to look away. He knew she did not mean those words!

"You must understand that I've been in the west for many years. I've learned to accept social customs that are not as rigid as ours. Your behavior seems entirely proper to me. And," he added with another smile, "no one else will know of it." Then he hesitated. "I would like to ask one question of you, before you leave. Your name, your little name?"

Softly her lips formed the words by which she was known only in her family circle.

"Sun Yi," he repeated. Then, to himself, "Yes. Angel. I'm not surprised that you have that name. That is how you appeared to me when I first saw you." He bowed. "And I am Lee Jung Ho."

"Forgive me my haste, Dr. Lee." A feeling strangely disturbing stirred within Sun Yi and she turned away, saying, "I must not be late."

She walked fast, not daring to look back, even once. Yet she was sure he still watched her until she was out of sight. Her thoughts confused her. What a strange meeting! But what an interesting person he was. He spoke to me as if I was completely his equal. And now I've done it again. I've broken another rule of women's behavior by talking with a man outside of my family alone. It will be my good fortune if we never meet again. I seem condemned to trespass against all the restrictions of my life.

The icicles were beginning to melt. Sun Yi stood by the window watching as drops of water fell onto the snow covered ground. For months the long cylindrical shapes hung from the curved eaves of the tile roof. Winter, longer and colder this year, was coming to an end.

She longed for the arrival of spring. Perhaps she could climb again to the summit of South Mountain. Her last afternoon there sometimes seemed to be nothing more than a fantasy. Had that meeting really happened or was it only a dream? If she returned to the place she would know.

Han Ju burst into the room, covering the distance with a skip and a bounce. She turned and the somber expression on her face transformed itself into a smile of welcome for him. This child never walked. He rushed toward every destination. And even though she'd been teaching him here in the cozy warmth of the ondol room all through the winter he still arrived eager to begin each morning's lessons.

Sun Yi, also, looked forward to these daily sessions. In the beginning she undertook them only as a way of speeding the passing of the days until she could return to her real life at the mission school but soon she discovered that her brother was bright and quick to learn. He hung on every word she spoke. Preparing his lessons became a challenge. She honed her skills as a teacher while she found new methods for developing his abilities.

The hours did pass swiftly but she found joy in his response while she filled his retentive mind with stories of Korea's past, its folk tales and its history. There were times when she thought of that book buried on the hillside near her school in Taegu. Was it still there? She'd like to have it with her now. She relished Han Ju's comments and observations as she shared this knowledge that he would never learn in a school controlled by the Japanese.

"Remember," she warned, on one of their first days together, "that the language I am teaching you is our own secret. This will be your own special, private way of speaking and writing. You must never allow anyone to hear you using it outside of our home."

"Why?" he asked with his usual inquisitiveness, his dark eyes wide with wonder at her admonition.

"Because we are not free to be ourselves. Those people who control us will be displeased to hear you speaking the language of our country. In school you must use only Japanese. But someday we will be free again. You must be ready. If you learn Korean at home you will be able to use it everywhere after the Japanese leave. Then it won't have to be hidden."

Sun Yi hoped that he understood, in some simple sense, what she was trying to tell him. At least he did promise, looking at her with his solemn demeanor, to keep the secret. The boy believed everything, implicitly, that this elder sister told him.

So each day she taught him a part of the Korean alphabet, hangul, and he absorbed it easily, imitating the lines she wrote with his own pencil as they sat side by side at the low table.

"You are fortunate. Did you know that?" she asked him one day, after praising his page of writing.

"Why?"

"Because hangul is possibly the simplest and easiest alphabet that any child can learn."

Again he wanted to know the reason.

"Long ago," she explained, "hundreds of years ago, in the fifteenth century, Korea had a king named Sejong. He was the third king of the Yi dynasty and the wisest of all. He was not only wise but also learned and he cared about all of the people he ruled. He knew that scholars could write the most complicated words in Chinese characters and read the classic stories written in Chinese. King Sejong. He was called The Great. He wished that everyone in his country could write the language spoken by them every day and read the wonderful stories that only the learned men knew. Most of the people worked hard every day and had no time for long hours of study, so the method of writing in Korean would have to be less complicated than Chinese characters."

She looked up. While she was talking Kum Seung had slipped in silently and she was sitting near the door, listening. With a nod to her Sun Yi went on, "So King Sejong called his most loyal scholars and told them what he wanted. With their help he invented this new alphabet, the one you are learning now. With this alphabet any Korean word can be written, just by combining the signs for each sound."

"Show me," he begged, and Sun Yi picked up her pen.

"Like this. He made a symbol for each sound in the Korean language. Sounds like 'oo' or 'ah' or 'ee' are called vowels. We have ten of those and each has its own sign."

She wrote the list for him.

"Now the other sounds, like 'k' or 'b' or 'sss' are called consonants and there are fourteen of them. Each has its own sign. When you put the signs together in any combination you will have the entire word. Even a long word can be written. All you have to do is to combine as many of these sounds as you need. You can write any word in the Korean language if you know these twenty-four signs!"

"Please show me how."

"Well, let's use the word for 'rice'. Pahp. Take the consonant sound 'p'. It is written like this: Then, the vowel sound 'ah', written like this: Next, the sound 'p' again: Combine all three signs and you will have the word: Pahp."

"Why doesn't everyone use this hangul now, if it is as wonderful as you say?" demanded her student.

"For one reason, many people still think it is better to keep the tradition of using Chinese characters to write our language, since it has always been the language used by the most learned scholars, who we respect highly. But many years of study, and an excellent memory, are required if one is to learn it well. Since the Japanese have come to our country they want us to use their language. They hope we will forget our own and become more like them, you see. That's why we are not allowed to learn hangul in school any longer."

He nodded his head. "So our language really is special, isn't it?"

Sun Yi glanced toward Kum Seung and smiled. She'd been telling her that this child was extraordinary and now she was witnessing the work of his brilliant mind for herself.

"The way the Korean language sounds is special, as well," Sun Yi continued. "And this is most curious. Listen carefully. Korean words do not sound like the Chinese, although China is our neighbor and has been our friend for a long time. Korean is somewhat like the Japanese spoken language but still it is different. It is more like the language of some people who live far from us."

Sun Yi stood up. "Look at this map with me." Opening the doors of a black chest that was covered with designs of inlaid mother-of-pearl, she unrolled a parchment and showed him the outlines of continents and oceans on it. Han Ju scrambled to her side.

"Here," Sun Yi laid her finger on a peninsula. "This is Korea, where we live." Her finger traced a broad arc as the pointed to the vast area north of China. "From this part of the world, many years ago, men took their families and traveled over great distances to make new homes."

She became aware that Kum Seung was looking over her shoulder.

"Way over here," she slid her hand to the top of the map, "is a country called Finland. The people of Finland speak a language that is like a cousin to our Korean. Although it is different, it resembles ours in many ways. And down here," her finger slid down,"is a place we call Turkey. The language of Turkey is also a cousin to Korean. And even over here," she raised her hand to indicate a portion of the area recently disputed in the Great War, "the language of the Hungarians has some resemblance to the manner in which we speak."

She sat back, appraising him. "Now how do you suppose all of these people living so far from each other could speak in way that are alike?"

Han Ju clapped his hands. "Maybe someone flew from one place to another, like a bird, landing long enough to show them how to talk."

Sun Yi laughed and Kum Seung joined in.

"What good ideas you have!" she praised him. "But it wasn't quite like that. Not a bird person, but many people, traveling long distances, looking for better places to make their homes, for many years. It's possible that all of them started up here in the northern part of Asia. Some moved this way," she laid her hand on the Korean peninsula,"while others settled in these other lands. In each place where they settled they taught the people already living there to speak the language of the newcomers. This took a long time, of course. Longer than the years you or I shall live. But in each of these lands the way of speaking changed, little by little, as the new settlers stayed put and didn't travel about much anymore, until now, when each way of speaking has become just enough different from the others' so we can no longer understand each others' speech. If you or I were to travel to one of these countries," she pointed to Finland, Hungary and Turkey on the map, or if someone of them came here he would not be able to understand what we are saying, either."

Han Ju's face turned sad. "Too bad," he murmured.

Sun Yi had a sudden impulse to hug him but she restrained herself, knowing that his dignity would never allow such a demonstration of her feelings. Instead she praised him again, telling him that today's lesson was one of the best he'd ever had.

Later, when they were alone, she told Kum Seung, "Now you've seen for yourself what this precocious child is capable of doing."

"I've seen what a natural teacher you are," replied Kum Seung.

"Perhaps, but it is a simple matter to teach when the student is extraordinary."

"For all of that, what kind of future will he have?" his mother demanded.

"What do you mean?"

"You know that no Korean man can hope to rise to a position of responsibility unless he is willing to cooperate wholeheartedly with those in control."

Teaching Han Ju was not the only way that Sun Yi found to pass the time during her winter of enforced seclusion. She surprised Kum Seung by asking to help with the preparation of food and learned how to make some of the complicated special dishes, such as sin su lo, and cut the shellfish, meats and vegetables artfully to develop the particular taste and texture of each, even simmering the combination in a delicately seasoned sauce that she prepared.

Sun Yi even developed the patience to sew. A quilt that she began before the first snowfall was nearly completed.

But most extraordinary was the way in which her father took her into his confidence regarding the business matters of their family. This first happened on the day when she met in the corridor just as he shut the gate after some departing guests. She saw the indescribable look of sadness on his face.

"Abuji," she spoke impulsively. "What has happened?" She followed him into the ondol room.

When they were seated he told her, "I've been forced to sell more of our land. There was no choice this time."

He explained how the Japanese, settling in ever increasing numbers in the province, were demanding land and setting their own price, never more than a small fraction of its true value. If he did not comply a great deal of trouble would follow. But without land to produce rental fees the family income would shrink.

"What of the farmers who live on the land?"

"They will suffer, also. If they're allowed to remain as tenants their share will be less. If they are forced off, they will become landless wanderers."

Sun Yi knew that her father, and his father before him, had always been a fair, even generous, landlord. Now all would suffer together from this sale and its consequences. Yet, who could put an end to it? Resistance was useless.

Her father had not spoken again of the arranged marriage plan. Sun YI avoided the topic, but she knew his intention was unchanged. Did he really believe, with many of his generation, the life of the your daughter and the course of a stream depend on what you do to guide them? She had no doubt that he did, for the minds of the elders such as he were hopelessly tied to the past.

Still she felt great affection for him. "I wish that I could do something that would help, Abuji," she told him now.

"You have already done more than anyone would expect of a daughter," he replied. His voice was heavy with sadness. "but we all know nothing has been achieved so far that will alter the determination of Japan to subdue our country."

Spring did come, finally, with a burst of green over all the hills. The last snow melted and all the fruit trees blossomed white and pink. Doors and windows were opened and sweet warm air filled all the rooms of their home.

Sun Yi could have recognized the season without these signs, for every corner of the house was scrubbed, swept and polished. Everyone, including the children, helped. Sun Yi supervised the mending of summer clothing. She suspected this task was given her to keep her out of the way. Even the yongpan paper in the ondol room was changed. Workmen came from the village to put down a glistening new layer of mulberry paper on the floor.

The house was immaculate, ready for the guests invited to the Tano festival. That carefree celebration, so ancient its origins were unknown, always happened on the fifth day of the fifth month by the lunar calendar. Everyone prepared for this official welcoming of springtime with a contagious enthusiasm. Even the oppressive rule of the Japanese could not subdue the spontaneous gaity.

First, early in the day, gifts of food are taken to the graves of the ancestors.

Next, a swing is hung from the largest branch of the fig tree in the women's courtyard, the hemp rope tightly secured. This for the one day in the year when all young women fling decorum and dignity aside to indulge themselves, releasing their spirits in a friendly competion.

Kum Seung looked lovely. Sun Yi watched her greeting the friends she seldom saw. She was still slim and youthful, though the mother of three, her black brows distinct against her smooth white complexion. Her cheeks glowed with a touch of rose and a quick smile lit her face after each bow.

It was exciting to see this house full after the quiet of winter. Women from all of the neighboring yangban arrived and their voices combined in a lively concert. Long tables in one corner of the courtyard were laden with red apples and golden pears brought out from winter storage. They glowed like jewels amidst the dried persimmons and platters of crisp namul, all arranged in careful patterns of color beside long strips of crackly dried fish and varieties of fiery kim chee.

Tables for the men were set with a similar assortment of tempting foods in the outer courtyard that Sun Yi helped to arrange earlier. Now the men of the yangban families were meeting there and she would not be allowed to appear. Only the serving girls could thread their way among them, offering platters of freshly broiled meats and steaming rice. Afterwards she listened to their voices blending in mirthful and increasingly raucous songs, spiced by free flowing yakju and the high spirited gambling games.

This was a day to rejoice in being alive. Forget past troubles, ignore the future. For the women the highlight of their day was the young girls' swinging competition. Sun Yi looked forward to the sheer exhilaration of participating in it herself.

Each girl tried to outperform the others, standing up on the swing board and pushing higher and higher, rising sometimes above the wall where it was possible to command a brief view of the men gathered on the other side.

The others, seated in a semi-circle, clapped in unison, cheering the girl on the swing to further heights.

Kum Seung, encouraged by the growing merriment, stood up and declared, "I can still do that!"

"Why don't you try?" called one.

Amid their laughter, she climbed up on the board, grasped the thick rope on either side and pushed away, swinging higher and higher, faster with each push, while the women below cheered and clapped harder. Her white chima billowed behind her.

Faster and faster, as high as any of the others had dared, she soared while the handclapping beat a rhythmic accompaniment to the motion and all eyes followed her path back and forth.

No one noticed the rope twisting from the branch, losing its tension. Sun Yi, standing to one side where she guarded the young children out of the swing's path, saw it slip, but it snapped before she could cry out a warning, and it gave way just as Kum Seung reached the highest point. She plummeted to the hardpacked earth. The board, swinging wildly, struck her on the side of her head.

She lay, crumpled, a heap of white, motionless. The others rushed to her side. Sun Yi saw Han Ju standing in the doorway, frozen with shock. She grasped him by the shoulders.

"Go quickly! Tell Abuji that Ohmanee is hurt. Hurry!"

Han Ju obeyed and he returned in a moment, bringing his father with him. Right behind them came another man, and he stepped forward with authority.

Those clustered around Kum Seung drew back when they saw this stranger. When he knelt beside the apparently unconscious woman Sun Yi saw his face and, her hand to her mouth, gasped in surprise.

How could he be here? He was the same man she'd spoken with on South Mountain months earlier. Dr. Lee, here, now, in her own courtyard! She would never forget that earnest, kind face. It must be he, though he wore the traditional loose white trousers and short jacket just like the other men.

Caught between the sudden desire that he give some indication of recognizing her and her fear of revealing before the others that they were acquainted, she edged back and hid among the women. Despite concern for Kum Seung, Sun Yi found herself in a maelstrom of emotions.

If her earlier encounter with this Dr. Lee became known she would disgrace her family. But would he give any sign that he remembered her? Sun Yi's anxiety faded while she watched him demonstrating his sincere attention only to Kum Seung. How foolish of her to even contemplate his doing otherwise!

Now she heard him speak to her father.

"It is best to move her to a more quiet place. She is only stunned by the fall."

Abuji suggested a room at the rear of the house, far from the sound of the frivolity, and Dr. Lee lifted Kum Seung gently, cradling her like an infant, while Sun Yi's father led the way.

Han Ju hovered nearby, a look of great distress on his face. Poor child! She'd forgotten all about him. She took his hand and smiled to reassure him. Together they followed his parents and Dr. Lee.

"Aren't we fortunate to have this doctor here? Your mother will be all right now." She whispered. "You must not worry."

But she did, and the cause for her concern was the return of that strange and unsettling feeling that seemed to make her heart's thumping audible.

Sun Yi pulled the silk quilts from the wall cupboard and spread them on the floor so he could lay Kum Seung down on them. In doing this she turned and faced the young man for the first time this day, and held his eyes for one brief instant before lowering her own.

She saw not one flicker of recognition in them. He didn't remember her. He doesn't even know who she is. Why did she feel disappointed? But how could he have forgotten? She recalled every minute of their meeting. She'd relived the scene time after time through the lonely months of winter.

Kum Seung stirred. Sun Yi bent over her as she opened her eyes and looked about. She was at first bewildered but when she focused on Sun Yi she seemed reassured. The doctor laid his hand on Kum Seung's forehead, the same hand that she'd watched moving confidently upon the silver flute. It had a calming effect. The injured woman relaxed.

"It's probably not a serious injury," he was telling her father, "but as a precaution she should remain here, resting, for a day or two, until we can be certain there has been no head injury. Is there someone who can stay with her?"

"I'll stay," Sun Yi spoke for the first time since entering the room. "if you can tell me what I must do to care for her."

Abuji gave her a sharp look before he acknowledged her reluctantly.

"My daughter, this is Dr. Lee. He is related to the Lee family near Yongju and spending some time with them."

He did not introduce her to the doctor.

Though she was not aware, the bright spots coloring her cheekbones enhanced the darkness of her eyes and gave her a striking beauty. She only knew that her heart was beating again with a vibrant intensity.

Dr. Lee told her of the signs she must watch for in the patient and cautioned, "Send for me at once if you notice any of these changes."

After Kum Seung begged them to assure the guests of her well being and to continue the festivities he and Sun Yi's father left.

The long rays of afternoon sunlight filtered through the latticed window. Kum Seung slept. Sun Yi sat, motionless, on a cushion nearby, feet tucked under her chima and chin cupped in her delicate hands, with a rapt look on her ivory face that was both sad and thoughtful. The room was still but she heard the distant murmur of the Tano guests' voices, an occasional burst of laughter, some singing. She was pleased that the accident, since it was not serious, had not ruined the holiday for the others. Kum Seung must be recovering, or Dr. Lee would have shown more concern. Nevertheless she continued to watch her carefully.

Han Ju peered from the door occasionally but a smile and a wave of her hand from Sun Yi gave him the encouragement to believe all was well and he would skip away.

All was not well, actually, for his sister was attempting to understand the dread and anticipation that battled within her after today's unexpected events. Though she had met the young doctor only once before, she found his presence comforting and familiar. She trusted his ability, his judgment. Perhaps she felt this because the memory of their first meeting refused to disappear, haunted her, and sometimes even returned in her dreams.

Today she was wide-awake. This was no reverie. Seeing him in this unexpected manner transformed her usually calm demeanor into an excitement that she feared must be visible. Thankfully she had this excuse to remain out of sight.

When she next looked at Kum Seung she found her awake and staring at her.

"You look much better." Sun Yi wanted to distract the attention away from her. "Your face has color again."

"It was a foolish stunt." Kum Seung shook her head from side to side on the pillow, wincing as the pain returned with the motion.

"That doctor is a kind man. How do you suppose he happened to be here?"

Sun Yi shrugged, as if the question were of little interest. "Abuji told me he was visiting relatives, the family of Lee." She did not trust herself to speak further of him.

In early evening her father looked in, telling them that the doctor would stay the night, in the event that Kum Seung needed further care. He could be summoned immediately.

Long after the other guests departed and late into the night, Sun Yi listened to the murmur of voices in conversation. The sound came from the ondol room. She laid out some quilts for her own sleeping comfort but sleep would not come. She turned from one side to the other, alternately dozing and waking, until the gray light of dawn.

Dr. Lee made one last observation of his patient before departing, reassuring Sun Yi's father that his wife had no further complications.

He did not even acknowledge Sun Yi's presence.

Kum Seung did recover quickly. There were no ill effects, except perhaps the realization that she was, after all, no longer a young girl.

Springtime was glorious, with long light evenings after the rains ceased. The green leaves of all the growing things in the fields pushed up under the heat of the sun and Sun Yi welcomed the passing of each day as bringing her closer to the time of her release from the confinement of house arrest.

When her father summoned her to the ondul room one morning, she hurried to answer with a light step. She'd sat there often in recent weeks, discussing with him the plans and concerns for the household. Today he was seated on the raised platform at the far end and she took her accustomed place on a cushion near him after bowing in greeting.

He looked quite pleasant as he returned her salutation.

"Daughter, I have received welcome news today," he began. "As you know, it has been a matter of grave concern to me for some time that I make the best possible arrangement for your secure future. At last the matter is settled."

A hard, dry lump of fear choked her breath.

"As you, yourself, recognize, a person with your history is not easy to match with a suitable arrangement. First, there is the matter of your education. Most men believe that interests and knowledge such as you have will only serve as a distraction to the important tasks of the home. In fact, I have freely admitted that you lack the usual training for running a household. Even if a man is willing to accept an educated woman as his wife, there still remains the problem of your activities in the underground independence movement. That makes you highly visible to the authorities and subject to their inquisitive observation. Then, there is the matter of your unfortunate birth year. That has been a concern from the beginning, of course. A girl born in the year of the Tiger, one who is destined to wield power. This is, to say the least, difficult, and at best, a challenge."

He took a deep breath and sighed. "It must be a man who also has a birth year with the qualities that will balance, counter-influence, or compensate for the characteristics you have. But at last I have found such a person, and willing to take responsibility for the burden you will bring. He seems to think neither your education nor your birth sign will be detrimental to a harmonious household."

Sun Yi wanted to cover her ears, to block out his words.

"Fortunately, he was not caught up in the independence movement. And, finally, his year of birth was that of the Dragon, the noblest of all animals, the only one capable of contending with the Tiger. I consulted fortunetellers about these omens and it has been confirmed today that all signs favor this match.

"I am so well pleased that I wanted you to know immediately."

Sun Yi barely managed to say, "Is it not possible for me to learn more about this man whom you have chosen for me?"

At this impertinence her father's face grew stern. "You have been told all that you need to know." Then, as Sun Yi remained silent, his voice softened and he added, "At first I was reluctant to accept this arrangement because it will take you far away from your home, but after much consideration I concluded that there will be no better solution for you. I have sent our acceptance. Your marriage will take place as soon after your release from house arrest as possible."

There was a secluded corner in the women's courtyard where Sun Yi stole a few moment each day to sit in contemplation. A trellis hung heavy with wisteria leaves in summer, providing shade even on the warmest of days. Large earthen jars used for storing soy and hot bean sauce stood here, blocking the view from anyone who might pass by. Only the afternoon breezes could enter, cooling the air and swaying the hanging branches.

Since she learned the impending plan for her marriage Sun Yi retreated more frequently to this hidden refuge. Motionless for an hour or more, she meditated. She could not shake this despondency. The feeling sweeping over her was much like that she'd suffered in prison but there was one clear difference. As a captive she'd retained hope that the future would bring eventual freedom. Now she envisioned nothing but endless captivity.

A stranger! Soon she would marry someone she'd never met, be taken into a household where her only function would be to serve the other members.

Impatiently she brushed stray hair back from her forehead. The sleek black hair pulled tightly away from her face was knotted into a single braid that reached nearly to her waist. Soon she would be required to wrap it like a coiled rope around her head. An apt symbol that her freedom was ended! The light summer linen of her white chima billowed with the cooling breeze. She sat very still, but her hands, tensely clasped in her lap, betrayed her turmoil.

Abuji had told her so little. All, he said, that she needed to know. That this prospective mate had been carefully studied. His family was of a good and ancient lineage, prominent and respected, with no history of serious illness or weakness. She must realize that parents, with their mature wisdom, were best able to choose the companion for a life long marriage. It had always been so. In time she would do the same for her child.

Still, she did wish that she could know more about her future. In September her year of house arrest would end. In just a few weeks she would be married.

"May I intrude upon your thoughts?"

Sun Yi's reverie broke with the sound of Kum Seung's voice. She smiled her welcome as the older woman sat near her.

"What peace you have here!" Kum Seung sighed. Even one moment of repose was rare in her active day. "I've been able to learn more of your marriage plans." Her smile was teasing.

She doesn't know how I really feel, thought Sun Yi. She doesn't even suspect. But she leaned forward to hear what Kum Seung might tell her, golden brown eyes kindling with curiosity.

"The go-between came with the request for this betrothal." Kum Seung paused and waited for so long that Sun Yi cried impatiently for her to continue.

"It is unusual. This man is quite a bit older than you. He was once betrothed in the usual way to a prospective bride who was older than he was by several years. She died of a sudden illness. For this reason he never married, as men usually do, long before the age he has reached."

How old is he? Images of men with white beards and tall horsehair hats filed through her head. "What of the sa-ju? Has that old custom been followed also?"

Kum Seung smiled broadly, eyes again lighting with mischief. "Oh, yes. That, too. As you know, you were born in the year of the Tiger, and what man wishes to face the prospect of being henpecked by a woman with a will stronger than his? But even the sa-ju is favorable, since this man is born in the year of the dragon, a mythical creature of great power. Thus your signs are compatible for a harmonious future. He shall have the wisdom and patience to curb your natural dominance. Perhaps he is destined for greatness, as well."

Sun Yi listened to all of this in silence. The influence of all her years of schooling caused her to doubt the value of these old beliefs, the gunghab. Despite her skepticism she wondered if there might be a grain of truth in the ritual.

"There's more." Kum Seung whispered, leaning close, "The sasung, the letter from his family, with the proposal of marriage, arrived. Your father answered it today, agreeing on the date for the ceremony."

"Can't you tell me more about him? Sun Yi pleaded.

"I can! He is a second son!"

"Oh! I'm so glad. You can't imagine how that worried me."

A second son might establish his own household. He would not have to live with his parents. She would not be under the constant surveillance of her mother-in-law.

For the first time in days the heavy dread lifted from Sun Yi's heart. She feared, intensely, the prospect of obeying a woman of old fashioned ways who might find a multitude of ways to shower resentment upon her.

"Perhaps my life will not be as stifling as I had anticipated," she admitted. "Still."

Kum Seung, sensing the meaning behind her reluctant response, asked. "Is it love that you are seeking?"

Sun Yi's color darkened.

"You will find that love grows between two persons who are well suited to each other, especially after you have a child. Then you will learn to love the father who has given you this beautiful human being to nurture."

"If I could believe that."

"It is impossible to ask anything more."

Sun Yi accepted her words but was not satisfied. "I cannot help feeling that I am stepping back, just as I hoped to become a part of the new movement to help women in our country." She waved her arms. "There must be more than this. You know, as I do, that women have no rights. Only responsibilities. We are told to obey our fathers, our husbands, and in old age, our sons. Why, I know I am as capable as they are. I proved it by my studies, by surviving that prison."

Her voice rose and Kum Seung pressed a finger to her lips.

Sun Yi lowered her voice. "It simply isn't right. I have no choice in my marriage."

To herself she added, I cannot admit, even to this woman who is my closest confidant, that I will be married to someone while I love another man.

Aloud, she continued, "And look at you. If my father were to die right now, leaving us alone, you would have no right to inherit his land. It would all be taken from you, given to some distant relative, until Han Ju comes of age. You would be at the mercy of another, like a child." Sun Yi trembled with anger. "I feel so helpless," she told her stepmother. "I see these problems but I have no way to change them. Now here I am, about to step back into the old customs myself."

"You may not be as powerless as you think. With patience you may find a way to influence the treatment of Korean women."

"I wish I could believe that."

"Just think of it! At least you're going to be in Seoul."

Kum Seung said this with a bit of wistfulness but Sun Yi didn't notice.

"Seoul? I'm going to Seoul?"

"I thought you knew that."

"Ohmanee. Ohmanee." Han Ju was calling.

"I'm coming," she answered, leaving Sun Yi alone in the shade of the wisteria.

Seoul! If that were true! His description had many similarities. But no. It was impossible. He didn't notice her on Tano day. And he couldn't be that much older, could he? He might even be betrothed to someone else. Perhaps that was the reason he could not acknowledge her. There certainly were other men sufficiently like him in this vast country.

She would not even dare to dream of such a possibility.

A few days later a large box arrived. An old man brought it and his shoulders were bent by its weight on the chige. Kum Seung watched while Sun Yi opened it, removing many layers of straw matting before she uncovered two wooden ducks. The traditional symbolic gift to a bride from her prospective husband.

Despite her misgiving about the approaching marriage, she was forced to admire the life-size carvings. Their mellow brown was worn to a dull smoothness with the patina of their great age.

"So very beautiful," murmured Kum Seung. "This is a real treasure."

"Look at the eyes, so alert that it is a surprise when these creatures remain mute." Sun Yi caressed the feathers, each curve outlined in delicate etchings. "These must be ancient, and priceless."

The skies were blue, the time of hanuri nopda, on the day of the marriage ceremony, but Sun Yi didn't see them. She remained in her room with Kum Seung and the maidservants helping her. The wedding costume was composed of many layers and dressing took time.

The bridegroom was on his way by this time and she envisioned his caravan on the last segment of its journey. The walk from town might take thirty minutes. There was only one road, a lane of packed earth. When his party neared her village it would cross the river on the pole ferry, for the Naktong River curved in a tight scenic loop around three sides of the settlement. The village wall, a strong barricade of stone and earth, harmonized with the countryside.

From there he would approach her home and first notice, within its gate, the round columns that supported the graceful curving roofs of green and gray lichen-covered tiles. Under the roof the massive exposed timbers accented the rice paper walls. The maru surrounding it was built of hardwood and worn to a fine polish by the tread of generations. Several separate buildings within the enclosure were set apart by lesser walls and designated the sections for servants, men, women and children.

Would this seem grand to him? Or shabby by comparison with his own fine home in Seoul?

"Remember," Kum Seung whispered before she left Sun Yi, "you must not smile today, or all your children will be girls."

Another of the many teasing remarks between the two women, perhaps the last, Sun Yi realized. How she would miss her!

The muscles of her face were stiff with the coating of white powder but even if she was free of this ceremonial makeup she would not smile today. Sun Yi believed she would never be truly happy again.

Kum Seung returned, carrying a box wrapped in silk, heavily embroidered in many colors.

"So. He is here." Despite the heat of the autumn day an icy chill shook her.

As wife of the head of their household Kum Seung must be the first to inspect this gift, and she opened it eagerly. Inside she found many folds of silk, delicate as tissue, in shades of pale pastel, and the letter of matrimony on top, which affirmed the marriage.

Outside, the main courtyard had been prepared early in the morning, its earthen surface raked smooth and covered by a straw mat that transformed it into a ceremonial hall. A large, low table stood upon the mat with two candles in brass holders at each end. Two celadon vases of shimmering blue-gray held branches of pine and bamboo. Brass bowls heaped with chestnuts, jujubes and dried persimmons completed the display.

Sun Yi's two uncles stood at each end, one holding a hen and the other, a rooster.

When the groom entered the courtyard was filled with family members, some neighbors and in the rear, the servants. He walked slowly under the weight of his stiff coat and heavily embroidered belt, balancing the tall black hat made of horsehair on his head. The fullness of the coat disguised his slender figure.

Once inside, his elder brother, who'd accompanied him on this journey, handed him a wooden duck. He placed it on the table and bowed before it twice.

Kum Seung stepped forward, took this duck, the symbol of fidelity, and carried it into the house.

When she saw her Sun Yi clutched her sleeve. "Must I?"

The older woman only nodded and led her to the doorway where a maid waited. The jeweled coronet on her head swayed and the veil hanging from it obscured her face. She could not see anything. The hanim guided her to the table and left her facing the groom. Her dress, long and heavy with many layers of silk in glorious colors, crimson, emerald, yellow, gleamed with gold embossed designs on hem and sleeves.

Sun Yi saw a shadowy outline of a face and the tall black hat. She bowed four times toward that apparition, following the protocol in which she had been instructed. He bowed twice in response and then cups of wine were placed before them. Three times they passed the goblets to each other, sipping. Her hand trembled, feeling the touch of the vessel as he guided her in raising it. The brew was bitter to her taste.

This completed the wedding ceremony. The merriment began for all but Sun Yi, a time for all of the guests to enjoy the banquet, to drink, sing, laugh, dance. She was left alone, to sit still and quiet. while the groom changed into less restrictive clothing, for he was free to participate in the celebration. She listened to the music played for them on the sogonghu, a thirteen stringed instrument similar to a harp, but she did not eat and she still could not see. Her vision remained blocked by the opaque cloth that hung before her face. While the hours passed and the sounds of frivolity continued she grew numb with sitting still and remembered the days in her prison cell when she feared unknown punishment for changing her position.

A room had been prepared for the bride and groom, decorated with delicate branches in vases and a table set with food and wine, cushions and quilts in place and when evening came she followed her husband to it, walking slowly for all she could see was his heels moving ahead of hers.

She'd dreaded this time more than any thing else about the day, for she knew the old custom was still followed by some of the more raucous voiced relatives. They'd cluster outside the window, calling out ribald comments and perhaps even poking holes in the rice paper.

After they were alone she heard her husband's voice for the first time.

"Won't you raise your veil and look at me?

He sounded kind, almost teasing. She hesitated and when she did not comply at once she felt the weight of the coronet being lifted from her head, allowing her to see for the first time the face of this man who was now her husband.

Yet it was not the first time. Sun Yi's golden brown eyes looked upon the one she'd given up all hope of ever seeing again. She caught her breath and trembled as his fingers stroked her cheek. She watched the smile flicker across his gentle face as he looked into those eyes.

"Didn't you realize," he whispered, drawing her close, "that once I'd met you there could be no other wife for me?"

Footsteps sounded outside with a rustling and the soft commotion of muted voices. Dr. Lee released her and strode over, picking up the decorative screen standing in one corner. He set it firmly in front of the window.

Then he returned to the table and, taking up a pair of chopsticks, stifled the flames of the candles that had illumined the room.

Part Two
1921 to 1926

"*A*ll roads lead to Seoul."

"Did you speak to me?"

"I was thinking out loud." Sun Yi's brown eyes, the only part of her that was not wrapped in the immense sigachima, sparkled with mischief as she watched this man, so recently a stranger and now her husband, lay down his book reluctantly in response to her words. She felt the heat creeping over her high cheekbones as she responded to his appreciative gaze, recalling the unexpected rush of passion that this man had aroused within her. Would it be noticeable to anyone else?

"Must you read now? I wish you to talk to me."

"What do you want me to say? It's been a long journey and I thought you must be tired."

"Oh, no. I'm so eager to see your city. Are we nearly there?" She rubbed the glass of the window with her hand, just as the train gave one more lurch. Turning back to face him, she smiled, then remembered that she must try to look sedate now that she was a married woman. It had been hard enough to manage the matronly hairstyle. She had first braided her hair, then twisted it into a knot at the nape of her neck. Not nearly as tidy as it should be, she reflected when she held up the mirror to it. Perhaps it would become easier in time. He, in contrast, looked proper and quite distinguished in his dark suit of wool, tailored perfectly. The white collar was tight under his chin; his dark hair combed straight back from his high forehead, clipped short in the new style. His hands, those marvelously dexterous but delicate hands that she had noticed on their first meeting, lay still in his lap, holding the small leather bound volume.

"What is this book that so holds your attention?"

"Oh, this." He shrugged. "Poetry. *The Odes of Horace.* One of my favorites."

"May I see?"

"Do you read Latin also?"

"No." She fell silent, reminded of how little she knew in comparison to his great learning, despite those few years in the mission school.

"What was it you said about Seoul?" he asked.

"Oh, that expression. I've heard it since I was a child. All roads lead to it. Now I do believe it is true. Tell me again what I shall soon see."

"You know it has always been the center of life for all Koreans."

"Of course. Since 1392, when the first king of our Yi dynasty seized the throne. It was he who made it the capitol and gave our country its name. Chosun. Land of the Morning Calm."

"Yes, but the town grew because it was close to the Han River. Once it was only a small market town but when the ships sailed so easily up from the Yellow Sea—only fifty miles or so east, you see—it quickly became an important city of its time, the center of all commerce and learning. And with the land near the river being rich and fertile the farmers could grow all the food needed to feed a large population."

"The Han River! Won't it soon come into our sight?"

Dr. Lee smiled at the impatience in her voice. "Yes, but first notice the hills." He gestured through the grime of the train window, and had to catch his own balance as the car swayed. "There is a great circle of hills around Seoul. It sits as if in the bottom of a great cup. Soon after it was proclaimed our capitol a wall was built encircling it, to protect it from invaders. Why, in time that wall extended to seven miles in length, twenty-five feet high in some places and wide enough on the top to serve as a road if needed. You can still see some portions of it today."

"I'd like that. How many persons live in Seoul now?"

"Oh, I think about 350,000."

"That many!" Sun Yi was silent, remembering the two among that great populace who would have the greatest effect on her future life. She must greet her husband's parents for the first time in just a few hours. What would they think of her? She would have to remain in their house for the three days of official greeting. Thankfully, she would then be able to move on to her own home. Although her husband had said it was only a short distance from them, in the same district, it would be a separate place. "I hope they'll like the gifts I bring." She nodded to indicate the boxes and tied-up bundles at their feet. The rest, household furnishings and other gifts followed in the baggage car.

"It must be a great city," she murmured, trying to shift her thoughts from the coming meeting.

"It was laid out on a grand scale from the beginning," the doctor continued. "It followed the pattern of Chinese cities of that era, with wide avenues on a square pattern. Wait until you see the gates! There were four large ones, of stone and wood, really massive, and some lesser gates in between. All of them were once closed tightly each night and in times of turmoil. The main gate is Namdai Mun, the front door to the city. Since 1396 that South Gate has stood, even though it has long since ceased to be of practical use. It is a magnificent monument to the craftsmen of the early days. But you know," he went on, taking up her hand in his enthusiasm, "the true essence of Seoul is the culture and learning that exists within its gates. That is our real pride. You'll see."

"Tell me about them again. Your mother and father."

"Don't worry so much. You won't have to say anything. You know how to bow to them, and you look perfect."

She smoothed out the folds of her hanbok. It was woven of fine white cotton and her only ornament, a brooch of delicately carved jade, glowed in its pale green translucence at the point where it fastened her narrow white collar in a V below her throat. She did want to make a proper appearance on this special day. Fate had been kind to her, after all, for she had a husband who truly cared for her, not simply as an instrument for continuing his family line, but as a person in her own right. She treasured the memory of his words on their first night together, when he told her of how the image of her face had remained with him from the time they first met.

"I knew that you were the one who must become my wife," he confessed. "For years I resisted the efforts of my parents to marry me to an unknown person but until I saw you I thought I had no alternative, ultimately, but to bow to their wishes. Still, it took all my powers of persuasion to convince them that a marriage with a provincial family could be to our advantage in any way."

Then he took her hand, much as he did now, placing the palm against his. She felt the beating of their pulses in unison and knew that good fortune had at last brought her happiness. She listened as he told her that the calm strength of her beauty and her spirit had lingered with him. He could not forget her, for she had truly captured his heart. "I will honor my pledge of fidelity as long as I live," he'd promised.

Now, while the train rocked and swayed, he continued to hold onto her hand, firmly, as if it belonged to him. Abruptly, he leaned closer and whispered "Do you trust me? Absolutely?"

"Of course I do." Sun Yi impulsively covered his own hand with her free one, wondering, fearful, at the sudden agitation in his voice.

"Then I may cause a breach in that trust," he stopped, caught his breath, and went on. "I was not completely truthful in my interview with your father."

Sun Yi's eyes grew wider as she watched his face, but she did not withdraw her hands from his. "Tell me. I don't understand."

"I assured him I had not participated in the March 1st demonstration. That much is true. You must remember how I told you that I was en route home, aboard ship, when that occurred. I allowed him to assume that I did not participate in political activities."

"That was one of his reasons for allowing our marriage. He's concerned for my safety."

"Yes, I know. He doesn't want you to suffer the horror of prison again. Neither do I."

While she waited for him to continue he searched her eyes, perhaps expecting to see in them her true unmasked reaction.

"If he realized the extent of my involvement he would have never given his approval."

"Does that mean.?"

"You must know, yet never let anyone realize that you know, for your own safety."

He went on to tell her that most of the leaders of the Independence Movement had been driven into exile, some to the soviet-controlled areas of northern Asia, Manchuria and Siberia, others to Shanghai where they were attempting to organize a provisional government, and the remaining few to Hawaii and America. Then he pulled his hands from her and buried his head in them for so long that she finally cried out.

"Please go on. There's more, isn't there?"

"Yes," he admitted, then lifted up his head to look directly at his wife.

"There are some of us still here in Korea, however, and we are determined to do all we can to preserve the cause of freedom for our country. We need to communicate, to be informed of what is happening elsewhere, to be strongly organized. It is imperative."

Sun Yi looked at her husband as though for the first time. The determination in his voice amazed her. I have much to learn about this man, she realized. Before, she instinctively admired him. Now she was seeing a new side of him that reaffirmed her convictions. When she looked up her affection expanded with a warm and glowing sensation. "That is your role." she stated simply.

"My commitment." He reached out to her. "That, and you."

"And you want me to work beside you?"

"Yes."

So now they shared two secrets. No one else would ever know the circumstances of their first meeting but more importantly to her, this man was as devoted as she had ever been to the efforts to regain their country's freedom. This knowledge, shared by them alone, would bind them forever. Her feeling of happiness expanded until she thought she could not contain it. If only she could shout her joy! She would still work for Korea's independence. For now, this knowledge was enough.

He bent to pick up the book, which had fallen to the floor. Watching him turn another page, she asked herself how could he keep so still? She fidgeted, touching her hair, smoothing her chima, impatient for their arrival, leaning toward the window to watch for the first signs. "Look," she cried. "There are lights everywhere!"

The doctor laughed quietly as she pressed her nose to the glass. Electric streetlights illuminated the city rolling into view in the subdued aura of early evening.

"They're like stars dropped to earth!" You didn't tell me it would be like this." Sun Yi fell silent. She must not disgrace herself by behaving like a simple country girl. After all, she was a member of the Yu clan, which had once been influential advisors to the court in this city. Then the broad Han River came into sight and she felt the rocking of the train crossing the bridge that spanned this great waterway. She caught her breath at the realization that she was high above the deep water. Around the city the flat plain extended in every direction.

Dr. Lee finally put his book away. "Most of the Japanese live in this southern portion of Seoul," he explained. "The railroad center here has grown rapidly. I was amazed to see it when I returned from Europe. Over there is the new hydroelectric plant that provides all these lights for you to wonder over. The Bukhan Mountains are to the north, and closer you can see our South Mountain, Nam San."

"There are so many rooftops," she remarked. The tiles seemed to overlap, all crowded together, over the one-story buildings. Only the lights from the street lamps marked the narrow alleys separating them.

"Follow me," he commanded, and for once she was pleased to obey, as he guided her through the crush of passengers and street vendors to a place where he could hail jinrickshas for each of them. The streets were clogged with vehicles of all sorts, a few automobiles, many other jinrickshas being pulled by wiry-legged men, some trolley cars hitched to overhead lines that kept them weaving along their tracks. Occasionally trucks attempted to push through with horns blaring and drivers waving their arms, but the effort was futile. The continuous flow of people, students and merchants, diplomats, missionaries, tourists, workers, the mix of a cosmopolitan city, seemed to be congregated in this place all at the same moment.

Sun Yi stared at the passing scene. Only three days had passed since her wedding ceremony in the yangban villa, but that countryside and all of its memories was quickly receding into the past. She could think only of what might happen to her next. If she may please his parents!

Carefully, slowly, Sun Yi removed her outer shoes at the entrance. This house was impressive, far larger and more elegant than she had ever before seen. She knew that it had been the home of Dr. Lee's family for several generations, but she'd never expected anything so grand.

It was located in the northwest section of Seoul, not far from Kyongbok Palace itself, and the original L-shaped structure had been expanded with the growth of the family until a second L-shaped addition was entwined with it, providing ample space for Dr. Lee's elder brother, his wife, and their five children, as well as for his parents.

Now she would meet them all. Sun Yi tried to slip on the loose house shoes the maid held out for her, but she was shaking and finally the young woman knelt down to place them on her feet.

"They're rather large," she whispered to her husband, with an attempt at a smile, as she realized she could only shuffle awkwardly in them.

"Don't worry," he whispered back. "You'll be fine."

But she thought he looked concerned. Her own father should be beside her now. Since he wasn't, she would have to face them alone. Why should this be any more difficult than standing before the Japanese police? She took one step toward the ondol room and hesitated, remembering that his people did not favor this marriage. Lifting her head, she walked on until she saw the elderly gentleman seated on a silk cushion on a raised platform. He wore the loose white jacket and full pants, bound at the ankles that were the traditional dress of a retired yangban but it was the sight of his dignified white head, the still thick mane of hair framing a face lined and creased with age, that forced her to catch her breath in fear. How could she ever expect him to accept her?

Then she noticed the woman at his side. She was tiny compared to Sun Yi and her pale face impassive except for the eyes. She stared at her new daughter-in-law with a gaze that seemed to slice her in half.

Sun Yi's knees gave way and she sank to the floor in front of them, with her head bending forward until it brushed the shiny surface. She was not even aware of her husband's presence beside her.

She held her breath and sat up slowly, remembering to avoid looking at them while they spoke the ritual words. The ceremony was brief. They wished the couple good fortune and many sons, and acknowledged her gifts of food and wine. She remained silent, as she should.

"My father and mother are skeptical of the recent changes in our society," the doctor tried to explain to her in the evening. "It's not that you are mistrusted. They fear the influence of the westerners in our country, After all, it is less than forty years since any outsiders have been admitted."

"But they did allow you to go to the west for training."

"True. It seemed useful, I suppose. My father is concerned-he fears the education of girls that missionaries have introduced will weaken our family system." He took her hand. "I assured them that your education has not turned you away from the traditional role of a wife. I promised them that you would be as dutiful as any daughter-in-law who had been cloistered in the usual way."

"You did that?"

"I had to secure their approval."

He smiled as if to reassure her. Or was it a way of warning, to guide her behavior in the days ahead?

Either way, Sun Yi tried to fill the role expected of her. After all, it was only for three days. Each morning she rose early, dressed carefully, and then greeted his parents with the accustomed respectful phrases. Throughout the day she tried to be as helpful as she could with all of the women's work, and she spoke only when addressed.

But she welcomed the move to their own home, small though it was. The narrow side street on which it was located was quiet, shaded by the overlapping branches of poplar trees, now golden in the autumn. Seoul's main avenue was not far away. It's tall entrance gate, set close to the cobblestoned pavement, was flanked by high walls of stone, and on the plain black wood hung a small brass plate engraved with the sign of a physician.

When she stepped inside the maid was already there. The elderly woman bowed to Sun Yi, and with a start she recognized her as one of the helpers in her mother-in-law's kitchen.

"My mother says she will be a great help to you, since she already knows how to run the household properly," he explained. "Let me show you where my clinic is located."

She followed him through the maze of small rooms at the front of the building, some with cushions for waiting patients, others cubicles for examination and treatment. The house was shaped in a U, with kitchen and storage at its center in the rear and, at the other side of the wide inner courtyard, their living quarters, with sliding panels opening into each of the rooms.

The kitchen was sunken below the level of the other rooms in the customary way, so that the heat from the fires in its ovens could pass through the tunnel under the floors and provide heat. Sun Yi peered into the small room, noting the buckets and baskets, the chopping blocks and low open fireplace in its dim light. Yontan briquettes were stacked nearby. It seemed that all had been prepared for her.

From the beginning her husband was busy. The stream of persons passing through the black gate seemed unending, even late in the evening. Sometimes he was called out in the middle of the night. She saw him so seldom that she looked forward to serving him his meal herself, bringing it to him on a low table in the ondol room when he dined alone, for then she could have a few minutes to speak with him.

The food was prepared by the maid, for Sun Yi soon learned that she was a far better cook than she and always presented his meals just as he preferred. Though Sun Yi was grateful for her assistance, she conceded ruefully to herself that the helper had been sent out of a concern that the son continue to be well cared for, rather than as a kindness to the new daughter-in-law.

"You are filled with questions," he protested during a late night meal.

"How can I help it? This new place is still confusing to me. Won't you have another serving?"

"No. That's sufficient."

"But you work so late and seem to eat so little. You are even thinner than when I met you."

"It's always best to stop eating while you are still hungry."

She was silent, wishing that she could. Somehow, food had never tasted so delicious as that which came from her own kitchen. She had to admit that she reveled in the delight of supervising her own home. Each day she planned, sending the maid to market after instructing her, sometimes even going alone to inspect for the freshest fruits and vegetables. She excelled in bargaining for eggs and fish, inspecting each item displayed by the vendors, discovering new delicacies that she must taste.

All of the shopping was an endless delight. She filled the courtyard with so many flowering plants, shrubs, and small trees that at last the maid complained of being unable to locate the soy sauce jar in the midst of the jungle.

For a time Sun Yi occupied her days with these activities. Then, during his evening meal one night, Dr. Lee asked her with some reluctance, if she would be willing to serve his guests when he invited friends to share a meal. When he noticed her surprise he added, "It is better that the maid should never see these faces, for her own protection. No one would ever suspect that you should appear before my friends, so you will be safe from suspicion as well."

She did as he requested, and on those occasions she would listen to their voices after she left them, continuing well into the night, a low murmur that she heard even while sleeping lightly. She worried, though she could do nothing, for she realized now that not all of the persons who came into this clinic were truly in need of medical care. The man in the shabby workman's robe, hobbling on a crutch, the stooped old man with the heavily bandaged hand, and others, also, as the days passed. Some discarded the disguise once in safety or left as suddenly as they arrived when their mission was complete.

The underground movement was not defeated by the repression that followed the Mansei demonstration. It continued in a more secretive way now and her husband's hospital became a convenient gathering place for those who could not risk meeting elsewhere. Who would suspect that man whose head was swathed in bandages was actually a bearer of surreptitious information?

No one, Sun Yi hoped every day.

But would all of this brave planning and effort really make a difference? She often wondered, witnessing the rapid tightening of all aspects of their lives. Some Koreans were openly beginning to believe that cooperation with the Japanese rulers might be wise after all. Dreams of independence were fading.

The afternoons that Sun Yi spent with the women of her husband's family seemed a tame comparison. Her sister-in-laws and their friends treated her kindly, for she did try to play the role outlined for her when she was with them. Her reward came when she listened to a cousin's wife describe her despair over a daughter who could not pass the entrance exam for Ewha College.

"If only she had someone to guide her in studying, I'm sure she would pass," the mother complained.

"I'll be happy to help," Sun Yi offered impulsively, worrying later about the reaction of her husband to this singularly independent decision. To her delight he was almost as pleased as she at this opportunity to do the work she had prepared for, and he suggested that she seek additional students. Soon she was holding classes each afternoon for small groups of young women, coaching them for the strict examinations.

Everyone she knew hoped to gain admittance, for Ewha was the most prominent school for girls in Seoul. It had been the first, begun in 1886 by Mary Scranton, an American missionary, with only a handful of girls. Education for girls at that time was unheard of and the school succeeded only because King Kojong gave his full support. Now, in 1920, Ewha had a distinguished and formidable reputation. Every capable young woman wanted admission to its brick walls. The building, two stories high, was a prominent landmark on the northern edge of Seoul.

At last I'm teaching also, Sun Yi wrote to her old friend, Yong Soon. She was teaching in the Taegu mission school where she and Sun Yi first met, and supporting her mother. Her father, Rev. Lee, was never found after that March 1 independence demonstration.

Throughout the winter Sun Yi continued to meet with her classes. She enjoyed the involvement with serious study once more but she also found pride in earning money for the first time, to add to the household income. There never seemed to be enough and she could not understand why.

One day in the springtime she opened the cash box in the clinic to get some coins for the tobu vendor. It was empty!

She waited until after serving his dinner that evening to ask her husband. "How can this be?" she demanded. "You are always working. The line of patients stretches out past our gate. There should be more money to show for your efforts."

Dr. Lee smiled in his usual gentle manner and asked, "Do you really expect me to ask someone if he can pay me before I try to relieve his suffering? You know that the poor can't afford medical treatment."

Sun Yi shook her head. For the first time she felt angry, truly angry, with this man. "So they come to you, because they know you won't charge them?" In her outrage she spoke rapidly, without thinking. "Sometimes I think every poor person in Seoul is lined up outside of your gate!"

"We have enough for our needs," he reminded her.

"Enough is not enough!" she retorted. "How can we progress or improve our condition? How can we save for the future?" She could see that her arguments had no effect, so changing to a tone of supplication, she added, "You are too good. You really do need someone as mercenary as I to protect you, or we'd soon lose the roof from our heads. And where would your son live, then?"

"If only this will be a son! If only this will be a son!" Sun Yi whispered over and over, as the time grew nearer for the birth of her child. Rain fell often and she found herself repeating the phrase silently in rhythm with the drops that dripped onto the red tile roof. Sometimes she thought, instead, I really don't mind those cold eyes whenever his mother looks at me. But life will be more pleasant for him when I am able to take my full, respected place in my husband's family. I do want to please him.

Word of her success as a tutor to the young women competing for admission to Ewha spread quickly and she continued to meet with her students each afternoon until even the long, loose folds of her chima could no longer disguise her condition. She still hurried to complete the morning work, and would not allow herself the pleasure of preparing the day's lessons until every corner was in good order. I'll not leave room for any suggestion that I'm neglecting my first duties, just because I'm teaching.

Rain lashed against the shutters but it was pain, not the noise of the storm, that woke Sun Yi early on an August morning. Strange, sharp pangs wrapped around her midsection like a vise, at first infrequent, but by daylight so close together that she knew she must summon help. Still, she lay listening to the steady drumming of the downpour, holding her breath, pressing her lips together to prevent herself from crying out, for a long time before she finally called, "Yubosayo."

He slept soundly. She repeated it several times. He is so tired. I wish I could let him sleep longer. But I dare not, she thought, twisting the corner of the quilt between her fingers. At last she reached out to touch her husband, stretching to find his sleeping form. Nothing! Sun Yi raised herself on one elbow, opening her eyes. The place beside her was empty. Where could he be? She'd been awake for hours. Surely she'd have heard him getting up. She forgot the pain, struggled to her knees, calling for him again and again, until she collapsed with exhaustion.

Then the maid slid the door open, finally, her timid face filled with unspoken questions.

Sun Yi whispered, "Help me. Call for my mother-in-law."

After she disappeared Sun Yi wished she had not done that. The last person she wanted to see at this moment was that woman. I want my husband, no, what good is he at a time like this, I want my mother, she's dead, what did she do at my birth, if only I knew, no, the person I need is Kum Seung, if she were here she'd know what to do, she's so far away, but she might come if I call to her. I'll say her name, the name that only I know, and she'll recognize my voice. She'll come to me.

Sun Yi squeezed her eyes shut and repeated the little name of her step mother, the sound growing fainter as blackness crept in from each corner of her vision, leaving only a pin prick of light, and then nothing.

A hand stroked her forehead and at once Sun Yi became aware once more of her surroundings and felt comforted. She was no longer alone. But, again, sharp pain seemed to split her in half. She became like two separate entities. Her own face, as she'd seen it in a mirror, was looking down at her writhing body.

"Kum Seung!" She laughed. "You heard me! How good of you to come so quickly."

The hand felt cool. It was stroking her gently. "Stay with me. Don't leave."

One more great spasm tore at her and then Sun Yi was enveloped by an immense wave of quietness that brought oblivion and relief.

"I told my son it would be a girl. That's all I expected from her. Only charcoal sticks and pine branches would be needed for the garland on the gate. It was his idea to bring chili peppers to add to it."

She recognized that voice, always tinged with sarcasm. Why was her husband's mother in her room?

"It's time for you to eat. You must be strong to feed my grandson."

Grandson? Sun Yi smelled the aroma of fresh rice and opened her eyes.

Her mother-in-law stood over her holding a tray with two bowls on it. She set it down on the low table next to Sun Yi and turned to look at the small sleeping form of a baby lying next to her. Her face was inquisitive, yes, even a bit softer. Sun Yi was certain that the stern lines disappeared while she looked at the newborn child. A boy! How fortunate! Now her life with this woman who always chilled her with a cold voice and hostile eyes would become easier.

"The garland is hanging on your gate," she repeated. "He insisted on bringing the chili peppers to add to it. He was right. This time."

She sounds as though she expects I'll never produce another son. A sudden desire to prove her wrong swept over Sun Yi. But not soon. How could she endure that ordeal again?

"Eat this," came the sharp command. "You must be strong to feed the child."

The older woman pointed to the bowl on the table, filled with the soup of the seaweed that would nourish her while she nursed the child. It was the custom. Sun Yi knew this. Yet she could not help grimacing when she looked at the tendrils of steam rising from it. She managed a smile and murmured kum up sim ni da to show her gratitude.

The day was already humid. She no longer heard the sound of rain. Though she wore the lightest of sleeping gowns, the cloth adhered to her body. Everyone said this was an unusually warm summer. A bowl of nang myun would taste wonderful. This was the season for cold noodles, not this. Brushing the damp hair from her forehead, she looked at the hot soup once more. She swallowed hard and glanced at it. Flat slices of the smooth, dark green keem floated on the surface and bits of beef lay beneath. The aroma overwhelmed Sun Yi. She glanced sideways at her mother-in-law, hoping the older woman would indicate that she was about to leave. If she were left alone for a moment she might, somehow, pretend that she had eaten the food. What else could she do with it?

A tall green plant grew in a clay pot in the far corner. Would she have the strength to cross the floor and pour the soup into it? What would that do to the plant? For a moment the familiar glint of mischief twinkled in her eyes. She suppressed a grin, turning to hide the dimple that would give her amusement away.

It was no use. The older woman sat on a cushion next to her sleeping grandson, with a look of satisfaction, ready to tend him, should he wake.

Sun Yi sat up and took one small sip. Eyes watched her while the silver head seemed to nod approval with each spoonful that she swallowed. She might as well become accustomed to this meal, for she knew there would be nothing else to eat for the next three weeks. Nor any visitors. That was the custom, probably a sensible one, for the child's good health. For her, however, it stretched ahead as a time of total boredom. How would she endure inactivity? At least she might converse with her husband during the time of quarantine that was symbolized by the garland hanging on their gate.

Her husband! Now she remembered. He was not with her on the morning of the birth. Where was he when she needed him?

As if in response to her thoughts, his familiar face appeared now in the doorway. It wore a look of concern. How could she be angry with him? Still, she had to know.

He entered and, after speaking a few words with his mother, she left the room. Then he came close to the place where Sun Yi lay. "I have only a few moments before Ohmanee returns, I had to see you."

"You left me during the night?"

"It was an emergency, a sudden situation that I had to take care of, to save some lives when no one else could be summoned." He looked puzzled. "You understand, don't you?"

She was weary. How could she cope with this now? "Why didn't you tell me? I knew only that you were not here when I needed you."

His eyes flashed in anger but this calm man, who rarely raised his voice, was still quiet as he replied, "You were well cared for. The midwife was here when I returned. And my mother. And the maid." He paused. "You, of all persons, must know that this country will not be a good place for our son's future unless we do all in our power to challenge the invaders who rule us. There was an attack on a power station. Men risked their lives. They might have died if I'd stayed with you instead of helping them. Bearing a child is a natural event, after all-their wounds are not."

She sighed. This was no time for a quarrel. He was hopeless, but she'd long known how it was with him, and wouldn't she feel the same if it were not for the new responsibility of this child?

"Don't you want to meet your son, then?" she asked.

Sun Yi watched his face as he peered down at the tightly wrapped bundle. The light that entered his eyes spread until its glow seemed to touch her also.

"He's perfect."

"Of course."

The baby's thick dark hair was twisted into a damp strand at the top of his head. The red cheeks were plump and firm. Though his eyes were shut, he looked absolutely beautiful. Was this the feeling that Kum Seung had once tried to express to her? She wished that her stepmother could be with her now.

"Will you return soon?" she asked as he rose to leave. He nodded and slipped out just as her mother-in-law appeared again, this time to remove the tray.

Sun Yi marveled at the faithfulness with which this woman served her. No one could fault her. She prepared the rice herself, not only in the morning, but three times more during the day, and once more at midnight. Sun Yi felt compelled to dutifully consume each serving of this soup and rice, but how she longed for the taste of other foods.

She read the newspapers and books that he brought her and made plans for the lessons she hoped to resume while the child slept and her mother-in-law supervised the work of the household but it was the visit with her husband that she looked for at the end of each day.

Once he came with the announcement that his father had chosen a name for the boy. "He will be called Jae Soon."

"Jae Soon." She repeated her son's name. It had a fine sound, imbued with dignity and promise for a bright future. Now she would be known as "Jae Soon's mother."

But some days later her husband brought more sober news.

"Our prince has a son, also," he said, sitting down quietly near her.

"You mean the crown prince?" she asked with apprehension.

He nodded. "Yes. Princess Masako has presented Yi Un with the twenty-first direct descendant of the Yi dynasty." His voice dripped with scorn.

"It's not the fault of our Prince," Sun Yi chided gently. "You know that he was just a child himself when he was taken away to Japan after his father abdicated the throne."

"That man had no choice, either. King Kojong acted under pressure from the Japanese government." Dr. Lee's voice rose at the memory of the injustice. "He was forced to leave the throne to Yi Un's elder brother. And what power that weakling, King Sunjong, had, ended with the formal annexation in 1910. Yi Un was simply a political hostage, an eleven-year-old pawn in this power game."

"Think of that poor child," Sun Yi persisted. "He never returned to Korea. He has been raised in seclusion, with only old men for companions, I've heard. Then he was trained in a military academy."

"He's no ordinary soldier, I'll remind you. He was assigned to the Imperial Guard of the Emperor."

"Even so," Sun Yi retorted, "our Prince had no more choice in directing his life than your own son has at this moment."

She nodded toward the sleeping boy.

"He was warned by our loyal patriots not to marry a Japanese after the violence of the Mansei demonstrations. Are you being soft on him now that you're a mother?" he asked.

"He was set to marry before his father died," she reminded him "The wedding was postponed only because of King Kojong's death."

Dr. Lee pounded his fist on the quilt in exasperation. "You are so stubborn in holding onto your own ideas. If I didn't know of your role in planning the demonstration to begin with, I'd suspect you of becoming sympathetic to these barbarians. Don't you realize that the blood of his Japanese mother taints this child, who is heir to the ancient and honored throne begun by King Taejo? This birth may be a symbol to some of Korea's unity with Japan but you must know that all true patriots call it a disgraceful end to our distinguished dynasty."

Sun Yi had no reply but to pick up her son and hold him close, thinking that that even though she was a Japanese woman, Princess Masako's feelings as a mother could be no different from her own.

Dr. Lee's mother returned to her own home at the end of the three weeks and Sun Yi returned to her usual activities, discovering that she was eager to resume teaching. There was an entire class of new students seeking her help. However, she found to her dismay that she was busier than she'd ever imagined. All the care of the child must be undertaken by herself, but in addition to the peaceful moments when he lay in her arms while she fed him, a time when she allowed her mind to wander and meditate, she must cope with the unending stream of laundry, for the maid was fully occupied with the kitchen work. Eventually she established a routine, finishing the household tasks by mid-day.

She taught her students in the afternoon, meeting with them in the ondol room with one ear tuned for the baby who slept in a corner. Jae Soon was a healthy boy, so filled with smiles for her that she wondered how she had lived without his companionship. He was never still, once he learned to move about. She was convinced that he showed signs of extraordinary alertness and often, while holding her plump little son, she made plans for his education. This boy would have every opportunity she could provide him, no matter what conditions must be endured.

Sun Yi was happier than at any time she could remember. The early spring of 1922 was a beautiful season, with air so clear that the distant mountains appeared quite close. The fragrance of pine drifted from the tree-covered hillsides and azaleas, pink, rose, and lavender, bloomed wildly. To complete the perfection, she was able, more often, to spend a quiet hour in conversation with her husband after serving his evening meal. Sometimes he played his flute and she simply listened to its music.

On one of these evenings Dr. Lee announced the astounding news that Prince Yi Un would soon make a visit to Seoul, his first since leaving as a young child. The Prince was following the tradition of presenting his wife and child to his family and to his ancestors. This would happen in the latter part of April and early May.

"Obviously our rulers feel sufficiently secure to allow this," he commented. "We've been subdued. Their confidence for his safety may be premature, however."

"Do you really believe there could be violence against him? What could happen?" Sun Yi demanded. "After all, he is still our prince. No one wants to harm him. It's well known that he had no control over his life after leaving Korea."

Her husband shrugged off her question.

On Wednesday, the 26th of April, the royal family traveled to Seoul by train from Pusan after crossing by ship from Shimonoseki. They were made to feel welcome. All along their route school children were massed in each town and village to wave flags and shout "Mansei!" When their entourage arrived at Seoul's South Gate station it was met by the highest-ranking civil and military officers of the Japanese authority and taken in carriages well guarded by cavalry soldiers to Toksu Palace in the center of the city.

The other members of the royal family of Yi still lived in Chang-Dok Palace, the former king, Sunjong, his wife, the Empress Yun, and Prince Kang and Princess Tokhye, younger brother and sister of Prince Yi Un. The two-week visit was filled with ceremonial audiences, banquets, and receptions.

On the fifth day of May, which is celebrated in Japan as Boys' Day, a paper carp was flown from a high pole on the palace grounds to proclaim that a boy-child resided there.

All of these ceremonies were carefully reported in the official newspapers of Seoul. Sun Yi read of these events and studied the photos and her sympathy for the young princess, a mother like herself, grew stronger. "Princess Masako looks so timid and gentle," she told her husband. "Poor lady. She had no choice in her marriage. Why, I heard that she first learned of her engagement by reading of it in a newspaper. I hope she is happy now."

But on May 11, as the royal couple was completing the round of ceremonial appearances, one of Sun Yi's students burst into her home, crying, "The young prince is dead!"

At first Sun Yi refused to believe it. All of the pictures showed him to be healthy and alert, bedecked in court costumes.

Rumors spread, sprouting like rice shoots.

"I've heard the child was poisoned, just as his grandfather was," she told Dr. Lee.

Once again he only shrugged.

This death saddened Sun Yi as she would not have believed possible earlier. She felt certain that her intense dislike of the Japanese invaders was as strong as it had always been. Yet, while she held her own son close, feeling his warmth, his soft hair touching her cheek, his head snuggling close to her shoulder, she could think only of that tiny, sad princess who must leave the cold and lifeless form that had been her baby in a dark tomb on the hillside at Sungin-won.

The letter arrived on a fine morning late in the summer of 1923. Sun Yi was so delighted with its content that she tucked it into the sleeve of her chogori after reading it. She pulled it out to reread several times while she continued preparing the special foods for the important guests that Dr. Lee would entertain in the evening.

ॐ

My dear friend,

Though many months have passed since your last letter you are always in my thoughts and prayers. Teaching fills most of my hours. You might not recognize your old school in Taegu, for the number of students has doubled. I believe the time is not far off when the educated Korean woman will be commonly accepted.

But today I write for a special reason. My closest friend here is leaving us to join the faculty at Ewha University. Will you meet her when she arrives next week? This will be a great kindness, for she knows no one at all in Seoul. I am certain that you and Kim Tai Un will share many common interests, for she is as extraordinary in her own way as are you. As for myself, I have only sadness that I cannot join in an hour of conversation once more, such as we often enjoyed in our school days together.

Your loving friend,

Yong Soon

While Sun Yi chopped and sliced the vegetables she thought of Yong Soon. The bonds of schoolgirl friendship remained strong. They would always be close, no matter what distance separated them. There were times when she felt quite lonely despite having work that kept her busy from morning until night. Often, when these low spirits besieged her, she thought what she needed most was a good friend with whom she could talk. She interrupted these thoughts to call out to the maid.

"Wait, I'll prepare the meat myself today."

Beef was an extravagance and she must be sure that the choice morsels were prepared in the proper manner. Cutting it into thin slices with a sharp knife, she then scored each side carefully with delicate strokes, taking care not to cut it completely through. Next she kneaded each piece into the sauce, redolent with sesame oil and soy, garlic and black pepper, a dash of sugar and some finely chopped green onion. Freshly toasted sesame seeds glistened in the marinade.

She chuckled to think of what Kum Seung would say if she could see this, for Sun Yi's culinary skills were vastly improved from the time when she left her family home. Setting the bowl aside so it could wait for broiling over the charcoal fire later, she mused again. Yong Soon was always nearby in her student days, and when she returned to her family there was Kum Seung. She may have been a stepmother but she was a closer confidant than any sister was.

Now I'm a married woman, even a mother, and there is no one. All of my students must address me as teacher. None of them could ever become my close companion. My husband has his friends. When they gather at the far corner of the house I can hear the muffled clink of the black and white markers, while they play paduk far into the night, but I never see them.

She sighed. At other times her husband sat alone, playing his flute. She listened to the plaintive melody drifting across the courtyard, wishing she dared to join him. She never dared to intrude on his moments of solitude and meditation. If he wished for her company he would seek her out.

There was the baby, of course. Sometimes she talked to him as though he understood her words, but then she would smile at the child wriggling on her lap and warn, "You are the only one I have but I know you will soon be ready to join the company of the men, and you will leave me, also."

Jae Soon would put his plump fist into his mouth and stare back at his mother, his dark eyes like pools of infinite depth, solemn above the rosy cheeks as if he knew her meaning. Then she would hug him, clasping the small body to her, but it was not enough.

Memories of the infant prince's death still haunted her. Innocent suffering disturbed Sun Yi, yet she dared share these thoughts with no one, for she had no wish to create the suspicion once implied by her husband that she bore even one drop of sympathy for those who were determined to rule her homeland.

There were some, she knew, who managed to survive handsomely by tolerating, even acquiescing, to their masters, but she had carried this searing hatred within herself for so long that she had a strong need to talk with someone who might understand her sudden conflict. Was it possible that the obsession crippled her natural empathy for others? Early in life she learned never to look at a face, to see only the uniform, never to listen to a voice but to hear only that unnatural accent. The death of the infant prince shocked Sun Yi into the realization that some Japanese might not share their leaders' enthusiasm for oppression of Koreans. Could it be possible?

Sun Yi had only to recall the violence, the beatings, the deaths of thousands which resulted from the harsh ambitions of the conqueror and she swiftly counteracted this idea. The sorrow of the Japanese princess is only one more drop into the pool of human suffering created by greed and lust for power. Perhaps she would discuss this with Kim Tae Un. Tonight, after his meeting ended, she would tell her husband of the letter.

Dr. Lee's home was still thought to be safe, an unsuspected place for gatherings of the patriots who plotted acts of espionage. A strict limit on the number of persons who might meet in one place at any time was imposed by authorities, but by using the hospital he had, thus far, been able to circumvent that order.

One last chore remained before she left the kitchen. Sun Yi measured out the uncooked rice kernels, one spoonful for each member of their household, and dropped them into the basket that held the offering to Ch'ondogyo. It was a good reminder, this daily ritual, of the importance of that faith in their lives. As the rice flowed through her fingers she remembered the depth of her husband's commitment to the principles of this doctrine.

It was the driving force behind tonight's meeting. She was foolish to worry, for she knew he was always cautious. But the danger existed. Both of them knew it. He and the other men, each one the principal spiritual leader for his own district, consisting of ten p'os, each of them with thirty households, provided the leadership that kept the movement for independence alive.

When he'd first instructed Sun Yi in the importance of setting aside a portion of rice each day, she'd asked the reason.

"To feed the less fortunate," he'd told her, and to provide the funds that would pay for paper and presses to inform the people, a harvest of food for the mind, as well."

Later, in the part of the day she most enjoyed, when the world outside was forgotten, she asked him, "How did you come to follow Ch'ondogyo? Many men do not." Meaning: why are you different?

"My father was an early believer," he replied slowly, but I was a skeptic, until I returned from Europe. Then I understood how I could make those ideals the structure for my own life. He took up her hand, absentmindedly, twisting her gold rings, and continued. "At first it was a kind of reaction to the western influences of the latter part of the last century. It began as a reaction. The original name of the movement, Tonghak, means eastern learning, but the political turmoil of the time, when many men challenged the social conditions that oppressed the common workers, encouraged the Tonghak leaders to believe their teachings could create change. That began more than sixty years ago with our founder, Ch'oe Che-u."

Sixty years. A lifetime, Sun Yi thought, watching her husband's face attentively. She was flattered that he would speak to her of these serious matters.

"It was a combination of two forces," he continued, dropping her hand suddenly, the light in his eyes catching fire. "There were the yangban, the nobles who'd lost their positions in the royal court, and farmers. They were poor, hopelessly held down by taxes that grew higher each year. Together they hoped to create a new way of life in our country. Do you understand?" he asked, almost plaintive.

She nodded, not wanting to quench the flow of his words.

"It probably sounds too idealistic, but the hope was born that this new set of beliefs could promote an unselfish concern for one's fellow man. That's still the basic idea for Ch'ondogyo, to treat each person as if he is God."

"That must have been a strong threat to the Yi dynasty," Sun Yi ventured.

"It was," her husband continued, fixing his eyes on her with pride. "Tonghak is the complete opposite of traditional religion and ethics. Although it borrowed from teachings of Confucius and Buddha, even from Taoism, and it imitated some rituals that early Catholic missionaries introduced, still it is the only original religion in our country."

His eyes looked intense, riveting Sun Yi's attention on his face. This is the man I married, she marveled. He is brilliant!

"Think of its potential!" he continued. "To believe that man and God are one. If a man is sincere, if he gives his respect to all other human beings, rich, poor, scholar or slave, even women. This is how he lives in the spirit of God."

Now he grabbed her hand and squeezed it so tightly that she drew back from him. "That sounds like paradise on earth."

"Exactly! You have it. The important idea behind Ch'ondogyo is that we have the power to create paradise here, during our life on earth."

"But isn't that more than we can expect of human beings? Most of us are not perfect, after all."

You are, she was thinking.

"How can we live up to those ideals?"

"What is crucial is to make the attempt," he reassured her. "Our first leader was executed, after much persecution, for that very deed. He was charged with proclaiming the existence of a being superior to the King, much like the Catholics, who were persecuted at the same time.

As Sun Yi listened she wondered if any other husband would even consider discussing ideas of this serious nature with his wife. "But that didn't put an end to his teachings?" She wanted this marvelous conversation never to end. He was paying such exquisite attention to her.

"No. It's strong today. Now there are more than a million of us. And each one makes a contribution of rice every day. Most of the money for the independence movement comes from this voluntary act. And our efforts to free Korea continue."

"And you have an important part?"

"I have important work to do. It is through my group that the exiled leaders in Shanghai reach their supporters. We have the most extensive network in Korea. We can reach a wide circle of persons-quickly."

Sun Yi shivered. This was exciting but dangerous. But that was the reason for its thrill, wasn't it? She covered the rice basket and thought again of tonight's meeting. When he'd first asked her help in preparing for it, Dr. Lee said its decisions would determine the future purpose of Ch'ondogyo. The fate of more than a million people, and perhaps the future of their country, to be decided here, in her own home.

Suddenly she realized that no matter how good a friend Kim Tae Un turned out to be, she would never tell her about this part of her life.

Sun Yi was standing in the kitchen doorway, occupied by these thoughts, when her husband appeared, hurrying toward her.

"What brings you to this part of the house?" she called. Sun Yi had never seen him near the kitchen in all the days of their marriage. Now he waved a newspaper at her and, when he was closer, spread out the front page so she could read the headline for herself, while he shouted, "An earthquake has struck Tokyo! The entire city may be destroyed! It is all in flames."

All the next day she waited for more information, something definite to counteract the rumors spreading throughout Seoul. The doctor and his friends talked late into the night. She'd lain wide awake, listening to the sounds of their voices, wishing she could hear the words, as they discussed the implication this sudden tragedy might have for their activities against the Japanese government. When he finally arrived, she rushed to greet him.

"Is there any more news?"

"All we know is that the damage is extensive, not only in Tokyo but in many other places as well. The number of deaths is growing, and the homeless are too numerous to count. You know how fragile their houses are, not sturdy like ours. Some are as thin as paper. So fires are the cause for much of the destruction." He handed her his jacket, adding in a low voice, "There's been some mention of riots, as well."

"Riots? Why would anyone riot in the midst of such tragedy," Sun Yi demanded.

"That's precisely what we cannot understand. It's a rumor, of course, but it has been repeated, coming from so many sources, that we decided to send one of ours, a trusted person, to learn more. Perhaps he'll bring us the truth." He turned away from her, his shoulders sagging from an unseen burden.

"There's more, isn't there?"

He turned at the sound of her pleading. Their eyes met in silence for a moment before he said, "Nothing more. Except that for a brief time I foolishly held some hope that the consequences of this human misery might force those weanom to look to the welfare of their own. Then there might have been a bit of hope for us. But nothing will change."

His pessimism shook Sun Yi. She realized how she'd come to depend on him, with firm, quiet confidence, believing all he did was right, how her faith in him sustained her when she felt doubts. She'd worried while she listened to the animated voices last night. Their meeting was illegal. Had they forgotten? What would happen if they were discovered? What had happened to her reckless bravery? Was her caution a result of having the responsibility for her child now? This new hesitation. Could it be possible that her resolution was weakening? The threat of prison was real. It had happened to others.

She looked at this man with whom she now shared a common destiny and pleaded, "You must be more careful. If you were overheard last night. I cannot bear to think what might happen to you."

Her husband laid his hand on her arm gently, saying, "You need not be concerned. I always plan carefully. These things we do may seem small and insignificant but one day, when we are free, everyone will be thankful that we tried to preserve the memory of our heritage." He smiled, reassuring her. "Do you recall that ancient teaching? "If you are strong like a tree, with deep roots, the winds cannot shake you. You will flourish and bloom."

Then Sun Yi smiled back. Yes, he still had that irrepressible optimism. What's more, when their eyes met she could see a kind of softness in his, an admiration of her. Was she still as lovely as he'd once said? She recalled his telling her how the sparkling intensity in her brown eyes set her apart from the other young women. A rosy flush spread across her high cheekbones now when she thought of it. He was watching her quick movements as she brushed her sleek dark hair and wound it impatiently into a coil. She knew the simple style suited her well, framing the oval contours of her face.

"What are you thinking, Yubo?" she asked with a laugh, as he continued to watch her.

"Only that the arranged marriage may not always be the best way to choose a wife," he whispered, drawing her into his embrace.

She lingered in the circle of his arms, remembering the secret they shared. No one else would ever know how they had chosen each other. This spark of conspiracy continually reignited their mutual passion. The harmony discovered at their first meeting still existed, as strong a bond as in the beginning. Because she knew this, it was possible for Sun Yi to wrap herself into a cocoon of contentment, even when her husband was preoccupied with the friends and activities of his world, from which she was always excluded. She trusted him completely.

Soon after she received Yong Soon's letter, Sun Yi dispatched a note of welcome to Ewha University, inviting Kim Tai Un to call on her. The response was immediate. Would the following day be convenient? Sun Yi returned a note of agreement. Thoughts of this meeting filled her with new enthusiasm.

How long had it been since she had spoken from her heart to anyone but her husband? Even with him there were limitations, for he had no understanding of women's' thoughts. What man could? Perhaps this woman, Kim Tai Un, will be the one to share the place that Kum Seung and Yong Soon filled in her life.

She prepared her home swiftly, stacking Jae Soon's playthings in a corner, sweeping the courtyard. While the baby slept and the house was quiet, Sun Yi dressed with care in a crisp white cotton chima, fastened her favorite pale green jade pin on the chogori, and thrust a matching hair ornament, a pinja, into her sleek black hair.

Finally she sat on a cushion, fanning, welcoming the slight breeze that shook the wisteria leaves and brought relief from the still warmth of the afternoon, and wondering, again, about this lady. At last she heard the rumble of the jinriksha and rose impulsively to greet this new friend herself.

They bowed simultaneously. A wisp of a smile touched the lips of the stranger as they murmured the polite greetings, and Sun Yi relaxed. How tiny this Miss Kim seemed, standing next to her, and perhaps also a bit older than herself. But her eyes! They were the brightest, most penetrating Sun Yi had ever faced. This may be a person from whom she could have no secrets, after all. She led her into the pleasant coolness of the shaded room and beckoned her to be seated on a cushion there. The doorway was open to capture the wisps of wind from the inner courtyard.

While a young maid served cups of cool podi cha, the tea made from roasted barley kernels, to them and offered plates of fresh fruit slices and small rice cakes, Sun Yi made inquiries about Yong Soon. An awkward silence followed Kim Tai Un's polite response and she searched her mind for a new topic.

"What do you think of Seoul? Yong Soon told me you've never been here before."

"That's true." Miss Kim was choosing her words as thoughtfully as she speared the crisp pear on her plate. "It certainly is different from any of the other places where I've lived, not just for its size, but it is always bustling. The noise is constant, night and day, and I see, in every direction, something being built or demolished."

"Even those of us who've lived here longer think our capitol is becoming unfamiliar to us before our eyes. Streets are widened and old ones vanish. Did you know that more than five hundred of the buildings on Kyongbok Palace grounds have been torn down?"

"Why would they do that?"

Sin Yi felt some pleasure that she had managed to shock Miss Kim into an exclamation. "To make room for new government offices. I've heard they'll have two or even three stories!"

"Those Japanese want to copy the western styles in everything, even their palaces," Kim Tai Un told her indignantly. "I saw the new National Capitol. It has five stories, all granite and marble. There's not one portion with our traditional carved wood or tile."

Sun Yi discovered, while they continued their conversation, that Yong Soon was right. She had much in common with this remarkably expressive lady. She offered original thoughts on every subject and broadened Sun Yi's impressions with her own.

Finally, pausing to sip the tea, she looked about the room and said, "Your home is charming, but more. It is comfortable." She sighed and went on, "I'm not often in such a place, with this warm feeling. A real family lives here."

"Is your own family far away, then?"

"There's not been a family for me in many years," Miss Kim confided softly. In response to Sun Yi's puzzled expression, she continued. "My father died when I was an infant. Typhoid. My elder brother, also. My mother was left alone with me, forced to become subject to the domination of my father's only relative, a cousin. He took control of our family wealth, of course. My mother was miserable, constantly, treated as a lowly servant."

"How sad. It can happen to anyone. What choice did she have, though?"

"You may think she had none." Kim Tai Un's back straightened, became rigid. She sipped the tea once more, then fastened her intense eyes on Sun Yi's face, as if to judge her reaction to this story. "For most women, no choice. But my mother is strong. She chose independence even though it meant living in poverty. When she told the cousin she was leaving he gave her fifteen hundred won. Only fifteen hundred. He would let her starve. She tried living with her brother, a widower. That was just as unpleasant, so she made a home alone, for herself and me."

"How could she? Such hardship! Was she ostracized?"

"Oh, yes. You know what people think of such things. But," she tossed her head, "we are northerners, so it was possible. My mother is stubborn, determined. She never gives up. Nor do I. When Yong Soon told me your story," she added, with a sideways glance at Sun Yi, I suspected you were also a northerner. One doesn't expect a woman from the south to be as strong minded as you have been."

That must be intended as a compliment, Sun Yi thought.

The maid brought a fresh pot of podi cha but they scarcely noticed her entrance.

"Did you find your education just as difficult?"

Again that smile. "You must call me by my little name if we are to be such friends that I would tell you about that. Difficult? At first it seemed impossible, for girls had no school in our village. So my mother cut my hair," She paused for the shock to be absorbed, "and dressed me as a boy. I was only seven. It seemed like wonderful play acting. I mastered all their games, and often beat them."

In the silence that followed, the remote look on her face suggested she was remembering those pleasant times of freedom when everyone assumed she was a male child.

"As I became older the masquerade was impossible to continue, so we moved again, to a town where there was a school for girls, run by the Christian missionaries."

"But how did you live?" Sun Yi was thinking of the comfortable home that she had left. Even her life had not been this hard.

"Oh, she was a weaver, my mother, weaving night and day, cotton and silk. I can still hear the sound of her loom at times when I am alone. In summer she took me along, traveling about, selling her cloth, earning a little for rice and a little for more yarn. We survived, somehow." Tai Un smiled once more. "Now she has a small home of her own, in that same town, north of Pyongyang. Since I began teaching, I'm able to send her a bit. But my dream is to bring her to live with me. She will enjoy living in this city."

When she stopped talking Sun Yi spoke and the wistful note was barely audible. "You are most fortunate. You know exactly what it is you want to accomplish."

"And grateful for this opportunity," Tai Un was emphatic. "Soon Ewha will be a full-fledged college for women. The first in our country! I'm proud to be a part of it. I owe this to my mother, and the most meaningful way I have to show my recognition of her sacrifice is to work at creating the same opportunities for women of the next generation."

Her voice rose. "Girls are always the forgotten beings in Korea. It is like abandoning half of the population." When she leaned closer, she spoke with great intensity. "It is my dream to live to see the day when all women are educated, allowed to develop an interest in society, in its problems, then they may also find a way to stop the brutality of men. It is our best hope for the future. Don't you believe that, also?"

Sun Yi, swept up by her emotion, nodded vigorously. "There's not much else we can do. But," she added after a moment of thought, "how will you cope with the demands of marriage?"

"Marriage?" Tai Un was incredulous. "That has never entered my mind. There is no place for it in my life."

"Never?"

She shook her head. "And my mother accepts this. She will never force me to marry. To be cloistered within walls by a tyrant, while he seeks all the pleasures of the senses elsewhere? My freedom is too hard-won to exchange it for that version of life. I don't understand how you can accept it, but then you have no choice. You will always have to live with the knowledge of your husband's concubines."

Sun Yi's eyes grew wide. She was speechless. Her husband?

"You don't believe me?" Tai Un shook her head. "You are naïve, but you still have time to learn."

But Sun Yi's husband was involved in far more serious concerns. His political activities enveloped every free moment of his life now.

The pains pierced her sleep, wrapping her body in their convulsive vise. She cried out in her anguish, sitting up in the darkness, reaching out to be comforted, and stretching out her arm to the place beside her. Her fingers fumbled with the light summer quilt and found nothing, no one.

"Yubo? Yubo?"

Where was he at this early hour?

Then Sun Yi remembered. He had not returned yesterday. The nightmare from which she'd just awakened was not a dream. It was real. It had happened. They took him away, those men with the rough loud voices, who pounded on the gate, demanding the doctor's presence. He'd answered, believing someone needed him. She watched through a narrow crack in the door, holding her son back so the tousled and sleepy child could not see the two men in black uniforms when they tied his father's hands behind his back. Then her husband looked up at her with despair. She'd never seen such a look on his face before, a look of utter helplessness. She lurched forward, dressed as she was in her nightclothes, and clung to his arm.

"You must not let them take you!"

He had no choice. They shoved him about, their faces stern, devoid of emotion. She watched helplessly while he disappeared into the dark street with them.

Now all the memories, images of her own time in prison, flooded into her mind. Where had he been taken? What could she do to help him? She was alone with her pain. It was sharper now. Dragging herself over to the door, she slid it open, called for the maid, struggled to make heard the thin quaver that was her voice.

This time the pain came too early. Only August now. This new child should not be born before the festival of Chesu in October. When her strength ebbed she lay next to the open doorway and felt gentle hands lifting her, placing her on top of the quilts. Rain fell, a steady rhythmic sound on the tile roof, just as she'd heard when Jae Soon was born three years earlier. The monsoon continued for days. The warm air stifled her lungs, heavy and unpleasant. How much time passed? The maid took so long to return with her mother-in-law and daylight seeped into the shadowy corners while she waited.

This boy came more quickly. She heard his first cry and opened her eyes for a moment. Look at him! Small, but howling. He had a strong will to live. How could he be in such a hurry to begin this troubled life? She lay back, relieved that he was healthy, but wondering as she drifted into a deep sleep at the child's impatience to enter a world so filled with sorrow.

"The dream returns to me every night," she told Tai Un. A week had passed with no word about her husband. "So real that I am frightened again, and unable to sleep for hours. The pounding, the loud voices, the threats. Then I see him taken away, over and over again."

Her face was thin and pale. In a low voice she retold the terror of that day while she rocked the tiny child in her arms. Wisps of black hair, soft and moist, molded to his head. The wrinkled face was rosy, the eyes tightly shut. "He wakes often, hungry as a tiger," she said, "but his stomach is soon filled."

"I can tell that you are not sleeping." Tai Un was concerned. "You must have some help, for you do need your strength. Have you heard any word at all about the doctor? I still can't believe that someone like him would be arrested."

"I called for his father as soon as it happened. He's been trying to find out something, but all the officials will do is confirm that there is a Dr. Lee in Westgate Prison."

Tai Un took the child from her arms and Sun Yi buried her face in her hands, silent for a long while. Both of them knew the reputation of that place. Finally she asked, "Well, do you know any reason for his arrest?"

Sun Yi raised her head and stared at her friend. What could she say to this woman? How much dared she tell her?

"There are many reasons. But I should not tell you any of them, for if I do, I will be placing you in danger as well."

"Believe me. You can tell me. You don't have to bear this burden alone."

I want to confide in her, Sun Yi thought. She is already my good friend. Yong Soon sent her to me at just the moment when I needed her, and there's no one else.

"It could be the secret meetings he held here," she hesitated, then went on, "or perhaps it was because of the information he obtained about the treatment of the Koreans in Japan after the earthquake. People here learned of those atrocities because of his publication."

"Is that really true?" Tai Un sounded genuinely surprised. "Of course I heard the stories myself, though I thought them almost too incredible. How could anyone blame other people for a natural disaster like that?" The baby stirred and she rocked him slowly back and forth while she pondered aloud.

"Not the earthquake itself, but the fires and explosions that came after. The Koreans living in Japan were blamed for those. Rumors can spread quickly, you know, in such confusion. Thousands of our countrymen died at the hands of the mobs, for there was such resentment built up. This gave it a reason to boil over."

"What have those poor people done to deserve this? After all, they were just poor farmers who lost their land here."

"You're right," Sun Yi agreed. "But it's only recently that they've organized themselves, to demand better wages and working conditions. It sets a dangerous precedent. The government feared they'd have an influence on Japanese laborers. So the Koreans were a convenient scapegoat in this disaster. It was an opportunity to destroy their movement."

"And it was your husband who dared to publish these facts?"

Sun Yi nodded. "You must understand. My husband shares with me this dream, of a Korea free again one day. We are not alone in this wish, to become, once more, proud of our ancestors' achievements. But even more," she added, "to dare to hope for a time when everyone here can have a better life." She paused, wondering how to convey to her friend the depth of commitment she and her husband shared. "He first had the idea, to begin these newsletters, to inform the common people through them."

"Yes, I've read some of them. Clever ideas, not just political but extremely practical for daily living. I admire his purpose but."

"You question his wisdom?"

"Well, yes. See what has happened. He knew of this danger. And you and the children ought to have been considered."

"My husband always knew I did not wish to be an impediment to his goals," Sun Yi stated vehemently. "Of course he is not alone in this. Many other men, like him, are disturbed by the growth of the pro-Japanese home rule groups. Even newspapers like *Tong a Ilbo* printed stories and editorials calling the home rulers national traitors."

The baby stirred again and began to howl. She took him from Tai Un and held him to her breast. He sucked noisily while she continued explaining. "When the mass meeting of protest was suppressed last April he helped to plan the June conference that denounced the government." She shook her head, remembering the arguments that came from his meetings in their house at that time. "It was in June that he and others promised to continue their demonstrations against Japanese oppression, no matter what happened."

"What happened?" Tai Un echoed.

"They attacked the office where his magazines were printed, ransacked the offices, smashed the equipment. Oh, they tried every means to stop him but he could not be silenced. Until now," she added softly, and for the first time tears flowed down her cheeks."

"Perhaps he'll be released with a warning?"

It was Sun Yi's turn to be astounded. "You. You are naive," she exclaimed. "And much too optimistic. They realize the extent of my husband's power and influence."

"What shall you do, then, if he is to be in prison for who knows how long?"

"I?" She brushed a stray hair from her wan face and, for the first time that day, smiled. "I shall remain here and wait for his release."

"No matter how long?"

"No matter. I will still be here. This is our home." Then she whispered, for the mother-in-law must be nearby, "My husband's father has already told me to move into his house. He was astonished when

I refused. The men of his generation are not accustomed to disobedience from wives or daughters." The smile appeared again. "If you saw the expression on his face when I told him I did not intend to leave my home, even you would have been amazed. But I can't leave. Don't you see that would be an admission of defeat, that I've given up hope of his return. I would become one of those pitiful widows, condemned to live out my life under someone else's roof, eating someone else's rice like a pauper."

She paused, patting the baby as she rocked him, before she added, "Remember that old saying? A son-in-law is a guest for a hundred years; a daughter-in-law is an eating mouth until the day she dies."

Sun Yi lifted her head in the now familiar gesture of defiance. "No! I will stay here."

"How can I help you, then, since you've made your choice?"

Tai Un's offer was characteristically swift. Sun Yi was not surprised. "I must have more students. I'll earn my living by tutoring."

"Ah, that will be easy for me to arrange. Just tell me when you feel ready."

This woman's presence seemed providential. Whom could she trust more? Sun Yi began to thank her but turned at the sound of the opening door. Her mother-in-law came in, carrying her mid-day meal of seaweed soup and hot rice. She stopped when she saw the guest, then set down the tray near Sun Yi and left the room.

Sun Yi smiled, shaking her head. "I'm afraid she gives you all the credit for my independent ideas. Before you leave," she added, seeing that Tai Un was preparing to leave, "I have one more special request. My father-in-law told me that I had permission to deliver one package to the prison." She gestured to a bundle tied up in a square of cloth. "Some clothing, a little food, and" she lifted one corner, "this." Among the neatly folded layers was one small red chili pepper. "If he does receive this, he'll know what it means. Please?"

"Of course I will." Tai Un took up the package by the handle formed of the four ends of the cloth tied together and reached out with her other hand to pat Sun Yi's shoulder. "If only I could do more. I'll be back in the morning."

After she left, Sun Yi laid the sleeping baby on the quilt. She was thinking of the sheet of paper she had slipped into the bundle for her husband. Anyone could see that it was only a poem, not any kind of message. Perhaps he'd be allowed to have it. He would understand if he read it, would know her thoughts. She'd copied it out carefully, this verse by the great poet of the Seventeenth Century, Yun Son Do.

> "Heart wants to sing, but cannot sing alone;
> Heart wants to dance, but dancing must have
>   music
> Then lute shall play,
> For none but lute can strike the secret tone
> My heart would sing
> So heart and song are one;
> Then lute shall play,
> For none but lute knows what is heart's desire
> So heart may spring
> Into the dance
> And beat its rhythm out.
> Welcome, sweet lute, my dear, my dearest
>   friend,
> There is no hurt the music cannot mend."

He'd read this poem to her more than once. Now it would convey to him, more than any words could, her feeling of desolation.

Days passed, weeks passed. Leaves fell from the poplar trees, like bits of hope drifting away. The air became crisp and cool and then bitterly cold. Sun Yi had never received direct word of her husband's arrest. She was told only that his medical services were needed for the inmates for an indefinite time.

"You are a willful, stubborn woman," her father-in-law declared, after one last attempt to persuade her to give up her home for his. He shook his gray bearded head and left her alone.

How she wished she had learned to be frugal! Now she planned carefully to stretch the money she earned by teaching, but it was never enough. Yet she continued to set aside a cupful of rice each day, the donation for Ch'ondogyo. He'll be pleased when he learns that I still do this, she thought.

She'd sent the two young maids away, knowing they'd find other places, but when Sun Yi told the elderly woman who'd been with her since the first days of her marriage that she could no longer pay her, she refused to leave.

"Then you'll have a home here as long as I do," she promised, and wondered how much time would pass before she must capitulate to her father-in-law after all.

She often sat side by side, working with her in the quiet house. On one morning in late October Sun Yi was in the kitchen courtyard, chopping vegetables for the kimchee, when Jae Soon came to her.

"May I help you, Ohmanee?"

Imagine such a baby wanting to do this work! She smiled at his suggestion, then realized he was quite serious, and found a task for him. He was growing tall, already past three years, and his thin face always looked serious. Once he'd been so high spirited. The somber mood of his home had stifled him and she'd never given a thought to it until now. What could she do?

The baby, given the name Jae Yun, gave her little trouble. He was a sturdy infant who'd made up quickly for his small size at birth. She concentrated on preparing for the afternoons when she tutored her girls. Tai Un kept her promise and sent Sun Yi as many students as she wished. Her reputation spread among all their circle of acquaintance. Now she must find time for her eldest son. How could she have let herself neglect him?

What is there to celebrate about this year, Sun Yi asked herself when she awoke on New Year's Day in 1925? More than five months since he'd been imprisoned and she missed her husband as strongly as on the day he'd been taken away. New snow fell during the night and she pictured him in that frigid prison. The winter was colder than usual. Snow packed down, layer on top of layer, never melting, drifting on to rooftops and hanging over their edges like thick ibuls, but without warmth. She'd sent a bundle of padded cotton clothing to him at the onset of the cold season. Did he receive it? Each day a member of his family took food and once a week clean clothing and bedding was allowed, but there had been no word, no message, from him.

"Ohmanee! Get up. We'll be late for the visit to Grandfather!"

Jae Soon skipped around her bed, parading before her in the new set of clothes she'd sewn by piecing together parts of an old dress. The tiny jacket was a rainbow of silk, red, yellow, green and blue stripes, and his loose trousers were a matching shade of navy blue. Of course she must take him to the home of her in-laws today. This New Year was the first he could remember and she would not allow him to miss the festivities, no matter how sad she was.

Jae Soon's dark eyes sparkled with excitement amidst the sounds of the many voices, and opened wide when he saw the delicious variety of foods laid out on low tables for the men of his father's family. He bowed to each of his elders, as she'd taught him, and then ran to drop the coins he received from them into her hand, finding them nothing he could play with, and ran off once more. He and his young brother were the youngest of all that gathered for this holiday. The two of them were the target of admiring attention from all the aunts and cousins. It was good that she'd brought them here, after all.

She felt less welcome, herself. Sun Yi stayed in a corner near the kitchen, where she could offer her help and still listen to the conversation among the men. She caught the sound of her husband's name. Brief bits of dialogue intrigued her and she lingered near the door after she'd served them, wishing she dared to stay.

One woman among the cousins finally spoke to her.

"Have you any word of the doctor?"

Sudden tears stung Sun Yi's eyes and she realized how seldom she'd heard such kindness in a voice since all the troubles began.

"No," she replied, and forced a smile. "But I'm sure he's well treated because his skills are so desperately needed there." But, she thought, that is a two-edged sword. If he is needed, he might be kept indefinitely. "You know," she told the cousin, "My father-in-law made frequent protests to the prison officials."

"That won't help."

"What makes you say such a thing?" She wondered why she'd thought this woman kind?

"Look at him. See for yourself."

Sun Yi peeked into the doorway. The old gentleman was sitting in the place of honor, above all the others, and though he wore the tall black hat that was the symbol of his wisdom, he appeared disconsolate. His slender figure, draped in white, was all but ignored by the younger men as they talked to each other.

"His time has passed," the woman went on. "He no longer has the recognition and respect of his age. Even when he walks in the street, some push him aside, saying 'You're too slow, old man.' I've even heard that they sometimes shove him aside in their impatience. He can't help you now."

Sun Yi bowed to the cousin. "I must see to my sons," she murmured, moving away, in a signal that the conversation was finished. Her husband's elder brother, the one who had been at the wedding, was speaking and his voice rose above the others. She strained to listen to it while she rocked the sleepy Jae Yun in her arms. This man had just returned from Japan, where he'd been sent for training as a junior technician for a new factory.

"I tell you that I saw new methods and equipment being tested and used in every part of that country," he was saying. All of the men seated around him fell silent and listened, also. "This is the way of the future, whether you like it or not. Change, progress, western technology. If we are ever to begin, to pass beyond our current state, we must adapt to these new ideas in Korea as well. And if we don't begin soon, we will fall so far behind that it will be impossible for us to reach Japan's competence."

There was a chorus of protest, each man shouting to be heard. What would my husband tell them, she wondered? Surely he would champion the side of progress, wouldn't he? But would he be as brave as the elder brother, daring to challenge the traditional views of his father in his presence? He always showed the proper respect for an elder. That brother was quite a different sort. Considerate to a point, but outspoken with his views, especially since he'd traveled out of Korea. He was shorter, a bit on the rotund side since he was known for his love of good food and good times. She knew he went frequently to be entertained by the kisaeng. She noticed how his high forehead glistened in the warm room as the argument heated also.

There was the younger brother speaking now. His thin, hollow chest gave him a gaunt appearance, like an ascetic. The contrast in his ideas was equally great.

"You would persuade us to cooperate with the Japanese simply for the purpose of economic progress," he charged. "You!" He waved his arm in the direction of the elder brother. "You seem to forget the harm done to our land. We are slaves!"

"Not at all." The elder one's voice was low, calm. "It is just so we may avoid becoming slaves that I insist we must study western science and technology. This country is rich in coal and other minerals. If we can only obtain the means to develop the northern mountains ourselves, then we may prevent our natural wealth from slipping through our fingers into the hands of the foreigners. All we need is men trained so we can make use of what lies at our own feet."

Everyone turned when the father moved for the first time, raising his hand to silence the others before he spoke. Sun Yi forgot she was in hiding and slid over into the doorway.

"For many years our country has continued its own peaceful way. We've never attacked a neighbor, never carried a battle beyond our borders, only defended ourselves. We follow the classical learning and Confucian teaching that has been our tradition. Our one fault, and that only in recent times, has been to allow the rise of incompetent leaders who dispersed their energy in rivalry. They were weak men who yielded to foreign invaders." He paused and looked around at each face.

He is a proud, good man, Sun Yi thought. If only my husband was here to witness this! If I dared to speak, I would tell them that each of them is right, partly. Only a compromise between their views will give us the unity we need to wage a successful fight.

"What we need is men of good will. We need not change our traditions," he concluded with a voice that was loud, strong, and clear.

"With all respect, Abiji," the elder son spoke quickly. "You seem to have forgotten that we cannot select our own leaders. We are driven like oxen in the yoke of the Japanese. Every one, from the poor farmer who is allowed to keep only a small portion of his earnings, to those of us who manage the new industries. We all work only for the benefit of the Empire."

"Elder brother is speaking the truth," admitted the younger son. "We have lost the power to make choices. Some of us, however, can make use of the opportunity to learn the western methods. And if we do that, we'll be prepared for the time when we can regain our country, and our traditions."

How optimistic they all sound, thought Sun Yi, pulling back but still hovering near the door. I hope these confident feelings last until we realize the dream of freedom.

A cousin's wife tugged at her sleeve, warning her. Sun Yi realized that she was the only one of all the women who had listened to this talk. The others had all retired to their own portion of the house. The cousin gestured for Sun Yi to follow her. I must, she thought. I've given my mother-in-law enough reasons for criticism already.

As she stood up, the stimulation of this discussion ringing in her head, Sun Yi thought how she missed speaking with her husband on such topics. How much longer could she endure without him?

In all of the letters she wrote to her own family, down in Kyong-sangdo, Sun Yi reassured them. Her husband would soon be out of prison and, meanwhile, she was quite comfortable.

Nothing could be further from the truth. She closed off all the cold rooms but one, next to the kitchen, for the boys and herself, and another for the maid. This way, few yonton, small bits of charcoal, burned in the stove, yet were sufficient to warm the stone-lined ducts beneath the floor's shiny surface. They slept on the soft quilts that were rolled and packed away in the wall cupboards in daytime, when they took their meals at a low table in the same room. When her students arrived the same space became their classroom.

So this year's first warm spring days were more welcome than ever. Sun Yi always loved this time of year best of all, but now she only thought that the damp chill of her husband's cell would lessen.

Kum Seung sent her a letter, dictated through the hand of her eldest son, Han Ju, for she'd never had the time to learn to write, after all.

"I beg you to consider making a place in your home for your brother," she wrote, "for the boy has reached an age where he needs more challenging instruction than our village teacher can give him. As you may remember, he has an able and inquisitive mind. Your father and I will be saddened by his absence but we want him to have the best education and that can only be with you in Seoul."

That child she'd loved and taught during her house arrest was a boy of twelve now. What a fine companion he'd make for Jae Soon! For myself, as well, she admitted, and she wrote back immediately with her invitation.

Han Ju arrived on a warm day in April. Sun Yi hired a ricksha to meet him at the train station. Forsythia splashed patches of lemon color against the crumbling granite of the city walls and giant azaleas created a palette of pink, rose, and lavender on the gently sloping hills surrounding the saucer shaped hollow in which Seoul lay. Will the city seem as fascinating to him as I found it when I first arrived, she wondered? Pushing through the throngs of passengers, passing the pushcarts of vendors, Sun Yi searched for the face she remembered. He'd been sad when she last saw him, looking as if he thought she was deserting him, when she left her family home for the last time.

Over by a pile of baggage a tall young man was waving in her direction.

"Is it really you?" she asked, when he rushed to meet her. He was hanging onto a satchel of woven straw with both hands, with bony wrists extending from the sleeves of his dark jacket. Equally dark eyes darted about the crowd, shy, yet filled with curiosity. "I'm afraid I was expecting to find the same small boy that I left in Yongju."

She wanted to place her arm around his shoulder, to encourage him, but she dared not offend his dignity. Poor thing! He looked quite bewildered. No wonder. From his country village he'd been propelled into this huge city, all alone. Instead she smiled broadly. "Tell me about everyone at home. Do you think they miss me still? And how was the train ride?"

"It's an awfully long way," he said, brushing back a lock of shiny hair that slipped immediately back over his forehead.

"Well, now you'll have another ride, a shorter one this time," she told him, as they each climbed into a jinriksha. "Home is not far."

She looked back at him as they rolled along the wide roads of yellow-gray colored granite. The sky was intensely blue, under brilliant sunshine. Such a fine day to first see Seoul! They wove their way around the constant stream of slowly crawling oxen. The animals were laden with brushwood and led by men in dusty cotton clothing, wearing shoes of straw. Men sat in the doorways of shops and eating houses, smoking long pipes and watching them pass.

"Traveling makes you thirsty," Sun Yi laughed, as he drank the cool podi cha the maid brought to them. He stood in the doorway, looking puzzled as he peered up and down the narrow street. "Here you will see only walls. Our neighbors live beyond the gates. Our way of living will seem strange to you at first," she consoled him. "After you start school and meet your classmates, I'm sure you'll find this city as fascinating as I do. Well, what do you think of your uncle?"

Jae Soon hung onto the folds of her chima, peeking out from its security. He followed when Sun Yi led the way to the room Han Ju would have.

"This will be your own quiet place to study and sleep," she explained.

"I've never had so much space to myself before," he said quietly. Then he set down the straw bag he'd hung onto all the way from the station and opened it. He handed Sun Yi a small purse and a letter.

"Father sent this for you."

A message from her father! She opened the letter first. The money in the purse was intended to pay for the cost of Han Ju's schooling, she read, and for the expense of feeding another mouth. He hoped it would be enough. Enough! The sum she found inside was far more than needed for such purpose. Sun Yi rubbed her eyes. She seldom cried anymore, certainly not where anyone could see her. But to think that her family had chosen this way to help her survive difficult times without bowing to the indignity of asking for help! It would make a difference. Such a difference that now she was sure she would never be forced to beg from her father-in-law.

Jae Soon stepped forward and looked up at Han Ju, finally managing to overcome his shyness.

"This is your uncle," Sun Yi kneeled beside him to explain and grateful for such a diversion. "He's traveled a long way, riding all day on a train. Now he is going to live with us. He's come from the house where your mother lived when she was as small as you are now."

Jae Soon looked at him. A dubious expression crossed his face until the older boy pulled a wooden top from his pocket and, with a smile, took his hand.

"Come. I'll show you how to make this spin forever," he said, leading his nephew out to the courtyard.

Jae Soon followed him, not even looking back at her, Sun Yi noticed.

If her son needed her less now, she still had her friend. Tai Un was a constant visitor, like a sister. She was here today, soon after Han Ju arrived, but not to meet him. As usual, she headed first for the baby. Jae Yun smiled when he saw her and held out his arms, knowing she would pick him up.

"He always recognizes your face! I suspect I'm jealous," Sun Yi exclaimed. "That child comes to you as quickly as to me, his own mother."

Tai Un nodded, nuzzling the child's head on her shoulder before she settled him on her lap. She crooned the ancient childhood rhyme close to his ear.

> "Blue bird, blue bird, lovely blue bird
> Do not disturb the flow'ring bean plant.
> If the flower falls, no bean will grow.
> Jelly maker'll go home in tears."

She repeated the verse twice while Jae Yun laughed at the sounds.

"I remember that. My old nurse sang it many times," Sun Yi said.

Tai Un smiled at the baby then set him on the floor near her. Before she lifted her face to reply to Sun Yi the shadow of a hungry longing crossed her face but it was gone instantly as she turned, saying, "I have spoken to many people, as you well know, about the doctor's unjust imprisonment, ever since the first day of his captivity."

"I know I have no more loyal friend than you," Sun Yi responded quickly, feeling that she was being accused of something. What? Hadn't she done all she could, herself?

"I've always been certain that we can find some way to get him out of there. If only I could reach the right person. The one who can turn the key and unlock his cell."

Sun Yi nodded. "Someone like you, a teacher at Ewha College, can surely have more influence than an ordinary person."

Tai Un could converse politely with the Japanese of influence in Seoul. Nothing in her teaching was controversial. Who could fault elementary science? As a Christian she was in close contact with the missionary leaders, and of course, to those who knew her best, she was a patriot, a loyal Korean, as well. Many women secretly admired her achievements, her strength of will, her independence. Men recognized the importance of her role. She was impossible to ignore. Everyone listened when she spoke. But Sun Yi thought she knew her better than anyone else. When they'd first met she soon became a dear and trusted friend. If anyone could help with the release of her husband, it would surely be Kim Tai Un. And even though she had not yet managed to produce this result Sun Yi still felt complete and unquestioning confidence in her.

"Yesterday I spoke to the editor of the Seoul Daily Times, Tai Un began. "You recall, Chon Il Hong."

"That traitor!" Sun Yi interrupted, her words ringing with contempt.

"Wait," Tai Un spoke calmly. "You know that he has close contacts with important persons, the top level of authority."

"I'm sure he does. That comes as no surprise to me. One near ink gets black. He is a collaborator. He prints only the stories that please the Japanese. Not the truth, but only their point of view. That man no longer deserves to be called a Korean!"

"He is one of the few Koreans to achieve high position and power under the colonial government, that is true," Tai Un admitted. "But isn't it useful to us that a Korean man bears such responsibility?"

"I can't agree with you. I don't see that he has benefited anyone but himself. He has become a wealthy man. He lives well while others suffer in poverty because they remain true to their principles. I can never believe that his sympathy lies with our grievances."

Tai Un sighed and paused to sip her tea. She then arranged the folds of her long white chima with care, searching for her next words while Sun Yi, across the table, sat up straight, rigid, her mouth and chin set in firm disgust.

"Wait a minute. I understand your feelings," Tai Un continued in a gentle manner. "It does look that way to one who doesn't know him well. I have strong reasons to believe that Mr. Chon can be helpful to us. I have shown him some of your writing. He may be able to arrange for its publication in that new woman's magazine. She paused with the silence hovering over them, knowing Sun Yi would find the prospect tempting. "I'd like to arrange a meeting where you could speak with him. He wants to help you but he says you must ask him yourself."

Sun Yi was anxious to see her writing in print. She'd worked so hard on it. She knew it was good. And she also knew that Tai Un was deliberately tempting her. If Abuji had not sent that money!

"You are suggesting the impossible," she retorted, with a proud lift of her head. "We do not need him. Our family can have no dealings with such a person. Mr. Chon is the most despicable of all Koreans. He has willingly collaborated with the Japanese, simply to promote his own welfare. It is inconceivable that I could degrade our name by seeking help from him. I would be disgraced."

Han Ju stayed with Sun Yi but in August of 1926 he returned to his family home in the country for a brief visit, just as he was to begin his high school classes in Seoul.

Standing on a low ridge near Yongju on one hot and humid afternoon, he was thinking out loud as he surveyed the landscape around him.

"Yes, it is true. The countryside of Korea does look like a sea in a heavy gale" He'd once heard someone describe this land and now he could see the similarity for himself.

He'd missed the sight of this vista since he'd left it more than a year before. In the northwest mountains too numerous to count rose above the Naktong River basin. Green terraces of rice and barley marched up the slopes of lower hills on both sides of the river.

"Look!" His younger brother told him, extending his arm toward them. "Those Japanese settlers are using every inch of ground worth the labor with their new way of irrigating. They planted a lot of cotton."

"But there's still plenty of rice. I can tell from here."

"Oh, sure. There's still more of that than anything else. With our long season of warm weather it can be harvested twice a year. Did you know that Kyongsangdo is called Japan's breadbasket now? But they grow tobacco and soybeans, too. Beyond those fields you can see mulberry and apple trees."

"What's over there? Han Ju's voice rose in excitement as he pointed to an unfamiliar landmark.

"Railroad tracks! The trains go almost everywhere. All our crops can be loaded onto the freight cars straight from the fields and shipped to Taegu in hours."

"That's strange. We haven't noticed any improvement of the food delivery in Seoul."

"The food goes south. I thought you were a scholar. And you don't even know that! You must keep your nose in the books all the time. Most of the crops go down to Susan. Then they're loaded on ships. I've heard the crossing to Shimoneseki can be done in less than twenty-four hours if the weather is clear."

A long silence followed while the brothers looked over the scene. Han Ju felt strangely uncomfortable with this boy. He seemed much younger than the two years that separated them in age. It was not simply that Han Ju was so much bigger, though he had no idea how he'd grown until he stood next to him and realized he was a head taller. No, it was something more. Did city living change him so greatly?

Everyone in his family welcomed him back. His arrival was like a festival. He knew he'd pleased them by passing the entrance exams for Kyunggi High School. He would soon join the small number of young Korean men who could attend the prestigious school run by the Japanese, and it was the one certain route to success. But he sensed a barrier between him and the ones who stayed at home in the country. Well, it couldn't be helped. Instead of worrying about it, he would try to enjoy his short vacation.

"Say, have you forgotten why we came up here?" he demanded, punching his younger brother lightly on the arm. "Let's find the dragonflies!"

They'd made the nets together earlier, with Han Ju explaining the intricacies. "First, you tie the ends of the willow branch together. Try to find a thin one. It bends more easily. Next you fasten the loop to a long and straight branch. Like this." He tied a string of hemp around the two. "Now." He swung it in the air to test the knots. "We must cover the loop with cobwebs, as tightly as possible. Do you know where we can find good cobwebs?"

"There are plenty of them in the chicken house."

"Of course." How could he have forgotten that?"

When they emerged from the small building at the end of the kitchen courtyard not only the net but their heads as well were covered with sticky mats of the gray fluff. Laughing, the boys took turns brushing it off of each other and then ran to the crest of the hill.

Now they ran again, swinging their nets where the dragonflies swooped and droned among the wild grasses. For a moment they were children together as before.

After some time, though, they tired of their sport and tramped back down to sprawl in the shade of a pomegranate bush in the rear of the compound. In the vegetable garden nearby bees hovered over the blossoms of the cucumbers. Small green pumpkins and melons lay entwined in the vines. The boys splashed each other with dippers of cool water from the shallow well in one corner, then rinsed the dust from their faces and drank in great gulps before sinking down to rest.

"Tell me about Seoul," his brother asked. "Do you like it better than living here?"

Did he? Han Ju thought for a moment, wrinkling his brow in concentration. Finally he answered. "The water doesn't taste this good in the city. The air's sometimes dirty. The fruit and vegetables are old when we get them."

His brother nodded. This he could understand. Han Ju knew the rest would be more difficult to explain. He was happy to be home once more, yet he was longing, already, for the sights and sounds, the variety of activity that a young man could find in that fascinating place. He knew he'd never be satisfied to live out his days in this quiet provincial atmosphere. He could not tell his brother that, however.

Rubbing his hand over the smooth surface of the straw mat on which they lay, he wondered how to describe Seoul without causing his brother to feel a jealous resentment. His brother's place would always be here. His parents would not send both of their sons away, and he knew he'd been chosen as the one best suited for the challenge.

"Well, first you're on the train for hours, looking at nothing but open space, with farmhouses and villages along the way. Suddenly, just before you get to the city, the cars disappear into a long tunnel. You feel like you're being swallowed alive." He paused for effect. "You are under the Han River! When you see daylight again there are all kinds of buildings. You are in the middle of an enormous city."

"Really?" The younger boy had never ridden on a train but he squinted his eyes, trying to imagine.

"Now," Han Ju went on. "You know how the village near here looks, with all those stalls the Japanese set up on the main street, selling sweets and cigarettes and lamps with oil, and dolls and toys?"

The younger boy nodded. "Those men wear black and white clothing and they call out in loud voices, trying to make you buy, all the time making a din of noise with the clatter of their sandals."

"Right. Well, imagine not just one of those street fairs, but many. One long street after another! That's how Seoul is, in the southern district. The shops are filled with fancy things, all made in Europe or Japan. At night there's the sound of music, western music, coming from all the small restaurants. Violins, pianos, accordions, gramaphones, all playing different songs at the same time."

Watching his brother's wide eyes, Han Ju continued in a lower voice. "There's another part of the city. It's kind of sad to see it. Beyond all this, a night fair where you can buy all kinds of odds and ends of used stuff, really cheap. The sellers are old Korean gentlemen. They might have been rich and important once because they still try to look dignified, wearing tall black hats over their top knots. They all have long gray beards. But all you hear is haggling, arguing, while they compete just to earn a bit of cash."

His face brightened. "Then you come to the new Japanese section. It's a real ocean of lights, bright and noisy."

"Where do you live?"

"Elder sister has a house in the old Korean section, in the northern part, near Suha Dong. Nights are quiet and dark, like when you're asleep with the ibul pulled over your head. The East Palace is close. The side roads are twisty and narrow and lined with walls that are all grown over with moss."

Han Ju's voice drifted into silence. He recalled the first day he'd walked those paths, on his way to his school examination. The instructor, a Japanese man, stood to greet the boys, seated on benches before his table.

"When you speak of 'our country' you should think not of Korea alone, but of the whole Japanese empire." His voice boomed, giving the stern warning. "And when you speak of 'our countrymen' you should remember that you are talking not only of the Koreans, but of all the people of the Japanese Empire."

Han Ju had listened, realizing for the first time as he sat in silent obedience, what it meant, that expression he'd heard from older family members. "Kobul mok simnida" To eat fear. Yes. But more than that. It meant that one must refrain from speaking out when every instinct tells you to shout in protest. This closed mouth strategy was becoming a habit, a national trait. He was old enough to understand the goal of turning Koreans into second class Japanese. It would be achieved by leaving most of them uneducated and fit only to toil under their masters.

He would not let it happen to himself! Han Ju could see within his grasp, if he reached far enough, if he was diligent and had good fortune, the opportunity to be among those few to escape this fate. I will not be a tool of these rulers, he vowed. He would use his education to help his own country.

"Wake up!" The younger boy punched his arm, impatient with his daydreaming. "What's it like?"

"What is what like?"

"The place with those narrow streets."

"Oh, yes. Lots of houses, close together. Only a wall between them. Most are in an L shape and they have roofs of tile, not straw thatch. Vendors pass by with pushcarts, shouting about their tangerines, roasted chestnuts, dried squid, tobu, all sorts of things. Even the yut man comes by almost every day. You'd like that, with your sweet tooth. You can hear him by the clank of his scissors as he walks. In summer there is shade from all the trees, ginkos, paulinia, sumac."

Han Ju paused to think of something his brother would like to see. "The main street, Sejong Ro, is made of yellow granite and it is so wide that there is room for bicycles, streetcars, some autocars and trucks, as well as the men wearing chige loaded with yontan for the household fires."

His younger brother was listening to every word so he continued. "An enormous building sits on one side of this street. The outside is covered with white marble and granite and the inside walls are covered with Korean marble in many colors. In the middle there is a dome." He stretched his arms in a high oval to demonstrate. "This National Capitol took ten years to build and now it is so long that it would stretch from here to that willow tree on the far hillside, and it is five stories high. It is said it cost seven million yen to build it."

The younger boy shook his head. "I don't believe you. You're making up these stories. Let's play a game." He pulled the zbegi balls from a pocket. Each was made from a small coin tightly wrapped in bits of silken paper.

"I haven't tried this in quite a while," he remarked, "but as I remember, the trick is to kick these small balls up into the air with one foot, catch each of them with the other foot before it touches the ground, and kick it up again. He managed to miss several times.

It's a good idea to let this kid win, he thought. I'll probably never play this game again and he'll be proud to remember how he beat me. Han Ju was thinking that when he returned to Seoul in a few days he would put on the black jacket and the cap with its moon-shaped visor, pick up the satchel heavy with books. He could always hear the sound of his mother's voice in his head, admonishing him to "kong bu haera!" "Study!"

Each of the days at home passed in a similar way until the last one, when his mother called him into the cool shade where she sat sewing. He'd never seen Ohmanee with idle hands. Her slender fingers flew, whether it was the vegetables she was chopping for their next meal, or her needle flashing in and out as she prepared their winter clothing. He always pictured her in this way. He supposed he always would.

Kum Seung's face was usually serene but today he saw the lines of worry when she asked him, "How is your elder sister managing? It has been two years already since the doctor was placed in prison. Is there anything more that we can do for her?"

"She's very sad most of the time, Ohmanee, but she works hard. There is a houseful of students. There doesn't seem to be much that anyone can do, unless it is to knock down the prison walls and bring Dr. Lee home."

"There's no sign, then, that he may be released soon?"

"Oh, I've heard elder sister talking, many times, with that woman who is her friend. This lady tries to persuade elder sister to talk with some person who is a high authority. She tells her this man can help. Elder sister becomes angry. She always refuses."

Kum Seung sighed. Sun Yi hadn't changed. She was the same stubborn, determined person as before. "If only I could see her, even for one day! But you are the only one in our family who can be there, so you must help her in every way you can."

If Han Ju felt that the responsibility laid upon him was more than a fourteen-year-old should bear, he gave no sign. He reassured his mother that he would help Sun Yi.

When he prepared to return to Seoul Kum Seung gave him a large basket of the fine apples and gupo pears that were just beginning to be harvested. He took it, thinking that his carrying this gift of fresh country produce to her was perhaps the only real way he had of being useful to Sun Yi at this time.

Sun Yi looked at her reflection with a critical expression, ready to search for imperfections in her mirror image. Her crisp white chima shone, so carefully had it been ironed. The folds swept to the floor, with only the toes of her padded cotton slippers peeping out. The bow on her right shoulder was tied precisely. Her black hair, pulled back more tightly than usual, was anchored firmly into a knot at the nape of her neck.

She stepped closer, a frown creasing her brow. Was that a wisp of silver among the strands? No. Only a glint of light magnified by the glass created the momentary illusion. But she could imagine herself with a snowy white cap of hair. The words of the woman poet of the Sixteenth Century, Ho Nanserhon, came to mind.

> "Yesterday I fancied I was young;
> But today, alas, I am aging.
> What use is there in recalling
> The joyful days of my youth?
> Now I am old, recollections are in vain.
> Sorrow chokes me, words fail me."

Time was passing. Worries were a burden that never ceased. Yet she thought she would not become elderly so soon. She knew some ladies of twice her twenty-six years who were still youthful looking, or rather seemed to be ageless, with faces still smooth and clear. What would her mother have looked like now? Sun Yi would never know, for that lady had long been no more than a phantom memory. What were the next lines of that poem?

> "the flow of time and tide was sudden;
> The Gods too were jealous of my beauty.
> Spring breezes and autumn moon.
> Alas, they flew like a shuttle.
> And my face that once was beautiful
> Where did it go? Who disgraced it so?
> Turn away from the mirror, look no more."

Sun Yi raised her head, thinking that the long-dead composer of this kasa could have suffered no more sorrow than she felt at this moment. The face reflected to her showed translucent skin the color of ancient ivory, with cheeks almost crimson. A well molded face. Cheekbones slightly elevated, a similar lift to her almond eyes.

The general expression was quiet dignity and it pleased her. She would need it today. A blend of humility and pride, like amber ashes that might suddenly emit a spirited flame.

Why am I standing here? Playing with foolish thoughts! Sun Yi knew the reason well enough. Any excuse would do, if it would serve to delay this meeting. Relenting, finally, to Kim Tai Un's persistent pleading, she'd agreed to meet this Chon Il Hong. He was the editor of Seoul's leading newspaper and she would ask his help in getting her husband out of prison.

Today she must endure the confrontation, though it was contrary to all of her principles and, more importantly, her instincts.

> "Long is a day, cruel is a month
> The plum trees by the jade window
> Have blossomed and scattered, spring after
>   spring."

Four years. Four years she waited for him. Though he served as a doctor she knew he was treated as a prisoner, charged with instigating treasonous rebellion against the Japanese rulers of Korea. Not one of his friends or relatives had been successful. Left without other hope, Sun Yi turned now to the one person who might wield the influence to gain her husband's freedom, although he was notorious for his cooperation with the colonial regime.

Since she must face him Sun Yi wished that every detail of her appearance convey dignity, untouchability.

Tai Un called for her in a black touring car. It's for the use of everyone on the Ewha faculty, she explained. Sun Yi stepped up into it, hoping she looked at ease. In reality, riding in an automobile was a rare experience. She gave a cry when the driver threw the gear into first and held onto the armrest until they arrived at Ewha College.

Tai Un chose a public room there for the meeting. It was a respectable, neutral place. Rebellious though she might be in other matters, Sun Yi did try to preserve some proprieties. Speaking to a man not related to her was still a forbidden kind of behavior.

Ewha moved from its longtime location on Legation Street, within the city walls, a few years earlier. The new buildings of pale granite were set on hill surrounded by the In-Wang Mountains on the edge of Seoul. The light green of its roofs was a contrast to the dark pine trees surrounding them. Students dressed in dark skirts and white chogories drifted like flocks of quail along its paths. Under any other circumstances Sun Yi would have delighted to be in such an atmosphere.

Mr. Chon was waiting. Tai Un left her with him in the small reception room after the introduction.

"Will you be seated?" he asked, motioning to the three straight-backed chairs that were left as a courtesy to Westerners.

Sun Yi shook her head and sank to one of the silk cushions instead. He sat on one opposite, with an arrangement of chrysanthemums on the low table between them.

His modest manner in receiving her bow disarmed her. She was prepared for a pompous, condescending person. Instead, this slightly built man, graying at the temples, was meticulously polite, deferring to her, managing to convey an impression that her presence was an honor.

His hands twitched nearly all of the time. It was most distracting. She concentrated on his words.

"It is my honor to meet a member of the family of Lee, one of the most distinguished in the long history of our capitol," he began.

"Mr. Chon," she interrupted, "it is an imposition for a member of the Lee family to intrude upon your important duties. We come to you only as a last resort. We've been told, it is our hope, that you may be willing to persuade the officials who hold him prisoner to set our husband and father free. His occupation is a useful and honored one. Surely the time in prison has been sufficient. He can better serve everyone as a free man."

Her voice rose, each word tumbling after the other, propelled by the emotion she felt. Calm yourself, she thought, and she began to speak of the details of the doctor's career.

Mr. Chon waved his arm impatiently. "I know all about Dr. Lee. You must believe me when I say that I will be honored to do all I can to free this man. He has been long and unjustly imprisoned. You must trust me. Yet I cannot give you a promise of my success." He paused. His eyes narrowed. "I will gladly do what I can, without recompense of any kind."

Silence lingered after his words. Sun Yi dared to lift her head and look at him directly.

"However," he paused again, cleared his throat, scrutinizing her so closely that she averted her gaze, "I am not as powerful as you flatter me by suggesting. I am merely the conduit to power. There is someone else who must hear your plea. I can do no more than to arrange your meeting."

"Oh." She sighed. After all this, disappointment.

"Yes, there is another who may be the one to arrange your husband's release. He, unlike myself, may have some expectation of recompense."

"Mr. Chon, I am not a wealthy woman, nor is anyone in my family. You may say that silk clothing warms even a cousin, but there is no great wealth among my relatives either."

He smiled sardonically. "This man has no need of your money. Of that I am certain. But, as butterflies come to pretty flowers." His voice trailed off. "Well. So. You have come to his attention and he would like to do what he can to remove the sadness from your life. He tells me that he has never been inclined to help the Koreans, in all of the time he has been assigned to our country."

"He is, then, Japanese?" Sun Yi's voice faltered on that word.

"All of the authorities are, aren't they?" he replied, with a strange, bitter inflection, biting off each word. He pulled a white card from his inner pocket. "Here is the address. I assume you are willing. He will be waiting for you at two in the afternoon, tomorrow. Please be prompt. He does not respond well to tardiness."

Sun Yi sat still, stunned. She was not prepared for such a request.

"What does this man wish of me?" She managed to ask.

Chon leaned forward to catch her softly spoken words. For once his hands lay still. "I don't know."

She could not bring herself to tell Tai Un the outcome of this meeting. Sun Yi did not know, herself, if she would dare to keep this appointment. Yet she had led Mr. Chon to believe that she would. Would there be a repercussion for her husband if she did not appear? She dared not take such a risk.

No one must see her. Of that she was certain. A closed car was a necessity, though it was an extravagance she could not afford. Somehow she'd find the money to pay for it.

"Are you certain this is the address?" Sun Yi asked the driver.

"This is the number you gave me," he replied, in a familiar tone that Sun Yi was not accustomed to hearing. Perhaps that was the expected manner for addressing women who came here. It was a part of Seoul she'd never seen.

"But this looks like a private residence" She peered through the side window. The building was large, impressive, with an ornate entrance gate. Sun Yi took one deep breath and stepped out. How strange. She'd expected to find an office building.

A maid admitted her and asked Sun Yi to wait inside the gate while the mistress was summoned. A garden of luxuriant plants surrounded her, providing a cool refuge from the summer heat, and she thought she heard a distant splashing, gentle, like that of a waterfall. Brightly colored birds flitted from blossom to blossom, sipping the nectar, pausing to perch on a branch.

The rustle of silk preceded the woman's appearance. She was dressed in a chima and chogori of the palest lavender, with exquisite embroidered designs. She's not young, was Sun Yi's first thought, but she is lovely.

"I'm Mrs. Yu." she began.

"Yes, of course." The woman interrupted with a slight bow. "You are expected." Her smile did not extend to her eyes. "Please follow me."

She led Sun Yi through the first courtyard and then along a maru. Turning a corner, she led her into another open area, smaller but filled also with colorful flowers and plants. She stopped in front of a sliding door panel, opening it while Sun Yi removed her shoes.

"You will wait here, please."

The woman disappeared and Sun Yi realized that she had not identified herself. She blinked in the darkened room, waiting for her eyes to adjust to the change from the sunlight.

The room was not large. It was dominated by a long table of gleaming black ebony, with delicately carved legs and a surface smooth as a mirror. Cushions were arranged on either side, flat, square cushions of embroidered silk, the blues so intense, almost purple, and the scarlets brighter than blood.

Sun Yi dropped down onto one of the cushions. Overcome by a hollow sensation that drained her strength, she closed her eyes, resting her head on her knees. Why was she here? Could she leave now? It must still be possible. But she was engulfed by this isolation, and she did not move.

After a while she raised her head and looked about the room. Two matching chests of paulonia wood, highly polished, stood against the far wall. Two celadon vases, rare and delicate, rested on one, while on the other a bowl carved from translucent jade was displayed. Behind them the walls were covered with mahogany paneling. The rafters overhead were immense, solid.

In the silence all that she could hear was her heart, thumping like a drum. She brushed her face with her fingertips, feeling the cold beads of sweat on her brow. Moments passed. How many? She could not say.

The table was set for two, with delicate teacups, reminding her that someone else was anticipated. I'll leave right now, she told herself. Yet she remained, as if paralyzed.

Will my husband forgive me? How can I tell him? With each silent question she felt more desperate. Surely he will understand that she had no choice. She'd waited so long. His freedom was more important than anything else.

The door was sliding open. Sun Yi turned at the sound, her eyes widening with dismay.

Kim Tai Un arrived at Sun Yi's home late on the following afternoon, bursting with her usual good spirits. Sun Yi looked up from the school lesson she was preparing. She hadn't slept and there were dark circles under her eyes.

"How was the interview? Will Mr. Chon be able to help you?"

"You." Sun Yi spit out each word. "You. You are naive."

Sun Yi filled each day with a frenzy of activity. She did not know why, only that while she was busy she did not think. The house must be clean. It must be more than clean. It must be spotless. She kept the maid frantic with her incessant requests. Jae Soon caught her fever without knowing why and shouted orders to his baby brother. Han Ju was in school most of the time but when he did return he shut himself into his own room to escape the commotion.

The oppressive heat of summer changed to clear and sunny days of autumn, the time of high skies. She scarcely noticed, sleeping little, alternating between moods of elation and despair while she waited. Sometimes she dreamed that he had returned and woke in the darkness to clutch at empty air. At other times she saw his face while she slept, peering at her from a small barred window, pleading to be let out.

"I've done all I can," she cried silently. "What more do you expect of me?"

The students returned from the brief summer vacation and Sun Yi welcomed the routine of teaching once more. She tried to concentrate on preparing the lessons, pushing her worries aside. Yet they remained, like a constant festering wound.

Then, on an afternoon in early October, as she was in the middle of explaining a mathematical theory to the girls, the maid rushed in, calling.

"Mistress, come to the gate! Quickly!"

The elderly woman was there almost as soon as Sun Yi. Someone was pounding on the knocker. Together, they pushed back the bar. The heavy gate swung open.

"Yubo!"

Though she'd pictured this moment in her mind over and over, Sun Yi gasped when she looked at her husband, standing before her. A ricksha was rolling away. He stood quite still, as though he didn't recognize her. She reached out to him, grasping both of his hands in her own. The tears she'd held back through all the years of his absence flowed down her cheeks and she could not stop them. Scarcely able to see, she led him back into his home. He moved as if in a trance. She would not leave his side but called out, "Jae Soon! Come here! Quickly! And bring your brother."

The girls peered out from the doorway of the ondul room. She'd forgotten all about them. Jae Soon appeared, leading his younger brother. The six-year-old hesitated, brushing the shiny black hair from his forehead. Then recognition lighted his eyes and he stepped toward the stranger, kneeling, touching his head to the floor before his father's feet, as Sun Yi had taught him to do each time that she showed him the photograph of this man. "This is your father," she'd always said. "Someday he will return to us." Jae Soon believed her. Now the promise was come true.

Jae Yun remained next to the sliding door until Sun Yi scooped him up in her arms, lifting him so he could meet his father's eyes at last. Dr. Lee took the child from her and gazed at him, drinking in the first sight of his other son, but the four-year-old squirmed to be set free.

"Give him some time," Sun Yi consoled. "You won't be a stranger to him for long." She hung onto her husband's arm once more, tightly, as though she would never let go of it again. "How thin you are!"

Time and harsh prison conditions had ravaged him. Below his sunken cheeks, his jaw jutted with an angular shape to it that she'd not seen before. Only the glow in his eyes, when he looked at her, was the same. His worn gray jacket hung from his narrow shoulders and she tugged at it, saying, "You must bathe and change. Or would you like to eat something first?" She took his hands, pressing them to her cheeks, then gasped as she saw the scars, deep rings of white etched on his bronze skin. Those slender, tapered fingers she'd watched playing the flute or tending a wound were swollen at their joints, horribly misshapen. Covering her shock, she called to the maid.

"Heat some water. No, first, prepare the rice!"

The voices of her young students roused her to recall their presence and she spoke to them, sending them home. The doctor looked puzzled.

"Who are those girls?"

"Some of my students. Remember that I was doing some teaching?"

"Oh, of course. But so many?"

"How do you think I could afford to remain in this house? I've turned it into a small school."

"Ah, yes, I see." But he still looked puzzled and for a moment seemed to shrink back from the unfamiliar strength of this woman.

Dusk of the evening dimmed the daylight in their small room. Sun Yi kneeled to light the lamp. It flickered, casting shadows into the corners. Her husband, after eating a small meal, had slept briefly. He seemed weary, Sun Yi thought. But why shouldn't he? She served him again, bringing in the small table herself. Wisps of steam rose from the brass bowl filled with his favorite beef broth, kom tang. She lifted the cover from a smaller dish, revealing the pure hot rice, tantalizing in the aroma of its freshness, then presented the several small dishes containing the spicy condiments that he'd always liked so well.

He waved them away, telling her that he must eat simply for a time. She sat quietly, watching him savor each spoonful. So many questions crowded her tongue, yet she hesitated. Perhaps better not to force the terrible memories to the surface. Eventually he would tell her all that he wished her to know. For now, just being near this man was enough.

"Can you imagine what I'd like now?" A bit of a smile flickered in her direction, as he set the empty plates aside.

Sun Yi moved closer to him.

"In all those nights I imagined I was playing my flute. Do you still have it?"

"It has always been right here, Yubo," she replied, and she trembled as she opened the top of a small wooden chest. Then she unwrapped the slender instrument from the bit of silk in which she'd covered it four years before.

He lifted the flute to his lips. The first sounds came, muted, delicate. But then he brought forth the familiar trills he'd always used to warm it. The simple notes rolled up and down the scale and Sun Yi felt the rising sensation within herself that she'd nearly forgotten. He became absorbed in the tones. In the past, when she'd listened, sitting alone in another room, she realized that the deeper his concentration in this music became, the more he was lost to her. He drifted into another world, another time, without her.

Tonight was different. Sun Yi moved close to him, hypnotized by his fingers flying faster and faster back and forth over the silver flute. She was absorbed by its magic, not separated as before. For the first time she entered into this mystic realm with him. This could be the beginning of a better life. Perhaps all the unpleasant times could be forgotten. Perhaps he never need know all that she'd done for him, to bring this perfect evening into being.

A long time passed while he played. Sun Yi listened, unmoving. The first hesitant notes transformed themselves into one lilting melody, then another more plaintive, followed by a joy filled rondo, as his agility returned.

"It's almost as if you'd never been away," she murmured when he stopped. "Now we can resume our life. All will be the same, as if you'd never suffered in that prison."

"Yes, this is a time to savor. You must keep this memory secure in your heart, never forget this perfect serenity," he responded, caressing her cheek and pulling her closer. "No matter where we are."

Sun Yi pulled away. She sat up. "What do you mean? What are you trying to tell me?" Threads of apprehension gathered into a knot, tightening into a lump that choked her. "Why should we not remain here?"

He was still serene. Perhaps he intended to calm her. The effect of his words did not. "My dear one." He placed his hand on her glossy head. "I could not bear that place any longer. I was offered a choice. My freedom on one condition. I took it. I could not stay there another day. Another night. Can you understand?"

Sun Yi stared at her husband. "You were released because you accepted a condition? When did you make this decision?"

"It was some time ago," he answered. "Must have been late in the spring. Even after I capitulated the time promised for my release was drawn out."

Spring time! Before she met with that Japanese man! She felt as though she was sinking into quicksand. "What condition did you agree to follow, then?" She managed to whisper.

"There are many poor villages where the farmers live without a chance for good medical care. I promised that I would take a post in the countryside, far from any city. Next week we will leave Seoul."

"How long?" When Sun Yi looked into her husband's face she sought reassurance. "A few months?" He didn't say anything. "A year? Yubo! How long will our family have to live under those wretched conditions?"

His response, finally, was muted. "I'm not sure. I don't really know. Perhaps it will be for only a few years."

"A few years!" He might as well have said "Forever."

"How will we live out there? No schools? No shops?" Sun Yi bowed her head and pressed it against his chest when she saw his dismay. "Oh, forgive me! Forgive my hasty words! I should only rejoice that you have returned to me. Nothing else matters."

He wrapped her in his arms and she clung to him.

Within days word came that Dr. Lee was assigned to the provincial hospital in Shunsen, the center of Kangwondo. The poorest part of our poor country, thought Sun Yi. This place was northeast of Seoul, and bordered the East Sea, the Sea of Japan. Sun Yi shivered at the news, imagining she could already feel the chill winter weather of that mountainous region. She checked over and over to be certain that their warmest clothing and heaviest bedding was included among the items allowed in their luggage.

At Seoul General Station early one morning of the following week the four of them boarded the train. Watching the familiar scenery slide past her window, Sun Yi recalled her excitement on her first arrival in this great city. When would she ever see it again?

The spur of rail track was newly built. After the cars left the plateau outside of Seoul they began the winding climb up the side of one hill and down the other, only to immediately begin the ascent of another hill.

"We should be grateful for this train," she told the boys, patting the plush covered seats. "Can you imagine what it would be like to travel for sixty miles over all of this by any less comfortable way?"

It was a second class car, but a well heated steel coach nevertheless. The third class cars behind it were dingy gray, with no glass in the window openings. Showers of smoke, dust and cinders flew onto the poor passengers crowded together on long wooden benches.

Jae Soon and his brother began to bounce up and down with the rhythm of the clicking wheels.

"Look at the herons!" she called, distracting them by pointing to the snow colored birds standing in the rice fields. Who could blame the boys' excitement? Neither of them had been away from Seoul before and this was their first ride on a train. She watched as they pressed their noses flat against the glass. Clusters of small houses, maui, with rounded thatched roofs and low hanging eaves looked more like mushrooms against the cloudless background of bare hills and bleak valleys. Would the new home she was headed for now look like these desolate dwellings?

"Once these hills were covered with trees," Dr. Lee was telling his sons. His eyes were sad, permanently sad. "Now all have been cut down to feed the hunger of the new factories."

The two boys listened to him, their eyes solemn. He was still a stranger as far as they were concerned.

"Did you know," he asked, turning to Sun Yi, "that this land of Kangwando has been compared to an old Buddha sitting beneath a rock, a place that is lifeless, immobile, unchanging? Well," he added, almost to himself, "we'll soon learn for ourselves if that is a true description." He thought of its extreme poverty. It was a place, he'd been told, where man and mountain meet. Man was more frequently the vanquished.

The color of the soil began to take on a reddish tinge, unlike the fertile land of the valley. Among the small patches of arable land between the hills were fields of barley, with more stones than stalks of grain upon them. Small houses huddled as if seeking protection in their communal groups from the demands of the harsh landscape surrounding them. He noted that the roofs were covered with untrimmed slabs of slate anchored by lumps of rock.

Looking out at this, Sun Yi's spirits sank even lower. She was more depressed now than at any time since she learned that this remote land was to be her new home. She thought of all she'd left behind. The lovely chairs and tables of polished wood, inlaid with mother-of-pearl she gave to her mother-in-law's keeping. Faced with difficult choices, she'd placed extra padded clothing and bed coverings in the stack of possessions that was crated for shipment on the train. It really wasn't hard to consider her family's comfort and well being foremost. Jae Soon will be disappointed, though, when he finds those favorite playthings he'd added to the heap are not with us. Perhaps the fascination of this strange place will help him to survive without them. What she'd miss most was a person, not her possessions.

She thought once more of Tai Un's shock when she first heard the news.

"I can't imagine this city without you. Surely you'll return soon."

Sun Yi shook her head. "I'm resigned," she told her.

"You, resigned? Impossible!" Her friend had retorted. "Now tell me what I can do to help you."

You've already done enough, Sun Yi thought. But she could not harbor resentment toward her closest friend, knowing that many miles and immeasurable time would soon separate them. Tai Un had tried to be helpful, and she still believed that she was in part responsible for the release of Sun Yi's husband. Sun Yi would never reveal to her, or to anyone else, the subsequent events of that negotiation. She would live with her private shame forever but no one else would ever know. Never.

"How will you survive in that poor land?" Tai Un demanded, as the two women sat sipping tea together after a long day of packing.

"Truthfully, that does not worry me any longer. Living in Kangwando will be a challenge but at least we'll be together." She paused and added softly, "We must be grateful for this time of happiness."

"And what of Han Ju?"

"Oh, that is painful to me," Sun Yi admitted. "That brother has been my companion for three years. He was just a boy when he arrived but he has grown into a brilliant young man. Surely you, as a teacher, recognize his extraordinary ability." She paused to refill their cups with cool podi cha. "Han Ju will remain here, with my husband's family. He will have a great future, so long as he remains in Seoul and doesn't allow himself to be buried in a provincial town."

"You are critical of country living," Tai Un teased. "But write to me often. I look forward to your descriptions of Chunchon. ` What location could be more provincial than that one?" She asked this with laughter in her voice but the underlying tone was serious.

She'd stop laughing if she could see this place, Sun Yi thought, looking through the train window again. Chunchon. Shunsen. What does it matter how it is named? It's still the same dreary place. The settlement was renamed after the Japanese took it over, as was every other place in our country, but that can't change what it is. And I can't help still thinking of the place as Chunchon.

The train came to a stop "I can't see anything that resembles a town here," she told her husband.

Dr. Lee went forward in the train to find information. When he returned he said grimly, "This is the end of the line. From here we must ride a bus for the remaining mile."

No one said anything more. The boys looked at his face and kept silent. But they all helped to transfer the boxes and bundles to the bus that stood wheezing next to the track. Sun Yi covered her nose. Black fumes belched from the charcoal burner in the rear of the contraption. How could the heat of that stove nudge a vehicle carrying all these passengers into motion?

The crowd waiting to board was a curious mix. Old Korean gentlemen, slow-moving, tall-hatted. Small children wearing ragged clothing who stared at her well-dressed sons. A Japanese woman in a red kimona who clattered along in her getas behind her pompous husband.

"Yobu! Odega?"

A policeman bustled toward Dr. Lee, shouting in a rude manner. His uniform was dark and ill fitted, from the peaked cap on his head to the khaki-colored puttees around his short legs. A sword more than eighteen inches long dangled from his wide leather belt. With each step he took it swung between his legs, causing him to walk with an awkward gait, like a child in the costume of an adult. Jae Soon started to giggle. Sun Yi, horrified, clapped her hand over his mouth.

Dr. Lee turned slowly and stared at him, sucked in his breath and pulled himself to his full height. Looking down at the man, he replied in perfect, formal Japanese. "To Shunsen. I am the new doctor and I am going to live there."

"Sss. Name cards?"

He looked at their passes for a long time, then at his notebook. Sun Yi kept her eyes on the bus behind him. It was filling rapidly. If they were detained much longer there'd be no seats left for her family. Would this official, so puffed up with his self-importance, cause them to be left behind? If he heard a word of complaint he'd probably keep them even longer. She bit her lip while her impatience mounted. To be at the mercy of someone like this!

The bus was making the sounds of starting up when he dismissed them, handing back the papers to the doctor. She pushed the boys ahead of her up the steps, struggling with the oversized bundles she

carried at the same time. Once on its way, the bus jolted continuously over the earthen trail. How could she have been so eager to ride
on it? Such a decrepit vehicle! At least the boys were enjoying the
experience, as they had the entire journey. They had no idea what
was ahead for them.

This Kangwando, a land of wild, steep mountains with narrow
valleys between, seemed immense and endless, with hardly a town in
the entire two hundred miles of its length. A region best known for
spectacular scenery, high waterfalls, and the Buddhist temples nestled in secluded places. The King and Queen, in the last century, took
refuge in a palace built for them somewhere in these hills. Sun Yi
tried to imagine that early royal lady fleeing here. She'd have ridden
on a pony, or perhaps been carried in a palanquin, over these ribbons of trails. Could that highborn woman's misgivings been any
greater than her own?

Patches of white still clung to the highest peaks, snow that never
melted. Sun Yi shivered in the sunlight.

She'd listened to her husband telling that arrogant policeman that
they would live in Shunsen. That was not strictly true, for the house
was some distance away, near a small village. It had belonged to a
Protestant missionary family. They'd had to leave, of course. The
authorities were making life difficult for all the outsiders. So many
restrictions, more all the time!

The jolting stopped. Stepping down from the bus, Sun Yi sighed
and took a deep breath of the clean air. How pure and fresh it
smelled!

"Is this Shunsen?" Jae Soon was asking.

She took his hand, wanting to reassure him. But how could she? It
was a dismal sight, the main street of this town. Streets unpaved, of
course. Dusty with the dryness of autumn but marked with deep
ruts and potholes, evidence of the summer rains that had turned
them into muddy quagmires. The buildings lining each side were

drab, gray, undistinguished by any sign of grace or beauty. It was worse than she anticipated.

Dr. Lee hired an old man with a wagon pulled by two oxen to carry them for the rest of the way.

"This is the best part yet!" she heard Jae Yun tell his brother. Both boys were watching the driver closely as the wagon bounced along the narrow country lane.

They rode for more than two miles before she saw the house. Built in the traditional "L" shaped design, it had a thatch roof of mellow brown straw, not slate slabs, at least. There was a small courtyard, with mud brick walls surrounding it, a wooden gate in the middle of one side. In the distance some huts clustered on the flat land at the far end of this small valley. This will be my home, thought Sun Yi. How will I ever manage in such a place?

Dr. Lee was the first one down. He opened the gate for the driver to pass through. Sun Yi caught a glimpse of movement from within the house. In a moment a young girl appeared in the doorway. She approached, bowing low to the doctor, and told him she had been hired to prepare the house for them.

"Why, how could she do that? So few of our furnishings have arrived," Sun Yi murmured in a low voice. But she followed the girl, who looked like a child, surely younger than Han Ju, into the kitchen where she showed her the large pots and storage jars already in their places. When she smelled the delicious aroma of rice boiling for the evening meal Sun Yi remembered how little they'd eaten since morning. Only the simple lunch of rice cakes and pickled vegetables she brought from home.

At least she'd have someone to help. Sun Yi had worried about managing the house alone. The elderly maid was too feeble to follow them into exile. When her husband returned her to his mother's household he promised that he'd find someone to assist her after they arrived. Now it seemed that the matter had been settled for them.

She looked for the boys. They were chasing each other like puppies, exploring each of the rooms. There were four in addition to the kitchen, which was sunken on a lower level. Next to it was the most spacious one, with the heated ondol floor. Beyond that, three smaller chambers, each opening through paper-shuttered doors onto the maru that ran the entire length of the building. It rose on short piers above the hard packed earth of the matang. On the shorter portion of the "L" was one more, a larger space. It would be the perfect place if the doctor were allowed to treat patients outside of the hospital.

Beyond the kitchen Sun Yi glimpsed a small patch of neglected garden and a well. Thank goodness! That had been a worry. Suppose she'd had to carry water. Of all the potential problems to do with a country home, that had been first in her mind.

Dr. Lee was calling to her. "Just see how solid this house is!" he exclaimed. "It has a framework of stout beams," he went on, showing one to her. The walls were constructed of clay, a foot thick and tightly packed, strengthened by interwoven sprigs of willow, and the roof was heavily thatched with rice straw. "We'll be comfortable all through the year in such a fine building," he assured her.

Just as I suspected, thought Sun Yi. This move to the country does not entirely displease him. She looked around again. Well, the road into Shunsen was not bad, mostly smooth. It stretched across the floor of the valley like a ribbon. Beyond, a saddle shaped hill covered thickly with half grown pine trees created a splash of black-green color against the red clay hills. The sky was still brilliant blue in the late afternoon light, a sign of clear autumn weather, but among the shrubs bits of color showed, yellow, orange and red, suggesting that cool weather had already taken its toll of the green leaves of summer.

Sun Yi stood with her long white chima billowing around her slender figure, surveying her new home from every direction, breathing deeply of the pure mountain air. Was it possible? Could this remote valley offer the potential for a good life, for happiness?

Dr. Lee joined her, his hand brushing hers. "I wonder who our benefactor is?" he asked in a low voice. "The one who prepared this house so carefully for us."

Part Three
1926 to 1937

*C*louds of dust blew across the parched fields and swirled like puffs of smoke, blinding his eyes and filling his lungs. The past summer had been without the usual heavy rains and the path along which Dr. Lee was laboring on his bicycle was covered inches deep with loose soil.

He was on his way to meet the director of the medical program in Shunsen and he worried about this first encounter. Would the man be cooperative? Or would he try to bully him, treat him as a servant? And what of the young maid placed in his home? He suspected, believed quite certainly, that she was planted, to inform on him, and also on Sun Yi. A spy. What to do about her?

The lack of rain was evident everywhere, he thought. Stunted and dry stalks stood as if at attention in the rice fields along his way. By now, with the crisp air and clear skies of late October, no rain was likely before the first snowfall. Chusok would be a dismal holiday, with little harvest to celebrate this year. The rice crop had failed and even this glorious weather could not remove the shadow of concern on the face of every farmer.

They knew by experience that barley or millet would tolerate drought conditions better than the thirsty rice. Even cotton could have survived. But the men had no choice. Orders to plant rice came from landlords. They could not argue with such people. The doctor knew that the spring hunger was likely to begin earlier and last longer this year. Many would survive only by eating the roots and bark from trees. How was he to help to protect the health of these poor ones when a basic diet was beyond their grasp?

He braked the bicycle to a stop in front of the government building, a long structure of two stories built of wood in dire need of fresh painting. Perhaps it had once been light brown or grey. Possibly a pale shade of green. The remaining flakes were faded, peeling. He leaned the bicycle against the wall and slowly climbed the broad stairs leading to the entrance, stopping to catch his breath at the top.

Even Sun Yi's daily doses of ginseng couldn't restore his energy. Would he ever recover fully from the years in prison?

The man who greeted him was a Japanese, short, rotund, with thinning dark hair and a face that folded into creases when he smiled.

"Come in. Come in," he called, bowing to the doctor. "I'm pleased that a man of your fine reputation chose to come to our poor country station. We need you here."

The effusive greeting put Dr. Lee on guard. He certainly knows that I did not choose to come here, he thought while he waited for the other man to continue speaking.

"We hope you can begin immediately," he went on. "There are many who need care. As you know, most of these unschooled peasants wait too long before coming to us. Still rely on the herb medicine treatment, you know." He paused, arranging the papers on his desk into neat stacks, then looked up. "I hope you found your new home adequate. There is little housing of good condition, but we did our best." Without waiting for a response, he continued, "As you discovered, a servant girl has been provided for you. I arranged for her, told her to prepare the house." His eyes narrowed in the creases of flesh. "I feel certain you will wish to continue with her services. She is most capable."

He rose abruptly. "Let me give you a tour of our hospital, introduce you to the other doctor."

Daylight was nearly gone when he was dismissed. The day had been filled with new impressions and information and he was weary when he climbed onto the bicycle for the ride home. If every day were as hard as this one he'd soon feel like an old man.

"It was the hospital director who brought that girl here," he told Sun Yi as soon as he arrived. They exchanged glances, sharing a common thought. "Birds listen to daytalk and rats to nighttalk," he reminded her. "We'll have to let her stay on for now but later, when it will be less noticed, we must find a way to replace her." He already spoke in a soft voice. Sun Yi leaned forward to hear. Would it always be necessary to speak in this manner, even in his own home?

"Well, her name is Kim Hae Yong," Sun Yi replied. "I was correct in guessing her age. She is fifteen, nearly the same as Han Ju, though she is so tiny you might think her younger. And she has been most helpful to me. So we must give her a chance."

"This child works very hard," Sun Yi told him a few days later. "I don't know how I would manage without her."

The girl seldom spoke, unless to ask a question of Sun Yi, so it was sometime later, on a day when she gave her some written instructions, that she discovered the maid could neither read nor write.

"Can you imagine that she's never been to school!" Sun Yi told him in the evening.

"Not unusual out here in the country," he reminded her.

"But she is so bright and quick to learn," Sun Yi protested. "She must have some opportunity."

He watched his wife's face, thinking that she must be recalling her own childhood, when she had wanted nothing more than to be educated. Now all of her sympathy flowed to this young country girl. He smiled, shaking his head. "Don't tell me. I know already. You intend to be her teacher."

"Well, I did think of giving her a few lessons. Just some simple things. When we are not occupied with the work of the house."

It was good to watch as the eager expression return to Sun Yi's face. For the first time since they'd arrived in Shunsen she looked happy.

"If you can't find someone to become your student," he told her, smiling in the darkness and pulling her close, "I believe you would teach the alphabet to the chickens."

On a cold night in November when the outside was dark and they lay huddled under the thick quilts, Sun Yi woke suddenly from a deep sleep. She thought she heard some scratching on the oiled paper window. Could it be the wind? The sound persisted. At last she shook her husband's shoulder. Gently. He was so tired. But a sudden dread gripped her. She tried to waken him by whispering into his ear. "I hear something, coming from outside. Could someone be out there?"

It was the sound of fear in her voice that finally roused him. Drowsily he tried to reassure her. "Don't be worried. It's nothing. But I'll look."

She lay listening to his slippers shuffling down the walkway on the outside. Her heart was thumping all of the way down to her toes. Why should she be afraid?

But he soon returned. "I'll need your help," he whispered into her ear. "It's all right. Just come to my office, as quietly as you can."

Sun Yi struggled into a loose robe and followed him, wondering but trusting. When she reached the room sometimes used by the doctor to care for patients from the village she saw two young men sitting in a corner. They were both bearded, gaunt, dressed in shabby clothes. The doctor motioned for her to come closer.

By the light of one candle she watched him remove the jacket from the one who looked more like a boy. A bloody hole gaped from his bare chest, near the right shoulder. He winced when the surgeon's fingers touched his skin.

"Bring the candle closer," her husband whispered, handing it to her. "Hold it steady so I can see."

Sun Yi tried to keep her eyes on his hands as Dr. Lee cleaned and bandaged the wound but she winced and had to turn away when she saw his scalpel probe the raw flesh, digging for the bullet. She fought the nausea, realizing that this was the first time she had actually watched him at his work since that long ago day when Kum Seung fell from the swing. It was not her province to involve herself with his work outside their home. Life was changing, every aspect of it different now. The old traditions would never return.

When the bandage was in place the doctor draped the jacket over the boy's shoulders. The other man, who had watched in silence, slumped in the corner for the entire time, stood up and led his companion to the door. Still he said nothing but, raising his hand in a silent gesture of appreciation, he left as quietly as he'd arrived.

"Now you know," Dr. Lee whispered, before snuffing out the candle. He motioned for Sun Yi to precede him in finding her way back through the familiar passage in the dark. But when she returned to the still warm bed she lay wide awake, her mind sifting the questions she dare not ask.

She knew that bands of guerrilla fighters had been resisting the Japanese in Korea for years, especially since the time of reprisals for the March 1st demonstration. These patriots, mostly young men, did whatever they could to disrupt supply and communication lines, seeking refuge in the countryside, or in the mountains, where they could mingle and disappear among the farmers, and also receive aid from them. There were many times when their efforts appeared to be futile but still they persisted, a constant annoyance to the rulers of the country.

In the morning she could speak, though still in a whisper. "Is our home to become a haven for all the wounded and ill among these men, just as you used our house in Seoul for the relay of information? Is that what happened last night?" Her tone demanded an answer. "Why didn't you tell me before?"

He raised his dark eyes to her, proudly. "Yes, it is. I'd been expecting something like that midnight visit for sometime. I didn't want to tell you. I knew you'd learn soon enough and be forced to share my burden."

"But our children!" Sun Yi responded. "Have you thought of the danger to them?"

"I intend to be cautious," he replied. "My only concern is that servant girl. Do you think she could have heard? Would she be able to see the glow of light from her room?"

It was at the far end of the kitchen, a space no larger than a closet, where she slept.

"No, I don't think so," Sun Yi tried to reassure him. But she wondered. More nighttime visits would occur, surely. They could take no chances. Their house was probably under some kind of surveillance. Anyone could be seen entering or leaving it in the daytime since it was in an open area. But the girl was the only constant presence.

"She must leave!" he warned. "We'll replace her with someone we can trust."

The only alternative was to stop helping these brave young men. He'd never do that. But how to protect his family at the same time?

"She's a good worker," Sun Yi protested. "Both boys are happy in her company." Her brow creased into a frown. "Surely she will do nothing, knowingly, that will harm us. And the truth is that I have grown quite fond of her," she added. "Give me some time to think of a solution."

"It may be quite true that she does not intend to act as a spy," he replied, attempting to sooth Sun Yi, "but if she is questioned she may reveal information unwittingly about the things she's seen here. It may be that she does not even tell anyone but her own family. Then someone else may, in turn, betray us. She comes from a home that is desperately poor. Her small earnings must be needed badly, or they would not have farmed her out to strangers."

Sun Yi's face brightened. "There may be a way." she began. "Yes! What do you think of sending her to school?"

"To school?"

"Of course. We could do it. In Shunsen there's a mission school, you know. The fees are modest."

"How would you know that? I see. It seems that you are prepared, as usual."

Though he scolded, there was a note of pride in her husband's voice. He knew he need never to worry about Sun Yi's self-reliance. She'd always been resourceful. The knowledge sustained him during his imprisonment. "Have you thought about her father, though? How are you going to persuade an old-fashioned country farmer that it is worthwhile to have a daughter who can read and write? He needs her to earn a wage that feeds his family."

"I'll find a way," she promised with a toss of her dark head. Sun Yi's eyes sparkled in the old way. "Maybe," she added with a sly smile, "I'll offer him both." She rose, filled with enthusiasm for the challenge. "Today the family of Hae Yong will have a visit from her employer."

Later in the morning Sun Yi started out, with the boys, to walk to the maid's home. Jae Soon and Jae Yun soon tired of her slow pace and ran ahead, returning from time to time to share with her some treasure, a stone, and a bird's feather, discovered along the way.

The two were close companions now. This solitary life bound them more firmly here than in the city. For this, if nothing else, she was grateful. Today was their holiday; freed from the schedule of lessons she usually imposed upon them. Their education was her primary concern and she'd become their teacher, a strict taskmaster.

Watching their matching footsteps kick up a cloud of dust, with the younger boy keeping up to his brother's long strides, Sun Yi told herself she would never complain, no matter how she detested the isolation and primitive living, if the sojourn in Kangwando forged a lasting friendship between her sons.

She smiled to herself, recalling the look on Hae Yong's face when she told her of the day's destination. She was lighting the fire for the morning rice and a light sprang into her eyes, transforming her usual placid expression when Sun Yi asked, "Have you thought of going to school?"

"There's nothing I wish more, Mistress. I know it is impossible."

"I'll ask your father, myself, if you desire to learn."

The girl appeared startled. No wonder, thought Sun Yi. Who ever asked her wishes about anything before?

"He'll say no. But you are kind even to think of doing this for me."

"Just tell me how to find your house, Hae Yong."

We've been walking for half an hour, thought Sun Yi. That must be the place, just ahead. The huts were clustered in a circle, open fields stretching out on all sides while the mountains in the distance, ragged patches of snow clinging to their sides, framed the scene. The sky was clear, with only a few wispy puffs of white suspended in the still air.

My family's home is the closest, Hae Yong said. But can that be it, so small? It does look solid, permanent, somehow.

A wall of woven straw as high as its roof separated the place from its neighbors. The house was in three sections, enclosing a matang, a kind of courtyard, of packed brown earth. The gate on the fourth side gave it a sense of seclusion that reminded Sun Yi of the kitchen courtyard in her childhood home. The roof of thatch, not slate, hung thickly over the battened earth walls, like a boy's hair, trimmed around the edges but thick at the top.

The red chili peppers spread out to dry on a straw mat caught Sun Yi's eye first. Every inch of space in the matang was covered with shiny pods. Then she noticed the woman tending a clay jar in the corner and she seemed to be aware of her visitor at the same moment. Setting down the soy sauce container, she started toward her but abruptly stopped. Perhaps seeing the fine quality of Sun Yi's dress, she drew back and began bowing, low, before her.

A single brown chicken sauntered between them, swooping to swallow an insect. A breeze shook the few dry leaves on a slender wisp of tree. In that instant Sun Yi, sensing her confusion, quickly introduced herself.

"My name is Mrs. Yu, wife of Dr. Lee. I am the mistress of the house that employs your daughter."

"Is my daughter well?"

"Your daughter is in excellent health. Please don't be worried."

The countrywoman was tall and thin, the angular bones of her face hard under the taut skin, darkened by seasons of labor under the hot sun. Her simple cotton chima was roughly woven but immaculately white. She tugged at the hemp cord that was tied around her waist to keep its long folds out of her way while she worked, saying, "It is an honor to offer hospitality to the kind lady who offers my child shelter."

"She is a good girl," Sun Yi replied, "and I apologize for disturbing your serenity."

She looks suspicious, she thought. I can't blame her. Perhaps this is all a mistake. She'll think I'm interfering. And she'll be right.

"Boys, please be still. You are guests in this home. These are my sons," she began to explain. Jae Soon and his brother were stalking the chicken, one at either side, and driving the creature to distraction. "With your permission, they'll wait outside while I speak with you. A matter of great importance," she added with emphasis on the last words.

"Hae Yong's father is at work in the fields," she replied, not moving.

"Then I may talk with you."

Shrugging, Hae Yong's mother relented. "My home is simple but if you will come inside I will bring you some refreshment. Then you may tell me the message so I may relay it to him on his return."

Sun Yi bowed, wondering how effective a communication that would be. Slipping off her shoes, she ducked to enter the central room and blinked until her eyes became accustomed to the dim light. The woman disappeared and she looked around. A tiny woman hunched down in a shadowy corner, seated on a cushion. Her sparse gray hair, twisted into a tight knot behind her head, framed a face crisscrossed with an intricate pattern of lines and creases. While her bright eyes fastened on the stranger and followed her, she said nothing.

Hae Yong's mother reentered, bringing a clay pot and an earthenware mug on a small wooden tray. Kneeling before Sun Yi she poured cold podi cha and said, with a shrug in the old lady's direction, "That is halmoni, mother of Hae Yong's father."

She did not speak to the mother-in-law. I suppose she prefers to ignore her now that she is infirm, thought Sun Yi. Living in such a crowded space must create even more tension between these two than the usual difficult relationship. She could understand. The old woman may have tormented her in the past, but she looks pitiful, lonely, now.

"Dr. Lee and I wish to ask a great favor of Hae Yong's family," she began, after accepting a cup of the barley tea. "As I have said, the daughter of this family is a good girl. You have trained her well. She is most helpful to our family."

The woman nodded, saying nothing, but she looked pleased.

"Have you other children?"

"Yes, she replied softly. "Two are living."

"Are your sons in school?" Sun Yi tried to put the question gently. She did not wish to insult this proud person.

She shook her head in reply. "There was no opportunity."

"You can be proud of a properly behaved child," Sun Yi continued after sipping the cool drink. "Hae Yong is also intelligent. If she could attend school she might herself become a teacher one day."

The woman shook her head again, this time sadly. "We are grateful for your kind words," she said, adding, "but we are only poor farmers. There is no money to spare for schooling. Even with our daughter's earnings, there is not enough to pay all of the debts."

"I understand," Sun Yi told her gently, not wishing to offend this woman, who owned more of pride than any possessions. "But wouldn't your family be honored to have one of its members educated?" Without waiting for a response, she went on, "I have come here to ask Hae Yong's father's permission that we may send his daughter to school. You will still receive her wages, just as though she continues to work in our home. She'll not be far away, only in Shun-sen, and she will come home to you whenever there is a holiday." She ended the speech with an encouraging smile to the mother, who was looking uncertain.

After a long silence, Hae Yong's mother looked up. "In any case, her father must decide. He will be told of your offer." She looked down again and Sun Yi leaned closer to hear her next words. "It is time for our daughter to be betrothed. Soon she will be married. A proper marriage is difficult to arrange for an educated woman."

Still? Sun Yi wanted to cry out, to protest. "No! She is too young!" She bit her lip and locked in her rage. Will these customs never change? Masking her true feelings, she smiled, rising and bowing, and said only, "Please speak to Hae Yong's father. Tell us when he decides."

Stepping into the bright courtyard, she called to the boys to join her for the walk home.

"I really don't know what to expect from today's visit," Sun Yi reported to her husband in the evening. "It's understandable that her family is reluctant to accept the changes that education will bring to Hae Yong's life. Their pride, also, may cause them to hesitate before our offer."

"There are many farmers like them now," Dr. Lee remarked. "Once they may have been able to care for their own needs, even save a little. Each year more of them are forced into tenancy on their own land, each year slipping into more debt to the landlord."

'What causes such disaster?"

"There are a number of causes," he began, thinking that most women would not concern themselves with such questions. He didn't mind. He welcomed her interest. "One is the need for irriga-tion. Rice won't grow here without water, and there is never enough rainfall, except in summer. The farmers are forced to join a coopera-tive association. Each of them has to contribute his share of the cost for developing the system. Even if the crop fails, he's still responsible for the expense of the water." He paused, holding out his cup for Sun Yi to refill. "This can grow into a mountain of debt in no time. An insurmountable debt!"

"Then what can he do?"

"Give up his land. Become a tenant. More and more of the farmland is held by fewer landlords, while the tenant farmer works land he can never hope to regain for himself."

"How much does he pay, then?"

"Half the year's crop. Sometimes more."

"That's outrageous!" exclaimed Sun Yi.

"Well, that's not the end of it. The farmer also pays land taxes and the cost of the water, and he must deliver the landlord's share of the harvest to him, no matter where he lives, after paying a fee for inspection of the rice and supplying the seedlings, fertilizer and animals to haul it."

"I understand. I had no idea it was this bad."

"There's more. The agent for the landlord may order the harvest whenever it suits him. Their contract is only oral. The rent may be raised or eviction ordered at any time. Why, most farmers are fortunate if they have one-fourth or one-fifth remaining to them of what they work so hard to grow." He raised his hands in a gesture of futility.

"Life must seem hopeless under these conditions."

Dr. Lee nodded. "Do you know that more than half of Korea's farmers live under this system. More become tenants each year, as the Japanese continue to force them from their own land. The number of kadenmin increases constantly."

"What is kadenmin?

"I forgot. Your life in the city hasn't prepared you for this knowledge. Fire-field farmers. Kadenmin are those who have lost their land through eviction, or never had any to begin with. They wander from one spot to another, finding a bit of marginal land, perhaps some with only trees or shrubs growing upon it. They burn off that growth and plant a crop. The soil is too poor to produce more than one year's crop, so they move on in search of another that will sustain their life for another year, repeating the cycle."

Seeing her confusion, he went on to explain how nearly impossible it was for a man to regain his land. "Now the wage for a laborer is fifteen yen per month. If that poor man could save half of this, which he will never be able to do, it would take twenty-four years for him to save enough to buy one cho."

"It seems hopeless," said Sun Yi, watching as her husband buried his face in his hands.

"It is until we rid our country of these foreign rulers. If the farmer can remain on his land, there is still no way he can afford the equipment he needs to produce more with less effort. He is destined to be in the field with his primitive plow and, if he is one of the fortunate ones, an ox to help him to pull it."

"No wonder you want to help the men who struggle against this cruel government. I understand now."

Dr. Lee folded the pages of his worn copy of *Tong-a-Ilbo* carefully after he finished reading the newspaper. Then he laid it carefully in one compartment of the brass bound chest in the ondul room. The publication had arrived earlier that day, delivered as it usually was among the layers of straw that shielded the bottles of medicine sent to the hospital from Seoul.

Tong-a-Ilbo was one of the three newspapers allowed under the Japanese rule. It had emerged recently from a long period of suspension and the doctor knew that it was heavily censored; yet he read it eagerly for it was one of his few contacts with the wider world beyond Shunsen. Sun Yi would read it later and then he would pass it on, sharing it with his small circle of trusted acquaintances. He felt that he must still be cautious in reading something so closely aligned with his former illicit activities.

Twisting the key in the lock, he dropped it into the celadon vase that stood upon the chest. That vase was Sun Yi's favorite decoration. He picked it up, musing on the way in which she had insisted on bringing it here, selecting it from among all the other pieces of china that must be left at his family home for safekeeping during their exile. Whenever she looked at it, she explained, she was reminded of a civilized manner of living.

He held the vase for a moment before replacing it on the chest. The translucent pale green, caressed by a network of thin lines that gave it the appearance of fragility, had survived since the Koryo dynasty, more than six hundred years past. No wonder the celadon was considered one of the greatest triumphs of the potter's arts. He set it down gently.

The doctor knew, from accounts in the newspaper, that the helpless feeling of many of his fellow citizens toward the centralized power of Korea was increasing. All men were preoccupied by this foreign domination, driven to either evasion or adaptation. For himself, all he could feel now was an appreciation of his profession. A doctor will always eat, though his good fortune is derived from another's misery. He would be able to care for his family no matter how the political situation changed.

And he would not cease to do all that he could to effect a change. Twice since that first time he was summoned in the night to treat the wounds of someone from the network of underground patriots. On each occasion he and Sun Yi tiptoed along the maru to the room at the end of the house, always hoping that their movements were undetected, that the maid would not see or hear. So far he had no sign that these incidents were reported.

The wind howled along the outside of the thick rafters and he pulled his padded jacket closer. The floor was warm but the air above much colder. Surviving their first season in these northern mountains was their major occupation since winter began in earnest.

"It is so cold tonight! Are you warm in here?" Sun Yi stood in the entry, holding the table with the steaming bowls of food for his evening meal. "I've brought your favorite hot soup to take away the chill." She smiled at him while setting the low table before him.

"Your presence warms the room," he said, looking up, and watched her color rise at the unexpected words. She was dressed in the usual long white chima. How could she manage to keep it immaculate in the primitive housekeeping conditions of this village home? Her feet, encased in thick padded coverings, glided soundlessly when she crossed the floor. She bent her glossy head and the smile again lighted her oval face as she uncovered the dishes one by one. How little she has changed since I first saw her. Only her hands. He regretted that they were roughened by the work she must now do herself.

While he ate the steaming food she sat in silence. When he finished she removed the table before speaking. "You were so late tonight that even the children were worried."

"There's more to do each day. Not that more persons are becoming ill or suffering injuries, but it seems that many country folk are hearing about our hospital and growing in confidence that it is a place where they can be helped. To turn away from the herbal medicines of hanyak is often thought of as disloyalty to our heritage, as you know. Only when they find it can be combined with the techniques of western medicine do they accept our way.

"Aren't you pleased?"

"I should be, but the problem is that I am expected to provide a new magic that will cure all ailments."

"You do, don't you?" Again, that mischievous smile on her face.

"Not always," he replied, reaching out in a rare gesture to caress her soft cheek. "Today was especially hard for me. There are many diseases for which I can do nothing. Lung ailments are often so advanced that nothing can be done but try to make the patient comfortable until the end. The only childbirth cases I see are those with complications. No," he sighed, "I bring no new magic, unfortunately."

Sun Yi knew what came next. As some men might draw upon a pipe for an evening's relaxation, he found solace in the music he could bring forth from his flute. After a minute of playing he stopped abruptly, asking, "Well, has there been word from that girl's family?"

Sun Yi shook her head. "Hae Yong says only that her father reacted in anger at the news of my visit. Perhaps I acted rashly, unthinking. It was my fault. I should remember that countrymen are even less ready to listen to a woman's voice than." Her voice trailed off and she bit her lip, fearing to explain further. "She says he is firmly opposed to the idea of sending her to school. It looks like we'll need a different approach if we wish to succeed in getting her out of here." Sun Yi leaned closer, lowering her voice. "While we were talking, however, she did assure me of her complete loyalty to our family, because of her gratitude. Do you know that one of the men you treated here recently was her own brother! He's a secret member of the underground. Hae Yong told me to have no concern. She'll never give you away, no matter how cooperative with the hospital director she may appear. I've been waiting all day to tell you this!"

To Sun Yi's surprise, her husband did not share her elation at this news. Instead, he warned, "Only time will prove that to be true." Then he admitted, "I've been worried, constantly, that my actions would be dangerous for all of you, though I can't see how I can act in any other way. I'd like to believe she is on our side."

Nevertheless, Sun Yi felt relieved of her anxiety. "Now," she went on, "there is another matter. Your elder son has so little time to see you. He's no longer a baby. He needs more than my companionship." She smiled at him in the special manner that she knew was always effective, looking at him from the corners of her eyes, teasing. "Tonight the boy as waited all of this time, hoping that you would give him a few moments with you."

He relented. He could never resist her intriguing glance. "Send him in to me," he said, thinking how determined she was to have her way. Some might describe his wife as stubborn, if it were not such an unfeminine characteristic.

Within seconds Jae Soon, who had been waiting at the door, appeared and, tired though he was, the father found the presence of his son reviving him. Perhaps it was true that he'd ignored the boy, but wasn't that natural? The relationship with his own father was always formal. He bowed in greeting on special occasions but only twice could he recall a private conversation with the elderly gentleman, the first when he left to study abroad, and the other when he daringly pleaded for his plan to marry Sun Yi. Such was the tradition between fathers and sons but perhaps this, also, was changing in modern times.

The seven-year-old, tall and thin, with his shiny black hair bouncing in his visible eagerness, stood waiting to capture his father's eye before bowing. When he had done so he sat near him, head lowered in shyness before the gaze of his elder, and waited silently for him to speak.

"Well, now. Your mother tells me that you have remained awake beyond your usual time for sleeping," Dr. Lee began.

The boy nodded, peeking at his father's face.

"Your mother tells me also that you have been a diligent student for her," he continued, "and this pleases me. There is nothing more important than to study and learn as much as you can. What is in your head," he tapped it gently with his flute, "can never be taken from you by anyone! Remember that!"

"Yes, Abuji," Jae Soon nodded again, this time solemnly.

"There's an ancient story, a myth, told about the beginning of our people. You may have heard something of it before, but it is important to remember and to understand, for it will help you to know why we have a close feeling for the spirits of all natural creations around us."

Jae Soon moved closer and Dr. Lee, seeing that the eyes of his son were fastened on him in close attention, began:

"There was once a wise and brave prince, son of the Heavenly King. He asked his father to grant him the beautiful peninsula of Korea to govern. The King granted his wish and he was dispatched to Earth, accompanied by three thousand followers.

"He first set foot on land under the sacred sandalwood tree on the Taebaek Mountains that are far to the north of us, and established a sacred city. He had three ministers to carry out his orders, Earl Wind, Chancellor Rain, and Chancellor Cloud, who were charged with the supervision of three hundred and sixty officials. They controlled all things, such as grain, life, sickness, and the determination of good and evil."

Jae Soon's eyes were still wide open as he listened, and his father continued.

"At that time a bear and a tiger were living in a big cave near the sandalwood tree. They wished ardently to become human beings. Each day they prayed so earnestly before the tree that the Heavenly Prince be moved by their sincerity. He gave them twenty bulbs of garlic and a bundle of mugwort, saying 'Eat these and confine yourselves deep in your cave for one hundred days. Then you will become human.'

"So the bear and tiger took the garlic and the mugwort and went into their cave. They prayed earnestly that their wish might be granted. The bear endured weariness and hunger and, after twenty-one days, became a beautiful woman. The tiger was not so patient. It ran away, for it could not tolerate the long days of sitting quietly."

The boy leaned against his father, eyelids fluttering, now open, and more often shut.

"The woman was overjoyed. She visited the sandalwood tree again, praying that she might become the mother of a child. Her ardent wish was granted. She became Queen and gave birth to a Prince. He was named Tangun, which means the sandalwood king, and reigned for a long time as the first human king of our peninsula. He established his capitol at Pyongyang and gave our kingdom the name of Choson, the land of the morning calm.

"This was four thousand, two hundred and sixty-two years ago. He reigned for more than twelve hundred years, and when he abdicated for the next king he returned to the spirits and became a mountain god."

His voice ceased and Jae Soon sat up.

"Were you listening?" asked his father.

"Oh, yes, Abuji," the boy responded. "Did that really happen?"

"It is a story meant to teach us a lesson, my son. So it is not important to know if it happened, but instead to understand its meaning. We have a heavenly father and an earthly mother, binding us to heaven and earth. In all of our actions we must always remember that and behave accordingly."

He opened the door and called to Sun Yi. Then he bent down and whispered close to his ear. "Come to see me again tomorrow night and you shall hear the story of Admiral Yi and his turtle boats. Then perhaps I shall also teach you to play paduk.

In the morning Dr. Lee remembered the newspaper that he had intended to give to Sun Yi to read. He lifted down the celadon vase to take the key, which would open the chest. But the vase was empty.

The whole countryside was covered like soft sugar frosting on a cake. Foot-long icicles hung from the heavy blanket of snow that formed a second roof on her house.

Sun Yi, on her way to the kitchen, had to stop for a moment to look, even though the crisp air of early morning sent a stinging chill against her cheeks and turned her breath into an evanescent cloud. Snow intensified the blue quality of the daylight. Even the lingering shadows reflected this color. The light of the dawn conveyed a special mood of calm, a freshness that never ceased to project hope for the new day. Choson, the ancient name given to her country, which the Japanese had revived, aptly described this day: Land of the morning calm.

"Yubo!" Dr. Lee's voice, crackling with intensity, could be heard the entire length of the corridor that ran along the outside wall of their house. As she hurried to respond to the urgency of his commanding call she heard the melodious tinkling as one of the largest icicles broke and fell against the side of the maru.

Dr. Lee stood in the ondol room, dressed to leave for the hospital. The heavy quilted clothing he wore was most practical for the Korean winter. The loose and baggy pants tied at the ankles and the long coat was padded with layers of cotton to protect from the biting winds of January. No one would take him for an outsider, a city-dweller, dressed in this way.

"Why did you call me?" The loud voice was unlike his usual soft-spoken manner.

"The key to this chest has disappeared," he replied. "It was here last night." He shook the vase again. "I put it into this vase myself after locking the newspaper into the chest. I've already searched this room," he continued, pacing in agitation, "but it is not here."

"Where could it be?

"There's no more time to look for it. I must leave. Try to find it, if you can."

She knew he was still suspicious of the maid. Could he be right? Sun Yi soothed him. "Never mind. I'm sure I'll find it. Go on your way and try not to worry. It must be here, somewhere."

He stepped outside to pull on thick boots and she looked at the chest. It was massive, standing nearly six feet high, and constructed of paulonia wood with inlaid designs on its doors. The handsomest piece of furniture in their home, it was a treasure that had belonged to his family for several generations, and was used to store their most valued possessions. Behind its doors bound by shiny brass hinges were rows of small drawers, each marked with the character for the medicine the doctor stored in it. In the lower compartments he kept papers and documents, including the newspaper of the previous evening.

She gave the brass lock on the doors a shake. It was certainly locked. Wherever the key was, the contents of this chest were still safe. No need for worry.

The remnants of his breakfast were still on the small table. Kneeling to pick it up, Sun Yi thought how every strange or unexplained happening seemed to upset him since he had been in prison. Now the missing key aroused his suspicions. Well, she learned to accept these outbursts calmly. I never dreamed I'd become capable of such patience, she thought, carrying out the table.

Jae Yun nearly collided with her. The four-year-old rolled and tumbled rather than walking most of the time. Behind him Jae Soon followed sedately, his dark eyes somber and the hint of a wrinkled furrow on his brow. He looked a serious little man at the age of seven.

The boys shared their lessons, for though he was younger, Jae Yun learned as quickly as his brother, his mind leaping as nimbly as his feet did. Today, however, he held back, sitting quietly behind Jae Soon. His eyes shifted from his mother's gaze when she looked at him.

First she told them of the missing key. "I need your help to find it. And if you do, each of you may have an extra portion of dried persimmon with your evening meal."

Persimmons were their favorite treat. She rationed them so the supply of the flat, slightly chewy sweet would last through the winter when no other fruit was available. Satisfied with their promise to help in the search for the key, she turned to their lesson for the day.

By evening it was still missing, though, and she dreaded telling her husband. But he came into their house with other news on his mind. With a letter in his hand and a gleam of anticipation on his face, he announced, "Han Ju is coming to visit us!"

"Wonderful!" Sun Yi exclaimed. They had seen no one from Seoul since arriving in Shunsen four months earlier. Han Ju was especially welcome, for her young brother would also bring news of her family in Kyongsang, far to the south. Perhaps he would also explain the background for recent political developments of which they had heard only rumors. "When?" she asked, expectation lighting her face.

"By the end of the week," he said, "though this is a strange time to travel, in the midst of winter. Why do you suppose he is coming here now? He says he is traveling with his classmate. They'll stay only a short time but he has important news."

Later he remembered to ask about the key. "Well, I'll just have to break the lock," he remarked, on learning that it was still missing. "I'll need some of those medicines."

Jae Yun was the first to spot him when Han Ju arrived two days later, for he was standing by the courtyard gate. Even on cold days he would not stay inside. The boy jumped up and down, calling "Ohm-anee!" when he saw the figures in dark school uniforms approaching along the frozen rutted road from Shunsen.

"I've brought my good friend, Choi Son Sil, with me," said Han Ju after greeting his sister and the boys. "We are classmates at Kyunggi. He's never traveled to this wild part of our country before, either, and has great curiosity about the way of life here."

Sun Yi welcomed them. The change in Han Ju amazed her. Not only had he grown taller in a few months, but also he'd managed to assume the demeanor of a confident young man. At seventeen he was no longer the small child, her eager student.

His friend, young Choi, was shorter than her brother was and although the broadshouldered youth greeted her with all the proper deference she detected a subtle attitude that disturbed her. Was it arrogance? Why? After all, she also was a resident of Seoul, not a country person, though she lived here for the present. His round face set upon a short, thick neck gave him a solid appearance. His eyes were veiled. He did not have the same boyish eagerness that Han Ju retained. Why should I have an uneasy feeling about a person I've just met, she wondered? After all, he is Han Ju's friend.

"Come inside, out of the cold," she said aloud, and they all hurried into the warmth of the house while she pushed aside her doubts in the effort to provide hospitable comforts for them.

While Sun Yi prepared the evening meal, with the help of Hae Yong, she thought again of the relationship between the two young men. Naturally the closest ties of friendship for a Korean youth would be with classmates of the same school. Her own husband still retained the friends of his student days. Han Ju, far from his family home, would gravitate toward such intimacy. With the constant fear of infiltration by some informer, the value of having a small circle of friends sworn to brotherhood was even greater. And these two, having gained admission to a school of the highest rank, as Kyunggi surely was, would soon learn to think of themselves as superior to others.

The maid handed a platter of chap-che to Sun Yi. She praised the artful arrangement of mixed vegetables and thin noodles. Hae Yong beamed. Well, the first impression of Han Ju's friend was superficial. She should try to know him better before forming hasty opinions.

When the men had eaten Dr. Lee began at once with questions of the student demonstrations. "I've heard only the sketchiest details," he explained. "Is this serious?"

"Yes, it certainly is," Han Ju told him. "The trouble started in Kwangju, down in Cholla province, but student uprisings spread quickly to other cities. More than fifty thousand are involved, and many of them are in jail now as a result of their actions."

"It's been a long time since anyone in this country has dared to protest. How did it begin?"

Sun Yi hovered near the door, listening while Han Ju described the situation, and remembered how she felt when she, also, dared to speak out.

"For more than two years the various leaders of Shinganhoe have been organizing people, as you know. It could become a real political party, but since there is no hope of that, the members sometimes resort to violence." Han Ju turned to his friend for confirmation and Choi nodded his head.

"So far it hasn't helped their cause at all," Choi remarked.

Han Ju continued, "Their goal is to create a national conscious-ness, a protest against the Japanese rule, but they also support reform of the social system." Taking a persimmon slice from the plate, he chewed it thoughtfully.

"Who is involved in this Shinganhoe?" asked the doctor, growing impatient for him to continue.

"There are many factions. Labor, farmers, women, and of course, the students. The leaders come from religious groups, persons in law and education, and the newspapers."

"Some are radicals," Choi added. "Trouble makers."

Ignoring his statement, Dr. Lee asked, "Is Chondogyo a part of it?" He missed the daily contact with the other members of his church.

"An important part," Han Ju assured his sister's husband. The vice-president is Kwon Tong Jin.

"Ah, yes," replied Dr. Lee, nodding in recognition.

"Communists are a part of the coalition, also," Han Ju went on, "but they are split into so many factions that their voice is weakened. Most of the others take a more moderate stand."

Sun Yi brought a cushion and sat closer. She wanted to hear every word. Would these reform movements go on without them? Stuck out here in the country there was no way to keep up contacts with these patriots.

"And the factory workers," Han Ju was saying. "They began the most recent disturbances. Nothing to do with wages or working conditions, just a strike against Japanese control. But their protest spreads like wildfire and the police are hard put to deal with it, for they cannot predict in which factory it will next break out."

"The farmers?" Sun Yi demanded. "How are they involved?"

"They protest against high rents and the unfair amounts of rice taken by their landlords. All they have left to eat is the millet, and not much of that by the time 'spring hunger' time arrives."

"But I've heard more about this Kwangju trouble," the doctor interrupted.

"Yes. It's the worst, elder brother. Last year, on November third, three hundred high school students had a battle with students from the Japanese school there, near the railroad station. They say an insult to a Korean girl sparked it, but you know how our people resent the superior attitude of those Japanese and their teachers. The explosion was just waiting for the match to set it off."

"Go on," said Sun Yi, filling their cups once more with sung-nyung. She made the tasty drink by adding water to the crusted rice left in the bottom of the cooking pan. It was soothing to sip on this cold night while the wind howled outside.

"There were many injuries on both sides. Now the police are on the alert everywhere." His voice broke. "And many are in jail." He leaned closer, eyes burning with intensity. "What good does all this protest do? I ask you. You've both been there. Prison is becoming a badge of accomplishment for Koreans. But where did it get you?" He swept his arm in a wide gesture indicating their home.

Sun Yi sat upright, shocked by her younger brother's outburst before his elder, but her husband remained calm.

"I believe," said Dr. Lee slowly, "that no where in the world is there so ancient and continuous a tradition of students participating in national politics as there is here. What would you do?" he asked, looking intently at Han Ju.

"I have already made up my mind," he replied immediately, with a sidelong glance at his silent friend. "That is why I am here. I wanted to say goodbye to you before I leave."

"Leave?" The words escaped from Sun Yi's lips while her face became pale.

"Yes. And I wanted, hoped, you would understand. I am going to Japan to study, to a university. Choi is going with me."

"You? To Japan?" Sun Yi echoed his words with disbelief.

"Elder sister, look at me. How far do you think I can rise in this country? The limits are clearly drawn. I have no wish to remain a low level functionary." He spit out the words. "With a degree from a Japanese university I will be allowed to compete in the national exams on an equal basis."

"You have permission for this?" Dr. Lee finally spoke.

"Yes, it's all taken care of, and I am prepared to leave."

A wave of shame and sadness engulfed Sun Yi. Silence filled the room, oppressive with its portent. He would no longer be a part of her life. He and how many others? Had she and her friends suffered for this? A new generation choosing quiet cooperation with the giant that had swallowed Korea? Would the bright and able ones of the future all choose to follow the path laid out by her brother and his friend Choi?"

While she pondered what she could say to change him the sliding door opened and a sleepy Jae Soon stood in its shadow. "Ohmanee," he called. "Jae Yun is asking for you. He is sick and he hurts. He hurts a lot."

When Sun Yi rushed to answer Jae Soon's imperative call she felt only mild concern. Her younger son brimmed with robust health. He'd never been seriously ill and she couldn't believe he was now.

But, kneeling to look at him where he lay on the thick layer of ibuls, she realized that he was truly suffering.

His pale face was wet to her touch, tousled dark hair clung to his forehead, and his eyes were sunken and wide with pain. He writhed constantly.

She held the lamp close. It cast a dim light amidst shadows.

"My stomach hurts," he whispered when he saw her leaning over him. Streaks from dried tears lined his soft cheeks. "I'm sorry, Ohm-anee."

"Why, illness is not your fault, my son. You should not blame yourself." She laid her hand on his shoulder.

"It is. It is," he repeated slowly. "I'm sorry."

Jae Yun's mother laid her hand again on his forehead. Cool. Too cool. "Try to lie still. I'll bring Abuji. He can make you feel better"

Dr. Lee was still deep in conversation with her brother and his friend, their voices subdued and earnest, when she returned to the room. Han Ju spoke in a soft but persuasive manner while the others, sipping the sungnyung, listened intently.

"Our second son is really quite ill," Sun Yi interrupted. "He needs his father." Turning to her husband, she pleaded, "Please come and look at him." Then she turned to young Choi. "Please excuse us. My younger brother can see to your comforts. Rest well."

She paused only to show Han Ju where the ibuls were stored in a wall cupboard. The two young men would make their beds on the heated floor. Then she hurried off to join Jae Yun's father.

"What do you suppose has caused his illness?" she asked after they left the ondul room. "He was so well earlier in the day." She recalled the boy's eager greeting for their guests.

Her husband went in to his son and she heard the sound of his voice, calm and low, probing for some explanation from the child. "Can you tell me how you feel? Then I'll try to help you."

He called to Sun Yi. "It seems that our son has eaten something disagreeable to him, perhaps dangerous. Don't worry. I have some medicine that can help, but all my supplies are locked into that chest!"

"Could you send Han Ju to the hospital in Shunsen for something?" Sun Yi looked at the boy, still moaning and thrashing on his bed.

"In this cold?" Dr. Lee shook his head. "He'd freeze to death before he'd return. I'll smash that lock right now."

The child moaned and she thought he was trying to speak. Sun Yi moved closer.

"Ohmanee, I'm sorry. The key. In my stocking."

"Is he delirious?"

Jae Yun repeated the words, adding faintly, "Look. In stocking."

Sun Yi noticed Jae Soon hovering in a corner, wrapped in an ibul. She'd forgotten all about him. She beckoned, asking, "Where's your brother's clothing?"

He brought her an untidy bundle and she pulled from it the quilted cotton coverings they wore inside their home. She held one upside down. Clink! A brass key landed on the floor.

"How did he get this?" She held it up, looking surprised. "Did you know about this?" she asked Jae Soon.

He shook his head.

Dr. Lee took the key and left the room. Sun Yi experienced a chill of premonition, caused not by the frigid air whistling around the corners of their house but rather by the expression on his face. She'd never seen this man lose his temper, but the sharp intake of breath between his clenched teeth told her plainer than any words that he was angry. He'd blame her. She should know what her children were up to at all times. And he'd been so quick to blame the maid!

Jae Yun lay with eyes wide open. She leaned over him, placing her hand on his forehead. It was still damp, sticky to her touch, and cool. Sitting back on a cushion beside him she waited, motionless, for his father to return.

Listening for the sound of her husband's returning footsteps, she reminded herself how much more the truly poor suffered, without the means to feed their young ones the food they need, sleeping in unheated homes. No wonder they are victims of every sort of disease.

Where was her husband? Why was he taking so long? She stroked her son's head. Was that his footstep on the maru? No, only the wind.

Few doctors were so compassionate as her husband. He'd insisted on giving care to anyone who required it and never considered if they could pay. Living even for this short time surrounded by the poverty of Kangwando, she'd observed for herself how so many of her countrymen suffered for every day of their short lives. "Please may it not happen to our son," she whispered into the darkness.

No one heard her. Jae Soon, toppled on his side, lay rolled into his covers, sleeping. The eyes of her baby were closed now, also. He's not my baby, she told herself, for he is already four years old. But he seemed younger, lying still and pale.

Sun Yi shut her eyes, willing that her strength should pass into him. He would become well. Both of her sons must grow strong, both in mind and body. She knew they were destined for great careers that would bring pride to their parents.

"Is our son awake?"

There you are at last, she thought, but only said, "I'll rouse him."

"Good. He should drink this. All of it."

Sun Yi raised the boy, supporting him in a half-sitting position while his father persuaded him to drink from the cup she held to his lips.

"That should take care of it," he told her as she released Jae Yun and he lay down. "By morning we can be certain."

"Do you know what it was that he swallowed?"

"Now I do," he replied grimly. "He told me that he took some of the herbs from that chest. I looked just now, and I could guess how many, and which, were missing."

"Yubo, please don't be angry with him. He's young. And he has such curiosity! She shook her head, remembering. "All day long he asks questions. About everything. even some that I am unable to answer to his satisfaction."

"Nevertheless, he's old enough to understand and obey," he told her sternly. He touched Sun Yi's shoulder. "Try to sleep. I'll stay with him."

Later she woke in the darkness, her mind still filled with the worry for her son. Our family has been one of the most fortunate in this poor country, she thought. The shadow of death has not touched our home. Kum Seung, also, has her three lively children. More than one third of all Korean children died before the age of six. Only half would live fifteen years. She knew her husband would take care of their young ones. She extended her hand to the empty space beside her. She was still alone. Tiptoeing soundlessly to the other room where her son lay, she peered in. There was her husband, still, sitting close by but drowsing. His head bent so his chin rested on his chest.

Sun Yi returned to her own bed. She'd heard often enough that the mother is gentle with her children, while the father must play a stern role in their upbringing. Perhaps, she thought, snuggling into the warmth of her covers, that is true in some homes. Not in this one, however.

In the morning Jae Yun was better. The herb remedy mixed by his father counteracted the poisonous overdose he'd taken. Yet she insisted that he remain quietly in his bed. Confinement in one place would be a far more effective punishment for this active boy than any amount of scolding.

Han Ju and young Choi had risen early. Sun Yi served their morning meal herself, for this was the one day of the month when she always allowed Hae Yong to visit her family.

Thinking of their abbreviated conversation on the previous evening, she found herself using a stilted and formal manner of address in speaking to them, even to her own younger brother. She blamed Choi for influencing Han Ju, though she knew that was unfair. How much did she really know of this friend? Her reaction was based on simple instinct.

"We're going to Shunsen to look around today," Han Ju informed her when the meal was finished.

"You'll not see much," she warned shortly. "It's nothing more than an overgrown market town, a place for the farmers from all the small villages to bring their rice and drink makkoli together. The streets are all nothing but rutted tracks."

"We'll see for ourselves," he rejoined. "Even jade has flaws in it. How many people live in the town?"

"Perhaps twenty-five thousand. More have settled there since the rail line opened."

"You're not happy here, are you?" Han Ju asked, lingering after his friend stepped outside.

"Did you ever think I could be?"

"How long will you have to remain?"

"That is not for us to decide," Sun Yi reminded her brother.

"I've sent something for you, elder sister. It should arrive within a few days. I can't take it with me to Japan, so I wanted you to have it."

Ah, a peace offering.

"It's my gramaphone," he explained. "A small one, but it's beautiful to listen to, and all of my records are with it, carefully packed. Take good care of them, won't you?"

Music! There would be music for her to listen to once more, for the children to learn to know. Han Ju was making a gift to her of his most precious possession, which he knew, also, meant more to her than anything else possibly could.

"We'll treasure it," she said at last, looking up at this younger brother who towered over her, "and take the best of care, until you return. When will that be?"

He shrugged and said, quietly, "Don't worry, elder sister. There has to be another way than going to prison to make our family proud of me. I intend to find it."

When there was a lull in the day's activities she came in to sit with her son.

"Listen, my little one," she began with a somber look. "We expected you to obey Abuji, always. You know how wrong it was to open that chest, don't you? She watched for some sign of contrition. "This behavior makes us sad. How could you do it?"

"Oh, Ohmanee, I just had to see what was in there. Then I only wanted to taste one, so I'd know what it was like."

These last words he spoke in a low voice, looking up at her with his bright eyes. Eyes that pleaded for understanding, forgiveness. And what else? Indulgence? Perhaps the clever boy knew she would yield to her tender feelings for him.

"I had to know," he added with a slight smile.

"In the future you'll be better off with some wisdom here." She tapped his forehead. "Think before you decide there is something you must know about the next time you're tempted to explore. Think! And above all, always obey Abuji."

Jae Yun nodded, serious, his eyes intent on her face. "I will," he promised.

But she wondered.

Sun Yi began to despair of Hae Yong's returning in time to prepare the evening meal. Late in the afternoon the girl finally appeared, out of breath. Her long braid swung back and forth as she hurried along the frozen path and her moon-shaped face was agitated, as Sun Yi had never seen it before.

"Forgive me for being late, mistress," she panted. "It was impossible to leave my home sooner. Halmoni was talking to my father and I had to wait until she finished."

Into Sun Yi's mind flashed a vision of that old woman, so old that her face bore more lines than a spider's web, who had sat wordless during her visit.

"Halmoni told Abuji that I must be allowed to go to school! She insisted that he give his permission. It's because she asked the mudang," she explained in response to the silent question on Sun Yi's face. The girl smiled in triumph. "Halmoni brought the mudang to our home to perform a kut, to relieve it of the evil spirits. She asked the shaman what must be done to restore peace within our walls. The woman told her that I must be allowed to follow the path intended for me."

Hae Yong's smile now was conspiratorial. "Halmoni told me that she wants me to have a different life from hers. She thinks that the world is changing and I can have a better future than anyone in our family has ever had. But only if I go to school!"

Sun Yi thought she'd never heard the girl speak this many words before in an entire day and when Hae Yong stopped to catch her breath, told her, "This news pleases me more than you can know. But what did your father reply?"

Hae Yong looked at her mistress in surprise. "Why, there was nothing for him to say. Halmoni is his elder. He will follow her wishes in every way."

"A hard winter is over
Where are the bitter winds now?
Distant hills are bathed in fog.
The mild air is still.
I will open a door and admire
The morning dyed by the spring mist."

Sun Yi recited the words of the poet Yun Son Do, written three hundred years earlier, to her sons. The lines sprang from her memory and onto her lips when she first looked out on this bright morning in the early spring of 1934. Such a joyous emotion spilling from her heart surprised her.

Four years since Han Ju's departure and all she had received in that time were some occasional cryptic messages. She buried this sorrow among her others, deep beneath the surface layers of events that preempted daily life.

A skylark cried its song into the pale sunlight. She called for her sons to listen with her, laying her hand on the silky hair of her eldest. Jae Soon, twelve years old, was nearly as tall as she was.

"Do you both realize that we are living in a most special time? This is yundal, the extra month that comes only once in three years by the lunar calendar. It's a time when we can expect good fortune for the special tasks we must do." She did not add that yundal was also the period considered most auspicious for the preparation of burial clothing. She would not burden children with such notions on this glorious morning.

"Is that why we are going to the temple today?" asked her elder son.

"And why we are taking our kites to fly?" asked the younger.

"Yes, to both of your questions," Sun Yi replied, smiling broadly. And because your father must rest, for a day at least, from his labors, for once, she added silently. "Are you ready?"

"Oh, yes, we've been ready for hours, Ohmanee." Jae Yun turned to her with shining eyes.

She believed him, for this nine-year-old was always eager, restless, unsatisfied. He'd anticipated this holiday from studies, an opportunity to explore the country he could glimpse only on clear days, when the distant peaks seemed close. She understood his feelings all too well.

"Then run and tell Abuji we can leave." She went into the kitchen to be sure the girl had packed the food they would need for the journey.

A bus transported them from Shunsen. It moved slowly along the winding road, as the way grew steeper. Sometimes all the passengers left it and walked up the slope, waiting at the top for the laboring vehicle, with its engine in the rear belching smoke from the charcoal fire, to catch up to them.

Even the bus went no further than an outlying village. From that place they walked, but the trail was often used and easy to follow. The two boys led the way. Sun Yi slowed her pace to stay beside her husband. He enjoyed pointing out the sights to her. The green shoots of winter barley pushed up on the high ground and everywhere signs of spring were abundant. Magnolias brightened the hillsides, wild-flowers of every shade blooming among them. Streams in the gorges and valleys overflowed with the clear water from melting snow.

She smiled at him. Together they watched their two sturdy sons hiking in lockstep up the slopes of Mt. Sorak.

Farther on the white ribbon of a waterfall plunged over a steep precipice and crashed into a fine spray on rocks below, where it bubbled over the stones in a stream bed. The forest was silent except for the chattering of their sons and occasional loud cries of the cuckoo birds. After some time they reached a clear meadow high in the forest where they stopped near a stream. It was time for the mid-day meal, but first the boys must unfurl their kites and test the wind. The brothers had constructed them during the long months of winter, making strong designs with the rice paper, hardy enough to withstand the tugs of fickle air currents.

Sun Yi rested, leaning against a tree trunk, watching the three playing out their lines. This day was a sliver of perfection. Every aspect was ideal, the temperature balmy but the wind sufficiently brisk. No one became overly tired during the long climb, and best of all, she thought the serenity she observed on her husband's face had erased all the lines of concern. If this day could last forever!

Later, when the lengths of string were reeled in and the last rice cakes eaten, the four of them resumed their walk, this time close together. Their destination was a Buddhist temple called Sinheung Sa. It nestled on the eastern slope of Mt. Sorak, facing the sea. A quiet haven for monks withdrawn from the world to perform meditation. The boys stayed close to their parents as they approached the contemplative atmosphere of the shrine.

"This may be the oldest Zen Buddhist temple in Asia," their father instructed, and the boys' now solemn faces reflected their respect for the venerable site. He told them that this ancient monastery was first constructed in this remote place almost thirteen hundred years before, during the Silla dynasty that nourished Buddhism. Throughout the Confucian Yi period afterward the temple was allowed to retain its unique character.

A fir tree lined path, paved with cobblestones, led the way to a structure of warm brown wood, modest in scale, with upturned grey tile roof. From the bluff on which it stood there was a superb view of the surrounding crags and peaks on all sides. The outside roof beams of the building were painted in intricate designs, blues, reds, and greens, all entwined in a floral motif.

The interior offered even more intriguing examples of artistry.

"Look, Abuji!" his younger son cried out, forgetting the reverent silence about them when he entered the building.

Two images of the "crazy idiots of the Seventh Century", Han Sup and Sup Duk, were portrayed on the northern wall, larger than life, their faces absurd and grimacing.

"What does it mean, Abuji? asked Jae Soon, puzzled.

"They are warning us not to be overly serious about this world," his father explained. "They are laughing at the absurdity of existence."

Both boys nodding, pretending to understand.

Sun Yi thought, yes, I must remember that.

The fantasy, a combination of shaman, Taoist, and Buddhist imagery, with creatures, half tiger, half leopard, writhing dragons, cranes, bats, was painted in brilliant colors on the ceiling.

Later Sun Yi and her family found lodging for the night in simple accommodations provided by the monks. Early in the morning they awakened to the sound of a bell tolling, breaking the silence of the dawn.

During their return, as they walked down the mountain, Jae Yun discovered some nesting swallows. Sun Yi smiled to herself at this happy omen. No one else was yet aware that another child would soon join their family.

Suddenly she realized that she was now like most of her country-men, finding her happiness in the small joys of her own family, thoughts of protest long grown quiet. Her greatest happiness was that her husband seemed recovered at last, filled once more with the vigor of spirit she loved in him.

Such an irony it is, she thought, that life continues in this way, despite the terrible years we have lived through. The Japanese took over our country twenty four years ago. That is most of my lifetime. No one can tell when, if ever, they shall leave us alone. Conditions for most of us have done nothing but worsen. We have learned to swallow our fear. Kobul mok simnida. We carry on. We survive. We create a new generation. For what? Shall they know better times? Will any of them stand up to the oppressor as we once did? Do we want them to?

Sun Yi recalled the words of Dr. Lee yesterday, when he explained the temple images to their sons. What did he tell them? "They are laughing at the absurdity of existence." Perhaps that was the best way to think of this time. Change, after all, was the one constant idea. Surely the future years would bring a better life.

Part Four
1937 to 1944

*G*reta Garbo, six times larger than life, stared down at Sun Yi. The colorful poster was attached to the wall of a five story building on one side of Chong-no, the main thoroughfare in the Korean district of Seoul. "Queen Christina" was playing at this theater. See it now! the bold black characters urged.

"But it's not Seoul now, Ohmanee," Jae Soon protested, when she spoke to him of the city they were touring together. "You must be more careful. It's called Keijo. Every place in this country has been renamed in the Japanese language. You know that. If you continue to use the old names you will be reported." He guided his mother through the throngs on the crowded sidewalk. "Life will be easier for you here if you do nothing that will call attention to yourself."

Sun Yi stopped look up at her eldest son. He was warning her how to behave? This young man, though only seventeen, was taller than his father. The close cropped haircut proclaimed his status as a student, as did his dark blue suit with high buttoned collar and visored cap. The small emblem pinned to his jacket indicated the name of his school. Kyunggi. Her face flushed with pride once again when she looked at it. He was now a part of that illustrious institution, just as her young brother Han Ju had been.

She'd missed her son's lively face. How many months since his last visit to Chunchon? All right. Shunsen. Now she'd see it every day. Was she really back in Seoul? She looked around her. Motor cars, busses, trams roared past. The few years brought great change to this city.

Time after time Dr. Lee sought permission to return. She'd nearly given up hope. The notice came suddenly, just a few weeks ago, and she told him, "I'll not accept the fact until we're on the train. Maybe not even then. Suppose someone changes his mind. That's quite likely, isn't it?"

He shook his head. The hair at his temples was silver and he moved more slowly. "This time I believe them. I've earned their trust."

"Well, you certainly should," she replied, thinking of all his years of devoted care for the poor provincial farmers of Kangwando.

With the aid of his brother, Dr. Lee established a small hospital in the northern suburbs of the now sprawling city where he could practice medicine and provide a home for his family. He would live in peace, for he was considered reformed of his rebellious fervor. The aid he gave to members of the underground movement had never been discovered.

So here she was, walking with her son on a public street of Seoul, an act she would never have dreamed of doing eight years before. How the place had changed! No one noticed her. The sea of white clad figures swept past, each one intent on some private purpose. Street noises drowned further conversation. Chong-no was paved but among the modern vehicles she noticed an occasional ricksha and sometimes a heavy wagon pulled by stolid oxen. A man wearing a chige laden with straw baskets jostled her arm, while another man followed, a dozen or more small tables stacked in a pyramid and strapped to his back. Women with infants tied to their backs pushed her aside.

"Thank goodness! There's the East Gate! I still recognize that. I think I've had enough sightseeing for one day. Could we find our way home now?"

"I was intending to take you to Kyongbok Palace first," he replied, sounding disappointed. "It's quiet there and the flowers are in bloom."

Jae Soon was more familiar with his home city than she'd ever been, she thought, following her son. Of course. He had the privilege of a young man to roam through it freely. Some things never change.

They stepped off the crowded streetcar near the Governor General's Palace, seat of government under the Japanese. The granite building was massive, with columns and steps of Korean marble. It dominated the slope before the mountains at the northern edge of the city. Behind it, nearly hidden, stood the centuries old home of Korean kings, reflecting unchanging permanence. Its upturned roof, once thought to be a means of keeping bad spirits from a home, framed the scene with its graceful lines. The drooping branches of aged willows and alders surrounding the lotus filled ponds and winding canals whispered of eternity.

"At least they left us this," she noted. "There were so many more of these lovely pavilions once."

Mother and son crossed a bridge and found a low platform in the Summer Pavilion where they could rest. Pools of water reflected the azaleas, in shades from palest pink to rose and scarlet. Few others strolled the paths here. There was a sense of solitude even though the bustle of the city could still be heard.

"You must see great changes," Jae Soon said, breaking the silence.

"Of course. New buildings, more people. But the real contrast," Sun Yi replied slowly, "is, to me, not so easily noticed. Our language, for example. It's gone. All the names, every place, every building, even the direction. Even our own names have been changed to Japanese! They've finally succeeded." She thought of that book buried on the hillside in Taegu. Would she find it there still if she were to look?

"Your father often reads the poetry of Goethe to me. The poet has a way of saying what I feel. 'Give me another tongue and you give me another soul' That is how I feel. And there seems to be so little opposition"

"No one dares to reveal his true feelings to anyone else," he reminded her.

Sun Yi looked away. "Perhaps it is true. We have another soul." She paused. "You know that the newspaper has been suspended again?"

"Yes, I heard." He nodded. "Not because of what is written in it, this time. Just as another way of discouraging use of the Korean language."

"That may be. It means, also, that only those persons who can read Japanese have access to a paper now. There is no other way for us to learn of the outside world."

"Have you forgotten my radio?" Jae Soon's eyes held a mischievous glint of light. "Others have them as well."

"Oh, that. Well, all I can say is that you'd better be careful not to get caught using it."

"I know as well as you that such things are forbidden to us, but I also know how to protect myself." Jae Soon was quiet for a moment, then added, "Be sure you tell Abuji. He should, also."

Sun Yi found that the quickened pace of city life, together with the increased responsibilities of supervising a large home, left her little time to think of the past years. But one evening as she glimpsed the sight of a full moon rising she felt an unexpected nostalgia for the country home near Chunchon. She recalled a similar night not long before her leaving, when she'd stepped out onto the maru to watch the glow on the horizon.

Though the night breezes of early April were warm she wore a shawl of light silk and as she stood by the railing the moonlight shimmered on the silver pinyo that she wore in her sleek, still dark hair. It held the knot at the nape of her neck in the nanja style. Her eyes followed the narrow valley from one end to the other and the words of the classic sijo, written by a kisaeng of the early Yi dynasty, came to mind.

> Night draws near in a dead village,
> A dog barks far away
> I open the cottage door and see
> The chilly sky, the moon like a bright leaf.
> Be still; stop barking at the moon
> Drifting, asleep over the bare mountain.

It might have been her home that Ch'on Kum was describing, this scene, so familiar after eight years of living through its sweltering heat in summer, the clear light of autumn, the frigid blasts of winter. Truly this was her home. Now another spring was returning and she was leaving it.

As if to remind her of this, a warm breeze brushed her shoulders. Yet she shivered and pulled the shawl close about her slender frame. A shadow of a cloud passed across the moon, bringing promise of rain by early morning, the "plum rains", soft and gentle, that would water the fields where the green spikes of winter wheat and barley were poking upward. The irrigation ponds would fill, slowly, and farmers would know that the harvest could be fulfilled this year.

"Of every three harvests, one is good, one is fair and one is poor," was the ancient way of foretelling the cycle of the seasons. Surely, this year the harvest would be bountiful. There! At last she thought like a countrywoman!

But she would not be here to see it.

She would miss the sound of the cuckoo birds and the cries of the ploughmen to the oxen as they guided their wooden plows across the pockets of flat land between the hills.

I've become a part of this land, Sun Yi realized. Perhaps I've forgotten how to live in the city. I'll have to learn all over again, just as I did when I was newly married. But we'll be all together. No more of those too brief visits from her older sons.

How difficult it had been to let them go. First Jae Soon and, a year later, Jae Yun, left to live with the grandparents in their Seoul home, so each could begin his high school studies. Jae Soon was a solid, sturdy boy while his younger brother had grown tall and thin. Such opposites. Yet they were inseparable, just as she'd wished. That was the reason for sending the younger one to join his brother after they'd been apart one year. They needed each other more than they needed their parents. How sad that Jae Yun had not been able to follow his brother to Kyunggi. She still could not understand how such a bright child could fail the entrance exams as he had done. Jae Yun had to settle for a lesser school.

A dog barked in the distance. Just as in the poem, Sun Yi realized with a shiver, turning to go inside.

Later, while she tucked her babies into their sleeping quilts, she remembered once more how fortunate she was to have them after all of this time. A second family. Her daughter, Jin Sook, was sweet. Timid, though, for four years. Perhaps the city life would change that. Jae Wan was too young yet. He'd never remember this country place. Neither of them knew their elder brothers. So many years between them. But that, too would change when the family was reunited.

But she'd miss the life created here in Kangwondo. Organizing a cooperative group for the farm wives of the nearby villages had been her best idea. She helped them learn how to market the handcrafted items they made so well. How proud these simple women became when they began to earn their own money! Hae Yong's mother would carry on her work, though. Fortunately it was well established.

Yes, it was a propitious time to leave. She'd see the same moon in Seoul.

"Where is Abuji?" demanded Jae Yun.

Your father has taken this holiday to meet with his friends," Sun Yi replied to her fourteen-year old, attempting to sound patient. "They're dining at the Full Moon Restaurant."

She tried to calm her third son long enough to fasten his jacket. It was the fifth of May by the lunar calendar, Tano Festival, and she was dressing the younger children so all of them could visit the Biwon. the Secret Garden on the Changdok Palace grounds, to see the cherry trees in blossom.

She knew the meeting was nothing more than an excuse. He was meeting his compatriots in Chon'dogyo again. He'd been back no more than a few months and he was involved once more in dangerous, illegal acts of patriotism. What could she do but to preserve the outward appearance of innocent revelry? Meanwhile, she'd enjoy this day of brilliant skies and unseasonable warm weather with her children and friends.

Kim Tai Un, still a teacher at Ewha University, was to meet them at the palace gate. Jae Soon, also, promised to be there.

Jin Sook teetered as she took hesitant steps, reaching out to her mother. This special hanbok made her self-conscious. "The silk is stiff," she complained.

"Yes, but you look so pretty, just like a real lady."

She did, thought Sun Yi. The miniature chima and chogori of vibrant red, yellow and green stripes contrasted with her glistening hair, worn in a long braid flaunting a red bow at its tip.

Jae Wan equaled her brilliance with his embroidered vest and the striped sleeves of his jacket, though he looked bewildered by the commotion around him.

By the time the four of them reached the Palace both Kim Tai Un and Jae Soon were waiting by its massive gate, the Tonhwa Mun.

"I'm surprised to see that hasn't been torn down like everything else," Sun Yi told her friend. Although it had been restored several times since its construction in 1405, the carved wooden structure was still impressive for its artistry and great age.

Once inside, they saw the entire range of gardens, radiant with pink and white blossoms. It was, truly, a masterpiece of the landscapers' art, with most of the curved paths bordered by cherry trees in single or double rows. Most were pink like the Japanese species but some varieties introduced from the wilds of Korea bore blossoms of pure white. Crowds of people roamed in every direction, the children's bright colors bobbing among the white clothing of their elders. Here and there families sat on straw mats eating their picnic lunches.

"It would be wonderful to see this in the evening when all of the trees are illuminated," Tai Un whispered, as they stopped to admire the beauty of the scene. "I have been told there is no finer sight, even in Japan, than this vast garden when all of the colored lights in the trees are glowing. Even that lovely pond is brightened by the concealed spotlights." She gestured toward the nearby stream from which divided streams of water gushed below an artfully arranged rock mountain.

Sun Yi had to smile at her enthusiasm. Tai Un, with her unquenchable spirit, was her true friend. She had never forgotten, during all the years of exile, to write notes of encouragement with her news of events in Seoul, sending parcels of small necessities and a few luxuries never found in the outlying province. She had not changed in spirit or appearance. Her gentle face with its delicate features was as unlined as a girl's. The dark hair, parted in the middle, was pulled smoothly back and fastened with a jade pinyo. Only her lively eyes, in which the sparkle could not be concealed, betrayed her attempt at sedate conformance to propriety.

"You're very quiet today," Sun Yi murmured to her son, stepping back to speak with Jae Soon as they continued to stroll the paths. "Something is wrong, isn't it?"

"You always seem to know what I'm thinking," he accused, but he tried to smile. "It's the new school schedule. We learned of it only today. Military drill and training will replace all classes. With the war in China continuing, more soldiers are needed, and that is what the school authorities intend to make of us."

Korea had fought no wars, except to defend itself, since 1592, when the Japanese, under the leadership of Hideyoshi, laid waste to their land for six years before Korean forces drove them out. The Hermit Kingdom earned its nickname by shunning contact with the world outside its borders after that time and, with the protection of its powerful neighbor, China, managed to avoid warfare. Even the soldiers who guarded the palace were few in number.

But when the strength of China ebbed Japan and Russia jousted for control of Korea, while some Americans also assessed the strategic value of this country. Korea became, once more, a shrimp caught between whales, and opened its doors to Westerners in 1882 with the signing of a friendship treaty with the United States. In came missionaries, teachers, doctors, and the message of Protestant Christianity to end the long isolation.

Unnoticed by his mother, Jae Yun hovered nearby, listening to her conversation with Jae Soon in the Secret Garden of Changdok Palace on that bright spring day. He shivered with fear when he caught the words "military training" and "no choice." Was he also to be caught in this net, like the tiny silver fish he had once watched fishermen scooping from the sea? Their words drifted away with the breeze and he heard no more of them, but already his active mind envisioned a scene.

Both he and his elder brother traded dark student uniforms for the ill-fitting clothing of a soldier. The arms they shouldered were no longer wooden sticks but real rifles, with hard, shiny barrels.

No one in her family had ever had to be a soldier.

Jae Yun knew that even when the Tonghak forces had tried in 1894 to reform the government only a fraction of the people were involved in the fighting. Now, he thought, we are ruled by Japan. Our peninsula points like a dagger toward it, and we will be a base for its power, a stepping stone while the Japanese reach out to conquer other lands.

This year, 1938, with a war in China well underway, the military machine demanded more men, more equipment, more supplies.

Jae Yun knew, also, of the fine new roads being built in such a hurry, of the railroad lines splitting his country. Koreans, moving slowly in their timeless costumes of white, had no need of these. It must be only for the fast transport of troops and the furnishing of war that each mile of road and track was laid with the sweat of forced Korean labor.

And he wondered how long it would be until he was among those men moving north.

The Lee's new home was in a small town called Uijonbu, about twenty miles north of Seoul's center. Uijonbu was a pleasant spot. Sometimes called "City of Ever Righteousness, it was in a broad and flat valley wedged between the rocky, harsh looking mountain, Tobongsan, on the west and the curved and flowing lines of Suraksan to the east. A commuter train stopped at a station nearby and both boys rode it to their schools in Seoul each day.

The spacious house wrapped itself around various courtyards where azaleas, lilacs, wisteria in shades of lavender and a profusion of other shrubs bloomed throughout the spring and summer. Dr. Lee's share of the family inheritance, waiting for him when he returned to Seoul, had made its purchase possible.

A separate wing extended from the L-shaped main building and this he used as his hospital. It was far larger than any he'd had in the past, so he hired a young doctor to assist him. He had a staff of six trained nurses as well.

Shortly after their arrival Jae Yun overheard his mother telling her friends that his father was content at last, performing the work he liked best. She said he'd cast all thoughts relating to the political situation out of his mind. The boy knew this was not true, yet when he listened to the sounds of the flute drifting across the courtyard at the end of the day he heard the soft and muted tranquility of its tones in contrast to the strident urgency of the past years, and he wished to believe his father had reached a state of peace.

On a morning soon after the day of the Tano festival Jae Yun was dressing hurriedly for school when Sun Yi came to his room with a note in her hand.

"Come and take this message to your father. He's in the hospital already."

"Yes, Ohmanee," he responded obediently. But he found it necessary, suddenly, to search for a schoolbook, and minutes slipped by.

Sun Yi appeared in the doorway again. "This message needs to be taken to your father now."

"I'm looking for my mathematics book. My train will leave soon."

"That's a good reason to do as I ask you right now," she told him.

"I hope I won't miss my train." Taking the folded slip of paper from her hand, Jae Yun walked slowly along the maru, his footsteps hesitating even more as he neared the hospital wing. "There'd better not be one there today," he said aloud, "or I'm not going inside." He looked at the paper in his hand and realized it was no use. He'd have to. He must find his father and give him this. He looked down the length of the maru again. The place might be empty. No, it wasn't. He could see the narrow table at the end of the corridor. There was no mistaking it. He began running as quickly as he could in the loose houseslippers before his fear overcame him, running softly, silently, until he passed that table with its bulky shape outlined under the draped cloth.

Not looking back, he slid to a stop at the entrance of the room where his father was peering through a microscope. "Abuji, Ohmanee sent this message for you," he panted. "He knows," thought Jae Yun, when he saw his father looking up at him, his eyes keen and observing.

"How can you become a physician like me if you behave in this manner?" he asked, taking the note from his son.

"I'll be late for school." Jae Yun inclined his head, bowing with quick, ducking motion, and darted out of the lab. He ran even faster back down the corridor this time. I'll never be a doctor, he thought, knotting his hands tightly at his sides. I don't want to see blood and pain and death.

He snatched up his satchel, heavy with books, and threw in the tin box that contained his lunch, then, stopping only to exchange slippers for shoes at the door, ran all of the way to the station. He swung onto the last car just as the train pulled away, a motion perfected from daily practice.

With his hair clipped short and his immaculate suit of closely woven blue cotton, Jae Yun was the picture of a model student. No one would ever guess the promise that he was repeating to himself as he sat down. I'll never become a doctor, he thought, over and over. Let my brother be the one to carry on. Looking down, he saw that his dark shoes were covered with dust from the run. He looked for a place where he might buff them unobtrusively, but the seats were of wood and the floor composed of only a thin layer of tin. Nothing to be done about them now.

Leaving the train when it reached the city, he hurried toward school. On a corner of the busy street two young men looking not much older than himself blocked his way.

"What's your rush, school boy?" one asked.

Jae Yun gave him a scornful glance. The uniform he wore was loose and too large, but he swaggered with the importance of his status as a policeman, and prevented him from moving on.

"I can arrest you for running on this sidewalk." He poked with his club at the satchel Jae Yun carried.

"I'll walk," Jae Yun muttered and attempted to pass by. He knew better than to provoke these bullies. When the officer attempted to stop him again a word from the companion turned him back to his post. Young toughs, he thought, walking on without looking back. There's no hope for any of these country boys. They come to the city with no schooling and take these jobs since there's no other occupation for them. Then they think they can use their raw power to push the rest of us around.

The school day seemed longer than usual since he'd begun it in such an ill humor. In class Jae Yun could not concentrate.

"Student Lee," commanded his teacher in Japanese history, "I have called on you twice to answer the question. Are you sleeping?"

Jae Yun looked down the length of the room toward the direction of the teacher's voice. There were nearly sixty young men sitting at high wooden desks in straight rows. His was located near the rear. "I apologize, teacher," he replied. But his mind still drifted.

By the time of final dismissal he was reluctant to return home directly. He decided instead to walk about Seoul, for the spring days were growing longer and the day still seemed early. When he finally looked at a clock he realized abruptly that the last train would soon depart.

Sprinting, Jae Yun pushed past the clusters of people in front of shops. All of the cars were crowded. He squeezed into the last one just as it began to move and found himself packed in, unable to find a seat until many of the passengers reached their destinations.

Finally sitting down, he became lulled by the monotonous swaying of the cars and could not keep his eyes open. Buildings and fields swept past in a blur. His head fell forward onto his chest and he slept.

He was marching and there were other boys on all sides of him, marching also. "Where are we going?" he asked one. No one answered. All kept moving forward, in step with a strange rhythm. To Jae Yun the cadence was saying, "To war, to war, to war." The chorus repeated, in tune with the rocking motion of the train and the sound of its wheels. He spotted the boys he'd encountered this morning on the street at the front of the line. Still dressed in those ridiculous uniforms, they were now prodding everyone to keep moving. All of the marchers seemed to be, like him, students. The police urged them forward, striking any who stumbled or failed to keep step. Jae Yun was tired. He must stop soon. How long would he have to keep walking like this?

With a jolt the train stopped. Such relief. He could rest now. There was silence and he was alone. Alone? Where was everyone? He stood up and looked around the car. It was empty except for him. He peered outside. All was in darkness and he recognized nothing. No town. Not a sign of Uijonbu. Was this part of his dream?

A lantern casting a dim yellow light swung from the rafter of a rough timbered building near the track. That must be the station. No other building in sight. Only open countryside. Did I come to the end of the line? No one saw me sleeping on this bench.

Jae Yun sat down again. He was famished. He remembered the tin lunch box and opened it. Only one small rice cake remained. He swallowed it greedily, then wondered why he'd eaten so much at lunchtime when, it seemed now, he had not even been hungry.

Well, this train went back to Seoul in the morning. All he had to do was stay on and ride back with it. If there was only some comfortable place to lie down. The wooden bench at the front end of the car was longer than any of the others so Jae Yun stretched himself out on it, using his book bag for a pillow. He almost fit.

He wondered if he would be missed at home. Ohmanee was so busy with those two young ones. Sometimes she didn't even see him in the evening. Perhaps she would not even notice his absence. Still, it would be pleasant to think that he was the cause of some concern. He closed his eyes and slept.

The chill of the morning air woke him. Jae Yun shivered and tried to roll over before remembering where he was and why his arms and legs should be so stiff. He'd lain on this cramped, hard bench all night long. His stomach rumbled and ached with emptiness. His own fault, everything. If it were not for his foolish carelessness in falling asleep during the ride home he would be lying in his own soft, warm ibul right now, and Ohmanee would have a fresh, delicious smelling breakfast of steaming rice and hot soup ready for him.

He stood up, stretched, then brushed futilely at his wrinkled uniform. There was nothing to be done now but to stay on the train and return to Seoul, back to school. He wished he might send a message to his mother, but he could think of no way to accomplish that while so far out here in the country. And he dared not miss school. Again he looked outside. Wide, flat fields on all sides, as far as he could see, dewy green in the morning mist. Small houses with thatched roofs clustered as if offering protection to each other. How quickly the city disappears, he thought. Surely it is no more than an hour's ride from our capitol, yet all I can see is the quiet countryside. It reminded him of the home in Chunchon, peaceful and unchanging.

"No! I can't sell you a ticket. Why can't you understand? Stubborn old woman. Go away!"

Jae Yun jumped down from the train when he heard the harsh voice shouting from the crude ticket office nearby. What could be causing such an outburst? He found an old woman standing before the agent, her head downcast, while he berated her. She was dressed in the white hanbok and she held a small parcel, knotted into a scarf, close to her frail body.

"What's wrong, halmoni?" Jae Soon whispered in Korean.

When she raised her face to him he saw that it was creased with wrinkles and darkened by her years of exposure to the sun. Her sparse gray hair was twisted into a braid at the back of her head. Looking both surprised and grateful, she spoke softly. "They tell me I must ask for my ticket in Japanese or they will not sell it to me." She shook her head slowly from side to side. "But I cannot speak properly in that language."

She seemed weary, though the day was still early. Judging from the layers of dust on her rubber slippers, he thought she must have walked a great distance.

"Don't worry, halmoni, he reassured her. "I can buy your ticket for you. Where are you going?"

Stepping over to the ticket window, Jae Yun commanded loudly, in Japanese, "Two tickets to Seoul for my halmoni and myself."

The seller complied promptly, as if he were grateful to have the responsibility removed from his shoulders.

Jae Yun carried her larger bundle, which was wrapped in a bit of coarse hemp cloth with the ends crossed and tied on the top so as to form a handle of sorts, and led the old woman to a seat. The engine erupted into an assortment of promising noises and the train started rolling. After she was seated he couldn't help but to glance at the bulky package he'd set at her feet.

Noticing the object of his attention, she asked, "Have you eaten?"

"I've eaten well," he told her, out of politeness.

But she leaned over anyway, and pulled a flat tray from her heap of possessions. Unwrapping several layers of rice paper, she removed a plate made of woven bamboo and gestured, "Eat."

The tiny rice cakes she offered were mostly barley, unlike the pure white rice he was served in his own home, but at this moment the barley tasted better. He couldn't remember when he'd felt such hunger. She watched him with her bright eyes while he consumed the entire plateful, except for one small piece that he left out of good manners. By the time he returned the container to her, with profuse thanks, the train was filling with passengers, jerking to a stop at each station along its route, then jerking to a start again. He had no further opportunity to speak to her as the aisles filled also, and the crowds jostled him. When the old woman left the train at a stop on the edge of Seoul he watched the small determined figure disappearing among the throng and wondered if she would find someone to buy her return ticket for her.

The sun was already high in the sky and the air heavy with heat when he arrived back at school to find to his great annoyance that it was to be a March of Flags Day. He had forgotten. Nothing to do now but to follow his classmates in their orderly procession to the great field in the center of the campus where hundreds of other students were assembling. Along with the others, he was given a small Japanese flag mounted on a bamboo stick when he passed through the entrance gate.

These ceremonies happened more frequently since the war with China began and he thought with annoyance of the way in which this senseless activity replaced his really important classes. He dared not speak his thoughts aloud. Who could tell which of his classmates might be an informer, eager to make points by reporting his lack of patriotism? There were many people forgetting what it meant to be a Korean. They rejoiced in the victories of the Japanese as if each was their own. After thirty years of domination the illusive dream of a free Korea was becoming a lost hope.

Jae Yun remembered that day last year, in July of 1937, when he first heard the announcement of the beginning of Japan's war with China. An excited newsboy was jumping up and down, shouting at the same time, "Special news! Read all about it! Japan at war with China!" Since then the patriotic ceremonies dominated the lives of all the school children.

The first day of each month, for example, was set apart for exercises intended to inculcate this patriotism. Early in the morning, before classes began, everyone assembled in front of the Japanese Shinto shrine to bow and pray for Japan's victory.

Now, he thought, another of these March of Flags days is about to begin. Well, let's hope this one won't last all day.

Speeches from the loudspeakers blasted his ears. All around Jae Yun the other boys stood in close formation on the field where on a better day they'd all be playing soccer. Instead they responded to the exhortations with the appropriate songs and phrases they had been required to memorize. The tirade continued for an hour or more. Next the students in charge led him and the others through the main streets of Seoul where as many people as possible would see and hear them. They waved their flags, chanting songs of victory, pausing before each government building to shout, "Banjai, Banjai!"

Jae Yun had to run to keep in step and not lose his place in the line. As he went on he felt more and more exhausted. He'd slept poorly and had nothing but that poor woman's rice cakes to eat. Now he dared not stop or even to slow down. The June day was growing warmer. Perspiration streaked his face. The visor of his tight cap stuck to his forehead like a steel band. He must keep moving. He would show no weakness before those who commanded him.

Weary, he moved like a robot as the parade continued, down one street, around the corner, and onto another avenue, noticing that the way was lined on either side by rows and rows of his countrymen. A sudden revelation struck him. Was it possible that all this pageantry would remind each Korean he was nothing better than a slave under these Japanese?

He recalled the time, two years earlier, when the Olympic competition was held in Germany and a Korean man won first place in the marathon. Only most people thought he was Japanese, for he wore the uniform of that country. Then, at the time for awards he tore off his shirt in defiance and there, underneath, he wore another shirt. The flag of Korea was emblazoned on it. It was an exciting moment. Everyone he knew expressed pride in the defiant spirit of this champion. He spoke for them all, rekindled a patriotic fervor that hadn't been seen for a long while. Could that spirit, the desire for independence that obsessed his parents, live again?

If that were true, he'd be willing to march all day.

But he didn't have to. The students were dismissed at last and he drew upon a final reserve of energy to make the dash to the station. This time he would not miss his train! Even the hard bench in the swaying car was a comfort after his day of constant motion. Jae Yun looked at his shoes. Their brilliant shine was no more. Both were scratched and scuffed, covered with dust. His uniform, immaculate when he started out yesterday, was a mass of wrinkles, spotted and stained.

But he was almost home.

Jae Yun met his elder brother inside the gate.

"Has everyone been looking for me?"

Jae Soon was sitting in the courtyard with his back to him. Without turning around he asked, "Looking for you? Why should they?"

"Well, I fell asleep on the last train when I was coming home last night," he rushed to explain. "I didn't wake up until it stopped at the end of the line. By then I was far out in the country and it was nearly dark. I had to stay there until morning. There was no way to send a message from that place, you know."

"To tell you the truth, younger brother, I don't believe anyone here even noticed you were gone. Far more important things have been happening."

"What do you mean?"

Jae Soon shrugged impatiently at his question. "Many of father's friends were arrested yesterday. That is what I mean."

"Not father!"

"No, luckily. But both our mother and father are working frantically to get them out. They're talking to everyone they know who could possibly be of influence. You see, the prisoners are in West Gate police station."

"West Gate!"

That was the worst in Seoul. Well known to specialize in the questioning, meaning torturing, of suspected members of the underground. A place where Korean patriots were beaten and worse, and often by their own countrymen, Korean detectives who collaborated. Such men operated without remorse. They outdid their usual tactics of cruelty when they seized a person of higher education, especially one who had studied in the United States. More than one suffering victim jumped to his death from the upper windows of this prison. He knew it took more strength of courage than most people had for a man to survive the confines of West Gate unbroken in body and spirit.

"I didn't know," Jae Yun said, turning away.

He felt crushed. While he had been so concerned for his own welfare, thinking of his empty stomach, sorry to miss one day's meals, even while he was marching through the streets of Seoul singing those idiotic songs and parroting the praise of Japan's victories, those friends of his father, the gentle, white haired Dr. Koh, dignified Professor Song from the University, and Mr. Roh, who always had a special friendly word for Jae Yun whenever he visited. These good men, and others, were suffering more terribly than he could even imagine.

"But why?" he managed, finally, to ask.

"It is because` of that organization. Tong-U-Hoe. They're all members. It's charged it was promoting special education and training for young Koreans, training that does not fit the aims of the Japanese Empire. Every one of them is charged with subversive activity. Father says he was told they must be imprisoned as a "precautionary measure.""

As the brothers spoke thunder reverberated ominously outside their house. Soon rain fell. Fat, heavy drops of water. Its tempo increased until the downpour cascaded through the streets, forming deep puddles in the courtyard. Monsoons of summer were beginning. Through the humid heat of July and August rain would fall often. The Han River would rise, its banks, denuded of trees, crumbling before the torrent, filling the homes of the poor who lived near with debris laden silt, flooding the carefully tended fields of young rice and vegetables.

As the river spread over the lowlands, creating destruction and famine in its wake, so the fear of subversion flowed unchecked through Korea. The rising tide of paranoia engulfed anyone who dared to speak or write an independent thought or disloyal idea.

Jae Yun rose to shut the gate against the violence of the storm but as he could not muffle its sound neither could he alter the course of events that caused everyone to fear for his survival.

In the next few years conditions of life became increasingly difficult. The few American teachers and missionaries still remaining in Korea were forced to leave as tension between Japan and the United States grew. Korea became even more vital to the support of its rulers, providing rice and other staples in addition to mineral resources for the production and maintenance of the war machine.

Military training instead of education was routine for Sun Yi's two elder sons. Her two younger children began elementary school knowing nothing but the constant indoctrination. Each morning they stood at attention and shouted three times, "Ten no hei ka ban zai!" "Hurrah for the Emperor!" Students who wrote the most strident essays condemning Americans earned prizes. Patriotism was rewarded. The title of "hero" was bestowed on any youngster who reported his parents' unfaithfulness to the Emperor.

Gradually parents came to limit communication with their children to the most perfunctory and mundane topics.

We never discuss any matter of true importance with our children any longer, Sun Yi realized one day. Is this to protect them? Or to protect ourselves? No matter. There is a wall between our generations now. And where will such habits lead this family that once was so close?

Jae Wan, returning from school, burst into the house on a winter day the year that he was six, eyes bright with excitement.

"Look, Ohmanee!" he called, hiding his hands behind his back.

"What is it?" she asked, willing to play his guessing game.

"A rubber ball, Ohmanee." Triumphant, he brought out one hand on which he held the toy, small and red. It bounced hard when he threw it onto the floor. "Everyone in the first grade got one!"

"Careful," she cried, and thought, it's a strange gift when little rubber is available for even the household necessities during these days of war.

As if in answer Jae Wan assured her, "There'll be lots of rubber for us from now on. The Emperor sent us a message. Now that we have Singapore in the Empire there'll be lots of rubber for everyone. Even for toys." He bounced the small hollow sphere with both hands, up and down, up and down, until she wanted to cover her ears.

"What is Singapore, Ohmanee?"

Outwardly life continued in its calm and traditional pattern. Seasons passed, rice was harvested, though most of it was shipped away to feed the armies, and Sun Yi supervised the making of kim chee each autumn. The large wagons creaked their way to the kitchen gate, laden with cabbages, just as in her childhood years in Kyongsangdo.

Yet change, imperceptible at first, affected her life. There were the buckets of sand and water. Each day she checked them herself, to be sure they were still near the entrance and properly filled. No one could predict when a policeman would set a fire in the street, just to test the vigilance of this neighborhood in controlling a sudden blaze.

A special entrance to the basement was excavated in the rear of the house. All the people in her household rushed in through it to take swift cover whenever the siren sounded for a practice alert. There were days when the entire family sat for hours in the crowded and dimly lit shelter, waiting for the sound of an all-clear signal, though no air attacks happened.

By 1944, when Jae Soon was a grown man of twenty-three and Jae Yun, twenty, both were students at Keijo Imperial University. By luck neither of them had yet been drafted, although they still drilled and trained each day after classes ended. The two of them lived much of the time in a small home owned by their family that was close to their school.

Sun Yi and her two younger children remained in Uijonbu, some twenty miles north of the capitol, where Dr. Lee continued to care for patients in his small hospital.

Kim Tai Un, who was still teaching at Ewha University, appeared there one day in July. It was a rare visit. Sun Yi hadn't seen her in months. She was shocked by her appearance. Tai Un had always been slender but now she was almost less than a shadow. Flecks of silver glinted in her dark hair. Was she being deprived of proper food? Sun Yi knew she'd never admit to it. And she realized how fortunate her family had been, so far. Dr. Lee was well rewarded for the almost indispensable role he filled so they'd suffered less than most from the shortages of wartime.

"I have a busy schedule. There isn't much time for anything but my work," she explained after Sun Yi led her into the garden. "But I had to see you before I leave."

"You can talk here, if you keep your voice low," Sun Yi assured her. "No one will overhear us. Where are you going?"

"The school is closing. My life will change completely," her friend announced in a whisper.

"Closing! What do you mean?" In her surprise, Sun Yi spoke out loud. "What will become of you?"

"We've just held the final graduation ceremony. No one knows when the school will reopen. I've seen it coming," Tai Un declared. "When the national emergency began we were informed there'd be no time for study of anything but subjects related to achieving the final victory. No music, no literature, or other such impractical subjects." She was silent, reaching out to touch a flower on a nearby branch. She pulled it toward her, inhaling the fragrance of the crimson petals. "What's this, a Rose of Sharon? Are you looking for more trouble?"

"No one will find it here," Sun Yi protested, "and it gives such lovely color to my garden. Why should a flower be banished?"

"No reason that I know of," admitted Tai Un, "except that our national flower happens to be a symbol, not just a simple blossom," she warned, allowing the branch to snap back. "A remembrance of the time when we knew who we were."

"But what of Ewha? What is happening there?"

"Well, first the four-year curriculum was reduced to one year. The only subjects offered were those considered appropriate for women, cooking, sewing, childcare. No more chemistry, biology." She sighed. "I began to feel quite useless. Now even that pitiful program is ended. However I am still needed. In fact, a new regime is designed for me. I am assigned to teach in a rural school, just as my students have been."

Sun Yi shook her head. "I don't understand. What can someone like you do in the country?"

"It seems the young, uneducated women in the villages are creating great confusion for the authorities. They can't handle the web of rules and regulations they must follow to produce quotas of food for the military. You know most of the young men aren't there. They're all in the army. So people like me are being sent out to every small settlement. 'Women's Training Schools' they're called, a way of quickly educating those without skills. We of Ewha, students and teachers alike, are to be the instructors."

"Incredible! For how long? Surely the university will reopen for the fall session."

"No one can tell when Ewha will open its doors again."

Sun Yi watched with a feeling of horror as Tai Un's face crumpled with a look of sadness, resignation, anxiety, perhaps even hopelessness. She wanted to comfort her. But what could she say? She'd never sensed this despair in her friend before, no matter how bad conditions were.

Before she could speak the bang of a door interrupted their conversation. That noise was followed by quick footsteps and muffled giggles. A young voice cried out.

"I'm first."

There was a protesting howl and the rippling melody of a scale played on the piano.

"Those children!" Sun Yi exclaimed. "Wait a moment while I speak to them."

Tai Un followed and peered into the room. A girl about ten years old, tall and slender, sat before the keyboard, her hands raised to play. Her glossy black hair was swept back in a single braid that bounced up and down over her white chogori as she energetically fluttered her graceful fingers bringing forth the rhythm of continuous arpeggios.

Jae Wan stood beside her, scowling. The eight year old's plump cheeks grew rosy as he fumed, "You always practice first! It's not fair. We should take turns."

Seeing his mother enter, he gave her a quick bow of greeting, then spoke again before his sister could say a word.

"I want to play the piano now, Ohmanee, so there'll be some time to meet my friends for a ballgame before the evening meal is served. Sister always gets here ahead of me. It's not fair!"

Sun Yi placed her hand gently on his shoulder and looked down at his pouting face. This youngest son of hers managed to get his way most of the time. She must be careful not to indulge him. She was tempted, for he knew how to charm her.

"If you want to be first you should come straight home after school." She gave the warning with a shake of her head.

"It isn't my fault that I'm late today," Jae Wan replied. "The teacher said I didn't bring enough dry weeds to school this morning. She sent me out to gather more."

"Dried weeds?" Tai Un's puzzled expression begged for explanation.

"Come along." Sun Yi led her son outside so Jin Sook could continue her practice session without distraction. "It's for the cavalry horses. Haven't you heard? All the school children bring grass and weeds to school each day now. When their collection is sufficiently dried it's shipped by train, to help the army." Seeing Tai Un's incredulous face, she suppressed a smile. Turning to her son she told him, "Go out to play now. Practice later."

Tossing her a grateful look, Jae Wan slipped away almost instantly.

"We do try to keep the children's lives as simple and happy as possible. Not easy in these days." The two women resumed their stroll along the garden path. "It's best for them if they are told nothing of our past troubles. Yet you can see that they are drawn, constantly, into the war. That boy was awake at five this morning so he could attend a fencing practice before school began."

"Fencing?"

"Well, it's called that. The children attack statues made of straw. They're named 'President Roosevelt' and 'Prime Minister Churchill'." She shook her head again, this time with sadness. "They don't really understand. There is so little real learning now. Why, last week his class was sent out to sweep the city streets, for all the street cleaners have been conscripted. Imagine! Next month, which should be a vacation for them, will be used instead to help with the gathering of the harvest. What can we do?"

Arm in arm, the two friends walked in silence until they heard someone entering through the gate.

"Why, it's Jae Yun!" Sun Yi cried.

Tai Un also brightened at the sight of the child she'd always favored. Meeting him today was an unexpected pleasure.

As if to confirm her thoughts, Sun Yi told her, "He's sometimes here on Sundays, when he has no classes but today is the middle of the week. Is everything all right?" she asked, turning to her son.

"Hello, Auntie," he greeting his mother's friend, ignoring his mother's question.

After exchanging a few more words Tai Un left them, promising that she would call on Sun Yi once more before she left Keijo.

Then Jae Yun led his mother into the middle of the garden and said softly, "Ohmanee, I came here especially to talk to you."

"Why did you leave the city on a school day?"

When Sun Yi turned to look at her second son she thought how tall he was suddenly, muscular and well proportioned. He'd always been thin, as if thought and motion consumed all his energy. He was handsome. And intelligent. His eyes flashed, sparkling with intensity. Only the student haircut, close cropped, detracted from his appearance. No longer required to wear the uniform of a high school student, he managed to look both relaxed and confident in his western style suit. The collar of his shirt was frayed, however, and a frown crossed her brow when she reached out to call his attention to this detail.

Jae Yun chose to ignore the remark concerning his shirt. Instead, he returned to her earlier question.

"Drilling, marching. That's all I missed today."

He went on, complaining that he could no longer use his record player. "Someone had a poor idea that a bamboo needle will replace a stylus of metal. It just doesn't work."

"Well, you should know there's not a sliver of metal left in this entire country by now," Sun Yi reminded her son. "There's no spoons in the kitchen, no rings on our fingers, no flagpoles on the buildings, no metal runners on the stairs, not even a nail to hold two boards together. Every piece of metal was collected long ago and transformed into weapons." She had to smile. "Someone warned me last week that it may soon be a mistake to open your mouth when you laugh. You will lose the fillings from your teeth if you let them be seen." Then she added, more seriously, "Besides, you know the playing of western music is no longer allowed. What do you want to play?" She sensed that his complaint about record needles was frivolous.

Jin Sook was still playing scales. The sound of the piano, muffled, came to them from the ondol room.

"Now." Sun Yi turned to her son, demanding, and "Tell me the real reason you are here today."

It was Jae Yun's turn to smile, briefly. He recognized her usual astute summary of a situation.

I suppose I came to say farewell, just as Ewha Auntie did."

When he heard her sharp intake of breath his words spilled out.

"Everyone in school is being called for military training. Soon I'll be drafted with the others." The young man turned to his mother, his eyes fierce, blazing with anger. "I won't go! I've thought this through and through. I can't become a part of the Japanese army!"

Helplessness swept over Sun Yi. She wanted to sit down, but she would not allow her son to see her weaken. If only she could still protect him as she had when he was a child! She would do anything, almost, to keep him in school until the war ended. Anything to prevent his joining that parade of disappearing faces. The tide of war would drag him along with all those others who did not return.

"I'll join the Russian army."

His words, harsh, ripped across her thoughts.

"If I have to fight, it will be against them, not for them."

Impossible, she thought. How can you? A thousand revulsions sprang to her mind as she clutched, horrified, for alternatives. Then she heard her own voice, a calm voice, asking, "How can you? The Japanese control the entire border area, all of Manchuria and North China, now."

"The Russian army has troops stationed just across that border, at the northernmost part of Korea," he replied.

Was that true? There were rumors, she knew, that Russia might attack Japan. Any Koreans who managed to cross over and reach their forces would be welcomed.

"You know, I've heard that there are already many Koreans in the north, serving in the Russian army," he was saying.

"Of course. Those who fled our country years ago." She'd heard this herself, of those whose only path of escape, when their land was taken, was this northward route. The same was true of the rebels, the guerillas who schemed and planned endlessly about taking roles of leadership when Korea became independent again. But was her own son to become one of these hopeless souls?

"I'll not turn traitor like Han Ju!" Jae Yun spat out these words.

"Han Ju! Have you heard of him?" Sun Yi trembled with a sudden chill, though the day was warm.

"He's in the Japanese army, isn't he?"

"You're only guessing. You don't know that."

Her brother had left years earlier to study in Japan. He'd come home at first, but only for brief visits. He passed the Japanese Higher Civil Service Exam after completing university studies. That much she knew. But no more. He must have stayed in Japan, or surely she'd have seen him again.

"The truth is, my son, that no one knows where Han Ju is," she told him sternly. "No one in our family, not even his mother, has heard a word from him since the beginning of the war with America. He may be in the army. He may not be. He may be. No one knows," she broke off, "but until we do know you should never, never consider your uncle a traitor."

This matter brought only pain. Nothing to be achieved by dwelling on the unknown. But what could she say now to this son? He was always stubborn, determined. How could she hold onto him, influence his mind? Wasn't he, after all, much like herself in the early days? She could not blame him, but only hope to guide him.

"You must have patience and confidence," she began. "Think of your family, of your future. Without education you will have no opportunity in this country. I believe," she added after a moment of thought, "that there is little time left for this war. Do you know how desperate they are? Little children collect seeds from the poplar trees so their silky fiber can be substituted for cotton in making explosives! How long can an army survive when it is relying on our young ones to supply materiel?"

She saw him begin to shake his head in disbelief but continued, warning, "This may be one sign, only one small sign, but I am sure it is an indication of fatal weakness. There is little time left for this war. I am sure of this. Promise me that you will wait a little longer before you try to leave us."

But when Sun Yi looked up at this tall young man she saw impatience reflected in his eyes and she knew that he'd already made his decision. The tears welled deep in her own eyes but she turned away, unwilling to allow him to see her, for this last time, crying.

Part Five
1945 to 1949

On the morning of August 15, 1945, Jae Wan rose sleepily, as usual, and after eating his breakfast met two other boys outside the gate of his home. Together the nine-year-olds walked to their school near the center of Uijonbu, chattering companionably as always.

To their surprise, however, when they approached their classroom, a teacher directed them, instead, to the auditorium. The large amphitheater was already crowded with children, all talking in soft but excited tones. Even the first graders were joining in.

Their Japanese teachers stood at the sides of the room, silent, waiting. For what? Then Jae Wan noticed a woman near him crying. An extraordinary sight. He could not take his eyes from her face. What could be causing such outrageous behavior? Even he knew how to control his emotions in public.

The principal stepped up to the speaker's podium and a hush of silence followed.

In a moment he began, "His majesty, the Emperor." His voice faltered and all the boys looked at this man, feared until this moment of weakness.

He started over. "His majesty, the Emperor, is calling a temporary halt to the war. In order that our soldiers may rest. It is true that a new kind of bomb has been dropped on some of our cities in Japan by the Americans. It has had a great and deadly effect. However," he continued, his voice rising, trembling, "we shall continue to fight to the last man! Do not be discouraged by this temporary cessation of the war."

Then he walked away, out of the room, his back to the children and his head bowed.

Jae Wan looked at his friends. Their faces reflected his own bewilderment but, true to their training, the boys began to follow the others out of the room in the usual orderly procedure even though no one was guiding or watching them. A sudden voice burst from a loudspeaker dismissing the students.

As if it was a signal, everyone began talking at once, standing in clusters, asking questions in loud, excited voices. Questions that no one answered. Then, realizing that there really would be no classes, they rushed into the street.

It was already filled. With Koreans. Jae Wan had never seen people in such frenzy. Some of his Japanese classmates were asking, "What does this mean? Have we lost the war? What will happen to us?"

Their answer resounded all around them.

"The war is over! The war is over! Korea is free! Free!"

Flags waved from doorways, banners that Jae Wan had never seen. Every Korean person seemed to have one, not the emblem of the rising sun, but with a circle that was divided into red and blue on a background of white. There was a design of black bars in each corner. What was it, this strange new flag, and where had so many of them come from suddenly? Never had he seen a flag waved with such exhuberance.

He was afraid. Inching forward, he tried to edge toward the fringe of the crowd. In the wild excitement hundreds of bodies surged forward, pushing, shoving, moving, always moving. And he was carried by the motion. He lost sight of his friends. In a few moments he felt himself squeezed up against the wall of a small shop. He stopped resisting and allowed himself to be swept along with the current of humanity.

At last he saw the gate of his own home and struggled, shoving cautiously and steadily until he was freed from the tide. He collapsed inside, breathing in ragged gasps. He was exhausted and confused. Why was everyone cheering? Were they happy to lose a war? Hadn't all of these people been shouting support for the emperor until this moment? Why, then, were they elated by defeat?

Though he could not know, the events Jae Wan witnessed in the streets of Uijonbu were being repeated in every town and village of his country at that same moment. Like champagne spurting from a bottle as the cork is freed, so the spirit of every Korean, no matter whether wealthy or poor, burst into a long suppressed display of joy. Smiles wreathed faces long unpracticed. Joy, incandescent, intoxicating. It flowed as if from a bottomless spring. All day long and into the night people paraded, sharing their happiness with strangers, waving their hastily constructed signs and banners. Hundreds upon hundreds of Korean flags were pulled out of hiding to wave and whip in the free air. Newspapers that had been forbidden, silent for years, appeared in almost instantaneous editions.

Liquor vats were opened and those spirits flowed freely as well.

But there was another emotion that day, and in the days to follow, and it could not be contained. Revenge. The hated Japanese must leave. Anyone suspected of collaborating in any way must be punished. In the initial fury few thought of the future, of who would operate the mines without the Japanese supervisors, who would guard the streets without the police. For as long as anyone could remember, all of these matters were performed with efficiency by the Japanese bureaucracy. Their martinets would leave. Most were packing right now. But where would immediate replacements, trained and responsible, be found so life could continue?

Meanwhile, the Japanese, nearly a million of them, had a different kind of worry? How would these Koreans, whom they had dominated for so long, treat them now?

Jae Wan was home for only a short time when his sister arrived. Her story of the morning was much like his. Throughout the afternoon he watched as the building next door filled with new arrivals. It was a spacious house, often used as an inn for travelers, but how could it hold all these persons? Most entered reluctantly, forced by Koreans in the street who suddenly took charge. By evening he heard the din of voices inside.

Only a high wall separated it from his home. While he looked at it and wondered a familiar voice called to him from the other side.

"Jae Wan! Jae Wan!"

"Toshio!" He ran closer and saw his school friend. "What are you doing there?"

"We're prisoners," the boy called down. "We're not allowed to leave and there's nothing to eat. I'm starving."

"You just wait. Don't go away. I'll bring you something."

Jae Wan dashed toward the kitchen. To his good fortune there was no one there to question him. He rummaged until he found some cold rice left from the midday meal, some pickled vegetables, and after some searching, a handful of dried cuttlefish. It was his favorite snack. He packed all of this into a tin lunchbox and rushed back to the wall. He couldn't climb up so he tossed the box to Toshio.

"This is all I could find," he told him. "I'll bring some more tonight."

Later, as it began to grow dark, he packed some of the food from his evening meal and again fed his friend.

Now the last slivers of daylight slipped from the summer sky. Almost midnight. Wednesday, August 15, 1945, was nearly ended. Jae Wan lay on his ibul, shifting restlessly from side to side. He tried to find a comfortable way to sleep but that soothing state eluded him.

He had had a terrible day. Now his damp cotton shirt stuck to his slender chest, causing more misery. The air was still humid, though the intense heat of day was subsiding.

He had just rolled over once more, trying to find a comfortable position for sleeping, when the glass of the window above him shattered. He heard the thud as some object landed nearby on the straw floor mat.

Jae Wan leapt up. More breaking sounds of glass splintered into the silent layers of darkness. Then, a different sound. Loud voices. Shouting. An angry roar. And cursing. Words never heard in his mother's gentle home.

He ran to the window, pulled back when he felt the jagged bits that framed the opening. He peered through, shading his eyes as if to bring the scene into sharper focus. He saw the blurred outlines of many figures in the dim light, filling his courtyard and spilling into the street. How many? There must be hundreds. The crowd grew larger while he watched.

What's happening? Why are those people on his land?

Turning away, eyes wide with fright, he ran out onto the maru that bordered the inner courtyard. Jin Sook emerged at the same time, her long braid swinging. The two nearly collided. She grabbed his hands and clasped them tightly, asking, "Tell me, brother, what is happening?"

He could not speak. He only shook his head. The din grew louder. Brother and sister clung to each other, unable to move.

Swift footsteps.

They both turned toward the sound. It was their tiny housemaid. Abandoning her usual slow shuffle, she swooped down to gather one child under each protective arm.

"Sh-sh," she warned as she guided them toward the air raid shelter beneath the house. They'd never used it except in practice. On the way they passed the entry leading to the front gate and he saw his mother standing in it. Alone! Sun Yi stood erect, facing the mob. Their shouting was louder now. She clutched the folds of her long white chima and held her head high.

Jae Wan had no more chance to question the commotion, for the maid pushed him down into the dark room beneath the house. She pulled the door shut and the three huddled in the cramped space together. For some time the only sound was his sister's sobbing but he heard his heart thumping and tried to calm the rapid beating of his heart by taking shallow breaths. Finally he spoke and his voice came out in a husky whisper.

"Why are those people around our house? Why are they throwing rocks and shouting?"

"They are angry because they say your family helped the Japanese," the maid told him, hesitating before repeating the dreadful accusation.

"We never did!" Jin Sook, shocked out of her crying, retorted.

"They say your family had everything while their children were hungry. They say you go to Japanese school so you must be friend of Japanese," the maid continued.

"You know that's not true, don't you?" persisted the girl.

"Who listens to me?"

The maid was interrupted by another crash of glass. The shards of a bottle scattered on the tile roof.

Jae Wan himself had no answer for these charges. He felt confused. How he wished his mother and father were here to help him to understand. But Abuji had left in a hurry after the evening meal, saying he must meet with his friends, and he'd not returned though it was late now. Ohmanee was standing alone, confronting these shouting faces. His elder brothers were absent also. Jae Soon lived in Keijo where he taught at the university, and Jae Yun had been gone for months. He'd crossed the Yalu, they said, and traveled north, away from his country. Since his departure Ohmanee looked sad most of the time. She seldom smiled, even to him. Jin Sook was with him, of course, but she was only a girl even though she was older. He would have to take care of her as well as himself.

"Can't we open the door just a sliver. I can't breath." Jae Wan pushed the handle. But he heard the sounds of the angry mob rising and falling, and an occasional crescendo of breaking glass above the din of voices, and he shut it with a tremble of new fear.

"Don't worry, little brother. Ohmanee will know what to do."

Jin Sook was patting his hand. She'd stopped crying. Now she was trying to comfort him !

"Remember how she spoke to your school principal last year when he had you beaten?"

He did remember. Sun Yi had been so outraged that she'd gone to the office of the Ministry of Education in Keijo with her complaint. Within a few days a new man took the place of that one. After that he believed his mother was capable of controlling any situation. But this time there were many persons against her.

Jin Sook continued, as if she was telling a story, speaking in her soft voice. "Ohmanee will never allow anything bad to happen to us. She always knows what to do. When the girls in my school see her at the gate they always say, 'Oh-oh. Here comes Jin Sook's mother again.'"

Jae Wan had, meanwhile, thought of an answer to the maid's accusation. "We go to the Japanese school because it is the best one." His voice was defiant. "Ohmanee says we must always have the best school."

Now here he was, growing stiff and tired from crouching in this hole in the ground. What could be happening to his mother? Hours must have passed since he and Jin Sook took refuge. More glass shattered and rocks landed with dull thumps on the grass outside. He tried to stretch his stiffened legs and thought, all at once, of the food packages he'd tossed to his friend earlier in the day. Could that have caused this trouble? Was it possible that he was responsible for the hostile crowd venting its anger on his family's home?

At the time he did it, helping Toshio seemed like the only thing to do. It still did. But his stomach grew queasy when he realized that his good intention may have brought on disaster. Perhaps someone, a guard, in that house had seen the food and questioned his friend about its source. But why should a boy suffer? Toshio was a child like himself, a classmate, someone he played soccer with after school. He'd done nothing to deserve the punishment of hunger.

Somehow, Jae Wan thought, if only he could talk this over with Ohmanee. everything would come out right.

Sun Yi rushed out to the front at the first sounds of shouting, not considering the danger. Now she stood on the steps above the gate, alone, while in her outer courtyard and beyond it as far as she could see into the street, figures clad in white surged in the shadows.

Stones landed on either side of her. A voice shouted.

"Go inside! Women belong inside!"

Another, more distant, astounded her. "Destroy the pro-Japanese! Betrayers of the people!"

She a pro-Japanese?

Indignation rose within her, surmounting her terror, fueling her will to resist. Imagine the boldness of these hooligans! Entering her home without invitation! Calling out these proposterous accusations! She would not turn away.

Another stone slammed against the side of the house and she raised one hand high. Her long full sleeve cast an arc of white in the darkness. She heard, vaguely, a scuffling behind but did not turn. It must be the children. She'd had only a moment to summon the maid, to bid her to look after the children. Now she must confront this mob without distraction.

All men. There would be no women, of course. They had a better sense of proper behavior. She must become the master. But how would she force them to listen? Where was her husband? He should be home at this time of night. He may be an important leader but I need him here, now. What would he do? A man knows how to placate ruffians.

Beads of perspiration formed on Sun Yi's forehead, beginning to roll down her cheeks. Hastily she brushed at them, then realized that her entire body was bathed in sweat. Be calm. Be patient. Be dignified. The thoughts flew through her brain. Yes, she could be all of these but even more. She would show no fear.

The mob still swayed and jostled but few stones were thrown. Each moment seemed to last an hour. Voices, lower, called out. Vile words.

Sun Yi remained still, her feet in their slippers planted firmly on the top step. Once again she was pleased with her height, for she was as tall as most of the men who confronted her. With the additional advantage of the stairs she created the illusion of towering over them. Thus far none had dared to approach any closer than at the beginning.

Perhaps, if she could single out one person, she might breach this barrier, this human wall that threatened to engulf her. She wanted to remind each man that he was still responsible for his own actions, not part of a mechanistic monster, unthinking and unfeeling. She leaned forward, peering into their upturned faces, and recognized the shopkeeper who sold her many daily purchases.

"Why, Mr. Ahn," she began in a voice gentle yet intended to carry beyond his ears. "What brings you here tonight? You should be celebrating with your friends. Today is a time of happiness for all of us. This is no occasion for anger."

He appeared to be startled by her recognition, her direct question, her quiet words. Good. Instead of replying he turned away, shriveling, drawing himself in as if he resisted being singled out.

Sun Yi, boldened, continued, speaking to another who stood close to him. "Why aren't you at home looking out for your family? Instead, you disturb an honest man's rest with your noise and destruction."

She hoped no one would notice the tremor of her voice. This second man also shrank back upon feeling the probing of her gentle words addressed directly to him. Her confidence surged, freeing her from apprehension. Recognizing another face, she called, "Mr. Shin! How is your wife? Did the medicine that the doctor gave you, without charge, cure her ailment?"

Stung by the reminder of the largess received at this gate, Mr. Shin turned and began to push his way through the throng as though he would hide his shame. Several others turned to watch him retreat and then, with hesitant motions they also began to weave their way backward, searching for an opening in the press around the gate. Then the crowd gave way, others assuming there must be some good reason for the exit of these men.

Elated, Sun Yi spoke to some of the men nearest her. One, she knew, made great profit by selling his ware to Japanese clientele at inflated prices. Then, to another, who dealt in antique art objects that he was always willing to part with for sufficient compensation, she managed to convey her contempt by reminding him of his practice.

The voices subsided into a low murmur as men watched their leaders disperse. There were still many crowding, pushing outside. Danger was not yet ended. She could not relent in her efforts to deflate their anger. What was it that caused men to behave so differently in a mob than they would when alone? Each of them, she knew, was kindly and helpful on an ordinary day. Now good sense left their heads. Why, they moved like the legs of a centipede, repeating the motions of the one in front, never missing a step, as if each had no head!

Somehow she must hold back this human tide, must show them how mistaken they were in attacking her family. Yet who would listen to a rational explanation? It was easy to find someone else to blame for life's misfortunes. Much easier to destroy than to work and build together. They were caught up in the feverish heat of raw emotion, finding an easier path by allowing themselves to be captured by this force, asking no questions, wishing no answers, desiring only to follow someone who made decisions for them.

Sun Yi continued speaking in a quiet, pleasant, yet authoritative manner, almost as if she was their hostess, to each of these neighbors poised to destroy the sanctity of her home. She controlled the tone of her voice, never raising it though sorely tempted, but allowing it to carry clearly to each listener. Somehow she covered the sound of fear and anger that was shaking her inwardly. To each one she gave a reminder of some small way in which he had profited or been protected under the regime that was ending, until each man, humbled by her persistent needling, turned in shame to depart in haste.

At last the crowed diminished, some perhaps disappointed at the failure of the promised excitement to materialize, others unwilling to press forward without a leader, still others beginning to admit the shame of their action.

Finally Sun Yi stood alone on the stairs. The moon was rising. She saw the solitary gate etched in its pale yellow glow. The scene was peaceful, bewitching. Had all of that turmoil really happened? She was still there when her husband arrived.

Startled by the unexpected sight of his wife, Dr. Lee rushed to her. "Yubo! What are you doing out here? Alone, in the middle of the night!"

When she tried to speak she found her tongue reluctant. Would he actually believe that her speech alone was sufficiently powerful to turn away the wrath of angry men?

Puzzled by her silence, disturbed by her distress, the doctor guided her inside.

Then she remembered. The children! Where were they? They must be frightened. But she found them in their rooms, safely asleep. The maid had cared for them well.

"I thought you'd never come," she said to her husband at last, and then the words spilled out. She described what she'd tried to do and he listened, then reached out to her with comforting arms.

"The meeting went on for hours," he explained. "I had no idea what you were enduring. We're all worried. How will we keep peace and order now? What happened here may also take place everywhere."

"What can be done?"

"We're trying to organize a provisional government that will include all the factions, from left to right. But we may not have enough time. Russian troops have already come over the northern border."

"Is that true?"

"Yes, and they're moving quickly. Pyongyang is already occupied."

Her son! Where was he? She asked the question silently. Aloud, she said, "But what of the Americans? Won't they have a part in this occupation?"

His answer came wearily. "The Americans are supposed to arrive soon but no one seems to know when. We've heard there's some confusion as to which of their armies will be sent. At any rate they'll probably supervise only a small part of Korea, in the south. It doesn't matter. None of these foreigners will remain long. You can be sure of that. Soon we'll take control ourselves. Remember that message? The one that was smuggled in by the provisional government when the world leaders met in Cairo two years ago?"

"Of course. Who could forget? My copy's nearly worn out, I've read it so often. In it they promised to make Korea independent immediately when the Japanese were beaten."

"Yes, it rekindled our hope," Dr. Lee reminded his wife. "When we heard those words we knew that the world had not forgotten us, even after all these years."

While her husband spoke, describing his expectations for their future, Sun Yi still trembled, even with the lulling sound of his voice. He noticed and drew her to the shelter of his arms. There he comforted her throughout the remainder of the night.

But the new day dawned in pale light before she could surrender to peaceful sleep.

The Cairo Declaration of 1943 had, in fact, used the English phrase "in due course" when it referred to Korea's independence. It was in the translation by the Korean Provisional Government that it came to read "immediately."

But Sun Yi and her husband did not know that. Like most of their countrymen they assumed that Roosevelt, Churchill, Stalin and Chiang intended Korea to become independent when the Japanese were defeated. What else? Now that the war had ended it seemed logical for them to cooperate with the incoming military forces that they believed were on their soil only to help Korea to establish its own sovereignty once more.

Just five days earlier, five days before fighting in the Pacific ceased, lights had burned late in the Pentagon on the banks of the Potomac in Washington D.C. as Truman's advisors conferred. The man who had been President of the United States for less than four months knew the end of the war was imminent and he faced a multitude of decisions, all crucial.

Among the many was the question of Korea's future now that its oppressor was defeated. The phrase promising independence "in due course" was undefined. No one among the military leaders knew when or had even given serious thought to the issue.

Some, including W. Averill Harriman and James Byrnes, argued for a greater commitment in Korea while others, led by General George C. Marshall and the Joint Chiefs of Staff, displayed a lack of interest in the about-to-be liberated country. They did agree that Korea must be divided between the Russian and American troops for the purpose of accepting the surrender of the Japanese there. The question had not been discussed at the Yalta conference. So a compromise was in order.

Two colonels, Dean Rusk and C.H. Bonesteel III, were sent to another room to select the line that would be practical from a military standpoint. Rusk and Bonesteel looked over the map and returned with the recommendation that the 38th parallel, a short distance north of Seoul, looked like a fair place to draw the line. In that way the Americans could be sure the ancient capitol city would stay within their perimeter.

So it was done.

Major General John R. Hodge was a tired man. He'd led his troops in the successful attack on Okinawa, one of the final battles of World

War II, and now he looked forward to his return to the United States. Other orders came instead.

"The 24th Corps of the 7th Infantry Division will proceed to Inchon, Korea, to accept the surrender of Japanese in the area south of the 38th parallel."

Code name of operation: Black List Forty.

General Hodge was not the first choice for this assignment. General Wedemeyer had been considered because of his familiarity with the Far East but he was needed elsewhere. General Stillwell was highly recommended until the Generalissimo Chiang Kaishek vetoed the presence of his arch enemy so close to the border of China. Hodge offered none of their expertise. His advantage was based solely on proximity. Okinawa is only six hundred miles from Korea.

The general was considered a tough man. He'd worked his way through the ranks without the benefit of West Point training. His brand of diplomacy worked well in the barracks and on the battlefield. When he heard these new orders he called an aide. "Try to find me someone who can speak Korean." There was no one. His troops had been trained to fight in the Pacific islands, not to occupy former Japanese territories.

The battle-weary 24th Corps landed at Inchon, the port city for Seoul, twenty miles inland, on September 8, 1945.

Hodge, meanwhile, ordered the Japanese general, Abe, to retain control and maintain order until the arrival of the American troops. Abe had been wondering how he would protect the six hundred thousand Japanese civilians under his jurisdiction from retaliation by Koreans so he was pleased to comply with this request. When he surrendered to Gen. Hodge he explained his predicament, then requested that the Japanese police be allowed to continue this role, fully armed.

"No problem," Gen. Hodge told Abe, and reminded his own staff, "I consider Koreans the same breed of cat as the Japanese. Treat them as conquered enemies."

Lee Jae Soon was deeply involved with his work of preparing and revising the chemistry curriculum for the change from the Japanese language to hangul, the Korean written language, when another young instructor at National University came to the door of his small office. The trim, wiry young man laid his steel rimmed glasses aside and rose to greet his colleague.

"Aren't you coming with us?" Rhu Bong Hae asked.

"Are you sure it will be safe? You heard the announcement. The Japanese police will shoot any Koreans seen on the street today."

"How can they do that? They lost the war, didn't they? They're just bluffing."

"You can't be sure, They might still try."

"Oh, come along. You don't want to miss the excitement. How often do American soldiers land at Inchon? Besides, I heard there's going to be a big group of important Koreans to greet them. We'll be protected by the crowd."

Jae Soon was easily persuaded. It was an historic day, and he wanted to be a witness to everything that was happening to his free country. In addition, he would be able to tell his mother about it later. She was always eager to hear the details of political developments. He followed his friend to the street, where they joined three other young men of his acquaintance and all of them crowded into a touring car of indeterminate vintage. Its frayed top was open to the air and its tires worn smooth.

"How are we going to get through the city streets without being stopped?" he asked, still wary about the entire undertaking.

"Leave it to me," his friend assured him, sliding behind the wheel. "I know the back roads all of the way to Inchon. We'll stay away from the main highway."

Jae Soon winced. He had a fairly clear idea of those "back roads." Unpaved, probably filled with deep ruts worn by the wheels of ox carts during the rainy summer just past. Still, the idea sounded plausible. He protested no further.

The deep blue sky of that September day was infused with a clear, warm light and when they arrived at the fishing port, covered with the dust of their detour route, all of the young men were in high spirits. No one had challenged their course of travel. Perhaps the warnings had been just that, Only a threat, one last attempt at intimidation. Leaving the auto parked on a secluded path near a fish warehouse some distance from the dock, they walked the remainder of the way.

"Look at that!" exclaimed Rhu as they turned the last corner. Even Jae Soon could not help giving a loud gasp of surprise. The troop vessel was the largest he'd ever seen and it was an impressive sight, even with its battle-scarred paint fading and peeling. It was anchored at some distance off shore in anticipation of low tides, though the muddy water lapped the docks now.

A gangway was in place at the dock but no one from the ship was yet in sight. On his left Jae Soon noticed the crowd, perhaps five hundred persons, waiting. All of them were in Korean dress and many carried bouquets of flowers. A few waved American flags that had the look of being hastily homemade. Others bore the distinctive white Korean flag with the divided circle, the yin and yang, red and blue. The entire group was cordoned off, a phalanx of Japanese police in uniform holding them back. Still, they were present. Apparently no official objected.

The Japanese authorities stood in erect formation on the opposite side of the pathway. ae Soon could see the gold braid on a dress uniform of one man who stood in the front rank. That must be the notorious General Abe.

A small boat left the battleship and steamed toward the dock. Martial music burst on the air and continued while a stocky man strode down the gangplank from the boat. That must be the American general. Hodge. He'd heard his name was Hodge. Jae Soon stretched to get a better view of the man they'd all been waiting to see. He was short, pretty much like a Korean, but his shoulders were thrown back, his head high.

A great cheer rose from the Korean delegation at the first sight of their liberator. The crowd surged forward spontaneously, waving their banners. This was a moment he never thought to see in his life-time. Too bad his parents weren't here to share it.

Shots exploded near him, at close range. Jae Soon leaped, turning toward the direction of the sound. The police were shooting! As he watched, white-clad figures crumpled to the ground, pools of dark blood spilling as they fell.

The pressure from persons in the rear continued to propel the people forward and those who were standing behind the wounded stumbled over them. A second round of shots spat from the rifles and more of them fell. The realization of danger struck everyone else at the same instant. They dashed in all directions, struggling to escape the next shots. Crushed flowers lay everywhere, mingled with the twisted shreds of bright colored cloth that had been flags waving proudly only moments earlier.

Jae Soon felt paralyzed. Horrified, he was unable to move. Then he was jostled aside by others fleeing and he lost sight of his friends. Shoved closer to the Japanese officials, he saw them still standing calmly in their places while General Hodge, also apparently oblivious to the carnage, continued the ceremony of surrender. His words were being translated to General Abe over the screams of the wounded. Jae Soon listened to him thanking the defeated officer for his effec-tive control of the mob. He praised the quick action of the police.

Astounded, Jae Soon thought, this is incredible. I must be dream-ing. Five bodies still lay motionless only a short distance from the general's feet. As the young man pulled back, stumbling, numb, and dazed, his friend Rhu grabbed him.

"Are you crazy? Let's get out of here!"

He guided a babbling and incoherent Jae Soon back to the automobile.

The five made the return journey in silence. No one complained as the vehicle bounced and jolted over the rough roads. Each was lost in his own bewildered thoughts.

So much had been expected of the Americans. Jae Soon's parents had always reassured him, telling of the teachers and medical persons they had known before the war, describing their kindness and generosity, their unselfish serving of others.

What happened? What went wrong? He must talk to his father. Perhaps Dr. Lee could help him to understand what he had witnessed this day.

Though the same high blue sky, hanuri nopda, shone over them, the world felt solemn and grey. A senseless flow of blood had drained the day of its color and joy.

When Jae Soon appeared at the gate of his parents' home on the following day, having prudently waited for the official curfew to be lifted, Sun Yi was not surprised. He came often in recent weeks. She looked for his visits, especially for the information he brought to them of the latest events in the political turmoil that had continued since the day of liberation. He had many official contacts among the persons he met in Seoul.

What never failed to surprise her, however, was his interest in his young sister, Jin Sook. For years he'd virtually ignored the child. After all, thirteen years separated them, as well as the distinctive differences of their gender. Now, each time he came to their home he took some time for a special conversation with her. Watching their two heads close together, Sun Yi was reassured that families ties remained strong. Perhaps the two had some common interest. After all, they were much alike, quiet and devoted to studies. Neither was energetic and mischievous as Jae Yun had been and as young Jae Wan still was.

But today Jae Soon did not ask for his sister. Instead, he went straight to his father. Their two dark heads, so much alike in appearance now that her son was grown, were bent close together while they talked. Their voices rose and fell in muted tones, making it impossible for her to hear the words, though she found numerous excuses to hover near their door.

Word of the shooting at Inchon spread quickly. Five persons died and nine more were wounded. It was an outrage and she knew all about it. Sun Yi suspected the event was the topic of their conversation. What she did not know, however, was that her own son had been a witness on the scene.

Time passed. When the hour for the evening meal arrived she brought their dinner in to them herself, hoping she would be invited to remain. When she set the low table between them they barely acknowledged her presence, so immersed were they in their own conversation.

She withdrew. I'll have to ask my husband about this later. He'll tell me, she consoled herself, and she continued to supervise the evening tasks of her household.

Fresh air. If only he could fill his lungs, just once, with pure, clean smelling air. Then he might survive, Jae Yun promised himself.

But there was no room, not enough space even to twist his body and strain his head upward, so crowded was this railroad car. It might have held about a dozen cows. Instead, there were sixty, maybe more, humans squeezed into it. Children crying. Old men cursing. Women wailing. All of them so closely packed, standing all through the night, breathing that fetid air.

All in the name of survival. Reduced to this common level of humanity, who could tell now who had been the doctor, the landowner, the minister, the shop keeper? The only goal for each of them was to escape, to cross the border into southern Korea.

Early in the morning the train stopped at last, and he was still alive. Jae Yun wondered at the sensation of pleasure sweeping over him. The rocking, shifting motion stopped and he could leap through the open door onto the solid ground. Even the tiresome waiting all day at the rail junction, waiting for another train to continue his journey south, did not fill him with despair. He walked, stretching his stride, breathing deeply, cleansing his lungs, before he lay down, surrendering to blissful sleep with the warm sun on his face.

Then more riding on another train, this one so jammed with anguished refugees that he climbed to the roof, clinging to the flat top of the car, grateful to be outside.

"Get down! Down! Heads down!" And he was filled with gratitude to that anonymous voice of warning when he saw the high-powered electric lines above him. He learned to duck quickly and cling tightly, pressing his shivering body close to the swaying car until safely past this deadly source of energy.

In the night, with the moon full above him, Jae Yun stared at the crest of the Diamond Mountains passing by. He had not realized his country could be so beautiful. If only he had someone to share with him the wonder of it. The wind cooled as the train climbed higher and the scent of the pines enveloped him while the craggy peaks rushed past. He was grateful then for the crush of bodies surrounding him, protecting him from the chill air.

On the morning of the second day the train stopped. It was not allowed to cross the border. Guards from the north barred the way. The end of the line, twenty miles north of the 38th parallel.

For the first time in more than four thousand years the land of Korea was divided.

The passengers stumbled, crawled, or leaped from the railroad cars. To be so close to freedom. No one would give up now, so close, no matter how weakened he felt. Dazed, Jae Yun found himself following an old man who had appeared, offering to guide some of them over the remaining distance. For now they must walk. During the day he shuffled in silence, reserving his energy. By nightfall a drizzling rain began, at first light, then more intense. Soon the earth beneath his feet was sodden. His clothes, covered with mud and sweat, stuck to his skin. But he kept on moving. Everyone did.

Without warning machine guns opened fire ahead of them. The Russian border guards! Jae Yun dropped into the mud, crouched against the ground, terrified. He inched forward. Think of it! To be shot by our liberators. The world was insane. Those Russians would do anything to stop people from running from them. Bullets hummed over his head and he moved closer to the old man.

"How far now, haraboji ?"

"One more mile," the old man answered. "Only one mile."

But the mile was uphill all the way. Good thing the shooting had stopped. Slipping back, falling, crawling forward again, somehow everyone with him reached the summit, encouraging those behind to continue. The old grandfather had warned them, "You must cross the border before daylight or they'll shoot you."

And the sky was lightening.

Another mile. The old man had lied. This one was downhill, still in the mud, slipping most of the way. The boundary marker came into sight and he and all of the others forgot their hunger, their exhaustion. They rushed into the clear, cold stream that flowed at the base of the mountain.

He washed. His face, hands, clothing. Bouncing up and down so the mud ran in rivulets. He was drenched, soaking wet, but he was free.

And almost home.

Sun Yi busied herself with the evening tasks while Dr. Lee and their eldest son continued to talk. Suddenly she heard loud noises. They seemed to be coming from the outer gate. Well, every strange sound startled her now, caused a shiver of apprehension. She did not think her neighbors would attack again. Good sense seemed to have returned to them. At least there had been no more threats or rocks thrown. The windows were repaired. Yet, there was this commotion.

The gate rattled. Loud pounding on it followed.

Was there no one else to respond? She'd take a look for herself. Lifting the folds of her chima, she tiptoed cautiously. Opening the small door in the center of the gate, she peered out. The man she saw standing outside was dressed in filthy clothing. She began to turn away in disgust from the face shrouded in a black beard, hesitating when he spoke. That voice!

"Ohmanee? Don't you know me? I'm Jae Yun. I'm your son. Please open the gate to me?"

Sun Yi flung open the gate and he stumbled in, collapsing onto the hard earth of the courtyard. She could not move him.

"Yubo! Yubo!" she cried. "Our son is home!"

At the first sound of her voice the doctor rushed to her. This was a miracle! Only with great effort did he restrain his emotion while he and his elder son together managed to carry Jae Yun inside. He trembled as he laid the weak body on a soft bed of cushions. He'd given up hope long before that this son would return, for he was aware of the hardships the boy faced if he had, in fact, made his way north to Manchuria or China, the terrible conditions of that life. He'd never told Sun Yi. Rebel soldiers lived in constant danger and privation.

Together they removed the filthy clothing, wrapping their child in a loose robe that soon became drenched with his perspiration.

He was alarmed but only told his wife, "Hunger has weakened him. Feed him a bowl of sungnyung. No solid food yet."

The hot tea brewed from crusted rice on the bottom of the pan was a nutritious drink. Sun Yi called to the maid, impatient to do whatever would help him. She could not take her eyes from him. He'd never sent a message or letter in all the time since his departure. She'd ceased to even speak his name, though she was tormented each day by memories of her son. She'd always nurtured, silently, a secret hope for his return.

No wonder he was nearly unrecognizable, thought his father, leaning over him once more. He'd suffered. Now he was matured, even aged. At once he wanted to forgive the boy for leaving without a word of request for permission from his father.

Sun Yi sat beside her son all during the night, half drowsing but refusing to leave, for his restless form was racked by shivers. She watched him turn feverish, then chilled, and realized he suffered from more than poor nutrition.

Malaria, the dread illness of the Korean countryside, infected his body.

"Isn't there something you can do for him?" she pleaded, rousing the doctor.

He gave him a dose of quinine. She watched Jae Yun swallow and was comforted.

"Now, just let him sleep," he cautioned.

Her husband spoke so calmly. She supposed he knew better than she. He was familiar with this kind of suffering. She felt each tremor of her child as if it shook her own body.

A breeze broke the still night but it was warm and brought no relief. She fell into a light sleep and dreamed they were still living in Kangwando. Jae Yun was a young child. He'd done a bit of mischief. Yes. What was it? Oh, yes. Now she remembered. He'd swallowed some medicine from his father's supplies. So much curiosity. That boy was always asking questions. Restless, always getting into something. They'd waited through the night that time, also, she and his father, watching with anxiety for signs of his recovery.

Sun Yi struggled to open her eyes, reminding herself that Jae Yun was now a grown man. Would he always remain a cause for their concern? She touched his forehead. The fever was still high and he slept restlessly, twisting under the thin cover, breathing in deep, ragged gulps, occasionally moaning.

There were many questions. Where had he gone? Why had he never sent word to them? Not once. What happened to bring him home in this frightening state?

He was drenched with sweat and she feared this would bring on even greater shivering. She replaced his cover with a dry one. If only she could do more!

With the first daylight he opened his eyes. When she saw him try to smile at her she was glad that she'd never left him. Somehow he began to look young once more, despite the beard.

"Had to come home," he murmured.

She patted his hand in understanding, then touched his forehead again. At last the fever was gone. He would be better for a day or two, at least, before the chills struck him again.

A tap at the door and the young maid brought in a small table with a bowl of warm water in which some grains of rice floated. Jae Yun's face brightened at the sight of the pure white rice. Its fresh aroma filled the room.

She helped him to sit, then waited while he sipped from the bowl. Surely his serving himself was a good sign. When he'd finished and the maid left with the table, he began to speak, slowly and softly. She bent to catch the words.

"It's good to be home once more, Ohmanee. There were times when I doubted I'd ever see this house again."

"You did not have to leave," she reminded him gently.

"At the time I did think I must. I still think I was right to go. Then."

"But now?"

"So much is changing, so quickly. I'm confused. I was not alone, you know," he protested, struggling to sit up.

Sun Yi slipped another cushion behind his back and he relaxed with a sigh.

"I had some names, some contacts to make after I crossed the border. That's when I discovered many others just like me, who thought as I did, that we could not further the conquests of the Empire and must escape to the north. At first we shared a strong sense of unity."

"Where did you go, then, at the first." She prodded him to continue but he was silent and she wondered if he was too tired.

He was, in fact, only pausing while he gazed at her face, and he said, "You haven't changed," sounding satisfied.

Sun Yi's sleek, still black hair was brushed back and tightly bound with the jade pinja that she knew was his favorite tucked into the knot at the back of her head.

"When I left home I went first to China. In Linch'uan, I'd been told, I'd find a branch of the Chinese Central Military Academy where Korean patriots received training. We were called "The Glorious Recovery Army.""

The name made both of them smile.

"Later some of us went to Sian. There the American general, Wedemeyer, gave us special training. He prepared us to infiltrate back into Korea. You see, those in command seemed to expect a landing of the Allied forces in Korea. We were to carry out advance organization of reliable civilians, to do anything, everything, necessary for independence before the invasion happened."

She handed a cup to him, filled with the sungnyung, and he sipped it slowly.

"Of course that never happened. But there was no sacrifice we were not prepared to make." He slumped back against the cushion, closing his eyes. Sun Yi, at last believing him asleep, rose to leave for a moment, but then his eyelids flickered and opened. He resumed his story.

"At the first we all believed so strongly in our purpose that difficult living conditions didn't matter."

"How did you eat?" He looked so thin, lying with only the light cover over him.

"Off the land, usually. Sometimes we'd stay in one place long enough to find someone who'd provide for us. But more often the farmers were suspicious of stangers. You remember how they are. So we stayed out in the country on our own, tried to do what we could by ourselves. Other times we blended into the crowds of small cities. Much depended on our assignment, our mission."

"How long did that last?" Sun Yi felt a sudden desperate need to place him, to match his location with the occupation and ideas she'd had at the same time. In spring, when new life was springing up on the bleak landscape, did he notice the soft beauty? When monsoon rains of summer began, could he have been sheltered?

"Oh, weeks and months. Probably several months, altogether. You know, Ohmanee, I lost track of days at a time, living like that. We thought of time in terms of a mission to be performed, how long it would take to finish it. All of that changed, of course, when the Russian troops crossed into Korea. We'd known they were near, across the border, for sometime. When the war looked the most desperate for the Japanese it was a simple matter for them to move into our country."

"What happened to you, and the others, when the Russians moved in?"

"We lost contact with the Americans in China. We'd been told that the Russians would be in charge of the surrender in the northern part of our country so we'd better be prepared to work with them." He reached again for the cup and raised it to his lips. "It was easy enough for some to do that. They'd been involved with the Russians for years. It was no big change for them. Many had even served in the Russian army. Did you know that many Koreans live in Manchuria, Ohmanee? They've been settled there for years, most of them, since they lost their land down here soon after the Japanese took over."

He sat up straight and looked away from her. "It was different for those of us who had arrived recently, I suppose because we had this feeling of loyalty to the south, while those oldtimers had tied themselves pretty much to the Russian way of doing everything. People like me thought of being there as only temporary."

"So you were divided by different loyalties?"

"Yes. That was soon apparent to all of us."

He stopped speaking and took up a cup of cold podi cha that the maid had placed silently on the low teakwood table near him. The room was cool, despite the heat outside, and an occasional breeze drifted from the narrow opening at one side of the room, passing through the partial opening of the sliding door on the other side.

"Soon after the Russians arrived," he went on, "and they moved all over the north quickly. We began to see people preparing to leave, heading south, taking with them all of the possessions they could carry. I realized there'd be no place for me in the scheme of those invaders, either, if I failed to cooperate."

Sun Yi sighed. It was true. She'd seen it for herself, already. Floods of refugees in every market place and street of Seoul. Who could imagine such crowds? With less than a million her city was a comfortable place. But now? With all these homeless souls coming, more each day, from the north, that million would soon be doubled.

"Where else can they go?" She spoke her thoughts.

"Well, everyone who can manage the journey is on their way," Jae Yun warned. "In the north anyone who owns a piece of property will have it taken from him under the name of land reform. People's Courts are set up in every town and village. No landowner has a chance of surviving its edicts. Then you have the ones who worked for the Japanese. There'll be no mercy for them. In fact, any kind of western contact places one under suspicion."

"Your auntie has told me that Christians from the north are arriving every day," Sun Yi said, referring to her friend Tai Un. "She says many teachers and professors are fleeing, also."

"If this migration continues the north will soon be emptied of all its most capable people," he went on. "How will they live when they get here?"

Sun Yi had no answer for her son. After some moments he sat up and pounded the pillow beside him. "Nothing is happening as we expected, is it? We thought we'd have our country back when the war ended and the Japanese left. Now the Russians are in the north, taking control of every part of life. And here?"

Sun Yi told him, then, of the American arrival and the shooting in Inchon on the previous day. "Even those we most depended on to help us. here at last and they treat us as a conquered enemy, forgetting that they are out liberators. But when did you decide to return?"

"I always intended to come back," he insisted, "though I realized the family would consider me disobedient. I thought what I did would make a difference, but when I witnessed the confiscation of property, the false promises to the landless. Then I knew that nothing I could do would affect these changes. By then the rail service was broken. That made escape much more difficult."

He shifted restlessly. "Now every train stops at the 38th parallel and goes no further. This land is torn in half by that border alone. Some think it only temporary but I have no illusions."

Jae Wan spoke these last words slowly. Sun Yi leaned over to hear him and was reminded that he was still seriously ill. How could she be so impatient when he'd endured such hardship. She must pace her questions, allow him to rest and recover.

He was already asleep when she whispered, "Enough. Don't say anymore now. We only care that you're home with us once more."

Jae Yun was sitting in his favorite spot beneath the persimmon tree in the courtyard. Leaning back on the cushions that Sun Yi had arranged for him, he watched the patterned shadows formed by its canopy of broad leaved branches. The fruit, green globes awaiting the first kiss of frost to call forth their blush of orange, had looked much the same when he left home in the previous year. Strange how little seemed to have changed in his absence, while he believed that he was now an entirely different person from that school boy.

Yet all the while the tree continued to perform in its predictable pattern, the fruit swelling and ripening, the leaves dropping to reveal its hidden brilliance, then only the branches remaining, stark and bare, reaching skyward in the chill of winter, next forming buds that blossomed, to be followed by the glossy foliage of a new spring and summer.

Was it only he who had been transformed, while every other part of life remained the same? If that were true, could he ever be comfortable with the life he'd once known?

The cool days of autumn brought a resurgence of strength to Jae Yun and he felt restless. This morning he could bear the solitude of his room no longer.

"It seems forever since I've seen the light of day," he complained to Sun Yi, glimpsing the sunshine outside when she opened the sliding door one morning. "Don't you think I'm well enough to sit in the courtyard today?"

He could not tell his mother that his year of independence left him chafing and rebellious within the strict routine of the family's household. Her constant care was only intended to make him feel welcome. She neglected all of her other duties to minister to her son.

But this golden day of October was different. It brought not only the clear high skies but the time for preparation of kimchee. Such a task could be accomplished only with her supervision so she approved of his request with more alacrity than he expected. Soon he was seated comfortably under this tree, hearing only muffled sounds from the direction of the kitchen.

The crunch of steps on the gravel walk disturbed his reveried. Then followed the booming voice of his elder brother.

"Ohmanee told me I'd find you here. You're certainly looking much better than when I saw you last." His cheerful exhuberance matched his appearance. A rotund man in his mid-twenties, Jae Soon dressed to perfection in a dark suit of western style, the sharp creases of the trousers touching his shiny shoes. He sat down carefully near his younger brother, who was wearing the comfortable Korean style jacket and pants. "Putting on weight, too. Soon you'll resemble me."

"Oh, you know Ohmanee's ways.She thinks food is the only medicine needed to cure any ailment. Every day she tell me 'Eat! Eat!' I promise you that before you leave this spot today I'll be served another bowl of nangmyon."

"On this warm day I'd be pleased to share such a meal with you," Jae Soon told him, "but the real reason I'm here is to ask you if you're feeling strong enough to accompany me to the rally on the day after tomorrow. Rhee Syngman will speak."

"Rhee Syngman!" Jae Yun's surprise was genuine. "Is he in Korea?"

"Since yesterday. He was flown in on MacArthur's own plane."

"How do you know these things?" Jae Yun looked skeptical.

"My brother, you've been away a long time. While you were in the north I remained here and made many new friends."

"Still, that does puzzle me," Jae Yun said, ignoring the barbed remark. "I spent some time in Chungking last year and my impression was that the Korean government in exile there, led by Kim Ku. as you know. had the best chance of taking over here after liberation. All of the long time leaders who've worked for independence from their base in Shanghai are there with him. What will become of those loyal men if Rhee takes over?"

"Well, it's said that his roots in the independence movement as as deep as anyone else's," Jae Soon reminded his brother. "He was, after all, involved with Jaisohn Philip in the Independence Club as early as 1896. He's definitely an elder among our revolutionaries. It is true that he never received support rom the Americans when he sought it in the past." He smiled wryly. "I suppose Washington considered him a nuisance, like a fly that persists in buzzing around."

He swatted at an insect that was passing, as if to illustrate his point. "Now he's become useful to them as a strong anti-communist alternative to Lyuh Woon Hyung." He leaned closer and whispered, "The American military here fears the influence of the left wing committee set up by Lyuh. Wouldn't even talk to them when General Hodge arrived. They are looking for a figure who is less liberal that Lyuh, but with the same strong personality. A person who can compete with his popularity among the common people."

He became quiet, watching a shy young maid approach them slowly, bearing a small wooden table on which were two large brass bowls.

"Just as I predicted. Nangmyon."

Each bowl was heaped with thin noodles of buckwheat surrounded by a chilled broth and decorated with slivers of cucumber, yellow moons of hardcooked egg and crisp slices of gupo pear. Crunchy pine nuts crowned it.

"I wouldn't complain of too much food if everything is as tasty as this," Jae Soon told him, dropping a generous spoonful of red hot kochichang into his bowl. "Where did these come from?" he asked suddenly, tapping the metal bowl with his finger. "I thought all metal was confiscated during the war."

"Never underestimate the resourcefulness of our mother."

After the maid retreated Jae Soon continued, "As you well know, Lyuh Woon Hyung is a dynamic man. He's widely known and a great favorite with students. It will take a powerful personality to overcome that type of attraction. But today I saw for myself that Rhee has such power. A great crowd formed outside the Chosun Hotel where he is staying. Everyone shouted for him to appear."

Jae Yun pondered, then asked between spoonfuls of soup, "How did the American military leaders decide on Rhee?"

"My friends," Jae Soon paused for him to be sufficiently impressed, "my friends tell me that no one, no one, in this occupation government knows anything about our country. No one can even speak our language. They must rely upon those with whom they can communicate, namely the few older persons who were educated in the United States. Most of them are Christians, as Rhee is. While these honorable persons have good intentions, it is my opinion that they do not think in the same terms as the younger Korean men who have a different background of experience and education. The view of life offered by these elders is bound by tradition. They resist change."

There was a silence while the two young men gave their full attention to the nangmyon. Then Jae Soon spoke.

"Only time will show us how well this Rhee Syngman will succeed. For my part I would prefer there were a wider range of political ideas represented in his group. But I may prove to be mistaken." He looked closer to his younger brother. "You have changed."

"I'm still too thin, if that's what you mean."

"No, something much deeper than that. You're older, somehow. I find when I look at you, that I must remind myself that you are my inferior."

"Strange, but as you came in I was thinking much the same thoughts. I do feel that I am no longer the same person I was a year ago, yet the world to which I have returned remains as it was."

"There you are mistaken, though you perhaps have not yet had opportunity to observe the differences, confined as you are to this comfortable home."

"What would I see?" Jae Yun demanded.

"Well, the most obvious is the crowds. This city is flooded with newcomers. Refugees from the north continue to arrive daily. Young men, those taken to serve in the army or work in Japan, they're back. And all of the political prisoners have been released. There's no place in the countryside for any of these people. Every one heads for Seoul, especially young men. You should see the streets, filled with the idle and restless like you never saw in the past."

"What can all of these newcomers do to survive?"

"I've already seen some indications of what is happening to them," Jae Soon replied. "Gangs. Ruffians, banding together, prey on shopkeepers for protection money. In many parts of Seoul the streets aren't safe, night or day."

"There's danger all around us." Jae Yun nodded in understanding. "I thought I left that behind when I came down from the north," he added sadly, "but these times are chaotic. There's no one in authority, no leadership in sight."

"I've been wanting to ask you about that. How did you make your way? But you've been so ill that I dared not disturb your rest. I know the rail service between north and south was cut off soon after the Japanese surrendered and the Russians took over. How did you manage?"

A wry smile spread over Jae Yun's face as he recalled the scenes he'd witnessed. "I was in Pyongyang when the Russians arrived, and I thought I'd like to stay around for a while, to see what they were like. Everyone was in a mood to welcome them at first, for they had, after all, helped to liberate us from the Japanese. And they were extremely friendly, always smiling and singing. The most surprising part was the contrast between the officers and the soldiers. Russia is supposed to be a classless society but the officers were clean, neat, well-mannered. Many of them even spoke English or German. The ordinary soldiers were dirty, coarse, vulgar. They liked to boast of the things they had stolen from the Japanese since arriving."

Leaning closer to his brother, Jae Yun lowered his voice. "It was then that the native communists emerged. They formed a temporary local government and the purge began. Pro-Japanese collaborators, rich landowners, then the Christians. No one was safe from the verdicts of the People's Court. Many fled to the south, if they could, and I realized the time had come for me to leave, also. There were so many of us!"

He shuddered, remembering. "Everyone was trying to leave at once, desperate to get out in any fashion they could manage." He described his own journey packed into the rail car. Then he paused, as if to obscure that memory with humor. "Ohmanee would have been horrified if she had seen me. You know how she always insisted we should be immaculate when we were young."

Jae Soon smiled, remembering, but urged him to continue his story.

"The most amazing part is how quickly one's good spirits can return, once the goal is reached," he concluded, after telling of the border crossing. "So when you see those refugees crowding our streets don't forget what each one of them has endured, just to be walking freely here."

Jae Soon bowed his head and buried his face in his hands. His brother listened, astounded, to his voice, low and muffled and filled with sadness.

"To think that you have suffered through all these hardships with such strength and courage, while I." He paused. "I have been, still am, such a coward, even in matters that shrink in importance compared to what has happened in your life."

"Please tell me, elder brother," pleaded Jae Yun, distressed by this unexpected behavior, "what can possibly cause you this unhappiness?"

"It is my own lack of will that creates my despair," confessed Jae Soon, raising his head at last. "I have discovered a beautiful young woman. I want to take her as my wife yet I cannot find the courage to tell our parents. If I do not speak to them soon I'm sure I will lose her."

"Why? And why do you believe our parents will oppose you? You know they've always devoted themselves to our welfare. Is she unsuitable?"

Jae Yun found it hard to believe that this brother who'd always been a model of proper manners managed to get himself into such a situation.

"She is perfect!" Jae Soon responded without hesitation. "If only you could see her. When she appears it is to me like the glow of a moonrise brightening a darkening sky."

"Then why?" Jae Yun persisted. "Does she know of you?"

"Oh, yes. For some months we've been exchanging letters," he admitted. "You know I could never speak to her directly. Our small sisters are classmates. They carry our messages. I have no doubt by now that In Ja shares my feelings."

"In Ja? That's her name?"

"Yes, Song In Ja. And she is as brilliant and accomplished as she is lovely, a fine pianist. That's when I first saw her, playing for a small recital."

"Then she must be the kind of person our parents would choose for you themselves," Jae Yun persisted.

His brother shook his head sadly. "The problems are insurmountable," he responded. "Our mother has already chosen someone else for me. I know this, for she has made many comments to me on this subject. She is not subtle. I fear she has her mind set firmly. Not only that, but even worse. In Ja has an elder brother. He's a well-known supporter of the liberal forces aligned with Lyuh Woon Hyung. He is a definite leftist. He may be a communist! The liberals can't survive if Rhee Syngman takes power. It would be unthinkable to involve ourselves, even indirectly, in such dangerous company. I will not endanger our family."

Jae Yun shook his head in sympathetic agreement. It was an agonizing dilemma.

"I don't know why I am admitting my problem to you," Jae Soon confessed. "I've told no one else. There's nothing you can do to help me. Perhaps I have carried it within myself for too long. This simply overflowed with my emotions when I heard your story, seeing your display of fortitude. I applaud, no, I envy your abililty to follow your own convictions and accept their consequences. I deplore my own pitiful weakness. If only I had the courage to be more like you!"

On a Wednesday afternoon late in the winter of 1946 Jae Soon walked along one of the main streets of Seoul, his shoes tapping a brisk rhythm on the pavement. With a glance over his shoulder, he pulled the collar of his overcoat higher, hoping it would obscure his face so no one would recognize him. If he met an acquaintance by chance he would be expected to explain why he was not in his class-room at this time of day. That would be difficult without resorting to subterfuge.

His closest colleagues were, by now, accustomed to his unex-plained absences. They no longer asked questions. Two or three of his good friends were even willing to take over his classes on short notice, for they knew he would return the favor whenever asked.

He turned onto a side street as soon as he could. Even there the crowds jostled him on all sides. Hucksters called out their wares from small shops and stands midst the rumbling of ox carts, the jangle of street cars, and the blaring horns of some private automobiles. He swerved to avoid colliding with an old man bent under the weight of an A-frame loaded with firewood.

Even amidst the commotion this part of Seoul was quiet now, he thought, compared to the time of the street demonstrations around the New Year. The people of his country, divided about the recent Four Power Agreement thrust upon them, took to the streets, chal-lenging those who differed with shouting and waving signs. It was a plan that would stall independence by placing Korea into a trustee-ship for five years, Only the leftists, some called them Communists, favored such trusteeship. Noisy partisanship prevailed and the wounds were still raw. A dangerous time.

Children skipped around him and he swerved to avoid stumbling over one of the street urchins. The warming weather must have brought them out. Where did they stay when it was colder? Seoul was a contrast, more than ever, between wealth and poverty. A black limousine rolled past him, as if to illustrate his thoughts, blasting a path through the street people and assorted vehicles.

He stopped in front of a red brick building, imposing among the lesser structures surrounding it. This was the place. It had to be, for a

Rolls Royce was parked in front of it and a chauffeur stood next to the open passenger door waiting to assist the ladies who were emerging from it, dressed in furs and silk hanbok. Other women, similarly dressed, most of them looking middle aged or older, were climbing the steps to the wide entrance. He saw a few elderly gentlemen among the crowd but there was no one else like himself and he realized that he must stand out noticeably. A broad shouldered young man in a suit of western cut, with a head of thick dark hair. Even his quick step was a contrast to the measured pace of the others. Well, no matter if someone thought him an oddity. So long as he was not recognized. The reaction of these persons was no concern of his, for he had come here only to listen to the pianist.

He found a seat in the last row, as usual. The house lights dimmed. He always tried to time his arrival to the beginning of her program. Now he sat back in the semi-dark hall, anticipating the spotlight that would focus on her slight figure as she made her entrance.

She could not see him but she would know he was here. How much could a performer see from the stage anyway? Mostly a blur of faces. He looked around, wondering why everyone else did not watch for her as he did. Most of this matinee audience seemed totally involved, each group in its own circle, chattering with heads close together, almost until the moment when the first notes rippled from the keyboard. Did any of them appreciate the wondrous beauty of her music? He doubted they did.

There she was! Entranced by the sight of her lithe body moving gracefully, dazzled by her cameo face, he thought how charming was her manner of arranging the fullness of her silk chima as she seated herself before the ebony grand piano. The first notes struck. While his ears listened to the melody his eyes traced the outline he now knew so well. The sheen of her dark hair, woven into a tight knot at the nape of her neck, framed her classic oval face.

She was playing only for him. Jae Soon knew this. The opening notes of the Mozart sonata, the no. 11, were an invitation, drawing him into the enchantment of her dream world. Pure. Soft. Increasing intensity. Why had she chosen this one for today? She spoke to him through her music.

Sometimes her note contained no more than a cryptic date, time, place. She left him free to interpret her intention, her message, through the music she selected to play.

This passage was celestial, supreme. He heard a peculiar tenderness in it that he'd not noticed before. Jae Soon forgot the nodding grey heads around him. Only In Ja, leaning over the keyboard, and he were in this room. In Ja, the beautiful In Ja. The forbidden In Ja.

When he heard the Chopin nocturne, the op. 48 in C minor, the last of her program, Jae Soon knew she'd captured the richness of mood, the depth of its meaning, as no other pianist had ever done. He felt her transform the brooding beginning into a storm of protest. How could someone so ethereal in appearance play with such power? Lost in the intense final chords, he realized with the crescendo of applause following that In Ja was, after all, a vital and living presense to others was well as to himself.

He must, somehow, manage to see her alone, to speak with her, to be certain that her feelings were as strong for him.

They'd first met nearly a year earlier. Another concert but with a setting more intimate. He recalled how she acknowledged his presence, smiling gently in response to the kindling light in his dark eyes and the smile on his lips. He wrote to her the next day and asked his sister to carry the message. She gave it to In Ja's own younger sister at school. The two children delighted in this secret game and their correspondence continued until he thought he knew her well.

But still he could not speak to her openly. When they met by chance she'd greet him with a slight inclination of her head, her eyes flickering recognition before anyone could notice.

Damn her older brother! That communist! He was the problem. The man was too well known as the right hand man to the leader of the leftist element that struggled to take power in the months following liberation.

But this young woman! She'd come to mean so much to Jae Soon, was so essential that any risk, almost any, seemed worth the price. He thought night and day of what he might say or do that would convince her of his love and desire for her.

They met by the West Gate. In the first warm sunshine of spring he saw her standing, half-questioning, somehow sad, waiting until with a rush she recognized him. Jae Soon knew that dressed as he was in the well tailored dark suit and proper tie he made a distinguished figure, despite his youth.

He took her hand without a word and led her to the road outside the Gate. He followed her along a narrow and rocky path. After some time she stopped abruptly and turned to face him with her warm smile, her dark eyes soft. Yet her look was more proud than gentle and he felt his love for her rush until he thought it would choke him.

In Ja neither spoke nor moved. He looked at her sideways and watched the rose-pink flush mounting from her delicate neck to her cheeks. He smiled down into her eyes as if he might infuse her with his own daring.

She grasped his hand tightly, then, and once more stepped lightly. Beside him she walked, lifting the hem of her pale blue chima so it would not touch the dust of the path.

They turned toward the mountain, climbing the unshaded flank of the bare slope. The first pale blooms of wild azaleas lined their trail. Midway she halted to catch her breath and shaded her eyes with one free hand, looking out over Seoul. The high, rocky mountains surrounded the city, set deep in the circle of the valley. Far away the curve of the Han River outlined its edge under a sky intensely blue, cloudless.

"How beautiful this place is," she said. "I must always remember this view."

They left the narrow path and stopped beside an overhanging rock at some distance from it, seeking shade. Jae Soon spread his coat on the ground for her and they sat, side by side though not touching, each suddenly shy of the other in the still, private world.

She was so near that he could put out his hand and touch her. Her skin was cream white. The high color glowed in her cheeks. He became more intensely aroused by the sight of her lovely face so close to his own, her eyes lustrous and dark.

Jae Soon dared to put out his hand and take hers, placing their palms together. Each felt the pulsing of their heart's blood beating in unison. Then he lifted her face to his.

"What do I mean to you?"

"My love," she said at last.

He pulled the pinja gently from her hair and buried his face in the long dark strands unloosed, soft and straight, inhaling the delicate scent. He embraced her, clasping her close with his renewed passion, till she cried out.

"Let me breathe!"

Jae Soon loosed her but she remained lying in his arms.

"Why are you so silent?" he asked, laying his cheek against hers.

"I fear for our happiness. I know it cannot last."

"It will last, as long as we live!" he denied her premonition fervently.

"Do not make fun of me!"

"I do not. I am only waiting for you to continue, to explain your meaning."

"Why do you look at me like that, then?" she asked, sitting up.

"How am I looking?"

In Ja turned to one side and he reached out to tilt her face toward him and look into it.

"You are not telling me something," he whispered. "Tell me."

She looked away. "Soon I will be married," she said, her voice husky with sadness.

A dark fury spread over his face and she added, hastily, "not to any man. I will be married to my vocation. To my music."

Then she told him her parents were sending her to America to study. The plans were all arranged. Even the visa was ready.

Jae Soon looked into her face, admiring the beauty he thought he could not hope to possess. "So that's the reason you dared to be with me here today?"

"Yes. You know we cannot be married. Your family will never allow it. You are taking a dangerous risk, the chance of being seen with me, a member of a family with communist associations, today. But I had to speak to you before I leave."

"Does your family know? About us?"

"I don't think so. But my brother has alienated my family from everyone. And so I must leave." She stroked his face. "It's not only that. I have been given a gift. I cannot keep it to myself. I must share this gift of making music, unselfishly, with others."

"I'll wait!"

"No. I don't know when, if I will return. So you see it would be no use to wait for me."

He took her hands in his, touching one by one the slender, tapered fingers.

Then she added, as if admitting her guilt, "I went to a fortune teller and asked him about our birth years, if we would be compatible."

"As if you really believed that old superstition! What did he say?"

"Listen. Perhaps you will be pleased," she protested, and her smile was teasing. "He said you, the male, are the dragon. I," she placed her hand upon his breast, "am tiger. Dragon is stronger than tiger, but tiger is strong also, and she will fight you sometimes, though she can never hope to win, for the dragon sits above, always in the clouds."

Jae Soon pulled her into his arms, suddenly, and pressed her warm, soft cheek against his. "How can you leave me?"

"How can you let me go?"

They clung together as though they would never part. In Ja responded with such instinctive passion as he had never dreamed of, and he breathed a sigh of profound happiness. Was there ever such a woman as this one?

The wind whipped the tall grass, laying it flat on the hillside, carrying the fragrance of early blooming wildflowers sweet as honey on its breath. The sun slipped lower on the horizon.

When the exquisite moment had passed and they drew apart he felt closer to her than ever before.

"I'll always love you, wherever you are," he whispered into her ear.

"No, you will find someone else and be happy. I know." She sat up and wound her long hair into a roll, then searched for the pinja that had fastened it.

Jae Soon found it lying on the grass beside them. He handed it to her and watched as she poked it fiercely into her hair. He reached for her hands and buried his face in them. She pressed her cheek against his hair, gently, resting, and he tasted the hot brine of her tears.

Then he pulled her to her feet and she followed him down the mountain path, back to the city.

In the shadow of the Gate he held her hands again for a long time, then stood still as In Ja turned and walked swiftly away, watching as she disappeared into the crowd.

The silvery scales of the limp fish glistened and one bright eye gazed up at her when Sun Yi peered into the basket.

"But it is so small! Surely you could have selected one equally handsome but larger than this?"

She looked with dismay at the other food items the maid had just brought from the market and then at the few coins the woman handed to her.

"Everything is more expensive today, mistress," her servant tried to explain. "This is all I could buy with the money that you gave me. All of the prices are higher this week than last, and those were higher than those of the week before." She raised her gnarled hands in a gesture of supplication. "Like climbing a ladder, prices go up, up. Next week? Who knows how much the food will cost?"

"Well, you must return it and get another, I'm sorry to tell you," Sun Yi sighed. "This one simply won't do for tonight. I'll give you a little more money, for today we must have the finest, largest fish in the market." After a moment she added, "Did you offer to pay the first price asked?"

"Oh, no," replied the maid. "You know I wouldn't do that!" The old woman's honest face displayed shock at the suggestion that she did not know how to bargain.

Sun Yi pressed the extra won into the maid's hand and watched anxiously as the woman hurried through the narrow street, her long chima swaying as she disappeared. Then she turned back into the courtyard. How much longer will this continue, she asked herself aloud. Though there was no one to hear, she continued to list her complaints.

The cost of every necessity was rising constantly since the end of the war. Just before the liberation the Japanese flooded the country with excess currency. That started the spiral of inflation. Then, the American military government refused to place controls on grain prices. Now, in these early months of 1946, no one was able to predict the cost of anything from one day to the next. Each person struggled to survive and provide for the needs of his family.

She must discuss this business with her husband when he had time for her. When would that be? He was preoccupied much of the time, if not with the care of his patients, then with meetings of his friends in the Chondogyo.

Dr. Lee held a high position in that religious group, the reward for his long association with it. She respected his efforts, but she could not help wishing that he would show more concern for their daily hardships. Everything fell upon herself when it came to managing this house.

She stood in the courtyard enjoying the touch on her shoulders of the spring sun. Its light shimmered on the lavender silk of her chogori. Today she expected a definite answer. After months of discussion her plan would be confirmed. Sun Yi twisted the ring of white jade that she always wore and smiled, thinking of the perfect wife she'd selected for her eldest son.

Why had the matter taken so long to settle? She couldn't understand why the parents of this girl were reluctant. Jae Soon would be the ideal son-in-law. He was well established in his position at the Seoul National University. How satisfying it was to make these plans! She knew exactly how to arrange each of her children's lives.

All that remained was for the two young people to be introduced, and she would take care of that detail this afternoon. She had no doubt that all aspects of this union were harmonious. Didn't she know her son's mind and personality better than anyone? This young woman would be the perfect complement to his temperment. When he met her he'd realize that.

So she'd tell him tonight, when he came to Uijonbu for his usual weekly visit. First there would be a delicious meal, with all of his favorites. She could see his face now, surprised but pleased that she'd concerned herself for his happiness. Sun Yi's eyes, golden brown, sparkled as they had when she was a young girl.

Someone was pounding on the front gate. Sun Yi frowned. Such a rude disturbance on her quiet morning. She opened the small window. A slender young man in a suit of the western style was raising his fist to knock once more.

"Stop! I heard you. Who are you?"

His reply came in agitated phrases. "I'm the principal's assistant. At the school. Your son's school."

Ah, yes. Now she recalled the face from her past visits.

"Well, why are you here making all this commotion on a peaceful day?"

"Your son is not in school! Nor any of the others. Not one of them."

He caught his breath to continue speaking but she interrupted him.

"My son? Not in school? Where else would he be?" The idea that her son would misbehave! "He's not here," she declared. "He left quite early this morning, as he always does."

"I was sent to locate the boys," he told her. All he knew was the message found in the classroom. "It said they were on strike," he went on more calmly.

"Strike!"

"Yes. Until their demands were considered. I'm notifying all the parents. You must cooperate." He glared at Sun Yi. "This is a serious matter."

"Of course." What a presumptuous person! "I'll do what I can." A strike! The idea was preposterous. "But first, tell me how it is possible that such young children, they're only grammar school students after all, could possibly be on a," she hesitated, suppressing a smile, 'strike?' Children only ten years old?"

"Isn't everyone on strike? Why not?" Again he was agitated. "The street car drivers strike. Factory workers strike. Everyone takes to the streets with signs, shouting 'strike!'" His voice grew louder. "What can you expect? This country is in turmoil."

I'll have to calm him down, she thought. "They can't be far away. I'll speak to some of the other parents. We'll find them."

After he left, somewhat mollified but still muttering to himself, Sun Yi wondered how Jae Wan could have managed this mass rebellion, if that's what was happening. His school kept strict rules. If only her plans for the day were not disrupted. She was just beginning to feel cheerful. The dark days of winter, seemingly endless, glazed her spirit with pessimism. It had been a harsh season, bitterly cold. But today the burst of spring captured her feelings of gloom and lifted them into the sunlight as a gust of wind will twirl a heap of dry leaves.

She started out to find some of her neighbors, parents of the other children in Jae Wan's class.

There were times when each of her children presented a different set of problems for her. Jae Yun, for example. Where was he today? Still weak from malaria, he'd insisted he was well enough to begin work as a reporter for *Tong-a-Ilbo*, the renegade newspaper that resumed publication after liberation.

"What about your education?" she'd asked him. "How can you give up school?"

"It's too late," he'd replied. "I'm too old, too restless to become a student again."

And then he'd joined the street demonstrations. But the spirit of revolt touched everyone. It was an unforgettable scene, that New Year. Thousands in the streets, all protesting the plan that would pro-long the division of their country. Her son's rage was shared by most people. They wanted to be free! But when? In five years? Immediate independence was expected upon the defeat of Japan. Instead the United States and the Soviet Union organized this four-power trust-eeship over Korea.

Would her land never be free? Yes, she could understand her son's feelings. I'd like to shout in the street, myself, she thought. But those days are over and past for me.

Rhee Syngman was the one who called for the general strike. Three days of violence followed. At first most agreed with him. All the conservatives, certainly. Most of the moderates. Then, in the middle of the battle, the communists changed their signs. First it was "Down with trusteeship!" Then, "Up with trusteeship!"

There was a good lesson in that. The question divided people. Everyone looking for an instant solution. Problems only grow worse.

Even the young children knew what a confused world it was. Now Jae Wan and his ten-year-old classmates are striking. But can we blame them, when all of us are surrounded by conflict?

But where could that child be today?

As she called on the other parents who lived nearby she found each of them as baffled as she by their children's action, and equally appalled, but no one else knew where they were either. At last she decided there was nothing more to do but wait for their eventual return. Sun Yi knew her own son well enough to believe it unlikely he'd miss his evening meal. Consoling herself with this thought, she set out for the session with the woman who was arranging Jae Soon's betrothal.

"I saw some Americans!"

Jae Wan stood in the doorway. It was late afternoon. His uniform, pale blue for summer, was creased and covered with dust, his dark eyes bright with excitement. "Some American soldiers!"

Sun Yi was determined not to show anger. She'd first listen to his version of the day's events. "I've been told you were not in school today," she began softly. "Where did you see these Americans? Where have you been?"

"Playing baseball!"

His eyes blazed, the color was high on his cheeks. Then he turned away from her stern face. "Well, the teacher was treating us unfairly. We decided to stand up for our rights. Isn't that what Koreans have to do? We can be strong only when we act together. I heard elder brother say that. That's why we had a strike. Now that teacher will listen to us!"

"Tell me how all of this began. Why do you think you were treated unfairly?"

His young face was looking at her with such sincerity that she was compelled to hear him out. The truth is, Sun Yi reminded herself, I can never be harsh with this child. He is my youngest, my last son, and he might have never existed at all if the truth were ever known. Shadows flooded her memory of a time when she sat alone in a richly ornate room, trembling, so many years ago when her husband was in prison. Waiting for the screen door to slide open. She had to keep that secret. If it were known, she'd have been cast out, abandoned, bereft of her dear children.

She had promised herself that she would blot out the memory, never again think of that day. Yet now after all these years she still struggled against the vision, trying to sweep it from her mind as she would be rid of a dusky cobweb in her house.

Dimly she heard the young voice still speaking.

"Last week there was a fight," Jae Wan was saying, "a big fight, on the playground. It was between the boys and the girls. They were shouting at us and we were yelling back. Only the boys are to be punished. It was the girls' fault as much as ours. We're to be kept after school each day for two hours, for two weeks! And to be spanked each day, as well. The teacher refused to listen to our side of the story." Jae Wan's eyes hardened angrily at the remembrance of the injustice.

Sun Yi, still struggling with those cobwebs of memory, tried to be attentive. Sadness coated her words. "So you thought you would receive better treatment if you deprived yourself of a day's education? Who do you think was punished by that?"

She reminded him of how much better school was since the liberation. "You can speak Korean in public without fear. Your books are written in hangul instead of Japanese. You even have your Korean name again. Think of that! No one will ever call you by that Japanese name again."

He lowered his head, shaking it from side to side. "I can see now that it was the wrong thing to do." Then the head bobbed up. "But we still expect him to apologise!"

When she said nothing, he added, "It was such a beautiful day, warm, and so much sunshine. We had a really good game. Then, as I was walking home afterwards, I saw the Americans. It was the first time I've been really close to them. I could even hear their voices. They sounded deep and rough. They laugh a lot. There was one so tall." He stretched his arm high in the air to show his mother. "Taller than that, with red hair and blue eyes."

After a moment he added, "But there's something about them I don't understand. Their mouths are moving all of the time, even while they aren't talking. You've always told me it is rude to eat in the street, and I couldn't see that they were eating, but there was something in their mouths. They seemed awfully strange to me."

Silently Sun Yi thanked her son for restoring her to the present with his chatter. The cobweb visions were tucked away.

"Go now. Change into clean clothes," she commanded. "Your elder brother will be here soon."

He was late. The sun had set when Jae Soon stepped from the street car in Uijonbu and he hurried in the direction of his parents' home, urging his companion to keep pace with him, still unable to think of anything but In Ja.

Only a rim of light outlined the hills on the distant horizon to the east. The air was warm until the sun disappeared. Now the winds from Siberia were spreading a mantle of chill over the city again.

"I knew I'd need this overcoat for a few more days," he remarked, in an attempt to sound more friendly, as he pulled it more tightly around him.

"Yes," came the curt reply. "This false spring won't last."

The man beside Jae Soon was protected, also, by a top coat over his western style of suit, but it did not hide his lean, almost gaunt figure. Half a head taller and stightly stoop shouldered, he made a marked contrast to Jae Soon's robust silouette.

Again he asked himself why he succombed to the man's insistence and invited him tonight. He knew there was only one reason. Ohmanee would not be pleased. Until she knew that reason, also.

He saw Jae Wan by the gate, waiting for him. Not standing. That child never stayed in one place long enough to warrant that description. At one moment he was swinging on the gate and the next leaping across some imaginary line in the street.

"My youngest brother," he acknowledged the boy with a sweep of his arm. "Jae Wan," he said in a stern voice, "this is my classmate, Mr. Cho."

Jae Wan inclined his head immediately, bowing to the man who accompanied his elder brother. Then, turning to Jae Soon, he warned, "Ohmanee is waiting for you. You're late."

Sun Yi was hovering near the front of the house, her elder son noticed, though she appeared to be occupied and did not look up until they'd come inside. He greeted her, apologising for the delay, thinking of In Ja and how shocked his mother would be if she knew the real reason he'd been detained.

"I'd like to ask you to make another place at our table for my honored guest, Mr. Cho. He was my classmate. I've brought him to meet Abuji."

Sun Yi inclined her head and murmured the proper words of greeting and welcome to the stranger. Jae Soon detected an annoyance in her voice that detracted from its usual warmth. A fleeting frown crossed her face. He'd expected her to be upset but not to show her feeling. He observed, at the same time, the rigidly correct manner of Cho in returning her greeting, noting how sunken his face was beneath the prominent cheekbones. The high forehead, hairline receding, acccentuated his leanness. Only the remaining hair was luxuriant, brushed back in a glistening mane. Strange man, this Cho.

Cho Tok Su had attended Kyunggi High School with Jae Soon and later enrolled in the same university, so their acquaintance was lengthy, but they'd never been close friends. Therefore he was surprised when Cho began to make frequent calls, cultivating his friendship at every opportunity in the months since liberation.

He guided his companion to his father's quarters in the sarang-ban, to the left of the central hall and close to the front.

"Ah, a handsome room," Cho announced with approval, glancing around.

It was. A spacious place, with massive wooden beams across the ceiling, it contained a large writing desk at one end with long bookshelves on either side. Sliding doors between the wall cupboards emitted a filtered light through the rice paper panels.

Jae Soon motioned his guest to a low table in the middle. Plump silk cushions surrounded it and the ondul floor gave a welcome warmth to their slippered feet. He brought a bottle of makkoli from the cupboard and poured the rice wine into cups for Cho and then for himself, gesturing that he be seated. A plate of anju was set out to accompany the liquor.

"I'll be back in one moment," he promised, after seeing to his quest's comforts.

Sun Yi was still standing in the central hall. "I expected you to be alone tonight," she scolded. "Now there will be no opportunity for me to speak with you, since you must entertain this guest."

"I am surprised,Ohmanee," he replied. "You usually offer my friends a warm welcome. Has anything happened to upset you?"

He followed her onto the maru. On the narrow veranda twilight absorbed the last rays of sunlight and his face was obscured by shadows. She could not see his reaction to her next words.

"Only that I planned to tell you of your betrothal tonight," she said, "and not in this hurried way."

His hands at his sides clenched involuntarily. "My betrothal?" His throat tightened. I knew this was coming, he thought. Why should I be surprised now that I hear it.

"Yes," she said, and now she smiled with her pleasure and he saw the glow in her eyes.

"This has taken longer than I expected, my son, but I'm satisfied. I've found a young woman who satisfies all the requirements of a good wife for you." She patted his arm. "For you, it has to be a special person, and I am sure she is, for she comes from a family with a yangban heritage and she has fine accomplishments. Of course she will bring a dowry and good health. Her temperment will be a balanced accompaniment to yours and she is worthy of continuing our family line."

She paused, looking closely into his face while he remained silent.

He was thinking of In Ja on the hillside, saying her sign was the tiger. That would never do, according to his mother's standards.

"Her parents have agreed to accept you, as they certainly should. Now you have only to meet and we'll proceed with the arrangements for the wedding."

"This young woman! She's a stranger!" When he found his voice it trembled. "She may be a good woman, as you say, but how can you expect me to marry someone I don't even know?"

"I'm afraid you've been influenced by your contact with outsiders," Sun Yi replied, and she disguised the hurt with coldness, "or you would not say this. You've forgotten the traditional ways. Of course you will have the opportunity to become acquainted before you marry. Young people are fortunate today. In my youth it was not the custom for bride and groom to meet before the marriage ceremony." She softened her tone. "She is a lovely girl, my son. You will begin with a strong foundation for the future. Soon you will learn to appreciate her."

Opposition was useless. It would only cast him in the role of a disobedient, disrespectful, even ungrateful son. And for what? A soft wind blew through the passage between the house and the outer wall. Though it was warm, his skin prickled. He saw In Ja walking away from him and how he'd felt as the distance grew greater between them. He turned away, saying, "I leave it all to you. Do whatever you wish," then added, "I brought this man here tonight only because I believe he may know where Uncle is. I hope to learn something from him."

"Your uncle!" Sun Yi broke in. "You mean Han Ju?" Her voice echoed disbelief. He'd been away so long, and no word from him, the brother she'd taught when he was a child, the one who filled her with pride as he grew and became a brilliant young man. No one heard from him, not even his mother, Kum Seung. He'd gone to Japan to study and when the war with American began he'd simply disappeared.

Jae Soon laid his hand upon his mother's arm now, gently, realizing how much taller than she he was. I'm no longer a child, yet for her I'll always be one.

"I'll tell you later, but I can't promise anything yet. I must return to him now"

He called to Jae Yun as he entered the room. "Brother, I want you to meet my classmate, whom I've brought to share the evening meal with us. He's waiting in father's room. Come along."

The men dined alone, Dr. Lee having joined them. His two sons and Mr. Cho listened respectfully to the few remarks he made before beginning the meal. Then they concentrated on the enjoyment of the delicacies that were presented, one dish following after another. Sun Yi had made her best efforts with the ingredients she could obtain and there were many specialties seldom seen during the lean years of wartime.

The fish was a masterpiece, for the maid persisted and brought home a magnificent cod. It had been fried in its entirety until it was golden and crisp, then placed on a platter and garnished with a sauce of such delicacy that it enhanced rather than masked its robust splendor. Artfully trimmed and scupted vegetables in shades of orange, green and white surrounded it like floating water lilies.

Jae Soon looked on as the others, each in turn, lifted the morsels of tender flesh that fell from the bones at their touch until only the skeletal remains were left. The fish, once whole and beautiful, disappeared before his eyes. His throat constricted and he could not swallow, thinking that his own future lay also in shattered fragments.

When the last vestiges of the meal had been removed it was Mr. Cho who commanded their attention. He'd been in the southwestern province of Cholla during Rhee Syngman's recent six-week speaking tour, he said, and all of them wanted to hear his assessment of that man's political strength.

"I understand your original home was in Cholla," Dr. Lee began.

"Yes." Cho nodded as if he were reluctant to admit his provincial background. "My father was a member of the Posong there, one of the landowners," he hurried to reasssure them. "When he extended his business interests to Seoul before the war I followed. That's when I met your son at Kyunggi. We were students together."

Jae Soon resented the implication. They weren't close friends. But he said nothing. He found concentration on this conversation difficult. He could think only of In Ja. Was it really too late?

"Your father is still living in Seoul?"

Jae Yun, always the reporter, was questioning Cho closely.

"He is an elder of our group, the Posong," Cho admitted, "and highly respected for his success in business."

A mastermind of the conservative political movement is what he really means, Jae Soon was thinking. What did this man want from him? Could he lead him to Han Ju?

"An advisor, also, to the Korean Democratic Party," Cho added proudly.

The man had no shame. The same thing, thought Jae Soon. It's still Posong. Only a new label, taken to impress the American military leaders here. These men are afraid of the communists, no more, no less. Afraid of losing their property under the land reform programs. He was no communist himself. Why did this Cho create antagonism within him? Why was he attempting to revive supposed school ties with Jae Soon and through him with his entire family? For some time these questions intrigued him, ever since he became aware of Cho's angling for an invitation to his home. That was a gesture usually reserved only for close friends. Did he really have a connection with Uncle? It was a tempting bait. Jae Soon could not resist it. Now he wondered if this was merely a devious tactic to ensnare his family in the political intrigue.

Tonight Cho neatly sidestepped all questions on the matter. Instead, he continued to describe the reception of Rhee Syngman with enthusiasm.

"Great crowds cheered in every place where he spoke. There's no other leader in Korea with such a strong and secure base of support.

"And your party, the Korean Democatic Party, supports him? Jae Yun was probing again.

"Absolutely. The Korean Democratic Party is convinced that Rhee Syngman will lead this country to progress and independence. There is no greater patriot."

"Progress for everyone?" Jae Yun sounded skeptical.

"Of course." Cho spread his hands out flat before him as if to encompass that population. "As you know, our goals are simple, but vital to the survival of Korea. We believe in just reform of land and industry, with adequate compensation to the owners when it is redistributed. And we want an independent South Korean government as soon as possible."

He was persuasive, insisting that support for those programs would benefit all of the Koreans. Finally he paused and Jae Soon reminded him of the promise to provide information about his uncle, Yu Han Ju. Once more Cho assured him that he would make every effort, through his connections, to locate their relative.

Still no definite commitment, Jae Soon realized. He looked at his watch. "The midnight curfew will catch us if we miss that last tram."

Jae Yun had been silent, appearing thoughtful during the latter part of Cho's remarks. Now he spoke. "Elder brother, there's a private matter I must discuss with you before you leave."

The two brothers stepped out onto the maru, where the night air stung their faces.

"How could you give in so easily?" the younger one demanded. "Why didn't you tell Ohmanee how you really feel? Tell me, why are you willing to marry this stranger without a word of protest?"

"So you were listening." Jae Soon shrugged and turned half away. "Isn't it my duty to obey my parents?"

"You are evading my question," Jae Yun persisted. "What is the real reason? You could have explained. Ohmanee would understand. She always does."

"The matter of my marriage is of no importance to me now," Jae Soon told him. "As far as I am concerned, it is a family matter, not mine. In Ja is leaving the country. I'll probably never see her again."

"Leaving? Where is she going?"

"Shh." Jae Soon warned him to lower his voice. "She is going to America to study, to become a concert pianist. Her parents have already made the arrangements. I can't do anything about it. As I told you, it is hopeless for me. Now it doesn't matter who I marry now, so I may as well please our parents by obeying their wishes. Perhaps our mother is right when she says that I will learn to love the woman who is my wife." He broke off with a short laugh, mirthless and bitter. "Someday I may tell even you, if that should happen. Take warning now. You'll be better off if you don't challenge tradition."

Jae Yun laid his hand on his brother's arm as Jae Soon turned to leave. "Speaking of warnings, I'd watch this Cho if I were you. He'll have you snared in the net of political intrigue and rivalry if you aren't careful."

"You're warning me? After your own involvement with the underground?

"That's all the more reason to listen to my advice. I know what it is like. If you continue to have close association with this man you, or those close to you, could be in great danger."

"Wake up! Wake up!"

Jae Soon opened his eyes reluctantly, wondering if the whispering voice was part of his dream. For just a moment he believed he was still a child and his mother was looking down at him.

"Ohmanee!" He sat up abruptly "Why are you here? What time is it?"

"Sh-h." She laid a finger to her lips. "It's early," she admitted, seating herself on the floor next to his bed of soft ibuls. "But I knew how difficult it would be to locate you later, so I took this chance, though I knew I would disturb your sleep. Word came to us last night that your brother is in prison. I'm so worried."

"Prison!" Jae Soon exclaimed, rubbing the sleep from his eyes. He listened to her voice break on the last words and watched, amazed, as she buried her face in her hands. He'd never seen his mother when she was not in control of her emotions and for the first time he realized that she was as vulnerable as anyone else.

"You know we've had no word from him since he left for Taegu last week," she went on, "but that's like him. Secretive. One of his coworkers brought the news to us."

"What has my younger brother done now? I warned him Taegu would be dangerous," Jae Soon told his mother."With all the industrial plants down there it is a hotbed of unrest. When the railroad workers went on strike he decided to investigate the situation. I couldn't talk him out of it. He said someone had to write the truth about them and conditions were bad everywhere in the country. But I know there's massive unemployment around Taegu and with the inflation growing everyday its no wonder people are dissatisfied. How can they live?"

"And all those homeless refugees from the north, more than a million, I've heard," Sun Yi added.

"Yes," he said. "The political parties aren't finding solutions, just fighting against each other. I'm not surprised to see people protesting in the streets. The longer General Hodge and his American soldiers stay here the more hopeless the dream of independence seems. What do you want me to do about Jae Yun?"

"Well, find him, of course. Your father and I want you to go to Taegu yourself and see if it is true. If he is in prison, do whatever you need to get him out. Bring him home."

Jae Soon shook his head. This is so typical of my mother, he thought. Simply describe your wish and then assume that someone will make it happen.

"Taegu is more than one hundred and fifty miles south of Seoul," he reminded her. "The rail system is paralyzed by this strike. How can I get there? Furthermore, do you know how many persons are in prison? I may not even be able to locate him."

But he stood up, resigned, knowing he would try to follow her request. Of course he would. Sun Yi knew it, also.

Six months had passed since the evening in Uijonbu when Jae Soon learned of the marriage arranged for him by his mother. The wedding took place in late spring and although he and his new wife lived, in the traditional custom, in the home of his parents, the truth was that he remained in Seoul most of the time. He pleaded that the distance of twenty miles was too great to travel each day. He must be at the university for early classes and needed time for his research as well. The real reason, of course, was that he still preferred passing the evening hours with his colleagues.

He shared this simple house in the center of the city with Jae Yun but his brother was seldom there. News reporting assignments took him throughout Korea. Fully recovered at last from the malaria, Jae Yun worked for the leading newspaper, *Tong-a-Ilbo*. That publication was suspended during the latter years of the Japanese occupation and had resumed only in December of 1945. Now, eight months later, it was the most widely read newspaper in the capitol.

No trains were running. Absolutely nothing. How could he get to Taegu? After reassuring his mother, Jae Soon called a friend, another instructor at the university, hoping he'd have some ideas. Yes, he knew someone who had a friend whose family owned a truck that might be capable of a journey over those rough roads, if it didn't rain. And the friend offered to cover Jae Soon's classes for him, as well.

"But I can't drive!"

"Don't worry. The driver comes with the truck."

So by mid-morning Jae Soon was looking out of the truck's window at Suwon, a short distance south of Seoul. The old city was surrounded by massive walls, the fortress guarded by ornate gates with their double tiered roof lines curving toward heaven. Suppose King Chongjo, one hundred and fifty years ago, had been successful in his attempt to move Korea's capitol to this "Flower Fortress", as it was called? Jae Soon pondered the question while the driver guided the truck. It jounced over the unpaved road. What would Seoul be like today if that had happened? He'd be living somewhere else, maybe down here. All of this countryside was new to Jae Soon. The only place he'd ever traveled to before was Chunchon, up in the northeast. He'd been just a boy then. He still remembered his excitement in traveling there.

This excursion might have given him just as much pleasure if his reason for travel were not so serious.

Jae Soon and the driver covered more than half the distance by nightfall. They stopped in Taejon. It was a city of moderate size whose most prominent features were the smoke stacks of the textile weaving factories and the food processing mills. He found a yogwan after asking directions from a passerby. It looked like a comfortable inn. He took rooms for himself and the driver. After a simple meal of rice, soup and kimchee, he rolled himself into the thick quilts. Worrying about Jae Yun was useless until he could follow up with some action.

In the morning they continued south. Green and fertile valleys extended on all sides toward the ever-present profile of the hills. The road bypassed all the small villages with only clusters of thatched roofs to indicate their location.

The rice was nearly ready for harvest. This land fed a lot of people. Winter barley would be planted as soon as the land was cleared. Double cropping was common in this southern portion of Korea, due to the its more temperate climate and the extended growing season.

Jae Soon thought of his wife and found to his surprise that he had an unexpected longing for the sight of her face. Young Sa was a gentle woman, soft voiced and pretty in a delicate, almost ethereal way. She sometimes appeared as if she might be lifted into the air at any moment to drift about like an insubstantial blossom. She was always respectful and deferred to his wishes without question. He discovered soon after the marriage that she was pleased with the arrangement made by their parents.

But he could not stop thinking of In Ja.

For that reason he was all the more surprised that Young Sa's image should come to mind first today. He'd resolved months ago to cast all memories of the lovely In Ja from his mind. But he couldn't, although she was in America and he doubted he'd ever see her again. He never mentioned her name to Young Sa. Why should he? She need never to know about that part of his life. But did she have some knowledge of this other woman? He sometimes suspected she did, but it was not a question he could ask her.

Their wedding had taken place in May and it was simple, in keeping with the austere conditions of Korea in its first year of liberation. The ceremony was performed in the main cathedral of the Chondogyo, a long building of red brick with a tall steeple, located in the center of Seoul.

He remembered how she'd looked, with her dress of heavy white silk. On the skirt was an embroidered design of a Manchurian crane in flight, its red crest glowing, the black wing tips brushed in black. The symbol of fidelity. Near the end of the ritual he noticed her dark eyes beneath the western style veil that covered her glossy hair. They glistened with tears.

It was then that he resolved to try to be the kind of husband she expected.

They greeted the guests at a reception in the Bando Hotel, Seoul's finest. He'd changed from the dark western suit to a traditional brightly colored chogori and the pantaloons that he seldom wore in these modern times. Young Sa remained silent through all of this, as if she was determined to conform to the expectations of a perfect Korean bride. She did not smile. Her parents seemed more like grandparents to him. Well, she was the youngest of their nine children. Jae Soon could not imagine his own vigorous mother and father ever looking so frail and grey.

Later she'd appeared contented with the domestic routine, even though she was a recent graduate of Ewha University, even reconciling herself to his mother's autocratic ways, so he felt no guilt that he was absent from his parents' home much of the time. She never complained and always seemed pleased when he returned to it.

How strange that his recollection of her should be this intense.

They were nearing Taegu. The old truck lurched whenever it hit a pothole. Vast expanses of fruit orchards lined both sides of the road. The Taegu apple, valued through all of Korea and the neighboring parts of Asia as the queen of all fresh fruit, grew abundantly in this area. He still remembered a time when his uncle, Han Ju, brought some straw baskets filled with those apples to Seoul. Their pungent aroma perfumed every corner of the house. That was before the Chunchon time but he could smell them yet.

The family home of his mother and uncle was somewhere near here. She'd never returned to it, not once, after marrying his father. Well, times were hard then. Perhaps someday he'd ask her about those years, when there was a quiet moment, when the overwhelming details of daily existence did not press upon them as now.

Smoke, billowing clouds of it, filled the sky above the textile mills. Those provided work for the growing population, more than a quarter million persons, he'd heard. Easy to believe. Small houses crowded every narrow street.

How would he ever locate his brother in this place?

The city was smaller and poorer than Seoul. No wonder that Seoul was a strange and distant place to most who lived elsewhere. For some it was a mecca of opportunity and beckoned irresistibly. For others it was the source of alien customs and ideas and best avoided.

What was he doing here? He was a teacher, a scholar. He was not concerned with the dirty intrigue of politics. He'd resisted all the efforts of that Mr. Cho to involve him in partisan dealings. Only because of Jae Yun and his duty to his family did he travel now in this dust and discomfort. That brother! Always getting caught in the middle of whatever action was heating up. And it was always Jae Soon's obligation to rescue him.

In his attempt to locate him Jae Soon first called upon a former classmate who was teaching at the local boys' school. Mr. Min had once been his close friend but he hadn't seen him recently, so the man greeted him warmly. Together they walked to a nearby teahouse and sat down at a secluded table in a corner where they could talk in privacy.

After explaining the purpose of the visit, Jae Soon asked, "What's the situation here now?"

"Of course you know about the strike. But there are other problems as well," Min told him, narrowing his eyes in appraisal of the situation. "Other workers are joining the protest, the printers, the electrical workers, and more. Violence broke out when a right wing labor union moved its members in to replace the strikers. There was a battle between the two groups and some mass arrests took place. That might have been when your brother was picked up. If he was anywhere near that type of action he would have been swept in, right along with the others. The police don't ask questions."

Their two dark heads bent low and closer so that Min's words could not be overheard. He described the anger of the mob. Then he added, "As you may have already heard, the summer grain harvest is far below the amount expected and the rice crop, also, is predicted to be short this year. After last year's dreadful inflation everyone fears another year of hardship. Since the police have the duty of grain collection and the responsibility of setting quotas, they bear the burden of blame for shortages."

He called to the waiter to fill their cups again. "Rumors are that the American military government is favoring the police and anticommunist groups in grain distribution. It's even been charged that the United States is taking our rice, as the Japanese did, and leaving the cheaper, inferior grains for us to eat."

"That's news to me. Is there any basis for those suspicions?" asked Jae Soon.

"Who knows?" His friend shrugged. "What matters is that so many persons are willing to believe. Yesterday there was a protest. A big crowd demonstrated about the food distribution. It ended in violence, of course. A policeman was injured. Then a worker was shot dead. There are strong feelings on both sides."

"Well, all I want to do is to find my brother and get him out of here," Jae Soon said as they left the teahouse. "How do you suggest I start?"

"You can begin by asking about him at the central police station." Min gave him directions. "You're right to be concerned. That jail is no joke."

Jae Soon found the official building after a short walk through Taegu. Solid stone, he thought. Some contrast to the low and fragile buildings surrounding it.

He was standing on the corner looking at it when, without warning, men swarmed into the main street, flowing past him like a swift
current. More shouting resounded from the narrow side streets. At
the head of the crowd four men carried a stretcher. The body on it
appeared lifeless. They headed for the steps leading to the police station.

He watched, not thinking of escape, while police in uniform,
Koreans like himself, marched in rank. Why, it was brother against
brother! Each man brandished a wooden stick high over his head.

Those look just like the tools women use to wash clothes, Jae Soon
thought, but certainly more dangerous. When the sudden realization
struck him that he would likely be caught between the police and the
oncoming protestors he had only a moment to run. He crouched
behind the corner of a building, and watched the unfolding scene
with increasing horror.

The police waded into the front lines of the demonstrators, swinging their clubs as the rampaging men inched closer, striking down
the ones in close range. The sheer numbers soon overwhelmed them.
Some officers wriggled through the crowd in an attempt to escape.
Others were blocked and could not get away. The mob, infuriated
now, stabbed and struck at anyone in uniform, using axes, knives,
rocks, any object that could serve as a weapon.

At last they seized the police station itself and the rioters who
managed to enter it began to pass out guns, placing them into the
hands of men whose fury was now beyond any control.

A voice within Jae Soon warned him to flee but he could not
move. Nothing in his life had prepared him for the horror of this
brutality. The American tactical troops rolled up in their jeeps and
took charge, firing rifles into the air. Mesmerized and fascinated, he
watched until it was too late to escape. He felt the wrenching pain as
his arms were pinned behind him. He looked up to see a tall, red
headed man glaring down. In a short time the Americans rounded

up all the rioters and everyone else on the street, Jae Soon among them.

The jail cell was too small. So many were shoved into it that it was possible to sit only at the risk of being trampled. But once they'd calmed down these men seemed quite ordinary to Jae Soon. It was difficult to realize that less than an hour earlier they'd been shouting and beating the police. Now they looked like any workmen, dressed in loose clothing of coarsely woven hemp, men who struggled with heavy, overloaded chige on their backs in the streets.

He'd like to have a conversation with one of them. Too bad their dialect was impossible for him to understand. Besides, he was set apart by his clothing. They knew he was not one of them. Lean and hard muscled, these prisoners had faces burned red from long days working out of doors.

Not since he was a boy in Chunchon had he come into close contact with the farmers. A student and a teacher, he lived closer to books than to men. But his curiosity was becoming infused with a growing sympathy and he desired to understand them.

When he was first thrown into this prison Jae Soon wondered how anyone in his family would find him. He felt totally helpless. Particularly depressing was the knowledge that he allowed himself to fall into this predicament. Stupid! He should have kept his wits about him.

He thought of his father. What would he do in this situation? That man kept a strong faith in the teachings of Chondogyo. It had guided him through all the difficult times when he was imprisoned and then exiled into the harsh conditions of Kangwando. His father still maintained his belief that God and man are one, that other persons must be treated as if they were God. Nothing that happened to him altered his conviction.

How would his father expect him to behave now?

For five days Jae Soon endured. On the sixth day he was taken from the cell, marched down a long corridor and shoved into another room. When he saw who was waiting for him there he almost shouted, "But how did you get here?"

"Uncle! Is it really you?"

Astonished, Jae Soon looked at the man who awaited him in the prison reception area. He'd recognized him, only hesitating for one brief moment, though he'd not seen him for more than ten years. Older he surely was but Jae Soon could never have forgotten that high forehead on which the jet black hair formed a distinctive V, nor the sharp eyes that always twinkled, edged by laugh lines that were quick to form whenever he was enjoying himself. That had been often in the days when he shared the daily companionship of his mother's brother.

"How did you find me?" he asked incredulously. The words rushed out but his uncle did not answer. He, instead, warned with a gesture to be silent and then left to speak to an attendant waiting outside in the corridor.

The jailer escorted the two of them swiftly through a long passage leading to the main entrance where he left them and they passed through to freedom.

Pausing at the top of the steps, Jae Soon filled his lungs with fresh air. He took a deep breath, still thinking that this sudden and surprising release from that cramped and crowded, damp and fetid hole might be no more than a dream. He could not shake the feeling that he was still captive, and stepped briskly to disprove it, following Han Ju for more than half of the block before he managed to ask their destination.

"Where would you like to go?" was Han Ju's response.

"If it's possible, if you think there's one nearby, That is, what I'd really like more than anything is to bathe."

His uncle laughed heartily, sounding more like the man he remembered.

"Then we shall do our best to locate a place," he promised, and hailed a man passing by to request directions.

After being told that a mogyokt'ang was not far, the two men turned a corner and walked some distance on a narrow street with Han Ju stopping to scrutinize the sign of each small shop as they passed it.

At last he stopped, finding the famililar symbol, a canoe with three furled sails. Stepping inside, he spoke to someone and, satisfied that he'd found the right place, he poked his head out again and invited Jae Soon to follow him down the passage that opened onto a large room at the back. As soon as his eyes became accustomed to the blanket of steam issuing from the immense pool of water in the center he saw several men submerged in it up to their chins.

Little more was said until he'd washed and scrubbed himself with basins of water at the pool's edge. The red tile floor tilted outward with drain gutters around the edge that carried this away. Not until satisfied that he'd rid himself of the prison filth and odor did he climb into the massive hot bath.

Jae Soon eased himself into the water beside his uncle and gave a great sigh of satisfaction. "Now, tell me everything," he demanded.

"I had to be certain it was really you in that prison before I could take you out," Han Ju began. "That's why you were brought first to the reception area. I wasn't sure, even when I recognized your name on the list. It was hard to believe. After all you were only a boy when we saw each other last, but I should know that you'd follow your family tradition of spending at least a little time incarcerated." He added this with his familiar smile.

"All I have to say is that I am grateful to have that sojourn in autumn. Can you imagine that place in the heat of summer? Or worse, in the miserable cold of winter? And I would not have been there at all if not for my brother. I was searching Taegu for him and I ended by being snagged in the net of a mass arrest!" He sat up so quickly that a wave of water slapped against the side of the pool with a splash. "We must find him immediately! He may still be in the very place I've just escaped."

"Relax. He's already out and back to his reporting. It was his imprisonment I learned of first and I arranged his release this morning. We'll meet him tonight at my house."

"Your house? You live here? Does my younger brother know about me?"

"Not yet."

"Then how did you learn of this?"

Han Ju gave his nephew another one of those looks that meant clearly "don't ask." All he said was "I happen to be acquainted with persons who knew."

"If you can't tell me that, explain at least how you come to be in Taegu yourself? Why haven't you visited our family in Seoul? Don't you know how we've worried during your long silence? My mother, more than anyone. Have you thought of her?"

"Of course I have." A shadow passed over the face of the older man, peeling away all signs of his former jovial expression. "To see me now would pain her more than not knowing," he said after a moment of silence. "At the time I went to Japan to study, you must remember, all of us believed there would be no end to the domination of our country in our lifetime." He paused, then slammed one fist into the other so that the water leaped up. "I wanted to be somebody. Not a slave, not an underling." He calmed and continued. "I studied. All the time, until I became as much like the Japanese as it was possible to be, passed their examinations. I was on the way up, at that time, so it seemed wise to cooperate. After all, I was a good engineer. They needed me." He stopped, lost in thought.

"And when the war began." Jae Soon encouraged him to speak, recalling the early infrequent visits of his uncle, visits that had stopped altogether after the war started.

"Yes, when the war came into our lives I was forced to to face the reality of what I had become. I found it imposssible to continue playing that role. Not that I was a coward, but I could not become a cog in the war machine. So I chose to disappear; changed my name, wandered. How long? Who knows? It is unpleasant to think of that part of my life now."

"That's why you didn't communicate with us? To protect yourself from discovery?"

"Partly. But I also felt shame. I knew many would consider me a collaborator, when, if, I returned to this country."

"You did no worse than many others." Jae Soon found he wanted to reassure this man.

"To me that is no excuse," Han Ju declared. "Shall we leave now, if you are ready?"

"I feel completely refreshed," Jae Soon told him after he'd dressed and they resumed their walk. "Though I'd like some clean clothing." He thought of the driver who'd brought him to Taegu. What had he done when Jae Soon failed to return to the yogwan on that first day? He'd have to send a message, in the event the man still waited.

The long shadows of the autumn twilight shaded the street now. Many people hustled past him intent on their own errands. A sudden awareness of his great hunger attacked him and when he saw the sign of a poonsik jip he found the noodle shop too enticing to pass by.

A great brass bowl heaped with the mound of long myun in a spicy, steaming broth was set before him and he ate without interruption.

"This simple food never tasted so delicious," he explained when he'd finished. Then he asked his uncle, "When did you decide to return to Korea, then?"

Han Ju, who had been eating at a more leisurely pace, watched his nephew's enormous appetite with amusement. "A few months after the war ended. My wife wanted to see her family once more. She persuaded me to try living here, at least for a while." He leaned forward over the low table where he sat opposite Jae Soon and his speech became intense. "Can you have any idea what a stranger I felt myself to be? After so many years' absence? Fifteen years! I'd forgotten our customs, or so I thought. As for language, well, I speak Japanese with far more skill. My Korean is on the level of a school boy, but it is improving."

"So. You are married."

"Yes, and to tell the truth, that's another reason that I still hesitate to be reunited with our family. I married freely, by my own choice. My wife is the sister of a classmate whom I met while in Japan. She comes from the region near Kyongju, and her family is chungin, not on a social level with ours. How do you think she would be received by them?" He raised the cup of podi cha to his lips. "Times may be changing but I know that distinction is still important to them."

"Perhaps you are mistaken. This is a time of great confusion and uncertainty all over Korea," Jae Soon reminded him. "Anyway, I'd like to persuade you to reconsider. Ohmanee would be so happy. She's never lost faith that you would return. What am I to tell her?"

Han Ju did not answer. "Let's go," he said, rising abruptly.

The streets of Taegu were quiet, strangely emptied when Jae Soon and his uncle left the noodle shop, though the evening was still early. The American military government had imposed martial law upon the province in an attempt to control the violent demonstrations. Only the most vital traffic rolled on the usually crowded city streets.

"I'd like to return to Seoul as soon as I've seen my brother," the young man told Han Ju. "How can I manage that?"

"You should be able to take the train this time."

"How can I? The strike's still on."

"The American military is pushing some through. I'll get you a pass on one of them."

Jae Soon looked at his uncle, waiting for some explanation, but he could see that no answer was forthcoming. He should know by now that he'd never get one. Instead, the man said only, "You can sleep in my home tonight. Your brother may be waiting there already. It's not far from here."

After a short ride on the streetcar, Han Ju guided Jae Soon to a small house tucked in among many others of similar appearance on a narrow side street. Passing through the entrance gate, they crossed a small square courtyard and his uncle led him to the central room of the L shaped structure. Jae Soon shed his komusin on the maru, a long narrow corridor of polished wood that ran the entire length of its single story, and stepped in his stocking feet through the doorway after Han Ju slid it open. Revealed was a warm and pleasant room, lined with handsome wooden chests and offering the comfort of carefully arranged silk cushions.

It was the chests that caught his attention. He could see, immediately, that each represented the fine craftsmanship of an earlier age. The tall chaek jang on the far wall contained books on three upper shelves, while the panels of the doors below were inlaid with gingko wood. The burnish of its laquered surface contrasted with the smooth dullness of the brass ornaments and hinges, while the slender feet raising it above the ondol floor were intricately carved.

His uncle noticed his appreciation. "This one," he said, indicating a long, low chest, "holds paper. This," he patted the scholar's desk next to it, "is of elm wood." He rubbed his hand along the polished surface. "And this, of course, is a chest for blankets. This is my study and sleeping room, when I am not entertaining guests like you. A simple room, but it suits my needs. I'll ask the maid to bring tea."

Alone for a moment, Jae Soon reflected that he'd be interested in meeting the wife for whom his uncle had given up so much. However, he knew that was unlikely. Only a young servant girl appeared, setting a steaming pot of podi cha before him.

When Jae Yun arrived soon afterwards, his older brother's first reaction was to harangue him for bringing grief and suffering but he curbed his tongue on first sight of his gaunt figure. Under the best of conditions Jae Yun never gained even a kilo but his brief prison stay had altered his body to the point of emaciation.

"How could I know that you would follow me here?" he demanded, between bites of rice cakes. "I'm fully capable of caring for myself. You might have reminded Ohmanee of that. And you must remember," he added while reaching for another, "that if we had not come here and been tossed in prison, the chance of finding our uncle would have been zero."

"That's certainly true," Jae Soon responded, "and I never expected your gratitude anyway. I did this for our mother. Now, will you come home with me tomorrow?"

"Oh, no. My work here is not finished. There's been some violence in Yongch'on and the nearby villages, as well as in Chonju. Many are rising up against the police and the policies imposed by this military government. The resentment's been smoldering so long that flames may break out any where, any time." Pausing to sip cha, he raised his voice with emphasis on each word. "This revolt has the potential for a major rebellion."

"And you wish to be in the middle of it!"

"Not a matter of choice. I have to be here. It's my responsibility as a reporter."

"It's those communist agitators. They're behind the entire filthy business." Han Ju had been listening, silent until now. "The leftists stir up the workers with their speeches, making them discontented." He rose and began to stride back and forth.

The two brothers looked at each other with surprise. His accusations were harsh, yet neither dared to dispute an elder. Jae Soon shrank back on his cushion. He would allow his outspoken brother to frame the reply.

"The taste of meat comes from chewing, and of words from speaking," began Jae Yun, as if to soften the remarks to follow. "Uncle, pardon me, but you have been absent from our country for a long time. You may believe that Korea is still as it was when you left. Conditions are changed. Believe me. Greatly changed."

"Some ideas are permanent. The important ones never change."

"Allow me to explain, uncle. The lives of our people, particularly those in the villages, have been shattered since Japan began to use our country in its preparation for war. Forgive me if you think that I am speaking without respect for you, but I truly believe you do not understand the present conditions here."

Han Ju did wear an expression of disbelief while his young nephew lectured him, but he listened without interrupting.

"Young men left their homes in the country, often with no choice. Their hands were needed in the factories, in the mines, and for some, on the battlefield," Jae Yun went on. "Now the war has ended and what do you see all around us? Idle factories, with no materials, no parts, no skilled supervisors. Flooded mines, left to ruin."

"Yes," interrupted his elder brother, finding his tongue. "There are many today without the means to continue their daily struggle for simple existence. And more refugees crowd our cities, fleeing from communism in the north."

"There's no one prepared to give us the leadership for solving our problems," Jae Yun continued. "The force of resentment leaves no remedy but protest in the streets. Yes, there are communists among us, and they do offer one solution. But they do not gather the fuel. They are only lighting the fuse."

He slumped back, momentarily exhausted by the effort required by this speech. Jae Soon watched his uncle, silent and thoughtful, with apprehension. They were his uncle's guests. He'd rescued both from prison. Now he was being insulted within his own home. His position as elder was challenged. How would he react to this ill mannered behavior?

Calmly, it seemed. Speaking slowly, his uncle asked, "Tell me then, what is to follow? There must be some form of control. This country cannot be allowed to fall into chaos. Would you have this violence continue?"

"It's no solution to throw everyone who protests the wrongs into prison," Jae Yun insisted. "We must examine the causes and look for solutions."

"No one trusts anyone else. Suspicion flows like a swollen river through every city and town, Uncle," Jae Soon attempted to explain.

"The people say that what we have now is nothing more than an interpreter's government," Jae Yun went on. "The only Koreans with positions of authority are those with knowledge of the English language, those with connections, favored by the Americans. It's not our people making choices and decisions but only a handful of those persons who smell of butter!"

He spat out the words with a bitterness that surprised even Jae Soon. He'd observed his younger brother since they were children. Jae Yun was the one to look, always, for a better way, for an ideal. First he'd fled to China and risked his life with the underground. Now he wandered like a vagabond, sketching the scenes of his observation with the powerful strokes of his pen, protesting, endlessly protesting. But this bitterness was new. How long can he continue, wondered Jae Soon. He's wearing out his very marrow.

"Our liberation has become a nightmare," Jae Yun continued. "Only one month past, the newspaper *Chosun Ilbo*, which you know is the last to criticise, wrote that now the Korean people are suffering more than they ever did under the Japanese rule. If your idea, increasing the control, prevails, there will be more persons in our jails than there ever were during the colonial period."

"Do you deny the need, then, for the innocent to be protected?" Han Ju persisted, with his low, even tempered voice.

He refuses to argue on the same level with my brother, thought Jae Soon. He watched the dark eyes narrow as his uncle stated, "It is the people themselves who demand security, discipline, protection by the police from these ruffians of the Korean Communist Young Men's Association."

"Every political faction has an organized youth group, Uncle," Jae Yun countered. "The right uses theirs to harass the left and their tactics are equally brutal."

Their conversation continued in the same vein until their uncle, noting the late hour, finally quelled Jae Yun's vehement dialogue with him by observing that his nephew had become a strong willed and stubborn man with a powerful tenacity for defending his beliefs.

"But I'm still happy to have gotten you out of that prison," he told him. "I hope you can stay out. After all, we must remember that we belong to the same family and that is more important than any difference that may exist between us. It's safe for you to speak of these matters among ourselves," he cautioned Jae Yun, "but you must always guard your tongue when you are with outsiders."

In the calm that followed Jae Soon was compelled to ask his uncle, "How is it that you can remain habitually composed and cheerful, as I have noticed, after all of the trials and hardships you have endured?"

Another of those dark shadows passed like a ghostly hand across the face of the older man and he took some moments before he tried to answer.

"That is a proper question and it deserves a truthful reply. You may have expected to see my face prematurely lined with sadness," he said. "How can I answer? Am I happy? Sometimes, yes. At other times there is an infinite grief within me." He looked up at them and the laugh lines crinkled around his eyes. "I try to seize the fleeting moment before it is past, capture it, consider the reflection it casts, as if looking into a mirror, cherish its goodness before I let it go. Yes, some element of value does exist in each moment, no matter how grim it may seem at the time. If you try to be happy now, not wishing for a better future or lamenting the lost, golden past, well, then you may be able to see the joy of life itself in the present time."

He saw Jae Soon's look of skepticism and asked, "Could you not find something fruitful even in your prison hours?"

"Perhaps you're right." his nephew admitted. "Sometime during those hours when I felt that I could sustain myself no longer I became aware of my compassion for my fellow prisoners and I was grateful for the opportunity to know and understand them. Is that what you mean?"

"Yes. That's an apt example. Even the experiences of suffering may sharpen your senses, compel you to reach a greater awareness and responsiveness."

Jae Soon thought of his words on the following day while he sat upon the hard wooden bench of a railroad car rocking its way northward. He felt a longing to communicate with his beloved uncle, always, in such an intimate manner, but he knew it was impossible. Their life goals pulled them in opposite directions. He could not predict, even, when he would meet Han Ju again. He'd been unable to persuade the man that a welcome awaited him from his family.

This passenger car was a good deal more comfortable than the truck he'd used for the journey south, though it was ancient. Some of the windows would not close and each time the train passed through a tunnel he was enveloped in a cloud of black soot. However, he was grateful for its comparatively swift ride. With no unforeseen delays he would arrive in Seoul in the morning. He would waste no time in continuing on to his parents' home in Uijonbu. Imagine the glow of happiness upon his mother's face when she learned of his brother's and his safe release!

He particularly relished the opportunity to bring her the news of Han Ju after all this time, for he knew that this first substantial reassurance of his well-being, even if she couldn't see him, would bring Sun Yi immense pleasure.

He regretted Jae Yun's refusal to accompany him. He left his younger brother planning his journey to Kyongju as part of his news gathering mission. Jae Yun had encouraged him to go along, suggesting that a messenger could be sent to their parents. It was a strong temptation. For years Jae Soon had wished to visit this ancient city, capitol of the Silla kingdom. He dreamed of seeing the legendary Sokkuram Grotto on the side of the pine covered summit, its massive statue of the Buddha facing the East Sea. The white granite sculpture carved in the Eighth Century was the most perfect Buddha of its kind anywhere.

But now he felt an unexpected longing drawing him homeward. He refused the invitation with no regrets. The Buddha would wait.

From the window he saw a peaceful countryside with no hint of the turmoil occurring in the nearby villages and towns. Sometimes he watched a farmer patiently following his ox and plow in a field. A flash of brilliant yellow suggested a full blown valley of rapeseed. Clusters of thatch roofs indicated a village, and everywhere along the railbeds tall and spindly cosmos bobbed in the breeze, the pinks, mauves and purples bending to the wind on slender stems, swaying petaled heads with each gentle motion.

Presently his eyes closed and Jae Soon slept lightly, unsure of the difference between wakefulness and slumber, while the train's wheels beat a rhythmic sound that lulled him. He felt himself flying north, effortlessly, through the clear and warm air. He was surrounded by dozens of white cranes, each one a life-like replica of the bird embroidered upon his bride's wedding dress.

The crane, symbol of eternal fidelity, mated for life.

He moved easily among them as their wings beat steadily up and down, the black spot on each appearing and disappearing, the red crests moving steadily toward the north, bringing him closer with each stroke to his home.

Part Six
1948 to 1951

Sun Yi saw the speaker's podium clearly from the ring of wooden seats facing the capitol building, and she was on the shady side, an opportunity for which she was begrudgingly forced to thank Kim Tai Un. Most of the other spectators on the blistering summer day, the fifteenth of August, 1948, were being slowly broiled by the sun at high noon. Better than a deluge of rain, but still uncomfortable.

But she wouldn't think of missing this event.

Sejong-no was lined with people, thousands and thousands, all turned out to see whatever could be seen of the key figures in this inaugural ceremony. The noise was overwhelming, a din of voices blending with frequent blasts from marching bands, along the route. Yet no one would leave his vantage point for witnessing this day, long awaited in hopes and dreams.

She could even locate the old man himself, the first president of the new Republic, by his silvery hair. He sat in the center of the front row before the bank of microphones. When he rose to speak the frail voice of Rhee Syngman crackled through the loudspeakers ringing the Capitol Plaza.

"But, my fellow citizens, the final destination toward which we are all bound lies yet ahead, at the end of a road which may be both long and rough."

Yes, thought Sun Yi, although Korea is free at last, it's turned out to be only a partial freedom, with half of our country still in bondage to foreigners. All of my life I've believed that independence would solve our problems. Now I know that's not true at all.

"wearied and distraught though we may be from the struggles of the past, we can face the future with renewed strength, in the proud realization that we labor not only for ourselves but also for the peace and security of mankind."

When the president finished speaking he left the podium slowly, returning to his seat while the cheering, applause, and then more speeches continued. How grandiose, thought Sun Yi, but what do those words really mean?

After the U.S. general, MacArthur spoke, formally passing the Korean government from American into Korean hands, fifty thousand voices cheered as one. "Mansei!" May Korea live ten thousand years! Those were the words, the very same, that she'd shouted on that day in 1919. Nearly thirty years ago. Did anyone else remember? She'd marched in the streets of Taegu with her classmates, a young girl, pleading with all her youthful idealism for the freedom of her country.

Today she watched the dream becoming reality. A grandmother, with strands of silver shining in her black hair, she'd survived to witness the rebirth of her country. Perhaps she could do no more. Her children and the others of their generation. It was their turn now.

But how those difficult years had changed everyone! Sun Yi glanced at the members of her family. Beside her, rigid and silent, her husband. Dr. Lee appeared to be unmoved by this outpouring of emotion. She knew he detested the mass behavior of a crowd. Was he remembering his own years in prison and all of the times he'd risked his family's security to aid patriots in the countryside? Like so many others of his generation he'd devoted his full share to the realization of this day. Yet he'd not wanted to be here. He preferred to stand apart from any involvement in the politics of the present. Only because Kim Tai Un's invitation could not be refused had he finally agreed to accompany Sun Yi to this ceremony.

She looked at Jae Soon, feeling proud. Her eldest son was dressed in his dark suit despite the heat and managed to maintain his usual immaculate appearance, though some rivulets of perspiration lined his face. He was a youthful image of his father. The brief imprisonment in Taegu must have affected him, for he was now less involved in his career, more devoted to his family. She liked that, also. He lived with them most of the time and in the midst of that great snowstorm last December his delicate wife gave Sun Yi her first grandchild, a healthy boy. Sun Yi encouraged her son's wife to come with them today. Women in Korea, she told Young Sa, are entering a new age. We can feel free to appear in public. The young mother protested that she could not leave her child. She carried him with her, on her back, much of the day and he'd already learned to seize a moment of freedom, whenever she untied him, to crawl away from her. Sun Yi smiled to herself. Her grandson showed promise of a determined character.

Her own life was as happy as it had ever been. If only Han Ju were here everything would be perfect. To her great sorrow, he'd refused to return to Seoul and she consoled herself with the knowledge that he was, at least, alive and prospering, no matter what his current ambitions might be.

As for her second son, Sun Yi looked over the great mass of people and wondered where among them he might be. He was present, she was certain of that, but in his restless and inquisitive way he'd never remain long in one place.

On Sun Yi's left sat her old friend Kim Tai Un and she noticed that she held her head high today. She was a part of this government, one of the first women appointed to a position of real power. Her new prominence allowed her to secure the passes admitting them to the coveted seats close to the podium. Sun Yi reluctantly accepted her offer, for she couldn't risk inflicting further offense on her closest confidant.

She'd hurt Tai Un and she didn't mean to, but how could she, after all their years of friendship, not tell her what she was really thinking? The trouble began when Tai Un told her she would be a candidate for the Assembly in Korea's first free election, set for May of 1948.

It was a cold day in March, when she arrived with the news, soon after Gen. Hodge announced the date he'd chosen. Sun Yi tried to talk her out of running.

"Have you considered how your family and friends will feel if you lose?"

"I won't lose in this district. It's been promised to me," was her confident reply. "As for family, you know there's only my mother, and she's a thoroughly modern woman. She supports me fully, as she always has. You are my only friends, the only ones who really matter. Are you concerned that I'll fail you?"

"How can you say that?" Sun Yi began. "You know we're proud of all you've accomplished as a teacher, all the encouragement you give young women."

"It's for those very reasons that I must pursue this new goal," Tai Un interrupted. Her sharp eyes sparkled. "Think how much more I can achieve if I am a part of the government. I'll be an inspiration for them"

Sun Yi was shocked and dismayed over her decision. How could she convince her? It was useless to tell her friend that the political leaders were using her, a prominent educator, a pioneer, for their own goals. Politicians knew that her role as a leader of women covered her with a mantle of respect. The new constitution gave women the right to vote. They needed a woman candidate to satisfy the image of equality.

At last she said, "You'll be a token, a tool, nothing more than a symbol. You won't have a significant effect on policy. The men will see that any matter of importance remains in their hands."

Tai Un shook her head. Sun Yi was astounded that this brilliant woman could be so blind.

"You're an idealist," she cried, laying her hand on her friend's arm in protest. "Your idealism is shielding you from reality. Can't you see the hungry struggle for power? It's growing more intense with each day."

How do you know that?" Tai Un demanded, drawing back.

"I know because my husband and sons speak freely to me." Sun Yi covered her mouth with her hand but too late. The words struck her friend, reminding her that, by her own choice, she was an unmarried woman, alone, with no other confidant than Sun Yi. Aware of the damage she'd done, Sun Yi plunged on. "You'll be excluded from the conferences of the men. You'll not be allowed to know their intentions, their secret agreements. What will you do when you're pressured to vote against your beliefs?"

"If we support the party surely we'll be dedicated to its ideals."

Ideals? Sun Yi shook her head. "You are naive. Most of them have none. The forces of left, right, and middle share one common purpose. To hold the reins of power." She could not help but speak one last warning. "The first time you fail to cooperate the party will cast you aside."

Tai Un paled and pushed back her cushion, rising. "I never suspected you would fail me. I'll run for that Assembly seat, and I'll win. Then you'll see how wrong you were."

She left, angry as Sun Yi had never seen her before, and she believed their long friendship was ended.

As she had known, no woman stood a chance of winning. On May 10, 1948, in the first election in Korea's four thousand years, two hundred men were chosen, representing every town and village in South Korea. Those delegates elevated Rhee Syngman to chairman with a vote that was nearly unanimous. This despite the fact that no party held a majority. Independent candidates held more seats than any organized group.

Tai Un was rewarded with an appointment to a minor education office, however, and she basked in her new prominence. In a gesture of forgiving, she chose to forget Sun Yi's warning and invited her family to share the inauguration. On this day of celebration few people wanted to think about the problems awaiting the test of independence.

Though the new republic of South Korea might have achieved political independence, it still needed financial support from the United States. Shortly after those May elections the communist controlled forces of the north cut off all electrical power to the south, which had almost none of its own. Without the energy resources located in the northern mountains the fertilizer plants of the south were unable to produce the materials upon which millions of farmers depended. To avoid serious food shortages the government of Rhee Syngman was forced to seek even more aid from the Americans.

Sun Yi seldom talked to Tai Un in the months following the inauguration ceremony, for their lives followed ever more divergent paths.

But, on one particularly grey day in the cold month of November, Tai Un appeared without warning at her gate. She looked as bleak as the trees in the courtyard. The harsh wind had blown the last remnant of leaves from them, leaving their branches bare and uplifted as if in supplication, and her first words also begged forgiveness.

"It's a good omen that I find you at home. I need your help."

"You're shivering. Come inside right away," Sun Yi cried. Tai Un's face was pale, pinched with cold, the light faded from her eyes.

"I'll call for tea. When have you last eaten?" she asked.

"Eaten? Today? Perhaps I haven't."

Sun Yi, shocked by the vague response, so unlike her friend, urged her to sit down. She left to arrange for the preparation of some food. When she returned she found the other woman enveloped in such silence that she seemed unaware of Sun Yi's presence.

At last she lifted her head and looked at her. "I was a fool. How could I not understand your wisdom earlier?"

The admission was simple, blunt. How much pride it must have cost her.

"What's happened. Tell me!"

"Perhaps the most I can do is warn you."

Sun Yi laid a finger on her lips as the maid entered, bringing a small table and placing it in front of Tai Un. When she uncovered the brass bowls on it tendrils of steam rose from the soup and rice. The aroma had its intended effect. Tai Un ate hungrily. She waited for the maid to clear the dishes and leave before speaking again.

"Today a national security law was passed!"

Sun Yi gasped. "With the support of the president?"

"Yes. Everyone is suspicious of everyone else. Ever since the soldiers of the Fourteenth Regiment revolted last month at Yosu, they've feared another communist inspired conspiracy will happen. There were such speeches! 'We must destroy the responsible elements at their roots!' With that kind of talk the Assembly had little choice but to pass a strict law." She stood up, pacing the length of the small room, turning and pacing again. "I never anticipated such an action, never imagined I would be a part of." She did not finish the sentence, but buried her face in her hands, still walking back and forth.

"What does it mean, this law, to us? What will they do now?"

Tai Un lowered her hands to her sides, clenching her fists. "Don't you have any idea?" she cried. "Of course, more investigations, more arrests. Everyone will be more careful than ever. Public behavior, every word we speak, must be beyond reproach."

She walked close to Sun Yi. "Especially the teachers and newspapermen," she whispered. "They are the ones most open to criticism, the men who provide information and influence opinion." She grabbed Sun Yi's hand in both of her own. "Tell your sons. They will understand how to be cautious, won't they?"

Only a light snow was falling but gusts of wind from the north swirled each flake, frosting the air with a fine powder that clouded visibility on the streets of Seoul. Caught by this unexpected storm, Jae Soon decided to stay for the night. His younger brother lived in their small house in the city whenever he was not away on some assignment. Perhaps he'd be there.

He saw a glow of light when he stepped into the courtyard, confirming his expectation. Shaking off snow flakes from his topcoat, he called to Jae Yun.

"Too late and too cold for me to go home tonight!" The maid took his coat away to dry. "The warmth of this room makes me feel welcome."

Jae Yun rose from his table at the sound of his brother's arrival. "You are welcome. You chose a good time to stop here," he said, leading him into the room where his half eaten meal still waited. "I wanted to talk to you while I still have a chance."

"What makes you say that?" Jae Soon, assailed by a familiar sense of foreboding, glanced at him sharply. He could recall too many times coming to the aid of this younger brother, who, thin and wiry, always restless, jumped from one spot of trouble to another with the alacrity of a grasshopper.

"Forces beyond my control are closing in on me this time. My days of freedom are limited."

The young man ran his fingers, long and slender like his father's, through his thick hair, already tousled as if he'd repeated the nervous gesture often.

He fell into silence when the maid reappeared with another small table. She set it in front of Jae Soon and his nostrils quivered when she removed the covers from the bowls. "Ah! kom tang!" This soup was his favorite and he finished the entire serving while Jae Yun continued speaking.

"Do you recall the series of articles I wrote last month?" When Jae Soon nodded, he went on, "In them I described how our defense was seriously weakened by the pullout of U.S. troops last June. You remember I said they left us only obsolete weapons? M-1 rifles used in the war with Japan, trucks and jeeps that won't run? I predicted that our undertrained soldiers would find them useless if the North Koreans ever attempt that invasion they're constantly threatening."

Jae Soon nodded again, his mouth still full. It had been a heavy dose of criticism, no doubt of that.

"Our government wishes us to believe that our army is superior and well prepared to defend that border. That isn't true!" His dark eyes narrowed in anger. "It's not disloyal to write the truth if the purpose is to save the country. My words are genuine loyalty, not the false kind. My warning is intended to preserve our freedom."

"Even honey is bitter if it is served for medicine. Hearing the truth is often unpleasant. It disturb's one's good feelings. You should realize that," Jae Soon reminded him. "You are antagonizing some powerful elements. It's a wonder you've not yet been silenced." He pushed the table with its now empty dishes to one side. "If it is true, as you claim, that our army is unprepared and ill equipped, how did this happen? Why would the United States leave us in such a precarious position?"

"There are a number of reasons," Jae Yun countered. "Perhaps the American military governent does not know the extent of North Korea's preparation for war. Perhaps they do not wish to provide our president with the means to carry out his belligerent threats to unite Korea by force. Perhaps their attention is concentrated on the situation in Berlin." He stood up, shaking, and faced his brother. "Perhaps Korea is not important to them!"

Again those desperate hands ran through his hair, leaving some strands standing upright. "Have you read *Tong a Ilbo* tonight?" He thrust the newspaper toward his elder brother.

Jae Soon took it and, adjusting his glasses, read aloud:

"Washington D.C., January 12, 1950. United States Secretary of State Dean Acheson stated today, in a speech before the National Press Club, that it was important to defend Japan and that country would not be abandoned under any circumstances but 'the defense perimeter runs along the Aleutians to Japan and then goes to the

Ryukyus. The defense perimeter runs from the Ryukyus to the Phillipine Islands."

He looked up, puzzled. "There's no mention of Korea."

"Right. So now you are beginning to understand. Our country is without any defense."

"It still appears to me that the words you are writing can only harm you. You will be called a traitor. What are you achieving? You follow a dangerous path. Even you know that I must walk a tightrope each day I teach, even though I am not controversial, as you are." He leaned closer and in a soft but emphatic voice said, "I want to survive. To live. To take care of my family. Don't you?"

"Not at your price, elder brother."

"Then you must be prepared for what may happen to you. I can do no more."

Jae Soon took his bedding from the wall cupboard and unrolled it on the warm floor. He was soon asleep.

Jae Yun sat up for some time, however, and his thoughts were concentrated on what he knew he must do.

Two weeks later Jae Yun was arrested, and this time no one could rescue him. Sun Yi was not consoled that he was only one of thousands languishing in prison. She was haunted night and day by visions of her son being tortured, deprived of basic comforts, perhaps even racked by illness. None of her efforts to have him released were successful though she tried every ploy she could think of, appealing to every person she believed capable of influencing the responsible authorities.

Finally she was reduced to the one action still permitted. Each week she packed parcels of food and clean clothing, taking them to the prison office herself. She hoped that some of these items would reach her son.

He was charged with subversion under the provisions of the National Security Law. He was not the only one. Many other reporters and editors were, also.

Jae Soon tried explaining to his mother the serious nature of the crime his brother was alleged to have committed. He was cautious about involving himself in the case, however, for he feared his own indictment.

In December, 1948, the Ministry of Education had ordered personal histories of all teachers for the purpose of determining who held leftist views. The risk for him was too great to antagonize the ministry. He had the responsibility of his wife and child. Furthermore, he now knew the conditions of prison life firsthand. He wanted no more of them.

Jae Wan stretched and yawned, remembered that today was Sunday and rolled over in his cozy bedding. He listened to the rain beating on the tile roof, a rhythm that reminded him he'd neglected piano practice this week. But lying in bed was pleasant on this dreary morning.

He wondered what he might do today, the only time in the week free for his own pleasures. Six days out of the seven he rose early and now that he had begun high school he had more homework than ever.

Sun Yi's two youngest children, Jae Wan, fourteen, and his sister, sixteen-year-old Jin Sook lived in the small house on the northeastern side of Seoul most of the time, rather than riding the long twenty miles by train each day to their family home in Uijonbu. Sun Yi visited frequently but their long time maid cared for their daily needs. The children had little free time, for both were students at nearby Kyunggi High School. Classes were held five and a half days of the week and lesson assignments were long.

Jae Wan was proud of his dark tailored uniform with gold buttons and visored cap. Sometimes he missed his childhood home but the challenge of academic competition and the camaraderie of his friends made up for that. He thought Seoul was exciting. Despite strict rules that forbade students from entering its theaters and restaurants, he enjoyed the feeling that he was in the midst of hustle and activity.

But he did wish the rain would stop soon. Then he could play soccer in the afternoon. However, he knew that this storm, arriving in the last week of June, signalled the onset of the monsoon season, so he pulled the soft ibul over his head and drifted back to sleep.

Some time later he was roused suddenly when the covers were pulled roughly away. He opened his eyes. The maid looked down at him. Her face was distorted by fear. She shook him by the shoulders and, startled, he sat up. What was happening to this kind woman, usually so placid?

"Master!" she was shouting. "You must get up! It is so terrible! The soldiers are coming! I'm sure the war is beginning. Oh, what shall we do? Where can we go?"

"Stop that wailing!" Standing in his wrinkled nightclothes, Jae Wan rubbed his eyes, then covered his ears. "You know these little games are always going on. A little shooting from the north, a little shooting back across the border. Why do you get so excited?"

"This time is different! Something happened during the night. If you don't believe me, go look for yourself. The streets are filled with people and the police are everywhere. Oh. Oh. Oh," she moaned.

Jae Wan could not tolerate the sound of her crying. Dressing as fast as he could, he dashed outside. The narrow passageway outside his gate was deserted. He rushed toward the main street and stopped short. There was a crowd! Throngs of people, all of them milling about and looking confused!

A huge black car bearing the insignia of the police pushed through and, frightened by its failure to slow, people scurried backward to make a path for it. A voice blared from the loudspeaker mounted on its top.

"Listen! Listen! All soldiers! Return immediately to your post! Return immediately!"

It's Sunday, of course, Jae Wan said to himself. Soldiers must have been given leave for the weekend. But why would they be called back in this unusual way? The maid called it war. Could she be right? He walked on and spotted some men dressed in the drab uniforms and saw each one stopping a vehicle, anything, taxi, truck, wagon, so long as it was headed north, and begging a ride from the driver.

This part of Seoul was its northeastern section, closest to his home in Uijonbu, and that town was located midway between the city and the 38th parallel that divided his country into north and south.

That's where these soldiers are headed, right now, he realized and at the same time he felt a hard lump of fear growing in his stomach, spreading and tightening his muscles so he could not move but only stand and watch the men. More appeared at every moment, it seemed to him. Why am I afraid, he wondered. Everyone else is cheering. It sounds like the fans at a soccer game.

The rain still fell, a soft and soundless drizzle. The slender boy laid one hand on his bare head and felt its wetness but did not move. In that multitude of shoving, raucous bodies he stood alone.

Finally he asked an old man, "Do you know where they're going, haraboji?"

He was bent under the weight of his loaded chige and the wisp of white on his chin waggled when he replied shrilly, "To Uijonbu, they say. They'll chase those commies back where they came from in a hurry."

Was no one else as frightened as he? Jae Wan had heard the boasts, as had everyone else, of the South Korean Army's superiority. Now, in the face of this supposed invasion, it must be easy to be confident of victory. When those soldiers return they'll be big heroes. There's no reason to worry. He wouldn't, if only his mother and father were not somewhere out there in the middle of it, and his elder brother and his wife, and that mischievous baby nephew of his were there, also!

He remembered his sister, the only one of his family here in the city with him. She'd be waiting for some news. Well behaved young ladies did not roam the streets alone. Jae Wan raced back, grateful for this reason to seek the protection of his home.

Jin Soon was looking for him, standing by the gate, her cheeks stained by tears.

"Calm down," he called as soon as he saw her. "I don't know why you're acting so panicked. Don't you know we have an army to protect us? And all those tanks!" He hadn't seen any tanks yet, but there must be some. Every army has tanks.

They both jumped at the sound, like distant thunder, booming. Fresh tears coursed down Jin Sook's face.

All afternoon the two youngsters sat near the radio, listening for some news. They made a pretense of studying but could not concentrate. At last a voice, calm and steady, announced the outbreak of a dispute on the border between north and south. In a reassuring tone it described the bravery of the South Koreans in holding back the aggressors, and predicting a quick victory.

"See?" Jae Wan demanded. "I told you this is nothing." But he still felt fear. He was grateful that his sister hadn't seen what he saw in the streets.

It was nearly dark when Sun Yi found them there, their books scattered on the floor around them. Jae Wan tried his best to be nonchalant but Jin Sook clung to her mother, crying openly now.

"Is it true?" he demanded. "Are the soldiers fighting in Uijonbu?"

"Not yet," Sun Yi's voice lacked conviction. "But the wounded are coming to us."

Jin Sook begged her mother to remain with them.

"I can't stay. Your father needs me at the hospital. But I knew you'd be worried and I had to see you. Don't go outside. You'll be safer here than anywhere else."

"I'm old enough to take care of myself," he reminded her. "I guess I can take care of you, as well, if I have to," he added with a nod toward his older sister.

Jae Wan watched his mother leave. She'd promised to return whenever she could. He wished he did not have to appear brave, wished he dared call her back, ask her not to leave them alone, but he bit his lip and remained silent while she disappeared from his sight.

He woke early on the following morning. Should he go to school as usual? The streets appeared quiet, with only the usual routine traffic and people scurrying to their work, so he and Jin Sook decided they would carry on also. He'd have to hurry to reach Kyunggi before the first bell.

But he found the streetcars jammed. No busses in sight. It was three minutes to eight when he finally took his place in the school yard with the two thousand other young men. At precisely eight o'clock a siren sounded and the roll was called simultaneously by the leader of each class group. Then their voices rose in unison, saluting the flag of the Republic. The school band struck the opening notes of the national anthem and the entire student body passed in review before the principal, marching in step in their identical uniforms of summer blue with white caps. Forward they moved, into their classrooms, to await the arrival of their first teacher of the day.

Jae Wan had algebra and as his instructor entered the sixty first-year students rose as one, standing at attention and saluting him.

But during that first hour he could not keep his mind on the equations. What was happening to his family in Uijonbu? It didn't seem right that he should be here while they were in danger. Even if they escaped, what would become of his toys, his books? His piano! Would it be damaged?

The teacher completed his lecture and left the room. The Korean history teacher arrived. Rise. Salute. Be seated. What were his mother and father doing right now? He felt certain they could take care of themselves. But Ohmanee said yesterday that the hospital was filled with the wounded. Did that mean their soldiers might lose the battle?

From his seat by the window on the third floor Jae Wan looked out at the roof tops of Seoul and as his gaze wandered over the familiar scene he saw three planes hurtle past.

"Look!" he shouted, jumping to his feet.

Each of the other students rushed to the windows, to see for himself.

"Order!" shouted the teacher.

No one listened to him. All eyes fastened on the incredible sight. Airplanes glided low over the buildings and flames shot up behind them as they passed, followed by loud explosions.

"Wow!" exclaimed one boy. His eyes shone. "I never saw anything like that before!"

The teacher was shouting, scolding, but every student was on his feet, watching the aerial show as though it were an entertainment. Not one believed danger could touch them. They were observers.

Except Jae Wan. The tight feeling of yesterday spread into his chest, choking his breath, paralyzing his arms and legs. He saw the planes flying north, in the direction of his family's home. He heard the boys around him cheering. Why? They sounded exhuberant, joyful.

"What's going on?" He had to shout over the noise.

"School's been dismissed for the day!" came the answer. "We'll have a holiday."

He left the building feeling dazed. The streetcars were now overflowing with people so he walked, following the avenue toward his house, stopping now and then to read the wall posters with the latest news. All signs told of victory. Yet he was weighted by a heaviness that he felt down to the soles of his feet.

Jin Sook's school, also, was closed. She reached their home first. One glance at her face, terrified, sufficed to remind him of his responsibilty. "I'm the only man here," the fourteen-year-old told himself, and he determined to maintain a brave face, no matter how scared he was inside.

His reserve crumbled when the maid rushed in, this time telling of seeing refugees in the streets.

"You're mistaken!" he shouted. "It must be only the merchants selling their wares."

"Listen," she told the boy, "I may be only a maid but I know refugees when I see them."

Jae Wan ran to the corner to look for himself. What he saw dwarfed his greatest fears. He didn't want to believe the sight. Hundreds of figures streamed down from the hills to the north, many carrying bundles balanced on their heads. Others led children by the hand, pushed wagons loaded with furniture, sacks of food, old people. As some of them drew closer he found them so weary they were unable to speak or answer his questions. Finally he reached out and grabbed one boy by the shirt collar, shaking him, commanding, "Tell me where you are from!"

"Uijonbu," the boy replied. He was trembling.

"Why did you leave?" Jae Wan demanded.

"Because I want to live!" the boy sobbed.

Jae Wan released him, stunned, still not willing to believe, watching the exhausted parade. This can't be true, he told himself over and over. All of the reports say the fighting is taking place only near the 38th parallel, along the border. It can't be true!"

Early in the evening he heard the declaration of martial law. The radio screamed the warning. Sirens sounded and loudspeakers screeeched the words. No one was allowed on the street.

Alone with Jin Sook and the maid, Jae Wan sat waiting for more news. He now realized that his mother would not reach them tonight. No one could travel. Not his mother, nor his father, nor his elder brother.

Suddenly the house shook. There was an explosion and it was not far away.

"Play!" he shouted to Jin Sook. "Play the piano and don't stop!"

On Tuesday morning his school was closed. Vehicles roamed the streets with loudspeakers warning the citizens to stay inside.

Jae Wan had no desire to leave his home. It was still his refuge, safer than anywhere else, at least. Once during that interminable morning while he and his sister waited, hoping for a message from their mother, his curiosity overcame caution and he walked over to the main thoroughfare. Despite the orders that road was filled with people. Some were pulling or pushing carts piled high with possessions, others struggled under the weight of heavy bundles on their backs or heads, a few prodded oxen along. All were moving in one direction. South.

The only vehicles he saw headed north were trucks loaded with soldiers. The young men sang military songs while the wave of refugees receded to make way for them and roared their cheers. "Mansei!" Booming artillery sounded in the distance like the faint beat of a drum.

He remained with Jin Sook for most of the day. She was frightened and he could not leave her alone. Besides, his mother would expect them to be here when she arrived. But when? The hours moved as slowly as if each were a day in itself. He was surprised to find it was noontime when the maid served the mid day meal. His stomach was tied in knots and the lump in his throat prevented a single swallow.

The artillery fire grew louder in the afternoon. Thinking it was much closer, he slipped away to look at Chong Yang-ni Road. The confusion there was greater than ever. When he questioned some of those passing, he learned that their homes were even closer to Seoul than Uijonbu, but he didn't tell his sister. She cried often enough already.

"Please, master. You must eat," the maid begged, trying to tempt him with the steaming rice at the evening meal. But he only shook his head and ignored her.

"Ohmanee!"

Sun Yi appeared in the doorway just as daylight faded from the summer sky. Jae Wan jumped up, staring at her mudspattered chima.

"I walked all of the way," she announced before he could say a word.

His nephew was tied to her back in a sling. his small head resting on her shoulder, eyes tight shut. He helped to untie the boy and laid him on a cushion before asking, "Did you carry him all the way, also?"

"No, sometimes he walked, poor child, but that just slowed us even more. He's only two years old, after all."

"Where's Abuji ?" asked Jin Sook, as always fearful of the worst.

"Your father was still at his hospital when I left this morning," Sun Yi assured her daughter.

Her face, pale and drawn, etched with lines of exhaustion, shocked her children. The maid rushed out of the room, saying she'd bring something for her to eat.

"I stayed after everyone else had left Uijonbu, but finally I could not bear the thought of your being alone any longer. Your father has a duty to the wounded. He cannot leave them."

He could not take his eyes from the sight of mud dripping from her chima. Jae Wan had never seen his mother looking less than immaculate. Somehow her white dress now hopelessly bedraggled and soiled signified for him, more than anything else on this day, what was wrong. Nothing made any sense. His world was turned upside down.

Later Jae Soon arrived, bringing with him a basket of food and some clothing for his son.

"Where's your wife?" Sun Yi asked immediately.

"Isn't she here? I waited for her near the railroad station as long as I dared, for she promised to meet me there. When she didn't appear I thought she must be with you. She's not here?"

Jae Soon looked into each corner, as if he expected to find her. "Uijonbu was filled with North Korean tanks and trucks when I finally left."

Sun Yi told him that she'd last seen Young Sa at the hospital helping his father. She'd probably stayed. Wherever they were now, he'd look after her. But her voice lacked the confidence she was trying to convey.

Jae Wan pulled at a piece of paper protruding from his brother's pocket. "What's this?"

"Oh, that. It dropped from one of their planes. I forgot about it. What does it say?"

In large black print the words seemed to leap out.

Rejoice! South Korea Has Been Liberated From the Imperialists!

Jae Soon crumpled it and stuffed it back into his pocket, then picked up his infant son. The boy's eyes were nearly closed. He carried him into the adjoining room to sleep undisturbed. When he came out a few moments later he and Sun Yi began to talk in such low voices that Jae Wan could not distinguish the words, yet his instinct told him they were discussing the question that had been disturbing him as well. How much longer would this place be safe? He knew from the commotion he heard taking place outside that the neighbors were preparing to leave. If his family left also, where would they go?

Finally he dared to speak. "I'm old enough to help. Didn't I look after my sister for two days already?" He was tired of being regarded as a child simply because he was the youngest. He was almost as tall as his elder brother, if he stood up straight. If anyone deserved to be treated as a baby his sister did.

"You're right." Jae Soon came over and put his arm around Jae Wan's shoulder. "You can begin right now by helping us to pack. We're going to walk to Ewha Auntie's house on the other side of the city. We can spend the rest of the night there. It's close to the Han River. We'll get an early start in the morning, head for the south. Let's hurry."

The home of Kim Tai Un was located on the far southern end of Seoul. It was a considerable distance away from any main road the army might follow.

"Now?" Jae Wan's voice trembled. He'd not had such a sudden departure in mind. The night was moonless, the hour late. A light drizzle spattered the windows.

"Now," was Jae Soon's reply.

"What if Abuji comes here looking for us?"

"We'll leave a message for him, telling where we are."

Each carried what he could manage, a few necessities, some food, tied in cloth bundles. Jae Soon hoisted up his sleeping son and the boy nuzzled his head into his father's shoulder.

The streets, even in the middle of the night, were crowded. Their progress was slow. Traditional good manners disappeared as strangers pushed, shoved, and cursed. Though a curfew was in effect and the streets unlighted as a precaution against bombing raids, no one could enforce a law with thousands of people moving through the darkened city.

Midnight passed before they sighted the home of Sun Yi's friend. Tai Un was sitting close to her radio and she sprang up to greet them, shushing their voices almost immediately.

"Listen. The president is about to speak," she said.

The voice of Rhee Syngman, as if announced by her, began, sounding sad and weary. He read a short statement. The government was retreating from Seoul. It would move temporarily to Taejon, a town one hundred and twenty miles to the south, while the Army of the Republic prepared for the ultimate victory in which the enemy would be driven from their capitol. Admitting that the forces of the South were outnumbered and ill-equipped for battle, he beseeched the citizens to remember that the spirit was strong. He closed with a promise to return to Seoul soon.

As soon as his voice faded from the air Sun Yi turned to Tai Un. "Why are you still here?" she demanded. "Don't you know you will be in danger if you are discovered.? Anyone like you, with direct connections to the government, will be first on the list to be killed if Seoul is captured. Leave! Go to Taejon while there is still time to escape!"

"The assembly members voted on Monday night to remain but they changed their minds on Tuesday. You can do the same," Jae Soon added.

"Do you think I could run, when the rest of you are staying? I am not such a coward!" Tai Un stretched to her full five feet.

While Sun Yi continued her persuasion, promising to follow, to join her in the southern city as soon as Dr. Lee and Young Sa arrived, a great explosion rocked the house. Vases toppled. Wallhangings crashed to the floor. From the kitchen came the sound of smashing glassware. The baby woke and began to howl. Snatching him up, Sun Yi clasped her grandson to her breast and rocked him while over his head her eyes, wide with alarm, sought her son's.

When the second gigantic tremor, nearly as loud as the first, shook them, each person was rooted in stunned silence. Jae Wan was the first to move. He ran outside. He couldn't stand the tension. What was happening? He must find some explanation.

Rain continued to fall as though oblivious to the deeds of men. On the horizon tongues of flame were leaping up from the direction of the Han River, splitting and shredding the darkness.

Jae Soon followed and stood close to his young brother, watching with him. The boy looked up, hoping to gain some encouragement that this incomprehensible nightmare might have some end. His older brother was silent, however, only staring into the sudden brightness illuminating the night sky.

"What is it?" Jae Wan had to speak, to break this wall of silence.

"The bridge. It has to be the bridge," his brother muttered as if to himself. "I heard they'd planned to blow it up. But this is too soon. The army, people are still crossing. Too soon!"

The Han River, on the southern edge of Seoul, was three hundred yards wide and as deep as fifteen feet in some places during the summer months. The three lane bridge over it was the only way to leave the city, other than by ferry boat or the three railroad crossings. Jae Soon speculated that these may have been the target of the second blast.

Jae Wan's eyes grew wide with fear. "We won't be able to go south in the morning! There's no safe place for us."

Jae Wan must have dozed during the early hours of Wednesday morning but neither he nor anyone else, except for the baby in his innocence, could sleep soundly. At the first light of dawn Sun Yi's youngest son was on his feet. Before he left the house he filled himself with two bowls of hot soup and rice, enough to satisfy the maid, who hovered nearby watching him.

He'd promised his mother he'd be careful but he pushed through the crowded streets carelessly, hoping to discover what had happened during the night. Though he could see refugees still plodding through the city from the north, many, knowing there was no longer an exit, had stopped to sit in the roadways. Some looked bewildered, others simply confused or frightened. A few, bearing only blank stares, scared him and he stepped around them, hurrying on.

He heard the dull thud of artillery bombarding to the north, and though no one had said a word about it this morning, he knew that his father and his brother's wife were caught somewhere amidst the thundering explosions.

The boy, still wearing his student uniform of summer blue, rounded a corner and turned into the main avenue.

"Aigo !"

He was staring at a tank. The biggest tank he'd ever seen! It blocked the road, less than one hundred feet from him. That had to be a Russian T-34, although it was so much bigger than it had seemed in pictures. The front and sides were protected by thick armor plate and the turret was of heavy cast armor.

But it was the big red star on its side that startled Jae Wan the most. No doubt who owns that monster, he thought. He dared go no closer, for he could see uniformed soldiers beyond the tank. The wide cannon, sticking out like a snout, swiveled while he watched, cranking around in a quarter circle turn, and he listened to the whining noise it made, not realizing immediately that it pointed directly at him. When he did, he turned and ran as fast as he could, back to tell his family. Did he have news for them!

On the way he thought how suddenly quiet the streets had become. But those soldiers won't hurt us. We're all Koreans, after all. Would they kill their own people?

"The streets are filled with tanks and soldiers," he cried, pushing open the door. "But they're not shooting. It's more like a big parade. You must come out and see for yourselves!."

"We'll see enough when we walk home," said Sun Yi.

"We're going back?"

"Yes, since we can't leave the city. Your father will surely join us soon."

Before she left Tai Un, Sun Yi again warned her to be cautious and begged her to send frequent word of her well being.

As they retraced their path of the previous day crowds of people along the streets were already beginning to cheer. The loud clanking of their treads signalled the approach of more tanks. Some young boys even jumped onto the armored giants and rode with the soldiers, who were also cheering.

Jae Wan forgot the danger he'd felt earlier in the reassuring scene. He watched a few persons waving red flags.

"Some of those people have made a quick change since yesterday," he remarked to his mother.

She did not reply.

No foot soldiers were in sight. The only troops were those on top of the tanks. If it were not for the occasional sight of a building smoldering, Seoul looked much as usual. Encouraged, he kept reassuring his mother that they'd reach their home safely. Sun Yi only looked at him from the corners of her eyes. She was unwilling to be so optimistic yet.

His sister trudged along silently behind them, along with the maid. The baby bounced in his sling on his grandmother's back, staring at all the sights with his bright eyes.

Jae Soon had left, promising to join them later. He was still concerned about his wife and had gone to the home of a friend whom he thought might know where she'd taken refuge.

By mid-morning, when they were close to home, they heard a strange new sound. At first distant, it grew louder, closer. Marching feet, thousands and thousands of them. Soon he saw the first ranks of these foot soldiers.

"I never realized there were so many soldiers in all of our country!" Jae Wan spoke in amazement.

The sight was enough to stop him. He stared at these boys, for that is how they appeared to him, moving down the broad main street of his city. All sizes, all ages, all with guns.

"Ohmanee," he whispered. "That one looks younger than me!"

The youngster, no taller than he and far thinner, turned toward Jae Wan. Their eyes met for an instant before his head snapped back to attention.

He carried one large gun strapped to his back and balanced another rifle on his arm. The barrel trailed behind as he trudged on, leaving a long jagged line in the mud behind him.

Most of these soldiers smiled. They look friendly, even harmless, waving their hands to the cheering civilians who'd come out by now to line the streets.

"I thought they'd be cruel, Ohmanee. But they look just like us!"

He had different thoughts when, a bit farther on he saw the remains of a hospital building, flames still nipping around the gutted interior. North Koreans guarded its gate, guns ready, while they watched women and children searching among the stacks of bodies, all of the dead wearing the uniform of South Korean soldiers.

Sun Yi reached for her daughter's hand and gripped it tightly, hurrying her children past. No one spoke again until they were inside their own courtyard.

Strips of red cloth, already ragged, hung from every neighbor's gate, a sign of welcome for the invaders. Jae Wan dashed to his room, snatched up his red soccer jersey, tore it, and hung the remnants like streamers on their own door.

"Now," he told his mother, "we'll look like everyone else when they come by."

Sun Yi looked appalled. Have we come to this, she thought, that we are such cowards? But, alone, she could not resist. She would put all of their lives in danger.

There was no message from his father waiting.

"Let's walk to Uijonbu and find him," he suggested. "I'll go with you," and realized that for the first time his mother did not offer the protest of his being too young.

Instead she looked at her son and tried to smile at the efforts of this boy to behave like a man. But the muscles of her face were rigid. Would there ever be a time when she'd smile again?

She reminded him of the difficulty, saying, "The road is blocked by the soldiers, my son. Perhaps later we can try. Not now. Not yet."

Nothing to do but wait. Wait. The radio was the only source for news. Earlier there'd been a report that the Americans were sending help, air and naval forces promised by their president, Mr. Truman, to help defend Korea. Was it true?

He twisted the dials but found all radio stations controlled by the North Koreans and the only sounds were of patriotic marching music, interspersed with exhortations to rejoice in the liberation and to cooperate with the agents of their new government.

The orderly invasion met no significant resistance. Throughout the day an absence of noise, an unnatural calm, replaced the earlier booming of guns. The South Korean soldiers remaining in Seoul were more concerned with finding a means of crossing the Han River, the last barrier to their safe escape, than with meeting a useless death.

Jae Soon came to them, finally. He looked old, suddenly, nearly as old as their father.

"It's true," he said. "I saw with my own eyes. The bridge, blown by mistake all right. It had to be a mistake. There were so many dead everywhere, lying on the river banks, floating in the water. Not just the soldiers. All kinds of people. Is Young Sa here yet?"

He hadn't located his wife and no one was able to help him.

The droning of airplanes ended the silence, finally, late in the day. Jae Wan, standing at his gate, watched them flying low under the clouds. He strained his eyes to follow their course. One, two, three. Twelve altogether, in one formation. Small planes, with two engines. He could see the white star in a blue circle on each fusilage, below a bump that looked like a bubble near each tail. More small planes followed in new formations.

When these had all passed from sight, heading north, four more, larger than the first and each with four engines roaring, flew over his head.

Almost immediately, it seemed to him, a series of loud explosions reverberated through the thin walls of the house. What was happening now? The string of detonations, deep and booming, came from the north. Why? The fighting was supposed to have ceased up there with the victory by the Communists.

It's worse to be close to disaster, not knowing what's going on, than to be in the middle of the trouble, Jae Wan said to himself. We all know terrible things are taking place, but what are they?

He watched his mother's face. Would she console him? But no. She shared his suffering.

Together they walked to the top of the nearest hill, hoping to find a spot where they could see something to give them a clue, but daylight was fading fast. Jae Wan reached out for Sun Yi's hand, tightened his grip in response to her pressure, while they watched great clouds of grey smoke billowing higher and higher, mingling with the darkening sky, rising from the road that stretched toward Uijonbu, where she'd left his father.

After Dr. Lee persuaded Sun Yi to take the baby and leave on Tuesday morning warnings reached him that the North Korean forces were approaching Uijonbu. His immediate concern was for the wounded soldiers of the South Korean army. To save them from certain slaughter he must move the injured from his hospital before the enemy found them.

Young Sa, his son's wife, insisted on remaining with him and she, with the three nurses, helped him to find civilian clothing for those who were able to walk. After dressing in this protective camouflage the young men filtered into the crowd of refugees still moving south.

He moved the men with more serious wounds into the abandoned homes of his neighborhood, knowing their eventual discovery was likely. It was the best he could do for them.

The first of the invaders marched into town soon after the last patient had been transferred, swaggering with the confidence of their sheer numbers. They knew their forces, more than one hundred and fifty thousand men with the support of one hundred and fifty massive, heavily armored Russian T-34 tanks, would mow down the defenders. Furthermore, indoctrination had invigorated these men with the belief that the oppressed victims of American imperialism would welcome their arrival. They did not anticipate strong resistance.

Nor were these troops weary, for many of them rode, by train, directly into the center of Kaesong, the border town directly south of the 38th parallel, actually taking a position behind the beleaguered South Korean defenses.

At the sound of their approach Dr. Lee had time only to push his daughter-in-law and the three nurses into the underground shelter beneath the floor of the house before they banged open the gate and entered.

He turned to face six men. One, pointing the barrel of a burp gun at him. wore the insignia of a captain. Each of the others wore his sub-machine gun slung over his shoulder, with extra slings of ammunition beneath it like an elaborate chest decoration.

The officer held his gun on the doctor while he ordered the soldiers to search the house. Mud from their boots dropped clods of dirt onto the varnished floor and left deep scratches on its surface in each room as they passed through.

The doctor smothered his indignation at their crude manners, for he knew he must behave with caution and try to direct their wrath away from him if he were to survive. At the same time he couldn't help taking some satisfaction as he watched their expressions of amazement at the furnishings of this house. They sounded like country boys, with their rough Hamhyung accent, and their behavior betrayed them as exactly that. One ran his grimy hands over the piano keys and sprang back when the room rang with the medley of musical chords. Another seized Jae Wan's violin. His face shone with pleasure at the twanging when he plucked the strings. He tucked it under his arm while he looked around for more plunder.

In the kitchen one fellow scooped up the fine white rice from a large clay jar in the corner, letting the polished kernels flow from one hand into the other while the others stood around him admiring the glistening cascade. Then each man in turn filled his pack to the brim. One stopped to touch, one by one, the shiny utensils and containers of food.

Meanwhile, two of the others wandered into the vacant hospital rooms on the far side of the courtyard and emerged with some of his medical instruments in their hands. They pushed the doctor up against a wall and demanded to know the purpose of the mysterious equipment.

"You must be a member of the bourgeosie," accused one, poking his chest with the tip of the gun barrel. "You are one of the collaborators. An oppressor of the people."

What could he say? How could he make these simple country boys understand that these tools were necessary to the performance of his work? The folk medicine, hanyak, was probably all they knew. The metal pressed harder against his skin. He felt beads of sweat, cold, rolling down his cheeks and hoped they would not notice this sign of his fear. He searched his mind for the strategy that could save his life. He hesitated to speak, for he knew even the inflections of his Seoul accent could infuriate them. It punctuated the contrast between his comfortable way of life and their background of poverty, intensifying their animosity toward him.

"Wait!"

The captain appeared in the hospital doorway and the soldier stepped away at the barking of his command. The officer stepped closer and peered into the face of their captive.

"Don't shoot him yet," he ordered, while the others cowered under his wrath. "This man can be useful to us."

"You!" he addressed Dr. Lee, who was holding his body in a rigid posture to maintain his dignity under this threat. "You will serve us now."

He dispatched two of his men with an order to inform the commander about this hospital.

"Tell him he can bring the wounded here."

Then he assigned two of the others, one still clasping the violin tightly under his arm, to remain as guards while he took the last soldier with him to continue the survey of the area.

He had no choice but to give aid to the enemy. Thinking quickly, Dr. Lee agreed to their request but told them he'd need someone to help him. He could not allow Young Sa or the other women to reveal their presence while these enemies occupied their home. The cellar was a small place, uncomfortable at best, but it did protect them. He was overwhelmed with relief when he thought of Sun Yi and his grandson safe in Seoul with their younger children by now. If only she did not attempt to return!

He forgot his fear when he saw the many wounded. The procession seemed endless. Battered and bloody, the soldiers limped or were carried into the hospital rooms. Some looked even younger than his own son, Jae Wan. Though they were his enemy and he knew that not one of them would hesitate before killing him under other circumstances, the doctor's heart was touched by their suffering. After all, were they not one people, despite the indoctrination that separated the northerners?

He directed their placement, putting the most serious cases in one section where he could oversee their care, while those in less immediate need he relegated to the soldier-nurses who were ordered to follow his instructions. Soon even the maru was lined with bodies, some writhing in pain while others lay ominously still.

Darkness fell and still he labored. He was followed about by his guards, who watched with suspicious eyes the mysterious ministrations he performed upon their compatriots.

Young Sa and the nurses remained undetected but he dared not try to communicate with them. When a sliver of light began to outline the curved crest of Mt. Sorak in the east, the doctor stumbled with exhaustion and begged to be allowed to rest. He slept fitfully for a few hours but his restless dreams gave him little respite. He felt himself being tugged from one side to the other as the soldiers of the north and south competed for his attention. Awaking abruptly, he was immediately struck with the realization of his predicament. For when the forces of the Republic returned, as surely they would, he could be accused of cooperating with the invaders. Or, worse, the North Koreans would force him to go with them.

How could he escape either fate? He was doomed.

All day he moved about, doing whatever he could to help his patients, but thinking constantly of some way to evade his captors. Late in the afternoon of that Wednesday, just as he motioned to the soldier-assistants to remove one more of the recently dead, the doctor heard the loud droning of many airplanes. Before he had time to look out the window the building shook with a tremendous explosion. It was followed by another. Then the roof beams fell and the walls collapsed on top of him. Tongues of yellow flame flickered and ignited the crumbling remains of his home.

He heard, as if far away, screams of men trapped in the burning wreckage. The inferno ruptured from the center, intense, devouring every object in its path. Stunned, propelled by a power over which he had no control, Dr. Lee struggled to keep himself moving.

At last he came to his senses. He was dazed, yet unhurt, standing in his courtyard, and he was alone. Only a deep crater filled with black and smoking embers marked the spot where his house had stood. He listened to the booming of more explosions, inhaled the odor of burning flesh while bombers rained their instruments of holocaust over his Uijonbu, city of ever righteousness, and clouds rose from the consuming flames, turning the sky black.

In the streets the survivors ran, frenzied, seeking some escape. The doctor joined them but he walked, aware only of a strange center of calm within himself. He knew, somehow, in his bewilderment, that he had been given the gift of life while others died.

His daughter-in-law! Jae Soon's wife! She could not have lived. The horror of her fate, and those with her, overwhelmed him and he wandered to the edge of the destroyed town, walking aimlessly in his stocking feet until he lost track of time. Finally he found refuge in some collapsed debris and slept with the damp mists of night swirling about him.

When the light of morning woke him Dr. Lee sat up and saw only some of the people who'd lived in his town, now so utterly destroyed. He watched them wander, eyes glazed in fear and sorrow. No one knew where to go, or what to do. A few communist soldiers patrolled the former streets, blocking all of the roads leading away from the desolation. The destruction seemed to stretch endlessly in all directions.

Later, while he sat in a sheltered place attempting to recover his strength, he raised his eyes to the hills. Seoul lay on the other side. If only he had some energy! He would climb over them and find Sun Yi and the children.

Two figures were running toward him. He rubbed his eyes. Sun Yi stood in front of him, looking down, and beside her was his youngest son. Another dream. Then she called to him.

"Yubo!"

He stood up and threw his arms around her and she did not disappear. Without a thought for the propriety of such a public demonstration, he gathered them both into his arms.

At last he released them and stepped back. Sun Yi gasped. Then he looked down at himself and saw that his clothing was shredded, his feet clad only in cotton stockings. He began to laugh, shaking, sobbing.

"Well, it's not so bad. After all, it's a miracle I'm here at all."

He listened to Sun Yi's story. She and Jae Wan had walked since early morning, all of the way from Seoul. Twenty miles. They were determined to find him. All of the roads were blocked by the communists so they followed a path over the hills. Several times they hid from squads of enemy troops. That's why it took so long.

"There's still plenty of unexploded shells up there," Jae Wan interrupted, pointing to the hillside from which they'd come. They're marked 'USA'. I saw them myself. Does that mean the Americans have come to help us? Then why did they bomb our town?"

"When we reached the top of the that last hill," Sun Yi continued, "we could see where Uijonbu should have been, but instead there were only smoking piles of rubble all over with the land completely barren. I saw no sign of our home or hospital."

"It's gone. All of it." He tried to tell her gently.

"But why? I don't understand."

"The railroad cars at the station, not far from our house, you know?"

"Yes?"

"They were loaded with ammunition for the South Korean Army. It's possible that the Americans bombed them so the supplies could not fall into the hands of the enemy. Instead, some bombs fell on us."

"Well, where is Jae Soon's wife? Why isn't she with you?"

He shook his head and told her of how the young women hid in the cellar when the North Koreans came into their home. "She was still there when the bombs fell," he finished and reached out to touch his son once more as if unable to believe that any of them were together, reunited, after that catastrophe. It was a greater miracle than he had any right to expect.

"At least we still have the little house in Seoul. We can go there now." But he looked more closely at Sun Yi. She was exhausted, of course. "We can go tomorrow, after you've rested. Tonight we'll find someone to take us in. There must be some place of shelter left."

The next morning Sun Yi insisted on returning to the site of her former home.

"It will do no good. Why should you hang onto the past? That can do nothing but increase your sadness."

"Can't you understand? This must be finished for me. Only by doing this will I be able to accept what has happened to us."

The flames were out but some spots still smoldered.

"Phew!" Jae Wan kicked some ashes. "I think these were our phonograph records. They smell awful!"

Sun Yi poked at the pile of grey ash, still hot to her fingers. There was no other trace of the place she'd made their home for the past thirteen years. She watched a neighbor digging through the debris of his former residence, then reached out and took a charred splinter of wood. At first she dug at random, in a desultory way, but soon she moved as if frantic, plunging in with her hands when the stick gave way.

But, although she sifted through the fluffy residue for hours, all that she found was one pair of silver chopsticks.

"Why, Ohmanee? Why?"

On the following day, after he'd walked back to Seoul with his father and mother, Jae Wan demanded that Sun Yi explain. He somehow believed she could help him to understand.

"Why did this happen to us?"

He looked into her silent face. Did she hear him? He waited hopefully for some response from her. She moved through all of the necessary and routine chores without any show of emotion. He expected to see her, at any moment, turn to him with her usual quick smile and words of praise. But she never spoke.

Late on Sunday afternoon three young men appeared at the gate. Jae Wan went to meet the strangers. They told him they were members of the Youth Alliance and demanded to speak to his father.

What sort of organization is that, he wondered, as he led them across the courtyard.

Without the expected preliminary conversation the tallest one, apparently their leader, ordered, "Your son must return to school tomorrow morning at the usual time. Be sure that he does so." All three left without waiting for a reply.

How strange, thought Jae Wan. But about school. He felt happy to know that it was resuming. That made his life seem more normal again.

A little later a committee composed of older men called on them with a similar preemptory command, but this time for his father. He must report to work at a large hospital the next day.

Their takeover was amazingly swift. His mother had looked astonished to see the neighbor who'd brought the orders. And his father, equally surprised, asked why he should take orders from him. What authority had he? Dr. Lee said, afterwards, that he'd never suspected that man of leftist sympathies.

The neighbor told him that Seoul was now divided into five districts, with each further divided into units. The units were broken down further until every inch of the city, in clusters of ten or twelve homes, was placed under the supervision of one person who'd sworn to be loyal to the new leaders.

"It will be my duty to ascertain that every household in my territory follows the new regulations," he declared with haughty severity.

"That informer!" Sun Yi burst out.

She spoke! Jae Wan felt great relief to hear these words, her first in days.

"Who does he think he is, coming in here and telling us what we should do? Before the invasion he was a nobody. A nobody!"

"Shh," the doctor warned, shaking his head and laying a finger to his lips.

Just as Jae Wan was leaving, after the morning meal, she laid her hands on his shoulders and when he looked up at her he detected fear in her eyes. Her voice came as a whisper.

"Just do as they tell you. Try to do your best to study, the way you did before all of this began."

Why would she say that? As he dressed in a sharply pressed uniform of summer blue he wondered how different his classes would be under these communists. After all, how could they change algebra and science? It would be interesting to see. He'd not be afraid. In any event, he had no choice. Orders must be obeyed. He'd do nothing to endanger his parents.

Strangely he felt lighter, less burdened by worry, after her tirade last night. Perhaps that was because Ohmanee was behaving more like her self again. Nothing could be too bad if she was able to speak her mind in the old familiar way.

At the gate he met the neighbor again, and this time the man led four North Korean soldiers into their home. He didn't even ask permission!

"Show me where you store your rice!" he barked.

Jae Wan watched his mother stand aside, saying nothing. His father had to lead them to the small storage room behind the kitchen. The soldiers were skinny, looking no more than fifteen or sixteen. They struggled with the heavy sacks, hefting them onto their shoulders, tottering as they carried them to a truck waiting in the lane.

What will we eat now? That rice was supposed to feed the entire household until the harvest at the end of summer. He ran back, hoping some might have been left behind. The storeroom was nearly empty. All he could find was some barley, and not much of that. He recalled the many times when he'd pushed his bowl away, unable to finish the last grains in it. He feared that now there would never be enough to satisfy his hunger. They'd taken all of it and there would be no more for three months!

School! He'd be late! He ran out.

The streetcars were running again, but each was so crowded that many passengers were forced to stand. He squeezed into the last space and hung on to the railing. New wall posters, giant portraits of Stalin and Kim Il Sung, glared at him from either side of the street. Young men in drab brown uniforms swaggered along the sidewalks, swinging their dabal. He'd noticed already that every one of the invaders seemed to carry one of these submachine guns and plenty of clips hung from their belts.

Peering from under someone's elbow he saw that the air was clear after the heavy rains. The hills around Seoul were outlined against the brilliant blue sky, just as always after a storm. One might think nothing had changed. Yet the only home he could remember was gone, destroyed with one bomb, and his entire family crowded into a tiny house that was never intended to hold all of them at once.

His father'd told him to be patient.

"You must believe that life will be better someday. Keep struggling. Never give up. We will survive by living one day at a time."

How could it be? Already he'd learned the meaning of a new word. Dawai. It meant to plunder. To take another's possessions. Soldiers pounded at the gate, making demands in their crude Hamkyang accents. They took sewing machines, pianos, any object they could move, showing no respect for the gentleman or the elderly person. Where do all these things go? He'd asked this of his father, for now that they were reunited he followed him everywhere.

"Who knows?" He sounded sad all the time. "Perhaps shipped to the north. Perhaps not."

Objects, large and small, kept disappearing and that was all that mattered to those who lost their cherished possessions.

Jae Wan found some of his classmates when he arrived at the school yard.

"So you decided to return, also?"

One shrugged as they passed through the narrow gate together. "What else could we do? If I don't show up here my parents will be in plenty of trouble. What do you think will happen?"

"Relax." Jae Wan tried to sound confident. "We're only students. School is school. It can't be that different."

But it was. Much worse. First, a guard standing in the hallway directed them toward the auditorium instead of their classroom. Jae Wan took a seat toward the rear with the others of the first term. He saw some people sitting in the teachers' places on the platform at the front, but the familiar faces were missing. They'd been replaced by men he'd never seen before. The tall military officer at the podium wore so many medals and ribbons that half his jacket was hidden. This man in his trim uniform, standing so erectly, was the handsomest soldier he'd ever seen. The boy leaned forward when he began to speak.

"Greetings. I am Colonel Kim, your new principal. We have come to liberate you, our brothers, from imperialist America." In precise and drawn out tones he declared, "The Korean People's Army will bring equality to everyone!"

The cheering began, rolling through the auditorium as though the boys' voices were directed by the baton of an invisible conductor, while his voice boomed again. "You will experience complete liberty!"

He promised land reform and abolition of the tyranny of the family.

"No longer will you be forced to obey your father. Instead, you will make all important decisions by yourself!" he thundered.

Jae Wan brushed away a fly that was circling his face, buzzing near his ears. As the day grew warmer all of the heat from the bodies crowded in here made him drowsy. How long would this harangue continue? When would he be allowed to go to class?

He glanced quickly at the boys near him and thought some looked as weary as he felt, though the day was still early. On the faces of others, however, he saw enthusiasm. Shining eyes riveted upon the dynamic speaker.

The colonel's voice rose in a crescendo, reminding Jae Wan of choral class, when the gestures of their leader led their voices to an ever higher pitch, until the harmonious sound reached the dramatic climax.

"You will be given the opportunity to join in a noble cause!"

Some students down in front sprang to their feet. Wild clapping, loud cheers, echoed from the roof beams. Jae Wan looked around, then jumped to his feet, just like everyone else, and joined in the jubilant response. He dared not be different. Who might be watching and report his reluctant participation?

It's nothing but a big show, he consoled himself. There's no harm in trying to look like the rest of them. But he was glad his mother could not see him now.

One of the seniors marched to the microphone. The student body president! Students in Jae Wan's class were careful never to cross him. What was he doing here?

He raised his hands to quell the raucous shouting, then proceeded to lead the others in a round of resolutions that consisted mostly of name-calling condemnation of America. He asked for response by voice vote, or sometimes a show of hands. The boyish voices rose in unison, the auditorium a sea of flailing hands, according to his demands.

The place was in a frenzy! A student near the front jumped up and ran to the podium.

"Honored president, I move that everyone present here today join the Volunteer Corps!"

What was that? Jae Wan looked around. Suddenly the room was a cavern filled with silence. Did no one dare to speak? To question? To object?

His eyes fell on a soldier standing by the nearest door. He cradled a submachine gun in his arms. Another at each of the other exits! Fear, cold and paralyzing, spread over him. Who dared to dispute this order? What choice did he have? To cooperate now in order to die later? To be shot on the spot? To escape? But how? Did no one else share his fear? How could he carry a gun? He had never even touched one.

But there were many other boys, younger than he, in this People's Army. In fact it seemed to be made up of near-children, except for the leaders. Perhaps they'd had no more choice than he was facing now.

"Ten minutes!"

The voice warned over the loudspeaker.

"You have ten minutes for exercise before boarding for the training camp will begin."

The boys filed out, past the armed guards, into the school yard. Each one strolled silently. Alone. No one dared to speak. No one knew whom he could trust.

Jae Wan looked from the corner of his eyes at those nearest to him. Most of them were doing the same, looking around, eyes hidden by the shadow of their visored caps, watching, gauging how others would respond.

Outside, beyond the wire fence, a string of trucks, army-drab, waited with engines revving slowly. So this is how it happens. These students, the brightest minds in this captive city, will be removed. Carted away in the back of filthy trucks. The narrow wooden slats will enclose the human cargo like animals.

No time to tell Ohmanee. She will never know. Families are not important, they say.

He walked slowly. Tense. Wary. Head down. Avoiding even the eyes of the boys he believed to be his closest companions, true friends. In these few days Jae Wan had learned to trust no one. Some might be strict party followers. Some might cooperate out of fear they'd be charged as reactionaries, taken before the People's Court, from which everyone knew there was no return.

All shared a single goal. Survival. At any cost.

It happened in less than one week. Most of the people, warm, fun loving, trustworthy at one moment, suddenly changed, became rabid, self-serving, timid. He, also. He was no different. He was human, like them.

The only persons he could still depend upon were his family. He knew that, no matter what these invaders tried to drum into him.

And now he was soon to be separated from the only human beings who truly cared for him.

The ten minutes must be nearly ended. He continued to walk, slowly. Even paces. Unhurried stride. Edging closer. Closer to the gate. He saw the opening, saw the armed guard next to it. Now he moved, distracted by conversation with another soldier. Closer. Closer. Jae Wan saw the opening. It was only a few feet from him.

Now!

He leaped. He ran. He was outside.

Stretching his legs, he ran as fast as he had ever run in his life, feeling rather than seeing the presence of others doing the same, spurting off in all directions.

Shots fired, one, two, three.

They can't hit all of us.

Screams. Someone beside him falling. No time to look back. Keep running.

His shoes fell off, sucked by the oozing mud of the road. He was glad to be rid of them. They'd slowed him down, clinging, dragging.

The sudden feeling of lightness propelled him faster, faster, finding sources of new strength when he began to believe he had no more. He could not stop, though his dry throat rasped with the sharpness of a razor blade with each breath that he gasped.

Alone, he continued running, always in the direction of home, and he never looked back.

Jae Wan dared not leave his house afterwards. Each day he listened, ready to hide at the first sound of sudden footsteps. Each night he tried to sleep on the bed of ibuls where his mother hid him in a shallow space under the floorboards. Armed soldiers were fond of middle-of-the-night searches.

Sun Yi tried to disguise her worry but all of them knew the small supply of rice would soon be finished. Dr. Lee received his meal at the hospital but was allowed no other rations. By the beginning of the third week in July she was making regular visits to the pawnbroker.

"It is a whirlwind of fear, a whirlwind." The elderly man bowed before Sun Yi, repeating these words over and over, shaking his head.

She peered into the doorway of his small shop, waiting for her eyes to adjust to the darkness. It was a contrast to the bright sunlight of the city street.

He seemed pleased that she'd returned. The skinny wisp of beard on his bronzed and wrinkled face bobbed up and down in rhythm with the patter of his words. Meanwhile his fingers tapped on the table and his eyes shone with eagerness as he waited for her to methodically unwrap the parcel she'd brought.

Sun Yi removed the covering from her silver plate slowly. It was the last one. She gave it up, knowing it would take its place beside the others in this cluttered den until a new owner, one of those newly rich under this regime, would take it away forever. She was willing to let the old man ramble on, for he was in a position to gather all sorts of gossip. She never knew when she'd learn something useful. He seemed more well informed than most about events at the battlefront.

Which side does he favor, she wondered? There was no doubt he was prospering from the hardship of others but she would not blame him for that. Everyone did what was necessary to survive, day by day. His was a useful function, after all. How else could the possessions of a lifetime be traded for a day's food? Her own family would not eat if she preserved these empty plates.

"How is your family?" He took the plate, hefting its weight and appraising its sheen.

"I am alone," she lied, "with no one to take care of me. Please give me as much as you can."

"Oh, so you are alone."

Sun Yi watched his eyes light with renewed interest and quaked with a new kind of fear. Did she make a mistake in telling him this? Yet she would not permit him to learn of her husband, who was forced to work long hours at the hospital under watchful and suspicious eyes, or of her son, old enough by their standards to be a soldier.

At least Jae Soon had escaped. The last message said he was working as a translator for the Americans. Of her second son, Jae Yun, she knew nothing. Sometimes she fantasized that he'd been released from prison during those first grandiose days when the communists made gestures of friendship. There'd been no word from him, however.

The pawnbroker pressed the crumpled pieces of hwan into her hand and resumed the polishing of her plate. "You are a good customer," he beamed. "I give you fair value, very generous. Will you come back?"

"Perhaps." Sun Yi lingered, smoothing and counting the bills.

"You are fortunate if you are alone," he confided, leaning close. "You don't have to watch while your family disappears. One by one. Who will be next?"

She felt his sharp eyes pierce her with their suspicions and a tightness clutched at her, choking her breath.

"Those Reds are getting scared since the Americans began fighting them. Only a few now, but more coming soon, right? Maybe one of these days those Miguks will march right into this capitol city, drive those communists right back where they came from."

He paused, waiting for her to respond, but Sun Yi's face remained impassive. Did he really expect her to reveal her sympathies in this bold way?

"Doesn't look good right now, though. No one is stopping those North Koreans. They sure know how to fight. Heading right for Pusan. When they get there they'll have the whole country."

"Thank you," she murmured, folding the bills into a tight bundle.

"You come back. I'll give you a good price," he repeated as she turned to leave.

If only he knew how little there is remaining to be sold, she thought. If their home had not been lost in that first indiscriminate bombing she would have had many more treasures to bargain. She walked on in the marketplace, searching for some rice. How would she carry it home? Before this war began she always sent the maid to shop and the woman would hire a boy to carry her purchases. Today Sun Yi could not allow someone else to bargain. She trusted only her own shrewd ability to be certain her hwan would buy the maximum.

Only women were doing the buying and sellilng. No men in sight. Some sat before an odd assortment of items that could be only their own household goods, calling out, competing for the attention of passersby. Some offered roasted sweet potatoes, beans, or tobacco. So far she had not been reduced to that necessity. Among the shoppers it was a simple matter to identify those sympathetic to the invaders. They were the only ones with funds sufficient to buy all they needed, and more.

In a corner Sun Yi finally discovered a woman with some rice to sell. She handed her the sack she'd brought, requesting that it be filled.

"Very expensive," the old lady warned her. "Today I make no profit," she added with a shake of her head. She named the amount.

"But I can't pay such a high price," Sun Yi cried out in shock. "How can it cost that much? That's fifty times more than usual. You are trying to rob me!"

Though the day was still early crowds were already gathering in the space between the stalls, shoving and jostling each other to see what was available. The woman shrugged, her stolid face impassive. The lines around her eyes tightened and she replied, "I'll sell it to someone else, then." She pushed Sun Yi to one side.

Several more times Sun Yi attempted to bargain for a larger amount of rice for her money, but at each place the result was the same.

And to think that I worried about being able to carry the rice, she thought. At last she gave in to the demands of a vendor. Tears of shame stung her eyes. To think that she could do no more than this for her family! Even in the worst days of the past, while her husband was in prison, there had always been enough to eat. She tied the ends of the sack into a knot to make a handle and began the long walk back to her house. Its limp weight dragged, slowing her steps, but in her preoccupation with her thoughts she did not even notice.

When Dr. Lee returned late that evening his wife told him what had happened. She knew that he was exhausted but she could not restrain herself. The work of caring for the endless stream of North Korean soldiers was draining his energy and the daily scenes of death and severe injuries were sapping his reservoir of strength. He was thinner than ever and dark circles rimmed his sunken eyes.

"Have you heard any news of the fighting? The pawnbroker told me that the Americans are being beaten. Do you think that is true?"

The doctor shook his head. "All I hear is the information we are given each day in those required meetings. No matter what I am doing, even if the treatment is in a crucial stage, I'm interrupted and forced to listen to those lectures. We're always told the same story, that soon the entire peninsula will be in the hands of the People's Army."

Later, when Sun Yi and her husband believed that everyone else was sleeping, he took the shortwave radio from its hiding place under the floorboards in the kitchen. He never used it in the presence of the children. They were safer if they knew nothing about this illegal instrument.

He turned the volume as low as he could and pressed his ear to the speaker, listening to the words from Pusan. That port city on the southern tip of the Korean peninsula was the focal point of the small perimeter still not captured by the North Koreans. It was the entry for all of the military aid and troops sent by the United States and other members of the United Nations. Now the middle of July, more than three weeks since the invasion began, and still all the news was discouraging. South Koreans soldiers suffered one defeat after another, giving way before the superior numbers and weapons of their enemy.

He frowned. He could barely hear the voice of the newscaster.

"Too much static tonight," he told Sun Yi. "The same story, urging us not to lose hope." He listened to reports of heavy fighting along the wide battlefront. Both the ROK soldiers and the Americans were bravely withstanding repeated mass attacks led by tank units.

But where? Where were these battles? A line had been drawn, the announcer continued, as if in response, and President Rhee promised it would be held. No further retreat. From Kunsan, far to the south on the west coast, to Taejon, a hundred miles south of Seoul, on the way to Taegu, and over to Andong, near the east coast mountain range. He couldn't tell Sun Yi. Andong was near her old family home!

But she'd heard it herself. He could tell by the sudden fear in her face.

"Kum Seung!" she whispered.

Her step-mother, Sun Yi's aged father, and their second son still lived in the house she'd twice left. It could be in the direct path of battle. There'd also been a fierce three-day confrontation, the announcer continued, south of Chunchon.

The doctor recalled the poor farmers they'd cared for during their years in Kangwando and wondered if any would survive this new hardship. Their own difficulties seemed inconsequential by comparison. Imagine more than half of South Korea already in the hands of these invaders!

Intent on the muffled words, neither Sun Yi nor Dr. Lee heard Jae Wan enter.

"I thought of a way I can help."

At the sound of his voice, his father shut off the volume.

"Don't worry, Abuji. I know all about your radio." The boy turned to Sun Yi. "Ohmanee, I'm sure I can find some rice for us if I go into the countryside. And I'll buy it at a lower price." He stood in the doorway, dressed in his loose nightclothing, his dark hair tousled, and his eyes, though heavy with sleep, glowing in excitement.

"This baby, my youngest son, he can save us all."

"Don't say it. Don't tell me again that I'm too young! After all, I was nearly drafted into the People's Army."

Since that day when he ran all of the six miles from school to his home he'd not been outside. It was not safe to be seen. His restlessness grew with each day, but he knew he'd be captured if he walked through the streets. Every able bodied young person was conscripted. To dig ditches, defensive barriers around Seoul, to help with rebuilding the bridges.

Yet he needed to get out!

"Get me some white clothing, like the farmers wear, and a chige to put on my back." He walked around the room as if already bent under the weight of the A-frame. "I'll look like an old man. No one will ever suspect."

Sun Yi protested. His father, also, was reluctant, but Jae Wan persisted.

"Who else is there who can do this? You know you must be at the hospital every day. Ohmanee and Jin Sook can't roam the countryside. There's no one left but me."

He stretched as tall as he could and told them he'd leave early, before anyone woke, just at dawn. He'd forestall his return until the hour just before the curfew at nine, or even wait until the early hours of the next morning to come home. In the end his parents relented. With food enough for only one more day, they really had no choice.

Two days later Jae Wan slipped out of their house in the first pale light. On the previous day the maid arranged to have an old man, her relative, deliver a load of firewood to the kitchen. He'd departed without his chige and no one noticed. Now it was strapped to Jae Wan's back and, from a distance, he really did resemble a little old man. It was larger than he and even unloaded, it forced his shoulders to bend.

But to be more sure of his disguise he'd rubbed ashes from the fire into his hair, transforming it to a dull grey color, and Jin Sook, in a rare moment of playfulness, pasted a scraggly beard she'd made of twisted threads to his chin.

"I wish I could go with you," she admitted. "See what you can get with this." She placed in his hand the ring of gold she'd worn since her twelfth birthday. He added it to the trinkets hidden in the pockets of his loose white pants and jacket, promising himself that it would be the last object he'd use for trade.

Sun Yi couldn't sleep for worrying and rose early to watch him leave. Did he realize that this time he was no longer playing a game?

He took the shortest route out of the city, a precaution against meeting anyone up early who might find his appearance suspicious. Then, before the sun rose, he followed a rutted country lane in an easterly direction. The air was still cool, though later the heat of midsummer would bake the earth. He inhaled, welcoming the chance to breathe something fresh. That cramped hole where he'd had to sleep for the past two weeks smelled damp and musty all the time.

How far could he walk in one day? His bargaining power should increase with the distance from the city. If only he could find some farmer with rice he was willing to sell, or some barley, or even, he shuddered, a little millet. No one but the poorest of persons would eat millet. At least that is what he'd believed until today.

He'd felt stiff when he began. After all, he'd had no exercise in two weeks! Now, his muscles loosening, he began to enjoy the motion. He walked and walked, until the sun felt hot upon his head and he thought it must be mid-day. He should be nearing the village of

Wabu. Time to begin trading. No one else was on the road. People must be at work in the fields. Or perhaps the war caused them to stay in their huts.

At first the sound, a droning, was so far away that he didn't even notice it. The sound built to a roar and he looked up. A lone airplane, a small one, flew low and was approaching him rapidly. With the complete fascination of a young boy he stopped to watch.

Swooping! Diving! Turning! Coming straight back toward him!

He'd never seen a fighter this close. He could even see the helmeted head in the small bubble of a cockpit!

The F 80 turned widely, again, and returned. Its silver fusilage, between the red wingtips and the tail, flashed in the sunlight. Lower. Lower. Closer. Closer. Then its guns opened with even, repetitive shots sounding like a staccato drill. Little clouds of dust sprang up in the roadway as each bullet spit into the earth in front of him. That pilot was shooting at him! Throwing off the chige, Jae Wan leaped into the sodden drainage ditch next to the path. The chige splintered into fragments with the impact and the line of bullets traced a pattern of puncture wounds into the ground only inches from his prone body.

He continued to forage for food, dressed in his old man disguise, and no one shot at him again, although he saw the planes fly over every day and each time was ready to hide again. August was dry and hot. Temperatures soared and the monsoon rains failed to fall. He missed school, often wondering what had happened to his friends on that last day, but he lived a new life now, meeting the challenge of contributing to the survival of his family. Each time he brought home a few cups of grain or a bundle of fresh greens he felt pride and self confidence filling him like a good meal. But even with his help the truth was that he and everyone else lived with constant and gnawing hunger. How long could they live this kind of life? They had almost nothing of value left to sell.

The incessant propaganda of Kim Il Sung promised a victory for the north by August 15, the anniversary of Korea's independence from the Japanese, but that date came and passed without any change, except for the renewed promise that the United Nations' forces would be defeated by the end of the month. Reports of fighting in the south continued to filter through in the short wave broadcasts.

Each day his father seemed more weary, telling them that the number of wounded brought to his hospital was increasing. Did this mean that the People's Army was losing, or only that the fighting was heavier?

The boy relished the adult privileges that accompanied his responsibilities. When his father gathered with the few friends he still dared to trust they shared rumors and bits of information and he sat, silently, in a corner listening to their whispered conversation while his mother sent the maid in with cups of weak barley tea, all that she had to offer.

A particular excitement seemed to fill the room like electricity on a day early in September when they met. There was a quickening in the voices, an enthusiasm to interrrupt each other, a spark kindled where only the ashes of failed hopes smoldered.

"I tell you there is talk of an invasion soon. Seoul will be liberated!" It was Dr. Cho, who worked with his father, announcing the news.

"What good would that accomplish when there already are hundreds of thousands of puppet soldiers south of here?" demanded one of the other men.

"For one thing, the roads leading south can be sealed off. Then no supplies will reach those puppets. There'll be no escape route, either. They'll be trapped!"

"A dream. An impossible dream."

"Not necessarily," imposed Mr. Song, the chemist. "If the troops were to come by way of Inchon."

Laughing, a rare sound, interrupted him.

"Well, suppose Inchon were the place. It's the closest port to Seoul, after all."

"And twenty-five miles away. Do you really think the Seoul defenders will give an inch of that distance without hard fighting?"

Jae Wan sat up straight. His father was speaking and the others were listening without interrupting, for once.

"There are more than eighteen thousand North Koreans committed to maintaining control of this city. Ten thousand alone, in the 18th rifle division, thirty-five hundred Seoul city regulars, the ones you meet in the street every day," his eyes narrowed as he speculated the tremendous odds against the venture, "and another thirty-five hundred special troops being held for such a defense, plus the twelve hundred anti-aircraft regulars in positions ringing the hills."

You are well informed," Dr. Cho remarked.

"I've learned to keep my eyes and ears open one hundred per cent of the time, that's all," Dr. Lee commented.

"Well, that's not the only reason it's an impossible idea," commended Dr. Ko, the original pessimist. "You've seen those mudflats, stretching out to the horizon. It's the worst harbor in Korea! Shallow, shifting channels, tidal flats extending for six thousand yards. Hundreds of small islands break the wave action when the tide does come in. Did you know that Inchon has the second highest tides in the world? There's a thirty foot difference between the high and the low, and only two or three days in the month when the tide rises high enough in daylight to clear the mudbanks." He shook his head. "How could any army land a surprise attack under those conditions? And if they did manage to get that far, how would anyone climb those fourteen-foot seawalls that surround the entire harbor? While being shot at," he concluded, settling back, "and during the typhoon season."

"Granted, you all make it sound impossible," Dr. Cho admitted. "All I am telling you is that rumors are circulating everywhere that there will be an invasion somewhere. Soon."

Jae Wan shivered with anticipation. Suppose he could be right!

The saucy cry of a magpie on a yew tree outside his window greeted Jae Wan when he lifted the floorboards and crawled up into the room. The day was Friday, September 15, and he was tired. He'd walked a long distance yesterday. And discouraged. He'd brought home very little food for his efforts.

He leaned out, watching the bird preen its long tail feathers and cock its head, looking at him. Handsome fellow. He appeared well fed. What an omen of good luck! He must tell his mother.

He hurried to find her. There'd been no good news for so long. This might bring a smile to her face. She did nothing but look after her grandson, making certain he ate even when there was not enough for anyone else. She seldom smiled or spoke. He knew her ordinary world had disappeared. Danger was a daily threat. She couldn't seek out her friends and, worst of all, there'd been no word from Kim Tai Un. A week after the bridge blew she'd found her friend's home empty, silent. She'd disappeared. No note. Nothing.

If he could coax a happy look from his mother, just for a moment, with his tale of the magpie.

Sirens pierced the early morning stillness.

Jin Sook rushed from her room, struggling to carry the baby and brushing the sleep from her eyes with one free hand.

"What is it?"

"How would I know? Quick, let's find Ohmanee."

She tried to hide the radio when they came into the kitchen.

"Ohmanee, you know its useless to do that. We know where you keep that radio. Let's listen to it now, and try to find out what's going on."

As he spoke air raid sirens split the air again, sounding from all directions, competing in intensity for the attention of the people.

A faint voice crackled over the airwaves and Sun Yi bent close to catch the words.

"The invasion! It's begun!" she shouted. "This morning. Early. Near Inchon."

Hope ignited a sparkle in her eyes. Gone was her long passivity.

"Hurrah!" Jae Wan leaped up and down. "Father's friends were right! How long will it take the soldiers to get here?"

Her ear pressed to the black box, Sun Yi told her children, "There's hard fighting. We must be patient. The battle may last for days, it says. Oh, children. You must tell no one! No one, that we know this. No one."

The official broadcasts of the communist government in Seoul did tell everyone on the next day, however, with the added announcement that the "invaders had been pushed into the sea." All citizens were ordered to turn out for the victory parade.

Jae Wan did not dare to leave their house. He'd not been discovered yet. He could take no chances.

"You should have seen it!" Jin Sook told her brother afterwards. "I never saw so many people in the streets at once."

She and her mother, with the baby, watched from a street corner.

"They marched and cheered for the communist victory, all the old men and small boys, women and girls. There was no one your age in sight," she told him.

Sun Yi, torn between new hope and resigned despair, didn't know what to believe. Had the Americans been defeated? If not, why was it taking them so long to reach Seoul?

That was the question asked of anyone who could be trusted. There were no more official pronouncements from the communists and the rumble of distant gunfire continued. Few believed that anyone had been "pushed into the sea." Most knew that a fierce battle was being fought on the doorstep of their city. With possible freedom so close, impatience mounted.

In the first two days after the landing at Inchon the combined U.S. and South Korean troops gained only six miles, just enough to take Kimpo airfield, northwest of the city. Their next goal, the industrial complex at Yongdongpo, took even longer. Roads were mined, blocked with trees, sandbags, broken machinery. No vehicles could get through. Every soldier marched on his own feet every step of the twenty miles.

If Sun Yi dared go to the marketplace she hurried back to her house. Everyone feared the communists' actions when they finally admitted the city was lost.

Five days after the first news of the invasion heavy fighting continued with the North Korean defenders dug into the hills and hidden in the brush along the banks of the Han. When Yongdongpo was taken, finally, it was done with immense casualties.

To wrench control of Seoul from the communist forces the U.S. 24th Division had to cross the river. There was no bridge. Mines and anti-tank guns tore holes in their advance lines.

Two days later, and the U.S. Fifth Marines were locked into battle in the hills northwest of Seoul.

Sun Yi found no more rice in the market place, though she walked from one end to the other looking for it. She was ready to pay even an exhorbitant price now.

Another two days passed. Each hill was a major battle site.

On the morning of September 24 a low ground mist mixed with smoke from the burning houses to obscure vision. Unable to see, men fought anyway, with machine guns, mortars and hand grenades.

By mid-morning the haze lifted enough for air strikes. The U.S. 7th Division began to make some progress.

Ten days after the beginning of this invasion, five thousand troops of the U.S. 32nd Infantry and the Republic of Korea 17th Regiment entered Seoul. Their objective was Nam San, a large hill in the center of the city. A heavy fog over the Han River allowed a battalion ferried by amphibious vehicles to cross unseen into the northwestern section of the city.

Jae Wan had not left the small house in all of this time. His legs ached from lack of exercise and he massaged his muscles, thinking of his older brother. If this existence was like being locked into a prison, how had he managed to endure the weeks in Westgate Prison? Or had he? Perhaps he'd been dead for a long time and they didn't know, would never know.

In the final days of the occupation the North Koreans taught orphan children and vagrants how to set fires. They destroyed some of the finest buildings remaining in the city.

About this time, in the shadow of impending defeat, prominent citizens were rounded up, inmates roused from hospitals and jails, and all marched toward the 38th parallel, guarded by North Korean soldiers. Anyone who could not keep up was shot.

By the evening of the tenth day the United Nations' forces controlled half of Seoul, but fighting continued throughout the night, with an incessant flash of gunfire and crackling flames. There was no cessation and no sleep for anyone.

The walls of the house shook with each new bombardment and Sun Yi listened to the explosive sounds, closer and closer to them. She stayed inside, counting out the last remaining grains of barley and wondering how her family would eat when it was finished.

Every street, every intersection, was blocked by rubble, rice bags filled with earth, reinforced with rails torn from streetcar tracks. North Koreans with machine guns, burp guns, and some anti-tank guns manned each one. Machine guns and mortars were mounted on rooftoops. The battle went on, foot by foot.

The soldiers who'd come to liberate this city found every entry a potential trap. Snipers posed a constant threat.

To Sun Yi each gunshot sounded the cruel signal ending another life. Firing resounded continuously throughout the days while the defenders spent their ammunition in a futile attempt to retain control of Seoul.

While the soldiers, American and Korean, were stalled on the far side of the Han River their artillery fire and air strikes raked the city. No civilian dared to leave his shelter or walk the streets.

From her home in the northwest section she could se the silent range of hills to the north and wondered why some of the invading force did not try approaching from there while the communists focused on the obvious threat from the direction of the river.

Ever since the first reports of the Inchon landing's success she and her husband, with their children and Jae Soon's son, crowded into the cellar whenever they heard the sound of another air attack. The bombing raids pounded the streets and rattled the fragile buildings still standing.

Would this never end? In order to save Seoul, she told the doctor, their friends were destroying it. Their father's calm presence reassured his children and they clung to the tangible hope that his strength gave them.

Sun Yi said little but each day she portioned out the grain for one meal, telling no one else how little there was remaining. At last she cried out.

"Why is it taking so long?"

The thin fabric of patience was shredded. Surely this superior American army should have defeated the puppet forces by now. Ten days had passed since the first landing.

Throughout the night of September 25 and on into the hours of the following day the barrage continued, through the twisted streets of this strange city, with concrete roadblocks guarding every intersection and a deadly flow of howitzer and machine gun fire bursts at frequent intervals. After daylight the house to house fighting continued. The dead lay in the streets, hundreds and hundreds of dead.

Three days later a partial calm, an unnatural silence, settled over Seoul. Sun Yi dared to step outside and look around. By some good fortune the buildings around her still stood, but much of the city was flattened.

Radios and loudspeakers broadcast the announcement that President Rhee was returning and the American General MacArthur would be present for a formal and public ceremony to return Seoul to its rightful government on the three month anniversary of its invasion.

She had to see for herself. With Jin Sook she threaded her way through the rubble, sometimes losing her way in the once familiar streets. Crowds were everywhere, mostly old men and women and children, each face gaunt, pinched from weeks of deprivation. Did she look that bad? Thousands lined the main road. He was expected to pass through here on his way to the National Capitol Building. A path had been cleared last night, heaps of wreckage hastily bulldozed to the sides. He'd come from Kimpo airfield, to the northeast, first crossing the Han, on a crude bridge constructed yesterday, especially for him.

Would Seoul ever again look the way she remembered it? She felt weary, just thinking about the effort needed to clear away the mountains of debris. Ruin was pervasive. More around each corner. So many good and capable people were dead. Who would take their place, bring the talents to restore some semblance of the former life?

Many North Koreans had time to flee during the long battle. But there were others who stayed, changing to white peasant clothing, disappearing, mingling, waiting for the opportunity to renew their subversive efforts.

Sun Yi stopped, her way blocked by a cordon of military police. Only officers are permitted beyond this point, they told her. Ahead she could see the blackened shell of what had once been the preeminent landmark of the central city. She smelled death lingering near the pocked walls of the National Capitol Building. From far away she heard cheering. Jae Wan should be here. Her son would enjoy this spectacle more than anyone. He was still reluctant to be seen in public. She did not blame him. After these months of hiding, when he dared to go out only at night, trekking the countryside, his enforced silence. Of course he'd learned to trust no one. A harsh lesson for a boy of fourteen.

At the approaching sound of vehicles, Sun Yi stretched to look over the shoulder of the person standing in front of her. Five large automobiles, painted olive drab, rolled by. In each she saw the big nosed men, beribboned uniforms, visored caps. The license plate on the front of the last car had five stars. That must be MacArthur! Behind it a long line of army jeeps, spanking clean, making a startling contrast to the mud covered debris along the sides of the road. No sign yet, though, of the Korean president. This was to be Rhee Syngman's first appearance in Seoul since his hasty retreat on the second day after the invasion.

Suddenly she'd seen enough.

"Let's go home," she said, turning to her daughter as soon as the caravan had passed. She'd felt she must witness this sight so she could begin to believe the long nightmare was truly ended. But how could they begin to live again, when all around them was nothing but destruction. No food, no stores, nothing to buy and no money to pay for it, anyway, and no work for anyone.

The streets were filled with these strange foreign faces. American soldiers. Welcome but also an element one must deal with cautiously. She determined that her daughter must stay at home. Only sixteen. These strangers could not tell the difference between a woman of good family and a street person. Every girl might be assumed to be one of those camp followers, desperate to earn a few hwan. So long as she had a family to protect her, Jin Sook would be safe. But still, she must be kept out of sight.

One week later most of the troops moved out of Seoul, pushed north, following the battle line. The city was trying, in eary October, to resume some semblance of its former habits. Food, mostly barley, was rationed but available if one were willing to stand in line long enough and able to pay the price.

Sun Yi made the rounds of the markets, shrewdly judging where she might locate a little more to add to their meager store.

Refugees from the north, able at last to cross that border that had divided the country for more than five years, added to the crowds in the streets.

The United Nations' troops pushed north, crossing the 38th parallel on October 7, meeting little resistance. Pyongyang, the capitol of North Korea, was captured.

Dr. Lee was busy again. He had more patients than he had time to care for, but few could pay for his services. What else can I do? He asked Sun Yi this question when she reminded him of their slim resources. His skills were needed. Many ailments were difficult to diagnose, resulting from no direct injury, but as the result of weeks of malnutrition and anxiety. Little medicine was available. Perhaps that didn't matter. The best medicine would be a cessation of war, and he could not provide that.

General Walker' s 8th Army and the Republic of Korea Second Division advanced farther north in early October, the Korean troops in the lead, for the directive of the UN Security Council ordered United Nations' forces to stay clear of the vicinity of the border with Manchuria. The 7th Marines landed at Inchon and followed them, while off the North Korean port city of Wonsan the U.S. 1st Marines rocked on the waves for four weeks before finally stepping onto Korean soil.

Daily news reports fed the optimism that Korea would be free, even united, as the combined Republic of Korea and United Nations' troops continued to annihilate the enemy.

Jae Wan found work with the American Army headquarters in Seoul. Sun Yi was horrified.

"You're a schoolboy, not a laborer."

"But there is no school now, Ohmanee. If I do this I can earn some money and be a real help to you."

He knew that all their tradeable items had already been exchanged for food during the summer occupation, and that his father brought in no more than a pittance for his work.

Sun Yi looked up at him, her youngest. He was taller than she and the recent months had taken his childhood away.

"What will you do?" she asked, resigned. The words she'd used to encourage her children through the hard times echoed back to her.

You must survive. Since you were born you have a duty to survive.

She'd told them nothing could be worse than the times they were living through, but the future would be better. She doubted her own prediction but, if she could make the young ones believe it they might have a better chance of enduring the struggle.

"I'm to be in charge of burning documents in the communications center," he replied. The responsibility sounded important. Actually, what he did was to stand beside a fiery incinerator barrel hour after hour, periodically refilling it and watching that none of its contents blew away. The job was not so bad as the days grew colder. All of his warm clothing for winter had been lost in the bombing of their home. As long as he had this work he could be certain of staying warm.

When she complained to his father of his independent venture, Dr. Lee reminded Sun Yi that the times were not normal. The usual attitudes did not apply now, he told her. He was proud of this son who was showing the strength he needed to survive in the immediate future. Anyway, he consoled his wife, it was only a matter of time until the schools reopened. As soon as that happened the boy would return to his studies.

Jae Wan learned stray words of English while he worked. Near the end of October he heard a fragment of conversation suggesting that the Chinese army might enter the war on the side of the North Koreans. At first, when he mentioned these rumors to his father, they seemed only idle specualtion. But soon the idea became common knowledge, although official reports denied it.

Clouds of insecurity descended once more.

Intelligence officers learned, through interrogation of captives, that since mid-October as many as one hundred thousand Chinese soldiers had crossed the Yalu River into Korea. Hiding in caves and wooded areas by day, marching only at night, the men penetrated fifty miles below the border before the first of November.

By November 1 the first major confrontation with Chinese troops occurred when portions of the U.S. 8th Army and the ROK 15th Regiment were attacked at Ulsan. If this northern most location was taken, all the United Nations' forces in northeastern Korea would be cut off, isolated.

At the end of a five-day battle in this place six hundred American soldiers lay dead.

"What shall we do if the communists return?"

Sun Yi dared to ask, finally. She'd struggled for days with the question. Her face wore anguish, unceasing, permanent. Though they'd not yet admitted to each other, both she and her husband knew they could not endure, perhaps would not even be allowed the chance to survive, if the city were lost again.

We will leave Seoul. There is no alternative. But where will we go? How will we travel?

"For the first time in my life I feel completely powerless," Sun Yi finally confessed to him.

Dr. Lee took her hand.

"Always, always, whatever has happened, I believed that I could be resourceful, could find a way of solving problems. Now there is nothing that I can do!"

He looked at his wife, his eyes as gentle, patient, as on their first meeting.

"From the day I watched you climbing South Mountain I have believed that you have more life, more determination, vigor, and stubbornness than anyone else that I have ever known. When I was in prison I thought of your strength and it gave me courage. You still have that quality. I have faith in you, no matter how much more difficult these times may become."

Despite his words, his face was somber.

"All we can do is wait and hope that we will not face the choice of staying or leaving."

The 7th Regiment of the U.S. 1st Marines met Chinese soldiers in battle near Sudong, on the road to Chosin Reservoir in the far northeastern corner of Korea, on November 2. After that encounter no one denied their presence, but there was disagreement about their numbers. Then, curiously, the Chinese retreated. Nothing more was heard or seen of them for three weeks.

The country around the Yalu River is an endless expanse of utterly barren land, jagged hills, yawning crevices, in winter locked into a silent death grip of snow and ice.

During October and November three hundred thousand Chinese soldiers moved into North Korea, moving only in darkness, camouflaged, invisible to aerial photographers and observers.

Reports filtered through to Seoul. Rumors rolled through the city.

On November 24 the Chinese struck in full force, for the first time, hitting the ROK 1st Division and the U.S. 2nd Division of the 8th Army. If this battle were lost thousands and thousands of troops would be isolated in the frozen northwest corner of the country. At nearly the same time, in the opposite corner of northern Korea, Marines of the U.S. 1st Division fought in minus twenty degree temperatures in the Yudam Valley against massive and overwhelming Chinese forces. Each day more reports of defeat trickled down to the city and many began to doubt that the United Nations command would defend Seoul if it were to be invaded again.

During the first two weeks of December, while Siberian winds blew through Seoul in frigid gusts, Sun Yi watched her neighbors packing, leaving the wreckage of their former homes. She wondered each day, as she saw more of them departing on foot with awkward bundles fastened to their backs and balanced on their heads, when she would have to join the exodus. Everyone feared to live under communist domination. They all prepared to evacuate, although most knew no destination but to keep moving toward the south. The few trains still running were reserved for the military. Everyone else must follow the only trail leading to Pusan. It was a two lane unpaved road and already clogged with military vehicles.

Someone would have to carry the baby. A three year old could not be expected to walk without soon tiring. In those last days, filled with rumor and uncertainty, she worried over all the unanswerable questions. Only one point was definite. They must leave. Soon. Even the American Marines, caught in the trap of icy winter and the first harsh storms in the far nothern interior around the Chosin reservoir, were moving south as fast as they could.

On November 30 the 1st Marines left the Yudam Valley after taking many casualties in two days of heavy fighting, headed for a small village about ten miles south called Hagaru, the first stop on their way to the seacoast. It took three days, fighting, regrouping, fighting again, all of the way. On December 6, after resting, they continued. Sixty-seven miles to rescue.

"I'll leave with the army, Ohmanee," Jae Wan explained to his mother after their final decision, to leave Seoul, was cast. "It will be difficult enough for the four of you to find some transportation and keep together. I can ride in one of their trucks."

Sun Yi protested. Her son insisted. How could she argue with him? This young boy had become the mainstay of the entire family. It was useless even to try to give him parental commands now. He promised to join them in Pusan. They agreed on a meeting place, a point of contact in that far city where they would keep looking for each other until they met again.

On December 9 the 1st Marines, weakened by frostbite and dysentery but carrying their wounded and hauling their equipment, reached the village of Koto. Within forty-three miles of the sea they were submerged in the deepest snowstorm of the year. Five days later the first of them arrived at the port of Hungham where the ships were loading. One hundred thousands human beings waited there to be evacuated, not only the American soldiers but thousands of refugees as well, all headed for Pusan. There wasn't enough space.

Except for a few army trucks and jeeps, the streets of Seoul were deserted. Jae Wan found no streetcars or busses so he walked home in the rapidly chilling twilight, more than three miles. He'd continued reporting to work at the U.S. Army headquarters even after his parents and sisters departed. That was the only way he could be sure of a ride when the time came for the last troops to pull out. Now he remembered watching his brother's infant son walking sturdily beside the others. How long had he kept up with them before he demanded to be carried?

On the morning of December 20 he was standing next to the large barrel that was an incinerator with his stick in hand. Whenever he saw a sheet of paper flying out he poked at it and then watched it burn with the others. The heat seared his face and hands but his back was numb with cold. Two men of the crew from the communication center walked past. They didn't seem to notice him and the sound of their voices carried through the crisp air. They think I can't understand, he thought, and turned his head away. But he could. He'd begun to comprehend the meaning of some words in this strange sounding English language, and he listened to the soldiers whenever he could.

"Tomorrow, early, we pull out."

Pull out! Shivers, not from the chill wind but from fear, coursed through the boy. That meant leaving! If these men, who were the nerve center of the command, did that. Why, this meant all of the troops would retreat!

He had to find a way to get himself out of here. Despite what he'd told his mother, he knew that the only Koreans allowed to ride on the army trucks were the interpreters. His alternative was to walk hundreds of miles without food or shelter, and today the twentieth of December. He was living in a nightmare. There must be some way. Think!

Later that evening he returned to the headquarters, carrying the small bundle of possessions he'd rushed home to pack. There wasn't much. Extra clothes, a bag of apples, a notebook, the belt buckle from his high school uniform, a snapshot his father had taken of him with his brothers and sisters last year, the key to his piano lost in the fire, worthless to anyone else but to him irrreplaceable treasures.

He saw a truck driver walking past and, remembering that he'd been friendly to him, called out.

"Dan! Can you give me a ride?"

"You know the rules, Shorty." The young American, tall, with a shock of pale blonde hair, lean and red faced, shook his head. He leaned forward suddenly and whispered, "No promises but stick around. I'll see what I can do."

The other men loading trucks were hurried, tense. He stayed out of their way, watching. Hours passed. He was so tired. I"ll just take a short nap, he told himself.

The silence woke him.

Jae Wan sat up in the corner of the small, empty room he'd crawled into, confused, rubbing his eyes. He felt stiff. That floor was hard. He looked at his watch. Three a.m.! He jumped up and ran outside.

No trucks No men. Where was everyone? Only a single light left on, still shining from the top of a wooden post.

He'd been left behind.

Snatching up his precious bundle, Jae Wan ran. He knew where the motor pool was. All of the trucks had to pass through it before leaving the city. There might still be a chance. But it was three miles from here. He ran faster. The road was dark, icy, slippery. He fell, picked himself up, kept running.

"Stop!"

The voice, in Korean, shot out of the eerie stillness. The martial law. He'd forgotten. No one allowed in the streets after dark. Jae Wan looked back but saw no one. He kept running.

The disembodied voice called again. "Who are you?"

"Me! It's me, me, me!"

"Who the hell is me?"

He heard footsteps, saw a figure out of the darkness, and at the same time felt an object, hard, cold, strike his shoulder. Jae Wan stopped. He dropped his bundle, raised his hands high. The rifle was pointing at him. There were two men. One shone a flashlight in his face, took the identity papers from him, scrutinized them by its dim light while the other kept the rifle aimed at his chest.

Was all hope gone? Tears stung the boy's eyelids. He explained why he was here on the street. Would they understand?

"All right. You can go. But hurry! And be more careful."

New energy surged through his legs when he realized he'd aroused their sympathy and he ran even faster than before, the heavy bag bumping against his legs. He raced up to the gate of the motor pool and saw the long line of trucks still moving through. His breath, steaming in the cold, tore at his raw throat. Was he too late? A crowd of civilians clustered near by, each begging to be taken on, but the vehicles lumbered past like a herd of oxen, never stopping.

Jae Wan's eyes darted along the line of dull green. He would not lose this last chance! Where was Dan? Dan was his only hope. To all of the other Americans he was just another Korean kid among all the thousands of panicked refugees.

Over there! That looked like him, that white head in the driver's seat of a truck close to the gate, glowing in the pale light of dawn. It had to be Dan! Jae Wan shouted his name.

It was! Dan saw him! He raised his hands in hopelessness but then he pointed to the back of his truck, making a circle with his fingers.

OK! That meant OK! He sprinted for the gate.

His legs tensed. Could he be quick enough? The truck was moving. The guard, too close, scanned the clamoring crowd, moved, turned away.

Now! As the truck approached it almost stopped for one long second. Long enough. Jae Wan leaped into the open body, grabbing at a frame support, pulling himself up. With his other hand he hung onto his bag. He could not let go of it. It was all he had.

"Hey!" Another guard had spotted him. He was shouting, running after the truck, reaching out to pull him off. Jae Wan's heart pounded.

"Let me go!"

Did he shout these words, or were they only heard inside his head? Dan revved the engine, drowning out all other sounds, and they took off, leaving the guard behind. Rolling from side to side, he bumped into chairs, desks, typewriters, a jumble of furniture. Icy fingers of wind raked his body and when the speed settled down to a steady pace he hunched down between two filing cabinets. He was soaked with sweat and now he was freezing, his shirt stiffening in the frigid air.

Dan's truck followed the one in front at a steady pace, not fast, and Jae Wan looked out one last time at the city that had been his home. They were driving on Chang-ro, the main street. It was a silent place, filled with the rubble of destruction. He remembered times when he'd walked this road with his friends, filled with confidence, then turned from the pathetic sights as memories of those schoolmates struck him. He'd hardly thought of anyone since the last day of school. Where were they now?

The truck slowed as it approached the Han River and he recalled the night when he, with his mother and brother and sister, had intended to cross it during the invasion in June. The bridge blew up before they could use it for their escape but many other Korean people died on it when it exploded prematurely, people like themselves who were only trying to flee from forces they could not understand.

The broad river was frozen now. No bridge was needed. Anyone might walk to the other side. The communists would, also, when they arrived.

When the truck passed the railroad station further south, in Yong-dongpo, refugees swarmed in the yard around it, all of them waiting for the chance of a ride to safety. Most were women and children, their possessions tied up in sacks that they carried on their backs and on top of their heads. Then the wind blew, colder, more ferocious, and he hoped his parents were in some shelter. Or were they waiting somewhere like all these pitiful wanderers?

The caravan, moving south, seemed endless, with the people like a human river along the side of the road, moving slowly, walking over the snow covered rice fields. A somber, silent mass of the homeless marching toward the unknown.

In a land once peaceful, filled with natural beauty, he witnessed fear, hopelessness, bloodshed and death. Over all of this misery the eternal snowcapped mountains rose through the clouds and mist as though untouched by the distress at their feet.

All during the night he huddled in the rear of the slow moving army truck and the snow continued to fall on him. He'd never imagined this journey would be so miserable. He should have stayed with his parents, leaving when they did. Probably they were in Pusan by this time, warm and comfortable. The line of refugees was endless. They shuffled along the sides of the road, scurrying into a field or ditch whenever a truck demanded their space.

Some of the young women begged rides from him but Dan drove steadily on, ignoring their cries. The truck following his did stop once and Jae Wan watched two women climb into its back compartment. Were these what he'd heard called camp followers, or were they simply women desperate to survive? No one of a good family would behave that way before the war. Perhaps they'd lost their families. So many dead. So many missing. With no home, no money, what else could they do?

Each one struggles to survive in his own way, he reminded himself. He had learned that lesson. But the price for extending one's life could be degradation beyond hope.

What did his own future hold?

He blew warm breath on his frozen fingers. It was futile. They were without feeling. He shook the snow from his shoulders and shoved his hands under his jacket, then fell into a doze.

When, sometime later, he tried to open his eyes he found the lids frozen shut, coated with frost. He rubbed furiously, forcing them to open. The rice fields shimmered in a ghostly phantasm, the stream running along the side of the road was coated with ice, and the hills in the distance were dusted with white, fading into the grey sky. It was as though time itself was impaled on the hands of a clock that would never move forward.

When, sometime after daylight, Dan stopped at Taejon to refuel he signalled to him.

"Lay low," he mouthed, "or you'll be out."

He continued south, the truck lumbering along at the same slow pace. The snow changed to rain and mud flew from the wheels, spitting brown splotches on the people still walking along the sides of the road. Early winter darkness covered the caravan and still the truck inched along toward Taegu. The rain stopped and the air grew cold again.

He tried wiggling his toes and felt nothing. He'd never imagined such cold. Jae Wan lacked all desire to move. At least he was not walking and the jumble of furniture in the truck did provide some shelter from the wind. Those poor souls who stumbled along the way had nothing.

Yet, as the stiffness moved from his legs into his chest and arms, he began to wonder if he would freeze to death before morning, as he'd heard of the soldiers doing on the battlefields in the north. His tears flowed and froze on his cheeks as soon as they slipped from his eyes. He was unable to stop them. Not since he was a small boy in Chunchon had he cried like this. With the tears still rolling down uncontrollably he fell into a sound sleep.

Gentle shaking woke him and Jae Wan opened his eyes. The morning light was dim. He was still sitting in the back of Dan's truck. It was Dan who shook him.

"Hey, Shorty!" He pounded his back. "We made it! End of the trail. Taegu. Come on, Shorty! Wake up!"

His voice grew louder, the words more urgent. When Jae Wan still did not respond he picked up the boy in his long arms and carried him to a low patch of dry ground where he'd built a fire of some brush weeds. He sat down close to it.

Unable to speak, Jae Wan could not tell him how much he hurt. The warmth of the fire thawed his frozen body and the pain expanded, spreading, flowing through each muscle. He'd had not eaten in two days, but the gnawing pangs were forgotten in this new agony. The tears began again and Dan saw them. He took the boy into his arms, holding him like an infant, comforting him until the morning was bright.

Hunger replaced the searing ache. How could a can of beans, standard army ration, taste so delicious? Jae Wan spooned them out of the tin while Dan watched, nodding his approval. When he'd finished, the soldier insisted that Jae Wan put on a pair of his dry socks. The tips flapped loosely on his small feet and for the first time both of them laughed. They felt wonderfully warm, though.

Jae Wan understood that Dan could go no farther. He must remain in Taegu with his unit, unless the communists overran this place, also. Thanking this American friend, he managed to make him understand that he'd find a place in Taegu to sleep before continuing his march to Pusan.

But every street in the city was overflowing with refugees just like himself. Not even the poorest looking yogwan had room to spare. By midday he had not found any place to stay and he spent a large portion of his precious cash instead to buy a bowl of soup, heaping with noodles, from a small restaurant. At least, for the moment, his stomach was full.

Darkness was falling on this night, Christmas eve, and still he had no shelter from the cold. Finally, in desperation, he returned to the army base. Evading the guards, he searched for Dan. He could not find him. As the temperature plummeted he spotted one covered jeep that was parked away from the others and he climbed into it, found a blanket on the back seat and wrapped himself in it. Then he fell asleep on the soft, padded cushion.

A strong blow to his side woke the boy on Christmas morning. He opened his eyes. Two burly soldiers were glaring at him. One wore the insignia of a lt. colonel. Jae Wan leaped out the other side before that beribboned form could say a word and ran until he was out of their sight. No wonder the jeep was so comfortable! If he'd known it belonged to the unit commander he'd have searched further before taking refuge.

Jae Wan ran into Dan, finally, and told him of his bad luck. The young soldier was still sympathetic. "Why don't you work for me as my houseboy?" he suggested. "Then you can stay here until you find something better."

"What are you saying? I don't understand."

"I mean you can clean, you know, wash." Dan rubbed his hands together, suggesting scrubbing.

"Oh. OK." Jae Wan nodded his head. But that's women's work. He'd never washed clothes in his life. Is that what he'd come to? Besides, he wanted to get to Pusan. His parents would be worried if he didn't show up soon. He thought about the idea for a moment. He couldn't walk further without warm clothing and some better shoes. If he stayed here a few days and did this work perhaps he'd find someone willing to give him a ride south. Meanwhile he'd be able to show his gratitude to this kindhearted American. He nodded his head again.

"OK. I'll do it."

He scrubbed Dan's shirts and socks with enthusiasm, and while the clothing dried in the weak sunshine he polished his boots, rubbing and buffing the tips to a glossy finish. That he knew how to do, for he'd always kept his own shoes meticulously clean.

Look at me now, he thought, in these filthy, shapeless rags. How did this happen to me? That night he took the extra blanket and rolled up in it on the floor of the tent next to Dan's cot. For the first night since leaving Seoul he slept sound and secure.

But in the morning Dan was summoned to the commanding officer and dressed down for his violation of the rules. An MP had spotted the young Korean boy during inspection and reported his presence.

"Sorry, Shorty," Dan said when he returned. "Those are the rules. Guess the brass thinks all the refugees will come on base if he starts making exceptions. You'll have to find another place to sleep tonight."

Most of his money had already been spent for food. What he needed, in addition to a place to sleep, was a job. He walked the streets of Taegu all day but found nothing. With darkness approaching he dared not be seen on the street. Under strict martial law only the police were allowed at night. At last he peeked into a narrow alley where he'd be shielded from the wind. Several other persons huddled there already, shivering. He crept in among them and, for the first time in his life, slept on the street like a beggar.

There were no tears left. Only the heavy weight of despondence remained. He shared the suffering of all his countrymen who'd lost their homes and every material comfort that brought security to their lives through no fault of their own. All were victims, powerless.

If I survive, he promised, I will find a way to control my own destiny. Never again will I be at the mercy of faceless strangers who shove me like a pawn on the paduk board.

And I will survive!

Toward the end of the following day Jae Wan managed to smuggle himself back onto the base by jumping on the back of a truck and hiding under the canvas cover. Once inside, he returned to Dan's tent. He had to talk to someone, to find a familiar face in this city that was crowded with the uncaring.

"Sleep on the street! You can't do that!" Dan exclaimed, when the young soldier learned of his previous night. "This time you can sleep in my truck. Just be sure no one catches you. If they do, don't mention my name." He was in enough trouble already.

An anonymous army truck was more secure than a commander's jeep, the boy discovered. He slept undisturbed until the cold light of morning awoke him. He was still wrapped in his blanket when Dan appeared.

"Say, Shorty," he began, "I came up with an idea. There's a captain I know over at the 8th Army headquarters and I'm going to try to talk him into giving you a job like the one you had in Seoul. You're experienced, right?"

Jae Wan listened. He didn't understand all of those words, though Dan spoke slowly, but the message came through. If he could work for a while he might earn enough to make the remainder of the journey to Pusan without much suffering. At least he could pay for his meals along the way. This plan sounded like a good solution to all of his problems. Maybe he'd have a place to sleep, as well.

The immediate challenge was to smuggle him past the guards who stood at either side of the entrance gate. If he were caught! But Dan covered him well and the truck passed through without questions. Once safely inside, he knew where to find his friend. He told Jae Wan that the two of them came from the same town in the south. The captain had been his brother's classmate. Jae Wan must have looked worried. for he tried to reassure him, saying, "He'd a good guy."

Jae Wan watched the mans' face while Dan told the story of how he'd brought this kid down from Seoul with him. He promised the officer that he'd never find a better worker. At the end of his spiel the older man nodded his head. His grey eyes looked sympathetic and Jae Wan exhaled a sigh of relief.

The captain, a slightly balding dark haired man with well muscled arms, led them to his tent where Jae Wan could at last set down the heavy bag that he carried with him wherever he went. He did not dare to let go of the only objects on earth that belonged to him. He even slept with its straps wound around his wrist. He wished more Americans were as goodhearted as these two. They seemed to really care about the welfare of a stranger, a person who had no relation to them.

At this point Jae Wan looked up at Dan, realizing he'd be unlikely to meet this kind person again. He wished he could tell him that he knew Dan had saved his life.

"I'll never forget your kindness to me," was all he managed to say, the words spoken in his broken English, but Dan nodded. He seemed to understand.

"Here's a souvenir," he told the boy, pulling an American dollar bill from his pocket and handing it to him. He touched his young friend on the shoulder, patted it, said "So long, Shorty," and turning, walked away.

Jae Wan watched him until his pale blonde head was out of sight.

The captain's tent had a wooden floor and an oil stove.

"You can sleep here," he told the boy, pointing to a corner, "for now." He shared the tent with another officer, a tall, heavyset man who glared at the boy when he first saw him. When the captain tried to introduce him he walked out.

Jae Wan resumed his former job of burning papers and documents. During the remaining hours he tried to be as helpful as possible, keeping the captain's clothing and boots clean and in order. One morning, early, he watched the captain drinking straight from a bottle, tipping his head back while the light brown liquid slid down and the projection at the base of his throat bobbed up and down. Next the man downed a tall glass of water. Trying to keep warm, Jae Wan thought. He's not accustomed to this cold weather.

But the captain's face wore a constant reddish tinge and on some days he drank almost constantly, even when he was sitting next to the hot stove. However, he continued to treat Jae Wan kindly. He'd secured a gate pass for him so he could pass through freely and walk into Taegu for his meals. Two days passed uneventfully and just when he was beginning to believe his luck had changed for the better he discovered how unpredictable this Captain could be.

"Happy New Year!"

Jae Wan opened one eye.

"Hey, boy!" A foot nudged him. "Wake up! Happy New Year!"

The tent was in darkness. It must be the middle of the night, he thought, rolling over. Why all this shouting? Is this an American custom? He saw the captain pick up his pistol and leave. Too tired to get up and follow him, Jae Wan hoped he'd be able to find his way back by himself. He'd never been this drunk before. The boy fell back to sleep.

When the captain did return he stumbled over the sleeping form lying on the floor. He shook Jae Wan, trying to rouse him.

"I'll sleep on the floor," he insisted. "You take my bed."

He sprawled on the blanket that Jae Wan had been using. There was no way to argue. He was already snoring, so the boy lay on the bed, barely breathing, unable now to fall back to sleep. Minutes passed. A hand pulled at him, jerking his slight frame back onto the floor. Then a foot smashed into his side. Fists pounded against him. More kicks. He could not escape. Where could he go? He dared not resist, for this man was much larger than he, and dead drunk. The captain could not know what he was doing.

When at last he stopped beating the boy he fell back onto his bed, leaving Jae Wan, bruised and aching, on the floor. He pulled the blanket around himself, trying to feel warm again, and thought of other New Years. There was always a fine set of new clothes waiting for him, and more food on the table than anyone could finish. Early in the morning he would walk to his grandparents' home and bow low before the elderly couple, bending down until his forehead bumped on the floor. Then his grandfather would present him with some shiny new coins and crisp bills while his grandmother filled his pockets with candies. He was her youngest grandson and she made no secret of the fact that he was her favorite.

He felt half frozen. The heater in the tent must have gone out. The air was dry but so cold that he shivered until his teeth chattered. This was a New Year unlike any other and he was sure he would never forget it, no matter how old he might become.

This was also another working day, like any other. He stood beside the barrel, poking papers into the fire. A soldier approached. Jae Wan kept one eye on him. He'd learned to be wary. This man had a black skin. He'd never seen black persons until the American soldiers came to Korea and he noticed that most of them stayed apart from the white skinned men.

This black man came closer. When he was standing very near he reached out his hand to the boy. Jae Wan pulled back until he saw the bag of candy and the wad of Korean money in his hand, then looked up at him. What could he say? Seeing the man nod his head in a friendly way, he accepted this gift. The private saluted him and walked away.

As he had been thinking, all of these Americans were unpredictable.

All morning he pushed papers into the fire, enjoying the warmth it radiated. A gust of wind swept through, catching up a few of the papers lying on the top. As they fluttered to the ground a guard came over. Seeing them, he kicked Jae Wan. It hurt, but he did not flinch. Instead he bent over to pick them up. The butt of the M1 rifle cracked against his skull and he toppled over. Just before losing consciousness he felt the toe of the man's boot strike him in the face, smashing against his nose.

When he revived he was alone. He dragged himself to his feet and resumed the burning of the papers, but in a moment the guard returned and struck him again and again with the rifle. Ribbons of blood trickled down his face. Jae Wan gritted his teeth and stood, unsteadily but firm, resolved that he would not weaken before this bully. He'd heard stories of the ill treatment of Korean laborers who worked for the Americans, but he'd not believed it really happened until now.

He stayed with the job until it was finished, then staggered back to his tent and lay down. He couldn't sleep with the pain and he pondered his situation. How could he explain these opposing behaviors of the men sent to help his country? I suppose, he thought, they are very unhappy to be here in a place far from their own homes and so different. Life is almost as uncomfortable for them as for us. We're all together in a living hell, he concluded, that neither of us asked for or deserved. No one knows how long he will live. One more day? Or if he will survive to return to his home.

We've seen so many die since this war began, he thought, all around us. He could recall them all. We were told that the fighting would help to reunite our country. But it's torn apart more than ever. The communists are taking over in the north and in the free sections men turn against their fellow man in the effort to sustain life. One may be killed for a bowl of rice. No one trusts another, thinking he may be a spy or a guerilla, working secretly for the enemy.

Pain knifed through him and with it anger. Why should these men beat someone who did them no harm? He winced, moving gingerly to ease his swollen body. During these days he often remembered his mother's voice. Sun Yi told him, "You have a duty to survive!" Her words swam into his mind and he hung onto their sound as if it were a life preserver. He clung to them most during these moments of desperation. Where was she now? Had she and his sister and his father, and that baby, been able to reach Pusan safely? Somehow he must try again to find them.

There was no turning back. The war news was all bad. The communists were in the suburbs of Seoul, ready to take it over again. This time all they'll get is a ghost city, he thought, recalling the hundreds of thousands he'd seen in the midst of the frozen winter seeking the refuge of Pusan. They'll capture a place but not its people.

That was some small satisfaction for all of the suffering. But what would happen if they kept on coming, if no one stopped them, if the Americans pulled out, as some hinted they might. Pusan was the end of the line for people like him.

The next morning Jae Wan walked into Taegu and spent his last money, that given to him on the previous day, to buy a small bag of rice. When he opened it he found stones mixed with the grains, like confetti. He separated them, one by one. An hour later, when he'd finished, he cooked the rice in a tin can over the coals of a fire he built on the ground. It was one of his best meals in days.

Four days after the New Year the captain entered the tent while Jae Wan was in there alone. The boy looked up from the notebook in which he was writing his thoughts. Although the officer's face had a ruddy glow he appeared to be sober. He watched him warily, ready to dodge this time if he should lose his temper.

"Heard the news?"

The boy shook his head. "No news today."

"Well, those Reds hit your hometown again. Mopped it up and rolled right through." He sat on his bed, bending over to unlace a boot, not seeing Jae Wan's face. "Looks like they're headed right this way, moving fast."

An enormous lump settled in his throat. He felt the way he remembered feeling when one of the bigger boys plowed into him during a soccer game.

"Won't the Americans stop them?" he managed to whisper.

"Not me. I'm shipping out, back to Japan in three days."

Jae Wan sat up, pencil in hand. He looked at the captain. This man was the only friend he had. The strands of dark hair that he combed over the top of his head to cover the bald spot had slipped and he didn't look as young as he once had to the boy, but then maybe Americans turned bald early. Could be the alcohol that did it. What would he do without him?

The captain answered his unspoken question with one of his own. "Don't you think you'd better start looking for a ride to Pusan? Check out the train station?"

"What about the new general? Won't he make the armies strong so they can stop the Chinese?"

The captain shook his head. "Hard to say. Too early. It was damned bad luck to lose General Walker," he continued, referring to the jeep accident of the week before, in which the commander of the

8th Army died. General Ridgway had been sent out a day or two later to replace Walker. "Can't tell now if we're going to hold or pull out. Don't think anyone else knows, either, even the big brass. That's the reason I tell you that you'd better start looking for a ride south."

Good advice, Jae Wan thought, if only he could. The next morning he had no choice. He was told he'd lost his job. He wandered into Taegu and asked about trains at the railway station.

"Sorry. No civilians are allowed to ride the trains. Try the bus station."

But there were no busses, either. He returned to the Captain's tent.

In the evening the Captain surprised Jae Wan by asking, "Could you take me to a church?"

"Which church do you want to go to?"

"It doesn't matter. Any church will do."

Jae Wan recalled passing a Korean Protestant church each time he walked into Taegu. That was the only one he knew of, so he guided the captain to the small wooden building.

Inside, he watched as the captain fell to his knees, making the sign of the cross.

"Oh—oh," he thought, "I brought him to the wrong church."

A Korean minister came forward. He looked surprised to see an American officer. He became even more amazed when the man seized his hand, speaking in English, with tears rolling down his cheeks. The minister could not understand his words.

Jae Wan felt, under the circumstances, that he must say something.

"The captain is asking whether you mind his being in your church."

Nodding his head, the minister smiled, repeating, "You are welcome, you are welcome."

That must be all he can say in English, he thought. It seemed not to matter, for his words had a soothing effect on the captain, and when the two left together the older man had become more quiet, more gentle. He promised Jae Wan that he would not desert him.

The boy had learned about promises. I wish he would help me to get to Pusan, at least, he said to himself.

On the following evening the captain was already in the tent when Jae Wan walked in. He was lying on the floor and his face was covered with blood from a cut on his temple. Was it a fight this time or he did he fall? No matter. He'd have to help him. After washing his face and reviving him with cold water, Jae Wan coaxed the inert form into bed, wishing he could talk to him. He had some special news. But there was no possibility of communication. The captain slept soundly while Jae Wan packed his small bag of possessions. He'd made a decision. He would leave in the morning. There was no chance for a ride. He would walk.

When he said goodbye Jae Wan was overcome by his emotion, realizing that this was one more person he'd never see again. A good man. He owed his survival in the few days just past to him. If only he did not drink so much. The drunkenness frightened him. He could not predict the captain's behavior, nor prepare for it.

What to do next? He hefted the heavy bag over his shoulder and began walking south along the side of the unpaved road. Snow had not fallen for several days and the path was clear but blackened crusts coated the remains of the last storm and the horizon stretched before him, grey and dreary.

Jae Wan thrust his fist out, thumb extended, in the universal language he'd learned from these Americans, whenever he heard an Army truck approaching from behind him, but none stopped. Once he sat down to rest. He felt the cold even more, however, so he decided to keep on walking.

Much later a truck pulled up and stopped and the driver signaled to him with a friendly nod. What caused one person to be so kind when all the others ignored him, he wondered as he climbed quickly up into its bed.

He found some other passengers already huddled there, three small girls and a Korean soldier. The children were alone when he found them, the man, who wore the insignia of a private, explained. They couldn't tell him where to find their parents so he was taking them south where they'd be safe. They stared at Jae Wan in silence and he felt that their unblinking eyes reflected a depth of sadness without end. The oldest must be about seven.

Darkness was falling and the air growing even colder when the driver stopped the truck near a small village. It was no more than a cluster of grass roofed houses. Pusan was still far away. He told them he could not take them much farther. They'd be better off finding refuge here until morning. He waited while they climbed down from the back of the truck and then he drove off.

The soldier, also, said he'd soon reach his company. It seemed to Jae Wan that he'd been handed responsibility for these silent infants. They looked to him as if he were their guardian. He'd rather have only himself to worry over but he had no choice, for they had no one else. He asked a farmer to allow them the shelter of his grain storage shed for sleeping.

The old man hesitated, looking them over. Finally he nodded his approval. "There are communist guerillas in the hills. Sometimes they snoop around in the night. You'd better be careful."

"We'll take care of ourselves," Jae Wan assured him. He was wondering how when the soldier handed him a pistol.

"You can have this for the night, if it will make you feel safer."

He showed him how to point and pull the trigger. Then he stretched out on some straw, keeping his other weapon, a carbine, close beside him. Jae Wan had never fired a gun. He wondered if he could, but the thought of its nearness was comforting. Would his fear never end? He fell asleep with one hand wrapped around the hard metal of its handle.

As soon as the grey sky lightened Jae Wan woke and roused the others. Only the youngest girl resisted. She lay curled on her side with her thumb locked into her mouth. She must be near the age of his nephew, not even three years old. How had she managed to travel this far? He leaned over to shake her shoulder and saw her face, flushed and red. her forehead burned under his fingers. A fever! Jae Wan rolled her onto her back and then he saw the spots. Unmistakable. That rash meant measles. He could still smell the linseed poultices that his own mother had lain on his chest when his skin was covered with those splotches. How it had itched! He must have been nine or ten at the time. He lay in a cool, darkened room and there was always someone to bring him broth and other comforts while he recovered.

There was no food here, not even that. Nothing but water to drink. What could he do for this child? He wished for his mother. She always knew how to care for someone who was ill. Would her sisters catch her contagion as well?

"Look at this child," he told the soldier. "We can't travel today."

"Do whatever you choose," he replied. "I'm moving on. My company's not far from here and I'm going to catch up with them."

Retrieving the pistol from Jae Wan, he pushed it down into his belt, slung the rifle over his shoulder, and walked away without looking back.

Jae Wan called to the farmer and his wife poked her head out of their hut.

"This child is sick," he told her. "We'll have to stay here until she can move. Can you give these children something to eat?"

She shook her head. "No food. The soldiers take all." She disappeared inside again.

Was there no one to help him? He picked the child up in his arms. Her sisters sat on the heap of straw, staring at him. They seemed to be waiting for him to tell them what to do. He rummaged in his bag with one hand and found two apples, somewhat shriveled, at the bottom. He handed one to each girl and hoped they'd not be wasted. He'd like to have eaten them himself.

The baby flailed her arms in her sleep and he rocked her to and fro. The heat from her body seared his chest while his back shivered in the chill of the early morning. He closed his eyes and fell into a light sleep sitting up.

Later, he did not know how much later, he opened them and looked down at the child. She felt much cooler and lay very still. Not until her arms and legs fell limp did he realize her breathing had ceased. She'd died in his arms! Though he'd seen much death in the months since war began, he'd never been this close to it before.

The other children huddled together, staring at him.

"Sister?" he asked, pointing to the child still on his lap. They only stared, with eyes dull and expressionless. It was a long time before he could put her down. He laid her gently on the straw and spoke again to the old farmer. He found the man more amicable than his wife. He nodded, promising to give the child a proper burial.

When he began walking, holding each of the girls by a hand, he wondered if they understood what had happened. They'd shown no interest in their sister. If she was. He realized that he didn't even know that much about them. The roads were crowded, with everyone heading in the same direction. He doubted his chance of finding a ride now that he had these little ones to look after, so he left the roadway and, tying the younger of the two onto his back with his jacket, guided them straight up, over the mountain. It looked like a more direct route to the south.

Half way up the slope the older girl sat down on the ground.

"You can't stop here," Jae Wan said with exasperation.

"I'm tired of walking up this hill," the seven-year-old replied.

The other child said nothing, but the tears rolled down, leaving streaks in the dust on her cheeks. Jae Wan put her down and sat beside them. What could he do? People on all sides were passing, women and children with bundles tied on their backs or perched on their heads, plodding toward the only place they knew to offer hope of survival. A few young men hobbled among the refugees, barefoot, or with rags tied around their feet. No one even looked at them.

"Ready?" he shouted, jumping up. He'd make a game of this climb. "Follow me!" Remembering a poem his mother had once sung to him, long ago in Chunchon, he called out.

> Mountain!
> Mountain!
> Mountain high!
> Can you see?
> Can you see?
> The outmost edges of the sea?

It worked! The girls stood up and followed him slowly as he climbed higher. After hearing the poem a few times more they joined in chanting it with him, over and over, until they reached the crest and could look over into the valley on the other side.

> Mountain!
> Mountain!
> Mountain high!
> Can you see?
> Can you see?
> The outmost edges of the sky?

Toward evening Jae Wan searched for another friendly farmer who might offer them a refuge. With the apples finished there was nothing more to eat. This time the farmer and his wife took them into their house, making room for him and the girls on the warm floor, but they had no food to share. He felt so weak from hunger in the morning that he wondered how he would manage to walk all day.

"Are you traveling alone?" the old man asked.

When Jae Wan explained to him that he was hoping to find his family in Pusan and was bringing these homeless children along with him the old man's face creased in the pain of his sympathy.

"Aigo. Well then, perhaps you can get a ride on the train at the village south of here. We're too old to leave our home." He gestured to the tiny woman standing in the kitchen doorway. She was bent over, with a face as shrivelled as a dried persimmon. "All we can hope for is that the war won't touch us here."

With this renewed hope Jae Wan wakened the girls. It was still early.

"Today we won't walk so far," he announced.

The older one looked at him with a scowl.

"Soon you'll ride on a train," he added, and then even her eyes grew wide with wonder.

At least it was sufficient incentive to get them on their feet. They moved at a faster pace, though part of the trail was a steep climb. Even to Jae Wan the thought of a rail trip was enticing. He'd not ridden on a train since the beginning of the war.

The farmer was right. They found the railroad track passing through the village of Milyang and when Jae Wan inquired he learned that civilians might ride when there was space. He found a place for the children to sit while they waited.

"Don't leave this spot for a minute or you'll be left behind," he threatened, trying to sound fierce. He stationed himself near the track to watch. The day was more than half past before a train did arrive and he pushed the girls onto it almost before the wheels stopped rolling. It moved slowly and it was coated with grime, but for once he was moving without effort.

The windows had no glass. Each time he saw a tunnel entrance looming ahead he shouted, "Look out!" and the children ducked their heads, but it didn't help much. Smoke and soot filled the car and settled a layer of coal dust over all of them.

Pusan is a city built on hills. And now the furthest of them, the fringes of settlement, came into his sight. Shacks, constructed of nothing more than bits of junk, army surplus, with roofs of tin and even cardboard, covered every bit of open space. It was an instant settlement for the hundreds of thousands of refugees who'd crowded into this place, their last resort.

Thoughts of his parents flooded Jae Wan's mind while he watched the shanties roll past the train. Would he find them? They'd agreed on the meeting place, a park in the center of Pusan. At that time it had all seemed like a grand adventure. Instead he floated within this nightmare without end. He wished he could be a child again, without responsibility, protected, secure. Pusan was one of the few places in his country yet untouched by the terrible destruction. Could he feel safe here? Or would the surging tide of war continue rolling toward him, submerging all the life he knew, driving everyone into the sea?

The train roared through one last tunnel, then emerged into a narrow, flat land breaking on the huge East Harbor. This really was the end. There was nowhere else to go but into the water.

Once on the ground again, the girls clung to him. Jae Wan insisted they link hands.

"Hold tight! Don't let go!"

They cowered before his fierceness but did obey. He plowed through the crowded streets, pushing the children past throngs of people wearing nothing but rags, with anxiety stitched onto their faces. He wanted to find his family before dark. He could not face another night alone now that he was so close to the end of his journey.

When he reached the district where they'd agreed to meet he began to stop each passerby. Of course he could not expect to find his parents in the street but someone might know where they stayed.

"Do you know the home of the doctor?"

Each one shook his head, looking bewildered, and the chill hand of hopelessness crept over him. Perhaps they were not here in Pusan. Perhaps they'd never arrived. Most of these strangers looked at him with blank stares. Dead eyes. They all have dead eyes, he realized.

Hope is gone. The bodies shuffle along, fueled by the last vestiges of life, but the spirit is numbed, paralyzed.

No one could help him. He dragged the orphaned girls behind him, oblivious to their sobs until the smaller one sat down in the dust, refusing to move. He kneeled beside her, pleading, threatening.

An old woman stopped to watch. She balanced a basket equal to her own size on the top of her head and, pausing with one hand steadying the weight, she smiled at the child. A gold tooth flashed in her nearly toothless mouth.

"Is the child sick?" she asked. "There's a doctor up there on the hill. He can help you." She turned, pointing to an old house leaning against the slope, halfway from the top of the ridge.

A doctor! Jae Wan grabbed the child by her hand and pulled her to her feet. After running a few steps he looked back and called out "Kumupsimnida!"

The woman stared, made speechless by the form of polite address he'd directed to her.

He was panting, trying to catch his breath, when he reached the gate of the house, and he burst through without knocking. A strange woman sat on the floor of the room. Was this another hopeless chase? He stopped, recalling his manners, and told her why he'd behaved so rudely.

"Yes," she replied. "There's a Dr. called Lee here. Upstairs, at the back.

Up the rickety stairs he bounded, two at a time, still pulling the girls behind him.

They were all there, all crowded into one small room. His mother, his father, his sister, the baby. Even his elder brother. He saw them all as soon as the door was opened. But they stared at him as if he were a stranger. Didn't they know who he was? Then he looked down at his clothing. Ragged, filthy, crusted with mud and soot.

It only took a minute, though, for Sun Yi to recognize her son.

"Aigo!"

She sprang forward, folding him in her arms and hugging him until he gasped for breath. He couldn't remember her doing that since he was a young child, a baby. When she released him she asked, "Who are these children?"

The girls, reluctant to enter, were still in the doorway.

Sitting down, he tried to answer all the questions. Less than a month since he'd last seen his family, yet he was suddenly and completely overwhelmed by the vast gulf that separated him from them. He'd lived through experiences they would never know of, or understand. They thought of him as a child still, a fourteen-year-old, a high school student. He knew he was an adult. He'd never be a child again. In time, he thought, they may discover how I've changed.

But for now all that Sun Yi could think of was feeding him. While she set before him a steaming bowl of soup that she'd made herself he explained about these children, that he'd brought them safely all of the way from Taegu. There was no one else to help them, he said.

Sun Yi assured him she'd care for them as well and began by bringing bowls of soup to them also. She brought more food than he'd seen in weeks and even though the rice was mixed with a large portion of barley, it was white and pure and clean.

He paused with his mouth full and saw that none of the others were eating but simply watching him with satisfaction. They'd all sacrificed their meal for him!

When he leaned against the wall of their house the entire building shook and Jin Sook laughed at the look on her brother's face. There were only two small rooms that they all must share but it was a far better refuge than those he'd seen along the edge of the city, and it didn't matter, because they were all together once more.

Later Sun Yi attempted to ask him how he had traveled south and why it had taken him so long. He only told her "I traveled slowly, but there were no problems," thinking that he had no words now to describe that time. Perhaps there never would be. In that way, those days would be easier to forget.

The next day Sun Yi took her youngest son to a tailor shop where he could be fitted for a proper suit of clothes. Outwardly he looked like a schoolboy once again but inside he felt like someone who'd lived a long time.

The streets of Pusan, though laid out in wide avenues, were crowded, everyone hurrying, and among them, many beggars and orphans. That's what I looked like myself, a few days ago, he thought. He wished he could help each one to become as fortunate as he was now. And then he wondered how long his good luck would last. The communists were moving fast, unimpeded much of the way, while everyone retreated.

Later he walked about the city with Jae Soon. The hills ran directly to the sea, with only a strip of land less than half a mile wide that was level, next to the docks. Many vessels floated in the harbor among the fishing boats, freighters, destroyers, even an enormous battleship. Men scurried around the wharves, unloading crates and boxes, wheeling guns and other weapons of war. The main part of the city, Jae Soon explained as the brothers pushed through the crowds, the heart of Pusan, is behind the hill, out of sight. He told Jae Wan that Pusan had long been a small town. It was the Japanese who developed it as a port city. The harbor was a natural base for their operations in Korea when they took control back in 1910. Wharves were built, the port facilities enlarged. Few Koreans lived in Pusan at that time. It was only one day's voyage by ferry from mainland Japan and most of the populace was Japanese.

Jae Wan enjoyed this day of conversation with his brother. It was the first time he could remember that he'd not spoken down to him as a child. Perhaps Jae Soon noticed the change in him that no one else seemed yet to realize.

"Will you stay with us long?" he asked.

Only Jae Soon's salary as an interpreter for the U.S. Army made it possible for all of them to live in relative comfort here. His brother evaded the question, pointing out to him more sights. For the first time in many days Jae Wan revelled in the sensations of being well rested, well fed, well dressed. He strolled about as Pusan became familiar to him, exploring, even finding some of his classmates from Seoul who'd survived, as he had, miraculously.

But all around him was the talk of the war and how long it would take the communists to reach Pusan, for they were advancing on all fronts. And would the United States and others of the UN forces continue to fight on the tip of the peninsula. Or would the Koreans be abandoned after all this struggle? If that happened, where would all these people, these refugees, go?

Sun Yi was asking herself the same question. Almost everyone in Pusan was trying to leave, for constant rumors washed upon its shores and drifted over the coastal refuge. The communist troops were moving south with no one to block them. No army halted their progress. Within days the entire Korean peninsula would be in their hands. The Americans were preparing to evacuate.

Pusan was as far south as was possible to go, but wait! There was one more escape! The island of Cheju. It lay sixty miles off the coast. The place had always fascinated her. Isolated, with different customs. And warm. Almost a tropical paradise, she'd heard. So remote that Koreans on the mainland called it only "over there." A place famous for wind, rocks, and its women, the divers who harvested their living from the sea while men remained at home.

What an adventure it would be if she were to see it for herself! When Sun Yi learned that the United States Navy was using its ships to remove some of the persons crowding into Pusan, taking them across to Chuju, she rushed to tell her husband.

"You can go!" she urged him. "You're a doctor. They'll give you a pass. Then you can take all of us with you over there."

Dr. Lee gave in to her pleas and applied for passes for all of his family to accompany him to Cheju.

"Now we'll be safe, won't we?" She asked him over and over. It was her dream: to resume a peaceful life. She'd told Jae Soon the news when he returned to the cramped and shaking apartment that night.

"No," he replied. "I can't go with you to Cheju. I must remain here in Pusan until word comes from In Ja."

"In Ja? Who is In Ja?"

"In Ja is the woman I intend to marry. The one I always wished to marry. She's in America now and she's making the arrangements for me to join her there. She's finding someone to sponsor me and the child."

Then he told her the story of the pianist and himself.

Sun Yi stared at this man, her eldest son. He was a man, a father. She knew she could hold onto him no longer. If he made this decision by himself no one could change his mind. Perhaps once, long ago, his father might have been the one to persuade him, to cajole him into obedience to his elders. Too much about this country was changed, with different rules since the war began.

"How can you leave? You, our first son?"

He turned away from her stricken face. "There's no future for me here. No more." His voice was scarcely audible. "I want to live in peace."

"This woman. Who is she? How can she be a good daughter-in-law to me if she's on the other side of the ocean? I'll never see you again."

"Of course you will! When I'm settled I'll send for you."

"What would I do in America? I can't speak English. This is my country."

What would become of her family without the eldest son and his wife to care for them when she and her husband grew old, to carry on with the traditions? Lost! All of them were lost now. Sun Yi did not speak to Jae Soon again until the departure, when he'd promised to write, to send money from America, to return someday. Someday.

He was holding the boy and both of them were waving to her when she saw them last, from this very deck. The scrap of paper, with a strange foreign address, her only link to her firstborn and to her grandson, the only grandchild she had.

They were in exile and so was she now, but so far apart.

Chejudo has always been a place of exile for Koreans. Now the island is becoming my refuge, thought Sun Yi. The flecks of salt spray whipped through the air, stinging her cheeks, settling on her shoulders. She was standing on the deck of the U.S. Navy ship, pressed close to the railing by the crush of human bodies on the overloaded vessel. When would she see Mt. Halla? The horizon was obscured by mist. It was the highest mountain in the country, but the ancient volcano was only a dim shadow in the light of the early February morning. As the boat drew close to shore the clouds parted briefly and displayed its snowy cap.

Her husband and two children were somewhere on this ship. She'd seen them boarding, then lost sight of them while they struggled with the heavy cases filled with medical supplies for his mission here. Of course she'd find them when everyone was landed. As soon as the vessel left the pier at Pusan last night she knew she must remain on the top deck or she'd feel miserable for the entire voyage. The ship rocked back each time it plowed into a breaker and she recoiled with it, fighting her own waves of nausea. Conditions must be much worse for those below. Better to suffer the cold up here where she could breathe fresh air.

Both levels were so packed with people that no one had space to stretch his legs. Babies cried. Some religious persons huddled together, singing hymns and praying in loud voices. Yes, it was definitely better to be up here, despite the icy wind. Would it never stop blowing? She hugged her winter coat about her.

Wind, rocks, and women. All of her life she listened to tales of this exotic island only sixty miles from the southern coast. Over there.

Across. That is what Chejudo meant to the mainlanders, who considered the island people different, inferior to themselves. She'd always hoped to see this place.

But not in this way.

And where would she and her family go from here? From this deck the island appeared vast but she knew it was, at most, only fifty miles long and perhaps fifteen miles across at its widest point. All the refugees would not fit within such confines.

The sea breezes ruffled her hair. She listened to the sound of voices shouting, men's voices, rough, commanding, and wished she could understand the words. These American sailors were kind to her when she boarded, not like some of the soldiers who'd jostled her in the streets of Pusan, calling her a "mamasan", whatever that meant.

The ship's engines stilled, the throbbing ceased, but the land was still distant. Why? Ah! She understood. There, below, a flotilla of small boats rode on the waves and baskets swung out from the ship, carrying passengers, hovering over the pinpoint of deck, depositing screaming children and shrieking women upon each in turn.

Aigo! Suppose she must take her turn at that? The water must be too shallow for the ship to move closer. Twelve, she counted. Twelve small boats chugged from ship to shore and back, slowly, abandoning each refugee on a barren beach with its only backdrop the steep and dark cliffs of lava rising beyond it.

Sun Yi swallowed hard, preparing herself to take her turn. The basket swayed with the wind. I've come all this way. I can travel a bit further, even if my journey happens to be in a basket.

A stiff breeze caught it just as she stepped in, and she was compressed in its grip with all of the others while they floated out over the white caps and dropped down onto the waiting boat, to be spilled onto its narrow deck. Then the boat sped toward the beach. The ocean was a sea green, transparent over the the black coral of the reefs. She smelled the salt air and the must of seaweed and shellfish and stepped onto the refuge, wetting the hem of her chima.

Wind whipped the white sand, peppering her with its stinging grains but she remained near the shore, watching the arrival of each new boatload for sign of her husband and children. Hours passed. Hundreds of persons milled about before following the path that she'd been told led to a village. The noon hour passed before she saw them. Jae Wan and his sister accompanied their father and they still hung onto all the pieces of baggage they'd carried from Pusan.

"Why are we landing so far from Cheju city?" she demanded, as soon as he could hear her. "There's only one bus each day, I've been told, and all these people here, with nowhere else to go. What are we to do?"

Her husband scanned the horizon. He did not reply immediately. "The harbor at Cheju City is shallow," he explained in a voice heavy with weariness. "The ship cannot enter. Even here the coral reef prevents it from making a closer approach." He sighed. "I'm sure there must be someone to help us. They know the doctors are coming with this group. Perhaps in the village." His voice trailed off, uncertain words spoken only to comfort.

They climbed, the four of them, looking for some sign of a settlement. Reaching the top, they saw the network of low walls, built of lava rock, that laced the countryside, looking like windtorn spider webs. The houses were squat, walls of stone also, and their thatched roofs were lashed down with crisscrossed ropes of straw moored to the rafters like giant hairnets. A stiff breeze blew constantly, borne inland by ocean winds.

Jin Sook seized her mother's hand. "Ohmanee," she whispered, "there won't be any fighting here, will there? We left all the soldiers on the mainland."

Sun Yi looked at her daughter and then at her husband. Meeting his eyes, she squeezed her child's hand. "No, my daughter. Here we will find peace." She hoped she was telling the truth.

They asked a farmer in the village if he would take them in. Just for one night, they reassured him, and crowded into the small room that already held a dozen others. At least there'd be a place to sleep and something to eat. Sun Yi was so tired. Tomorrow they'd find a way of getting to Cheju City.

In the morning, though, Sun Yi was still exhausted, and Dr. Lee decided to remain another day while she rested. Jae Wan was eager to leave the confines of the hut. He and his sister watched as the farmer's wife made ready to go to the sea, preparing the tools of her diving trade, the straw basket and gourds. When she left they followed. Stories of the diving women of Chejudo were told throughout Korea. Here was an almost unbelievable chance to see one of them.

Heavy cotton clothing shrouded her. Even the woman's head was draped and bound by a cloth. Other women dressed in the same manner waited for her by the rocky shore.

Jin Sook hesitated. Jae Wan waved to her to hurry. Breathless, she fell in with his step. "I can't understand their language. Do you know what these people are saying?"

"The dialect of this island is peculiar," he admitted, stopping to shade his eyes and look out over the water. The ocean was smooth today, the color of turquoise, even early in the morning. "Abuji told me it's because they have lived so long in isolation, and also because the Mongols invaded their land long ago and their language got mixed up with the Korean. I suppose we'll get used to it after a while," he consoled her, meanwhile continuing to walk slowly upon the rocks.

"After a while? How long do you think we'll have to stay here?"

"Who knows?" He paused again, squinting to look toward the horizon. "If it's peaceful here I may never leave." These last words burst from him, as if held inside until he could no longer contain them.

Jin Sook nodded. From the high point on which they stood, side by side, they could see the bobbing heads, dozens of them in the ocean below. A head disappeared below the surface for what seemed to be a long interval, then broke out as with a splash and a shriek the diver exhaled the oxygen pent up in her lungs. She laid her prize, the shellfish or seaweed that she clutched when she surfaced, into the basket that floated, bobbing on the water near her. It never disappeared, being attached to her waist by a long hemp rope so that however long her dive she would find it when she emerged.

Jin Sook watched, fascinated by these women, strong and powerful in a way she'd never imagined.

"Maybe I will stay here," her brother teased. "It looks like a comfortable way for a lazy man to live. The women do all the work on this island, you know."

"Well, they make the rules also," she reminded him. "If you think you're ready to live under the thumb of a woman." She glanced sideways at Jae Wan.

He ignored her, walking on. Further down the path they discovered a statue of stone.

Jin Sook cried in delight. "Is it a grandfather stone?"

The carving hewn from rock was taller than either of them, a massive chunk of porous grey lava. Its body was a solid upright rectangle with arms and hands delineated against its stone torso while the face, with bulging eyes and a wide squashed nose, sat atop the shoulders. The lines of a rounded cap covering its head closely were carved on the surface.

Jin Sook put out her hand tentatively, touching the rough surface. "A nyung ha sim ni ka, haraboji." Her greeting bore respect. "What is it for?" she asked in wonder. "It looks as if it's been here forever. See how smooth and weatherbeaten it feels."

"I don't know. This is a strange place," Jae Wan shivered. The statue stood like a guardian of this island. Its large blank eyes compelled him to stare, fastening on him, seeming to ask silent questions. He turned his back on its hypnotic gaze.

That night before they slept Dr. Lee spoke outside with their host for a long time. Afterwards he called to Sun Yi and the children to walk with him. She did not mind the evening chill. This air was far warmer than that of the mainland she'd left behind.

"The farmer was warning me about the guerillas," he said. "Nightime is particularly dangerous. That's when they dare to come out of hiding. Sometimes they will raid for food and supplies, he told me, and sometimes they wish only to terrorize the poor people so they will cooperate. He wanted me to be prepared if it should happen while we are here." He patted Sun Yi's shoulder. "Tomorrow we'll go to Cheju City. It's a larger place. It will be safe. But it's better to know of this danger than to be surprised by it. Don't you agree?"

"Why, Abuji?" Jae Wan trembled. "Why is there fighting here? We left the war on the mainland." This place had seemed peaceful today, rocked by the constant rhythms of the wind and the sea and the women proceeding about their work.

"After Japan's war ended this island became a haven for communist supporters from the mainland of Korea," his father explained. "The hills provided a hiding place for them and they survived by living on the wild ponies that roam here, not so many now as before their arrival," he added.

"The land looks barren," the boy commented, looking toward the mountain slopes as if he might see the menace approaching.

"It is now. The government soldiers cut away all of the trees to rid the island of these trouble makers," Dr. Lee continued. "Until recently many of the people lived inland. Their villages were destroyed in this same campaign and they've been forced to resettle along the coast. They're not happy with the actions of either side in this struggle, naturally. And still the guerillas survive. It is said that if forty are killed on one day there will be forty more to take their place on the next day."

He frowned. Why should the young ones be told of these matters? To give them a chance to survive. Knowledge is the only power that can save them.

Darkness came and with it colder air. Everyone was sleeping, or trying to, in the crowded room. Sun Yi lay awake. So she was the first to hear it.

Gunshots. A woman screaming.

She sprang to her feet, stumbling over the prone figures. Dr. Lee followed, peering through the paper window.

In the road outside shapes and forms ran in a senseless pattern. More screams shattered the night stillness. Fearful cries of children, women. Sounds of shooting continued. Then flames roared into the sky. A second burst of flame, closer than the first, ignited the darkness.

"Hurrah for the communists! Everyone outside!"

Sun Yi clutched Jae Wan and Jin Sook to her sides. They huddled beneath the window, fearful their outlines would be visible to those outside. She could not move.

"Ohmanee!" Jin Sook whimpered.

"Shh!" she commanded, holding her tighter.

"Come out! Come out! Come out and join us!"

The strident calls mingled with the intermittent bursts of gunfire and screaming, while Sun Yi remained close to the floor. Her body rocked with anguish, locked into a rhythm that defied her mind.

The din went on throughout the night. Early in the morning she heard the roar of a truck's engine, the rushing of feet, and then it stopped. She dared to peek from a corner of the window. A phalanx of police marched through a corridor of rubble. No others in sight. The street was empty, with tongues of orange flame licking the still dark edges of the sky. Only the outlines of the fallen bodies remained to indicate the tragedy that brushed this place with blood and pain, and terror.

The farmer who owned her refuge startled her into reality with his outburst of fury.

"The same! Always the same! Those cowardly police never show themselves until the damage is done. They allow those communists to frighten us and show us what they can get away with. Who cares about communists or democracy? All I want is peace! Give me one night safe for sleep!"

"Yes." Sun Yi echoed in her mind. "Peace. That is really all any of us want."

The doctor found a wagon, on the following day, to transport the four of them to the small settlement called Cheju City, and a room where they could stay. He was immediately called to help, and worked nearly all of the time, for his medical skills were needed greatly in this place.

> "To the great shrine of Moon Soo Mul
> The god doth descend.
> Of the Ko Nahng Rock
> The departing ship takes hold."

Sun Yi watched, engrossed in the motions of the shaman woman, the simbang, as she began the ritual song of the ceremony, kut, her eyes closed and her body swaying in slow rhythm with the beat of the changgu. She'd been skeptical when her daughter persuaded her to observe this ceremonial service in a village near Cheju City, but now she was pleased that she'd accompanied Jin Sook here. The island of Cheju was the last bastion of these ancient rituals that honored the nature gods, one of the few places left in her country where the beliefs were still practiced with pure innocence. It would be a rare occasion for both of them.

"Please, Ohmanee, let us go, simply to watch," Jin Sook had pleaded. "I've never seen a kut performed, and these villagers are said to have great skill."

"Don't you know that those practices of shamanism are only the remnants of old superstitions?" Sun Yi protested when her daughter suggested this excursion. "Have you completely forgotten your own background? Educated persons don't follow these beliefs."

She reminded the girl that shamans, called mudang in other parts of Korea and simbang here on Cheju, were among the eight categories of "outcast" during the hundreds of years of the Yi dynasty. Along with Buddhist monks, artisans, butchers, funeral pall bearers, male and female entertainers, and servants, the shamans, mostly women, had been socially ostrasized for generations. Yet they'd persisted, endured.

The child had few diversions since coming to Cheju, or even since the invasion that began the war. Perhaps this ceremony would distract Sun Yi from her constant worries as well. She spoke to her husband about it. Dr. Lee, deeply involved in his medical duties, said only "Go if you wish. Such things have always been the province of women."

She knew he shrugged it off as mere entertainment.

The simbang swayed. The rich blue of her chima shimmered in the sunlight of the outdoor square. A large crowd, people from neighboring villages, created a festive mood. They made room for Sun Yi and her daughter near the front.

And then it began.

The man seated next to the shaman struck the changgi. It was a large drum, shaped like an hourglass and formed from a hollow tree trunk with hides of leather stretched over either end. He held it across his lap and slapped one end with his left palm, then hit the right side with a wooden rod.

The simbang stepped forward, eyes closed, head uplifted.

"The hae-nyuh at the upper place,
The hae-nyuh at the central place,
The hae-nyuh at the lower place."

The recitative style of her song, irregular in rhythm, was hypnotic. The hae-nyuh were women divers. They were another of the strange elements here that caused Chejudo to seem foreign to Sun Yi. Life here reduced needs to the simple daily routine while her existence in Seoul had been vastly more complicated. Which was better? The well being of the island depended on the gods of nature and their ability to provide the necessities of life, or take them away.

> "This offering, we beseech thee,
> Do receive."

The simbang performed the intricate steps of her dance in front of the kut table, which contained the ritual offering of chesa to the departed, heaps of rice cakes, seasoned vegetables, grilled meats and bean curd, pyramids of apples and pears, dates and chestnuts, and delicate pastries prepared with sesame oil and honey.

The guests will enjoy this feast later, Sun Yi surmised, and it will be a meal of rare delicacies for these farmers and their families. She was glad she'd been able to contribute to it.

Her daughter, sensing that Sun Yi's mind wandered, reproved her with a sideways glance. "Concentrate!" said her eyes.

> "The elder devotee,
> Forty and eight years doth be,
> The central devotee,
> Thirty and eight years doth be."

This simbang did not reflect the stages of ecstasy that she'd heard the mudangs of northern provinces would portray. Instead this woman was direct and confident in the steps of her feet and the motion of her arms. On this island the role of shaman was inherited, learned from a mother-in-law, handed on to a daughter-in-law, retained through a close circle of intermarriage. The mudangs of the north were more likely to be moved by a "spirit", to become possessed, bestowed with extraordinary powers that enabled them to communicate between the world of the present and the world of another level of reality.

Too bad she'd not had the opportunity to watch one in Chunchon. But she'd been reluctant to intrude. She'd always been an outsider there. Why were these persons, obviously endowed with great artistic talents, relegated to a low social status by the past dynasty? Sun Yi wondered if the Confucian Yi rulers wished to destroy the influence of this native religion over the common people of their time.

Each village had a god to watch over it, and shrines before which to demonstate their piety, and there were still many simbangs to perpetuate this tradition. It reflected the very character of Cheju itself. The rituals related the mythological origins of the island, a place without a vision of heaven or hell. The male gods in the mountains symbolized the bounty of nature, the use of animals for food and for their skins. The female gods emerged from the sea, bringing its offerings to the people.

Perhaps that is why the women have always been the divers here, she thought. Their basic purpose was created from these myths.

> "As the moon was setting
> In the afar-off sky,
> From the surface of the water,
> The head of a dragon
> Did suddenly appear."

The ceremony required the presence of a full moon, yes, and this kut was likely to continue for days afterward with bouts of dancing, singing, and feasting at intervals. The long, slow, involved recitative began with this plea to the gods to reveal the cause of the present trouble, and would end, later, with a supplication to them, an attempt to propitiate them, to drive away the evil spirits.

Well, she would remain a bit longer since it pleased her daughter, this opportunity to watch a folk ritual, but they must return home tonight. She did admire the skills of this woman and her prodigious memory. The simbang did not falter once in her repetition of the lengthy epic.

The accompanist beat the changgu louder, while he intoned a counter melody, a long drawn out series of "ahhhs."

The insistent and deep vibrations relaxed Sun Yi, transfixed her mind, then speeded the flow of her body rhythm. Her heart beat quickly, pulsating with the tempo of the drum. She began to sway in unconscious synchronization with the beat.

Suddenly her mind opened on a different reality.

The simbang twirled in a circle before her, the feather on her headdress whirring in a blur of color, each step punctuated by the striking of a cymbal. The discordant touch of the gong increased her frenzy as she whirled, faster, faster, preparing to meet the spirits with an empty and pure mind, to become a vessel, to transmit commands from a world real but unseen.

A second man joined in the music, adding the high thin notes of his piri. The sound of the reed flute heightened the eerie sensation.

The simbang fluttered her fan deftly, summoning the spirits to her. Then, with the help of another woman, she shed the pale colored top layer of her many garments, revealing bolder, more violent shades of red, green, blue beneath, while she missed not one beat of her dance. Her arms moved up and down slowly, their long, full sleeves becoming like the wings of a bird. In a dreamy haze she moved forward on her toes. Suddenly she gave a shout. She jumped and her fast left turn brought her around full circle.

Sun Yi's heart skipped a beat. She inhaled deeply. Before she could recover from her surprise the simbang jumped again and made another full turn. She stopped, her feet straight in line, facing Sun Yi. She looked directly at her with dark intense eyes now open, staring, drawing Sun Yi into communication with the forces she had summoned.

With a jolt of understanding Sun Yi knew what she must do. No proper recognition had ever been given to those she'd lost. How could she, when survival for the living demanded all of her energy? She'd done nothing to honor their memory. Of course she could not know their fate. She'd never be certain what had happened to her second son. Did he die in Westgate Prison or on the forced march north following the invasion of Inchon? Her dear friend, Tai Un? She knew in her heart that she would never see her again. Or her eldest son's wife, either, poor child.

Perhaps this was the reason she was here. This could be the proper place to bid them farewell and face the choices for the future.

The simbang danced again, shaking the bells in one hand, folding and unfolding the large fan in the other, as she leaped. Sun Yi felt that she was being pulled along with her. The woman began to dance the kori, with the changgi beating faster, faster, a dance to the ghosts of those who had died away from home or accidentally. It was sending off their spirits. And it ended abruptly.

All sound, all movement ceased.

The shaman's assistant stepped toward her, holding the garments she would wear in the next kori. Over her long blue chima there was placed an overlay of white silk, then a shorter dark blue silk chima and on top of that one of red silk. The woman pushed her arms into the long sleeves of a brilliant yellow robe. A wide belt encased her around the middle with a second belt of red added over it, the long ties dangling in front. Finally two pins of dragon design were set in her black hair and a multi-colored coronet of ribbons was placed on top of her head.

Sun Yi watched all of this through a haze, her eyes clouded, still encased in the web of surrealism.

For once the simbang was still. She did not dance. Instead she sat on a cushion and took the hourglass drum into her arms. First she struck the hand-beating end of it with the folded fan in her right hand. Then, with her left hand, she shook the bells.

The cadences of her narrative rose and fell, carrying Sun Yi back to a time when she was a child. Her nurse once took her to a similar ceremony in a village of Kyongsang province and she listened, wideeyed, to the raucous music and dancing and fell asleep secure in the arms of the good woman who'd cared for her as her own daughter.

The beating of the changgu continued with the accompaniment of the bells and the voice droned on while Sun Yi thought of the years that followed when she defied Grandfather to leave home and attend the mission school, of how she'd returned for his funeral and felt the pangs of remorse conflicting with her ambitions. She felt again, as if she were there, the damp stones of the prison cell where she sat after the March First demonstration for independence. If it had not been for the period of house arrest after that she might never have met her husband. What course would her life have taken if she'd always obeyed her elders?

The sun set and the simbang's chant intensified, releasing her mind to encounter thoughts long submerged.

There were her children. First the two sons. Jae Yun, a victim of the war. Would she ever learn his fate? Jae Soon, leaving to make a new life on the other side of the vast ocean, was now as separate from her as his younger brother, in his own way.

The time of struggle, with her husband in prison was a bitter memory. Did she make the right choice in her attempt to free him? She believed that she had but she would always be tormented by that doubt and she would never know that either, really.

So many uncertainties. Her life had traversed a long path, a tiring one, but along the way she'd learned to always let go of the past, to look to the future. What should she do now? Would she resist more drastic change in her life?

Strength. If only she had enough of it, so she would not be tempted to cling to the familiar. She'd created a home in remote Chunchon. She'd faced the departure of her second son and the loss of contact with her younger brother during the earlier war.

Gone. Everyone of them. Kim Tai Un could give her no more advice. There were the two younger children still, yes, but how much longer could she hold onto them? Or should she even try? She was exhausted. Weary. Perhaps she'd done all she could. There was her husband but now he withdrew from her. He was no longer willing to struggle, allowed himself to be carried with the tide of events without resisting.

Seoul was far away and there was no longer a home there, either. Who knew if she'd ever go back? The path of her destiny had led her to this place of exile, the last one. She would go no further.

But the children? Could it be possible that a different land would offer a future for them? All promise of life here was destroyed. As I left my home and family, so must my children, she thought. But could she release them?

The chanting voice slowed, halted. The drumbeats ceased. The bells stopped ringing. The moon was rising, clear and round and full, with the encircling darkness giving it a luminescence of its own.

The whirlwind created by the shaman enveloped the entire site of the ritual. There was a portentous silence. The simbang laid the changgu on the ground and leaned forward. She lit the three-wicked candle on the table before her, and its light cast a glow on the bowl of rice, on the incense burner, on the sheets of white paper that lay beside it.

At first it flickered, then it leapt upward into the darkness, illuminating the other world, showing the way. She called on the departing spirits to leave the blessings of good fortune, peace, and longevity.

Sun Yi sighed deeply. She felt the lightness of a release, as if the great weight oppressing her for a long time was rising. She knew now what she must do. What she could do. When she returned to her husband she would tell him. Her decision was made. Now she would show him that she still had the strength he'd admired within her. Their children would find their own way, like once captive birds set free.

Sun Yi recalled the lines written by the poet Yang Sa On. She'd memorized them as a child, the wisdom of hundreds of years past, and used them as her guide through other ordeals. Though she might never reach that summit, she would never give up the attempt.

> However high a mountain may be,
> It still is lower than the sky.
> Climb, climb again, and higher, who says
> You will not gain the summit?
> People claim it is too high,
> With no trial, no attempt, no will."

THE END

Note

This story is a work of fiction but it is based on many actual events, facts and personalities. The bibliography that follows will describe the sources of my extensive research, but all of my impressions, gleaned from observation and conversation for many years with my Korean relatives and friends, have contributed to the whole fabric.

I take full responsibility for my interpretation and apologize to them for any errors of culture and custom I may have inadvertently included.

About the Author

Beverly Johnson Paik was born to a Swedish immigrant family living in Massachusetts that settled in California when she was a child. She was graduated from Stanford University with a degree in journalism and special emphasis on Asian history studies and also earned a Master's in Education from Stanford. She has been writing since the day she learned to read.

While at Stanford she married a fellow student, Harkjoon Paik, who had arrived in the United States from Korea during the Korean War, at the age of fifteen. She has accompanied her husband as he completed law studies at Stanford and followed a legal career, including twenty-two years as a Superior Court judge in Monterey County, California, all the time gathering material for this book.

They have three grown childen and two grandchildren. Carmel Valley, California, has been their home since 1970.

Glossary

Family relationships:

Abuji, father.

Halmoni, grandmother

Haraboji, grandfather

Ohmanee, mother

Yubo, a term of familiarity used by husband when calling wife

Articles of clothing:

Chima, the traditional dress for Korean woman, loose from above the waist, full and floor length.

Chogori, the short jacket worn with the chima.

Chokki, decorative buttons that fasten the mens' traditional coat, the turamaji.

Getas, a Japanese word for wooden clogs.

Hanbok, a general term for traditional clothing of Korea.

Komussin, the shoe usually made from rubber and only worn outside.

Nanja, a married woman's hair style, with hair pulled back into a bun at the nape of the neck.

Pinja, a women's hair ornament

Pinyo, a woman's hair ornament

Sigachima, the coat or cape with hood worn by women that covers completely the body and head.

Turamaji, the traditional knee length coat of a gentleman.

Articles of food and drink:

Anju, appetizers usually served with alcoholic drinks.

Chap che, main course of bean threads mixed with shreds of meat and vegetables,

Daikon, a long white radish. When shredded, important ingredient of kim chee.

Duk kook, a soup always served with the New Year's Day meal, based on beef broth and containing thin slices of rice cake.

Kalbi, beef shortribs, cut into small sections with thin strips of meat attached to bone, marinated in soy sauce and spices, grilled,served hot.

Keem, thin sheets of a seaweed found in deep ocean water, prepared with sesame oil and salt, toasted until crisp, eaten with rice.

Kim chee, a basic spicy side dish with every meal, of Chinese cabbage or small cucumbers stuffed with shredded daikon, garlic, red pepper powder. Every family will have its own variation.

Kom tang, a soup with special flavor derived from ox tails.

Makkoli, a potent white liquor.

Mandoo, a dumpling with filling of ground meat, vegetables and spices. May be steamed, fried, or boiled in soup.

Nang myun, a soup served cold, served in hot weather, based on beef broth, containing buckwheat noodles, hard boiled egg, pinenuts, apple pears slices, various vegetables.

Pahp, word for rice

Podi cha, tea prepared from roasted barley kernels. Served either hot or cold.

Pul kogi, thin slices of beef, marinated in soy sauce and spices, broiled quickly over hot fire.

Sungnyung, a hot broth prepared from the crusted rice left in pan after cooking.

Tobu, bean curd cake similar to the Japanese tofu.

Yak ju, a strong rice wine.

Yut, a hard candy traditionally sold by street vendors who severed each piece with a long scissor.

General:

Ah nyun ha sim ki ka, a greeting.

Aigo, an expression of anguish.

Chaekjang, an ornate wooden book chest.

Chige, a wooden frame worn on back of carrier, shaped in an "A".

Cho, a measurement of land, about six acres.

Chondogyo, a religion or philospohy originating in 19th Century Korea.

Chonggu, a drum.

Chungin, the working class.

Chusok, the autumn festival, a time to visit ancestral graves.

Dawai, to plunder

Hamkyung, a rural province in present-day North Korea.

Hangul, the Korean alphabet.

Hanyak, traditional Korean practice of medicine.

Hanim, a housemaid.

Hanuri nopda, the time of clear, high skies in autumn

Hwan, term for currency.

Hwegap, a ceremony to commemorate sixty years of life.

Ibul, a quilted blanket.

Il yukka, oxcart.

Jongpan, specially varnished paper on heated floor of ondol room,

Kadenmin, landless farmers under Japanese rule.

Kam sam ni da, a ~~greeting~~ thank you with the familiar form

Keijo, name for Seoul under Japanese rule.

Kisaeng, woman entertainer.

Kori, a dance performed by a shaman, a dance of the ghosts, to commemorate those who died away from home or accidentally.

Kum up sim ni da, a ~~greeting~~ Thank you with the polite form.

Kut, a ceremony of the shaman women.

Kyunggi, the highest rated school for boys in Seoul.

Mansei, the name for March 1, 1919, nation-wide independence protest, also translated at "May Korea Live 1000 Years."

Maru, the long porch or deck surrounding a house.

Matang, inner courtyard of house.

Maui, small houses in countryside.

Miguk, America.

Mogyokt'ang, a public bath house.

Mudang, Korean name for shaman woman.

Ondol, floor heated by underground system leading from kitchen fires.

Ok dae gum, musical instrument of flute family.

Piri, a reed flute

Sarang, a room in a home, reserved for use of men.

Simbang, another name for shaman woman, used on Cheju Island.

Sijo, Classical poetry, usually of 16th Century.

Tano, festival to greet springtime, held on fifth day of May.

Tok, a large clay jar for storing food.

Tonghak, a revolutionary movement of 19th Century.

Weanom, savages, used to describe Japanese rulers.

Yangban, aristocratic class.

Yogwan, a simple inn.

Yontan, fuel made from charcoal.

Yundal, an extra month added to the lunar calendar each three years.

Zbegi, a ball often wound from rags by children, used in a soccer-like game.

NOTE: I beg to be excused by linguists who may find errors in my definitions of these Korean terms. Variable translations are always possible from the "hangul" script to English, but I have attempted to be as accurate as possible. For example, p and b are often interchangable in translation, as pul kogi is sometimes bul kogi and podi cha is also bori cha.

A word regarding names. In most cases I have used the family name first, in accordance with Korean custom, such as Yu Sun Yi. And, while traditionally Koreans would not address a person by their given name, but instead use a title of honor, such as elder brother, for the ease of an American reader I have taken the liberty of using first names in many scenes.

Bibliography

Adams, Edward B., *Through Gates of Seoul,* a complete guide to Seoul's vicinity. Taewon Pub. Co., Seoul, Korea, 1974.

Allen, Horace N., *Things Korean.* Fleming H. Revell, New York, 1908.

Allen, Richard C., *Korea's Syngman Rhee,* Charles Tuttle Co., Rutland, Vt., 1960.

Bartz, Patricia M., *South Korea,* a geography. Clarendon Press, London, 1972.

Berger, Carl, *The Korea Knot,* a military-political history, U. of Pennsylvania Press, 1957.

Bergman, Sten, *In Korean Wilds and Villages,* London, J. Gifford, Ltd., 1938.

Carpenter, Francis, *Tales of a Korean Grandmother,* New York, Doubleday, 1947.

Choi, Susan, *The Foreign Student,* a novel, Harper Collins, New York, 1998.

Choy, Bong Yong, *Koreans in America,* New York, Nelson-Hall, 1979.

Chin, Shin-yong, gen. ed., *Customs and Manners in Korea,* Korean Cultural series #9, Seoul, Korea, Sisayongosa Pub. Inc., 1982. Also #4, Folk Culture in Korea.

Chung, Kyung Cho, *Korea Tomorrow,* New York, Macmillan, 1956.

Chung, Kyung Cho, *New Korea,* new land of the morning calm, New York, Macmillan, 1962.

Clark, C.A., *Religions of Old Korea,* New York and London, Garland Pub., 1981.

Clark, Roger W., *Ride the White Tiger,* Boston, Little, Brown and Co., 1959 (novel of 1950-51)

Collins, J. Lawton, *War in Peacetime,* the history and lessons of Korea, Boston, Houghton Mifflin, 1969.

Covell, Alan C., *Shamanism in Korea,* Hollym Int. Corp., Seoul, 1983.

Covell, Jon C., *Korea's Cultural Roots,* 5th ed., 1983

Crane, Paul S., *Korean Patterns,* Royal Asiatic Society, Korea Branch, Seoul, Korea, 1978.

Facts About Korea, Ministry of Culture and Information, Seoul, Korea, 1969.

Fisher, J. Earnest, *Pioneers of Modern Korea,* the Christian Literature Society of Korea, 1977.

Gosfield, Frank, and Burnhardt, J. Hurwood, *Korea, Land of the 38th Parallel,* Parents' Magazine Press, New York, 1969.

Goulden, Joseph C. *Korea, the Untold Story of the War,* New York Times Books, Quadrangle, N.Y. Times Book Co., 1982.

Grad (jdanzev) Andrew J., *Modern Korea,* New York, Octagon Books, Farrar, Strauss, Giroux, 1978. (repr. from 1944 ed.)

Ha, Tae Hung, *Guide to Korean Culture,* Yonsei Univ. Press, Seoul, Korea, 1968.

Heller, Francis H., *The Korean War,* a twenty-five year perspective, ed. for H.S Truman Library Institute for National and International Affairs, Regents Press, Lawrence, Kansas, 1977.

Henderson, Gregory, *The Politics of the Vortex,* Cambridge, Mass., The Harvard U. Press, 1968.

Herlihy, Francis, *Now Welcome Summer,* Hawthorne Press, Melbourne, Australia, 1946.

Higgins, Marguerite, *War in Korea,* New York, Doubleday, 1951.

Hoyt, E.P. *On To the Yalu,* New York, Stein and Day, 1984.

Hoyt, E.P., *Pusan Perimeter,* New York, Stein and Day, 1985.

Huhm, Halla Pai, *Korean Shamanist Rituals,* Seoul, Korea, Hollym Int. Corp., 1980.

Kalton, Michael C., *Korean Ideas and Values,* Philip Jaisohn Memorial Paper #7, Memorial Foundation, 60 E. Township Line Rd., Elkins Park, PA.

Kahn, E. J., Jr., *The Peculiar War,* New York, Random House, 1951.

Kang, Younghill, *East Goes West,* the Making of an Oriental Yankee, Kaya Production, New York, 1997.

Kang, Younghill, *The Grass Roof,* New York, Scribners, 1931.

Keith, Elizabeth and Scott, and Robertson, E.K., *Old Korea,* the land of morning calm, London, Hutchinson and Co. Ltd., 1946.

Kim, Edward H., Korea, *Beyond the Hills,* Tokyo, Kodansha Int. Ltd., 1980.

Kim, Elaine, and Yu, Eui-Young, *East to America,* Korean American Life Stories, The New Press, New York, 1996.

KANG
~~Kim,~~ K. Connie, *Home Was the Land of Morning Calm,* a saga of a Korean-American family. Addison Wesley, 1995.

Kim, Helen, *The Long Season of Rain,* Ballantine Books, New York, 1997.

Kim, Nancy, *Chinhominy's Secret,* Bridge Works Publishing Co, bridgehampton, New York, 1999.

Kim San and Nym Wales, *Song of Ariran,* the life story of a Korean rebel, New York, John Day, 1941.

Kim, Yung Chung, *Women of Korea,* a history from ancient times to 1945, Seoul, Korea, Ewha U. Press, 1979.

Koh, Taiwon, *The Bitter Fruit of Kom-Pawi,* Philadelphia, John C. Winston, 1959.

Korea, its Land, People, and Culture of All Ages, Seoul, Korea, Hakwonsa, Ltd., 1960.

Leckie, Robert, *Conflict, the History of the Korean War,* 1950-53, New York, G.P. Putnam's Sons, 1962.

Ledyard, Gary, *The Dutch Come to Korea,* Seoul, Korea, Royal Asiatic Society, Taewon Pub. Co. 1971.

Lee-Chon, Seunghi, *Daily Pursuits and Timeless Values,* a woman's view in changing society, Seoul, Korea, Hollym Int. Corp., 1978.

Lee, Chong Sik, *The Politics of Korean Nationalism,* Berkeley, U. of California Press, 1965.

Lee, Helie, *Still Life With Rice,* Scribner, New York, 1996.

Lee, Man Gap, *Sociology and Social Change in Korea,* Seoul, Korea, Seoul National U. Press, 1982.

Lee, Mary Paik, *Quiet Odyssey, A pioneer Korean woman in America,* University of Washington Press, 1990.

Lee, Peter H., *Anthology of Korean Poetry,* New York, John Day Co., 1962.

Lee, Peter H., *Flowers of Fire,* 20th Century Korean stories, an East-West Center Book, U. of Hawaii Press, 1974.

Li, Mirok, *The Yalu Flows,* Michigan State U. Press, 1956.

Lueras, Leonard, and Chung, Nedra, *Korea,* Insight Guides, Hong Kong, 1981.

Mattielli, Sandra, *Virtues in Conflict,* traditions and the Korean woman today, Royal Asiatic Society, Korea branch, Samhwha Publishing Co., Ltd., Seoul, Korea, 1977.

McCann, David, Middleton, John, and Shultz, Ed. J., eds., *Studies on Korea in Transition,* Center for Korean Studies, U. of Hawaii, Honolulu, Hawaii, 1979.

McCune, George, *Korea's Heritage,* a social and political geography, Tokyo, Charles Tuttle Co., 1956.

McCune, George M., *Korea Today,* Institute of Pacific Relations, Westport, Ct., Greenwood Press, 1982. Originally pub. by Harvard U. Press, 1950

McCune, Shannon, *Korea, Land of Broken Calm,* Princeton, N.J., D. Van Nostrand Co., Inc., 1956.

McKenzie, Fred A., *Korea's Fight for Freedom,* AMS Pres, (orig. New York, Fleming H. Revell, 1920.)

Middleton, Dorothy H. and Wm. D., *Some Korean Journeys.,* Seoul, Korea, Royal Asiatic Society, Korea Branch, 1975.

Osgood, Cornelius, *Koreans and Their Culture,* New York, Ronald Press, 1951.

Pahk, Induk, *September Monkey,* New York, Harper, 1954.

Paige, GlennD., *The Korean Decision,June24-30, 1950.,* New York, Macmillan, 1968.

Pihl, Marshall, R., ed. *Listening to Korea,* New York, Prager, 1973.

Riley, John W. and Schramm, Wilbur, *The Reds Take a City,* New Jersey, Rutgers U. Press, 1951.

Russ, Martin, *The Last Parallel,* New York, Rinehart, 1957.

Rutt, Richard, *The Bamboo Grove,* an introduction to sijo, Berkeley, U. of California Press, 1971.

Rutt, Richard, *Korean Works and Days, notes from the diary of a country priest,* Rutland, Vt. and Tokyo, Japan, Charles E. Tuttle Co., 1964.

Smith, Robert, *MacArthur in Korea,* Simon and Schuster, New York, 1982

Solberg, S.E., *The Land and People of Korea,* `New York: Harper Collins, 240 pp.

Sook, Nyul Choi, *Year of Impossible Goodbyes,* Boston: Houghton Mifflin, 144 pp.

Stephens, Michael, *Lost in Seoul and Other Discoveries on the Korean Peninsula,* Random House, New York, 1990.

Stout, Mira, *One Thousand Chestnut Trees, a novel of Korea.* Riverhead Books, Penguin Putnam Inc, New York, 1998

Sunoo, Harold Hakwon, *America's Dilemma in Asia, the case of South Korea,* Chicago, Nelson Hall, 1979.

Toland, John, *In Mortal Combat, Korea, 1950-1953,* Wm. Morrow.

Voorhies, Melvin B., Lt. Col., *Korean Tales,* New York, Simon and Schuster, 1952.

Wade, James, *One Man's Korea,* Seoul, Korea, Hollym Corp., 1967.

Weems, Benjamin, *Reform, Rebellion and the Heavenly Way,* Tucson, Arizona, U. of Arizona Press, 1964.

Whang, Sun Won, *Trees on the Cliff,* a novel of Korea and two stories, tr. by Chang Wang Rok, New York, Larchwood Press Ltd., 1960.

Winchester, Simon, *A Walk Through the Land of Miracles,* Prentice Hall Press, New York, 1988.

Wong, Shawn, *Asian American Literature,* a brief introduction and anthology, Harper Collins College Publishers, 1996.

Yi Pangja, *The World is One,* Seoul, Korea, Taewon Publ. Co., 1973.

Yim, Louise, *My Forty Year Fight for Korea,* New York, A.A. Wyn, Inc., 1951.

Yoon, Suk Joong, *Half Past Four,* poems for children, tr. by Francis T. Yoon and David D. Lapham, F.T. Yoon Co., Los Angeles, Ca., 1978.

Zong, In Sob, *Folk Tales from Korea,* London, Routledge and Kegan, Paul, Ltd., 1952.

0-595-24098-4